PRAISE FOR SENI GLAISTER

'Seni Glaister's latest "up-lit" novel is perfect
for fans of last year's runaway bestseller
Eleanor Oliphant is Completely Fine' Hello!

'Classic up-lit – literary comfort food
for a cold winter's night' *Saga*

'A funny, feel-good tale' *Candis*

'Extremely charming' *Sunday Times*
bestselling author Marian Keyes

'A sheer delight – it will make you laugh and
cry in equal measure. Charming beyond belief'
Sunday Times bestselling author Veronica Henry

'A real gem' Fiona Harper, author of *The Memory Collector*

Seni Glaister worked as a bookseller for much of her career before founding WeFiFo, the social dining platform, in 2016. Her first novel, *The Museum of Things Left Behind*, was published in 2015. She lives on a farm in West Sussex with her husband and children.

Also by Seni Glaister

Growing Season

Seni Glaister

ONE PLACE. MANY STORIES

HQ
An imprint of HarperCollins*Publishers* Ltd
1 London Bridge Street
London SE1 9GF

This edition 2020

1
First published in Great Britain by
HQ, an imprint of HarperCollins*Publishers* Ltd 2020

ISBN: HB: 978-0-00-828502-9
TPB: 978-0-00-828503-6

Permission to use excerpt from 'Cut Grass' by Philip Larkin
granted by Faber & Faber

MIX
Paper from
responsible sources
FSC
www.fsc.org   FSC™ C007454

This book is produced from independently certified FSC™ paper
to ensure responsible forest management.

For more information visit: www.harpercollins.co.uk/green

This book is set in 10.9/15.5 pt. Adobe Caslon Pro

Printed and bound in Great Britain by
CPI Group (UK) Ltd, Croydon, CR0 4YY

For my daughters Poppy and Millie

And in loving memory of

Leila Rendel 1882–1969
Olive Rendel 1889–1973
Cecily Rendel 1910–1994

& the other women who
came before us

Cut grass lies frail:
Brief is the breath
Mown stalks exhale.

EXCERPT FROM 'CUT GRASS' BY PHILIP LARKIN
Permission kindly given by Faber & Faber

Prologue

Yew Lane was not exactly a lane, but rather a cul-de-sac. It led nowhere in particular but served as the peaceful access to a number of small detached and semi-detached houses. As a no-through-road, it offered few opportunities for passersby to chance upon it; its purpose was simply to deliver the home owners to their front doors whilst also offering a couple of lay-bys just wide enough to accommodate the increasingly frequent delivery vans that liked to turn themselves around indignantly after hurling their parcels carelessly over hedges.

Each home in Yew Lane had probably once boasted a much larger garden, but these spaces had proven very fruitful to land-hungry developers who could turn one plot into four, each with an easily maintained garden or off-road parking. Gradually those little in between spaces, the scraps of land, the allotments, the wooden framed single garages, the creaky lean-tos and the orchards had all been usurped, largely to the satisfaction of all, except, perhaps, the bees who rued the loss of blossom and the occasional deer who had once supplemented their diets with roses and winter greens but who were now thwarted by the high wooden fences that served to carefully cordon off one property from the next.

Broome Cottage was the furthest of the properties on the lane, the last before some scrappy woodland that itself led to some more substantial woodland and arable fields beyond. The garden of Broome Cottage was just small enough to have been ignored by prospectors so it remained intact, offering a nice patch of lawn behind the brick-built cottage with its pretty half-hung tiles. Like all the houses in Yew Lane, the garden had a high wooden fence on all sides. Broome Cottage, however, still boasted a small garage and a path led between this and the house to the lawn behind it. The front of the house was north-facing but the garden side of the house was south-facing and, to any future gardener, that was what counted. At the back of the garage, in the corner of the garden, a narrow wooden gate opened on to a public footpath.

Diana stood on the footpath with her back to these houses and to the woodland below her. She looked through a small gap between the fence post and the gate, quietly observing the arrival of the latest newcomers to Broome Cottage. She had first been alerted by the constant beeping of a removal vehicle reversing the length of Yew Lane and she'd been anxious to find out what sort of neighbour she would have on her hands. The previous gentleman had been elderly, he'd never given Diana any bother, even his ultimate departure had passed without fuss. And then the developers had come in with their skips and scaffolding and she'd watched with concern to see what atrocities they might bestow on the pretty little cottage. But fortunately the house and its small garden had survived the process unscathed.

Once Diana had begun her vigil, her interest had been

further piqued by the intriguing young woman who seemed to be coordinating the move. She was very young, not yet thirty, and appeared entirely in charge. But there was something complicated about her, Diana felt. She appeared confident when she greeted the removal men, issuing directions with a clear, happy voice and plying them with tea, demonstrating the genteel manners of a much older woman. But when Diana caught glimpses of her alone, off guard, her face appeared careworn and she often displayed a worried frown as she scurried from place to place.

Diana had taken up her watch post a number of times, and she was there when the removals van eventually left. She wondered, while she watched the driver gun the big vehicle's engine to life, why they were always called removal vans. Removal was only half the story. Here, on Yew Lane, it was surely an *arrivals* van, a vehicle conveying hope and new chapters, emptying out its promises into this nice, neat house.

Diana was watching, too, when the woman's partner or husband finally appeared. He was young also, and they were at ease together, but they were more like an older couple with their fire and their fury long behind them. To Diana the two seemed rather alike, physically. It was not the likeness of siblings, but of two pieces from the same jigsaw puzzle. Like her, he wore glasses and these he often pushed up his nose with an index finger, betraying a nervous tic. And like her, he often wore a concerned frown when alone. But Diana was glad to see him pull her into his arms, proudly, as they stood in the lane admiring their new home.

Diana finally stopped herself from spying on them when

the young woman glanced in her direction and seemed to stare at her worriedly, as if she could see right through the fence. Diana froze, then backed a couple of steps away, immediately ashamed of what she had been reduced to.

Diana retreated.

Chapter 1

Danny hadn't been sleeping but a guttural screech had yanked him from his meditative state of rhythmic breathing to one of immediate alertness. He swung his legs out of bed and was now peering between the curtains into the darkness beyond, his heart thumping wildly in his chest.

'What the hell was that?' he asked, his voice strained in the silence of the bedroom.

'What was what?' asked Sam, sleepily, beside him.

'Did you hear that noise? It sounded like someone's being murdered out there. I heard a scream. Did you hear it?' Danny let the curtains drop and stumbled around the bed, feeling his way around a room that was still menacing in its unfamiliarity. He fumbled in the darkness for his dressing gown, unhooking it from the back of the door and wrapping it around him tightly.

He returned to his watch-post, perching himself on the side of the bed, and once again he pressed his face to the glass, squinting into the raven night.

From her prone position beside him Sam answered him through a yawn. 'Probably just a fox. Or a cat maybe? Or an owl. It could have been any one of the holy trinity of night noises. Welcome to the countryside,' she said, with an exaggerated yawn.

Danny didn't smile, he continued to peer into the dark. 'That was no fox. I know what a fox sounds like. A fox sounds like metal.'

Sam, fully alert now, processed his logic and laughed, switching on the light. 'You idiot. Foxes don't sound like metal.'

'They do! They make a very distinctive sound. Turn the light off, I can't see a thing.'

'You mean the sound of dustbins? Foxes make the sound of metal because you've only ever heard them rooting through a dustbin? Jesus, Danny. We got out of London just in time to rescue you.' She turned off the light again and stared up at the dark ceiling above her, smiling.

Danny, feeling vulnerable in his boxer shorts, kept his dressing gown on and flopped back on the bed beside his wife. She was laughing at him kindly, he knew, but he also felt idiotic. His heart was still pounding which made him feel more exposed still.

After a few minutes of agitated pause, he sat up again and returned to his vigil. 'What else did you think it could be? A cat? What the hell do they do to their cats in the countryside? If it was a cat, it was definitely being strangled.'

'Sex. Cat sex. It's a very noisy business apparently and I don't think it is always consensual.'

Sam could see Danny's face reflected in the dark glass. She could see he was grimacing at the thought of noisy, bucolic, non-consensual sex. 'What about owls? Is owl sex noisy too?' he asked, fearfully, as if not really wishing to know the answer.

'I somehow doubt it. I think if the noise was made by an owl, it was probably just seeing off a predator. Or perhaps it had just made a violent kill, and is now swooping low across the fields with the small body of a dead rodent hanging limply from its outstretched talons.'

'Jesus Christ, Samantha. That's disgusting. If I'd known the countryside was so violent, I would have stayed in SW11.'

Sam continued to smile in the darkness. 'I'm teasing. I have no idea why an owl screeches or even if that's what the noise was, but I expect one of the neighbours will be able to tell me. All I know from my two-week advantage of living in the countryside, is that cats, foxes and owls account for most of the night noises around here.'

Sam reached her hand out to find Danny's. They lay together companionably as Danny steadied his breathing by matching each inhale and exhale to hers.

'Go to sleep, champ,' said Sam, conscious of Danny's unnatural breathing pattern.

'I'm not sure I can.' Danny's heart was still thumping painfully.

'You'll get used to it. Honestly, you will. Trust me, I barely slept the first couple of nights here.'

'Really?' he asked, reassured.

'Yes really.'

Danny wriggled closer and, taking her warmth to supplement his strength, his breathing relaxed into something approximating sleep.

Sam felt a flicker of guilt in the face of Danny's trust in

her. Once again, she had lied to her husband. The truth was, she had actually slept deeply from her very first night in the countryside. She loved falling asleep to the nocturnal babble, marvelling at the variety of sounds she'd been introduced to that she'd been quite unaware existed. She loved the darkness and this fortress of a house with no shared walls. In London she had been able to hear the coat-hangers rattling in her neighbour's cupboard. The cupboard must have been just behind her head and its owners must have been very uncertain about their outfit choices because they seemed to scrape the coat-hangers back and forth every evening and every morning with predictable and prolonged determination. Here, though, the house noises were *her* house noises and the punctuations from the outdoor world were welcome reminders that her domain had suddenly become so much broader.

Sam had moved to the new house two weeks ahead of Danny so that she could be there to oversee the tedious little tasks that would have rattled him. She'd upgraded the broadband, hooked them up to Sky TV and had found a plumber to turn the adequate shower into a power shower and to install a water filter under the kitchen sink. She had hoped that these little details would make it feel less traumatic for Danny when he eventually arrived. Ahead of her move, Sam had been dreading this period alone, imagining intolerable loneliness after her busy London life, but the chores she'd allocated to herself had swept up the hours comprehensively and completing these little missions had helped turn the house into her home immediately. She'd already come to love it inordinately.

Sam had campaigned for the move from London persistently and strategically, for as long as she and Danny had been married. But whilst her arguments for pastoral life were sound and important, they ultimately had very little impact on Danny's eventual agreement.

Sam had finally chanced upon her winning arguments when, in quick succession, she had stumbled across two important facts for the Home County she'd set her heart on. The first was a social media rumour that suggested a new train operator was being lined up to take over the existing service and, accompanying this speculation, there were soon whispers of dramatically improved schedules and greatly shortened commuter times. Any fool could deduce that the knock-on effect would be a positive impact on property prices along the entire length of the train line, but Sam knew Danny well enough not to spell this out. He loved to be the most cunning man in the room. Rather than draw his attention to the financial imperative, she'd talked about the improvement to his life that a shorter commute from the countryside would deliver and she had then stepped away from the conversation, allowing him some space to calculate the monetary benefit to the return on investment should this train service go ahead.

In a similar vein, whilst idly stirring a risotto at the stove she'd read an article out loud from a local estate agent's report to Danny, as he uncorked a bottle of wine. 'Heavens, there's a new John Lewis store opening up nearby,' she'd said. 'Listen to this,' she continued, 'a John Lewis or Waitrose store opening in a new area can impact property prices by seven per cent!' She allowed this fact to sink in before continuing.

'*Ludicrous*. Aren't people silly to let those sorts of things influence their decisions.' To demonstrate her utter disdain for consumerism she had tossed the paper in the recycling bin but she knew the information would have landed in her husband's calculator of a brain and, coming so fast on the heels of her train line propaganda, she felt confident that she'd hammered two impactful nails into the coffin that served as a basement flat in an up and coming area of South-West London.

And of course, her campaign had worked. Here she was, sharing the new king-sized bed for the first time with her husband, listening to the little creaks and groans that were the rhythm of the house she loved and, here she was, blending these with the outside noises and Danny's breathing.

She knew she should feel guilty every time she lied to her husband, but it seemed to Sam that he rarely wanted to hear the truth and that was probably because he knew he would not be advantaged by it. Some of the harder things *could* be spoken, but only once they'd been repackaged into a palatable bite, whilst other things were better left unsaid altogether. And there were more things, still, that Sam couldn't even admit to herself, let alone to him.

Outside, the barn owl, quiet now, alighted softly on a branch to take vigil. The night was clear and dry so she'd soon leave her watch-post to repeat her ghostlike rounds, her soft fringed feathers making no sound in the dark night air. Watchful, she waited, alert to the dangers around her, while all about her the unknowing creatures dropped their guard.

Chapter 2

Long after Sam had fallen asleep, Danny realised he was fully awake, unsure if he had slept or not.

It was 4 a.m. and it was still dark, and it would be dark for a while. Danny needed to pee. He lay in bed arguing with himself. If, he wondered, he gave in to his bladder's demands now, would he be making a rod for his own back? Would he become a slave to his bodily functions, destined to never make it through the night without a bathroom visit? On the other hand, he reasoned, if he ignored the urgent pressure then perhaps he might give himself a whole different set of problems. Perhaps he'd stretch his bladder or cause some sort of infection. His wife had certainly suffered from those, but he wasn't sure if men his age could get them too. But if it didn't lead to an infection, might it lead to something much worse? How did cancers in that area begin? He knew that bladder cancers were more common in men than in women. Perhaps not relieving yourself might be causal? He sighed, a little disappointed in himself for allowing the argument to escalate so quickly and with almost no opposing defence deployed by the reasonable bit of his brain. Getting up as quietly as he could, he padded through the darkness to the bathroom.

He still wasn't used to the house. It was so much bigger than their London flat, which he'd loved. It had been his bachelor pad for a few years before Sam had moved in. Not that he'd been *that* sort of bachelor. It wasn't as if he were entertaining a whole host of women in there. But the flat had been his and he'd been proud of buying his first property while still in his twenties, something he'd achieved quite independently of the inheritance that had then accelerated the move to Broome Cottage. There was no doubt that marrying Sam and sharing his flat with her had been the best thing he had ever done. She was there, every night, in touching distance and he would never tire of watching her sleep or waking up to her next to him. But her approach to domesticity was more chaotic than his own. She had arrived with very little, but clutter seemed to be attracted to her, following her home uninvited and finding space amongst his own ordered possessions. She never got around to explaining the purpose of the things that appeared on shelves or, increasingly, on every available surface, but they gave her such pleasure that he taught himself ways of coping, largely by seeing if he could notice a new item before it had formally been introduced to him. He would memorise the precise layout of each room as he left and scan it against his mental register on his return, discerning what was new, what was no longer there, what had moved. Eventually, when space became an issue and he could no longer see his apartment for her curious baubles, he realised he needed a longer-term coping mechanism. He advanced his plan to buy a larger house.

Turning on the light, he nodded in approval. This new bathroom was well-finished. The house was old – hundreds of years old according to Sam, but it had been fully renovated before being listed on the market. The kitchen was brand new and fitted, carpets had been laid throughout and both the upstairs bathroom and downstairs cloakroom featured good quality fittings. These were in an old-fashioned style, Victorian he thought, and they looked classy. More importantly, the taps worked and didn't drip, the shower (which Sam had upgraded before he arrived) was powerful and the heated towel rails were piping hot. It was a good bathroom. He was proud to own it. But he still wasn't *used* to it.

He turned the main light off and flicked the light on above the mirror, scrutinising his face. He was tired; the skin under his eyes sagged a little. He peered in closer and examined a couple of very thin lines on the side of his nose, trying to establish if they were broken veins. When did that begin to happen, he wondered, surely not in his thirties? He was technically a young man still, wasn't he? He pushed his hair back and looked at his hairline. That had definitely been creeping a little bit, there was certainly more forehead than he remembered. But he wore his hair quite long and it flopped forward so nobody was going to notice until there had been very much more retreat. He felt the top and back of his head, but it was ridiculous to try to ascertain if there was less hair there. Could he ask Sam? No, perhaps not. It was probably best if he didn't draw attention to his slow decline. She was so vibrant and luminous. Her skin had an elasticity that suggested she would never be diminished by something as mundane as aging and he didn't want to highlight her obvious superiority, in case it somehow weakened him in her eyes.

Danny knew he didn't sleep enough, and it was beginning to show in his face. It needn't impact on his career prospects – premature aging was a positive attribute in his line of work. Most of the successful partners could be mistaken for men ten years their senior. It wore you out, the constant counting and watching your back.

However, Danny was aware that long term sleep deprivation could impact on your physical heath and those were things that Danny needed to guard against. He knew that fatigue could be a symptom of cancer, but could it also be a cause? Poor sleep made you at risk to all sorts of diseases, he was sure, so it seemed very likely that cancer was one of them. Whether or not his bad habits were carcinogenic, he knew that there had been all sorts of studies that linked a lack of sleep with a poor outcome in life and Danny's rational brain knew he needed to get a grip and tackle his insomnia. His irrational one, however, conspired quite forcibly to keep him awake.

Danny turned the light off and his sombre reflection in the moonlight looked just as terrifying as his yellowed face had under the glare of the bathroom light. Now, the dim shadows picked out his skeletal frame, peeling back the flesh and revealing the gaunt core of him. He looked like his father just before he died. He and his reflection stared at each other, and Danny wondered if his path was already inalterable.

Chapter 3

Now that Danny had also moved in to Broome Cottage Sam found herself having to adjust once again to a new persona altogether: that of a wife of a man who commuted, a man who departed early in the morning, taking the car and leaving her and her house entirely reliant on each other for company.

As she watched the rear lights of the car disappear down the drive, the red orbs losing their definition as they became consumed by the morning mist, she felt a pang of guilt. Danny now had to leave home two hours earlier to arrive at work at the same time, and all so he could enjoy the many benefits of countryside living she had promised him. In reality, it was unlikely he'd enjoy the house in daylight until early summer and even then, though she'd promised barbecues and stargazing, evening strolls and late-night cocktails, she knew he'd only really feel the benefit of country living at the weekends.

She glanced at the kitchen clock. It wouldn't be light for another hour or so, and this sixty-minute pause stretched ahead of her like a yawn. Where Danny's day had been shortened, her own days were now unfathomably long, and since she no longer had a job dictating how she spent her day, the many different things she could do with her time were overwhelming.

Sam thought fleetingly about the career she'd left behind in London. She missed it. She missed the dizzying forward momentum that came with a full workload and the sense of belonging that came with a shared purpose. But she didn't miss the way it made her feel towards the end: the side glances and pity, the laughter that stopped when she walked in the room, the sense of rejection that came with being suddenly, unalterably different.

She shrugged away the flood of regret. This was better: small manual tasks that required no input from anyone else, jobs she could complete that made each day a little bit better than the last. These were the things that might make her feel whole again.

She climbed upstairs, her bare feet enjoying the carpeted treads. She had been busy at Broome Cottage since the removal vans had first arrived, finding a place for everything and ensuring the house achieved that fine balance of looking both lived in and orderly. She now admired her work but felt a little saddened by the way their entire London life had been so neatly absorbed by the spacious cupboards and plentiful shelves she now had at her disposal. In London, their small apartment had been bursting at the seams and her life had felt both interesting and complex. Books were piled on every available surface and vases weren't allowed to exist as empty vessels, they'd been stacked or filled with other small items. Here, everything had a place yet their combined possessions left the house looking hungry for more.

She wandered into the smallest of the three bedrooms, which sat immediately at the top of the stairs. This room was positioned neatly between the master bedroom with its en suite bathroom to the left and the guest bedroom and family bathroom to the right. Though small, it was a nicely proportioned, airy bedroom and was perfectly positioned for a number of purposes. It would be impossible to escape the notice of any prospective buyer that it was within hearing distance of the master bedroom and next to the bathroom, making it ideal for anyone with their heart set on a bigger family.

Sam sat at the desk and opened and closed the empty central drawer absent-mindedly. The furniture was well made and the mechanism was of good quality and the drawer slid open and closed silently in a most satisfying way. Next to the desk was a heavy filing cabinet, made of light oak, its pair of matching keys, guarded for transit with a bit of blue tape, still hung together from the top lock. The filing cabinet was solid and perhaps designed for bigger lives than theirs, but she could imagine filling up the drawers over time, watching the files become designated by her tightly printed capital letters, spelling out the nooks and crannies of a future that could not yet be named or anticipated.

When unpacking the huge delivery boxes, she had simply put the box files from their London flat into the top drawer of the filing-cabinet, but she realised now that sorting these more definitively was a job that would happily absorb an hour before she left the house for an exploratory walk. Sam had resolved to make walking part of every day and idly wondered whether Danny might ever soften on his determination not to get a dog.

Warily, Sam eyed her laptop, which sat on the top of the desk. She had paused when she had come to pack it, and she wished she'd had the courage to leave it behind her in London. Perhaps she could have thrown it melodramatically into the skip with all the other detritus that she didn't want any part of anymore. Better still, she could have hurled it into the Thames as they'd crossed the bridge on their journey south. But the logical part of her brain had won, telling her that the physical laptop wasn't the issue, it was merely a symbol, so she'd capitulated and brought it with her.

Ignoring the laptop, which seemed to glower from the desktop, silently insisting on attention, she resisted the urge to plug it in. Instead, she retrieved her own box file from the top drawer and began to sort the paperwork into separate piles on the grey carpet. Systematically, she shuffled the papers into the compartments of her life: one, the largest, for the letters, bills and documents that related to her health; one for receipts and guarantees; another for her driving licence, theory test and car documentation, a final pile for the paperwork associated with her academic career. This pile, the second largest, was surprising in its bulk considering she never felt she'd achieved anything much, but she'd kept her school reports for a number of years and she had her GCSE and A Level certificates in stiff card envelopes to protect them which added a little heft to the pile. Her degree was represented by a single certificate which seemed a rather flimsy portrayal of what was her greatest accomplishment to date. Sam had received a top degree from a respected university (not a *top* university, but one that usually won an impressed nod of approval whenever she mentioned it) and she'd worked very hard for her result. She'd eschewed the parties and club scene in favour of extra courses, and she'd worked diligently for three years, anxious not to waste the opportunity her parents had afforded her. And despite her admirable work ethic, she'd still had fun, met Danny, fallen in love and set herself on a course for life that seemed immutable now.

She looked up at the big cork notice board that had been fixed to the wall above the desk. From where she was sitting, its emptiness looked like longing. So far, the only embellishment she'd made to the board was a pinned strip of four identical pictures, showing herself and Danny squeezed into a photo booth, pressed cheek to cheek and giddy with happiness. Their clear-sighted younger selves showed no inkling of the impending set-backs on the horizon, instead, they both just grinned at her, their assumption of more good things to follow blazed unapologetically in both sets of eyes. The photos looked sad, pinned up on the board on their own and Sam dithered for a while, holding her certificate in both hands and wondering whether she could pin it up there too. But of course she wouldn't. Her degree was better than Danny's and it would look like she was showing off, something she really didn't deserve to do considering how well his career had progressed and how little she'd actually managed to achieve since abruptly ending her own. She shuffled the certificate to the bottom of her education pile and continued sorting out the many small mementos of her inconsequential adulthood.

When she was happy with the distribution, she transferred each pile of papers into its own cardboard file. Her medical papers needed two. The years immediately after marrying Danny, she could see quite clearly, measured her greatest failures, and the file was bigger, substantially bigger, than the sum of any successes. Sam was perversely pleased by these metrics. She liked to see what she had, and hadn't, done with her life so far and was amused by the neatness of her filing and the conclusions she had drawn. It was better, she thought, to know these things about herself and to file them away in a light oak drawer with a small key to lock it up, than to have them rattle around in her head, jeering or making her doubt or misremember. It had always felt important to her that she gave Danny the impression that she was as organised and as systematic as he was. She smiled at the idea, but her smile vanished quickly, replaced not quite by a frown but certainly by an instinctive correction. As if anyone could even aspire to be as organised and systematic as her husband.

Once she had finished, two documents were left unaccounted for on the carpet. Sam labelled a file 'career' and dropped the P45 and a signed leaving card into it. She barely glanced at these chronicles, the testaments to the conclusion of a career that had fleetingly seemed so promising.

Sam glanced up at the curtainless window. The sky had lightened since she last looked, taking on a wash of cool, bright light that beckoned her invitingly. She stood and stretched and using the sole of her bare foot, pushed against the bottom drawer. It slid shut, carrying with it Sam's successes and failures, and closing itself tightly with a gentle but reassuring thud.

Chapter 4

Danny, meanwhile, had entered the very specific realm of the commuter, a whole new component of the day in which he was neither quite at work or at home, but nor was he at leisure. He was now a bona fide suburbanite.

He sat on the train, watching the view race away behind him. The train was already crowded but it was still early and his fellow passengers, united by a collaborative hum of determined concentration, were thankfully quiet. Danny had felt engulfed by a sense of calm as soon as he'd secured a window seat near to the door. Though he had barely glanced at his laptop it was open on the table in front of him, creating a respectful frontier between him and his neighbours. The knowledge that there was now no need to move again until they pulled into the mainline station allowed him to imagine closing his eyes for an hour. This was his preferred seat and whenever possible, he resolved, he would always occupy it.

Danny had undergone a number of similar practice journeys before exchanging contracts on Broome Cottage. He'd trialled the prospective commute on each workday morning and evening at peak rush hour to ensure the vast amount of time he was going to commit to this journey would be commensurate with the benefits. Whilst calculating the cost (in both time and money) he'd worked on the assumption that he would make this journey between 1,440 times and 2,400 times, depending on the vagaries of the property market. It was entirely possible that he would spend the equivalent of 300 working days sitting on this train. He had methodically measured the cost of this time and weighed it up against the likely rise in the value of the house he was going to buy. He knew somewhere, in a part of his brain he chose not to access too often, that there were other incalculable tariffs that should be factored in, but for the purpose of this exercise he'd restricted himself to those levies he felt qualified to identify and name.

After his practice journeys, Danny felt he had begun to grasp the small nuances that identified travel patterns on different days of the week and though he knew that the months ahead would be filled with incremental improvements to optimise his journey, he already felt his preparation had been vindicated by his ability to position himself at exactly the right point on the station platform to secure this seat. Trains were refreshingly predictable and so too, it appeared, were the commuters.

As it transpired, Danny's move to the countryside had him arriving earlier to his desk than those years where his journey had him zigzagging London for a few short, but intense, miles from Battersea. Granted, this feat had only been accomplished by getting on a train earlier than strictly necessary, but the rewards were manifest.

Arriving earlier had been an unpredicted benefit of moving much further away from the office. Danny's work could only properly begin when he was at his desk, logged on, with a fierce frown on his forehead to ward away the frivolous conversations that tended to cluster and tangle like weeds in a riverbed, slowing down the onward journey of fruitful productivity. The idlest of chat happened in the small kitchen while people loaded the fridge with their Tupperware boxes full of home-made lunch (salads, grilled chicken breasts, chickpeas and other healthy options associated with a successful career) and while his colleagues made themselves their first coffee or tea of the day. These puerile, nebulous interactions were hard for Danny to navigate and the constant sharing and swapping of news of how they'd spent their hours since they'd last spoken was particularly baffling. The sheer banality of the conversation could send Danny's pulse racing and he was constantly on guard, prepared to deflect any attention that might swing, scimitar-like, towards him.

Danny recognised that piloting a confidently nimble course through these exchanges was an essential part of career progression, so he was careful to be polite and maintained what he hoped was a courteous interest in the conversations around him, but he really preferred not to blur the boundaries between his work and home. Experience had taught him, however, that even if he successfully dodged the endless questions asking him what he had achieved since the previous day (Monday mornings were the worst, with a whole weekend of updates required), common manners would demand that he reciprocated with a 'and how was yours?' Over the years, the answer had remained fairly constant, though the context had changed. From 'knackered, mate, on the lash Saturday night' through to 'exhausted, we're teething at the moment,

God help me'. Regardless of their stages in life, it appeared to be a competition about who could arrive at their desk on a Monday morning with the greatest sleep deficit.

Had Danny been truthful in his responses, he would probably win *that* competition hands down. He'd not actually had a solid night's sleep for some years, but he did not feel that this was a competitive arena he ought to enter, particularly armed with truthful responses. Over-sharing fed the cesspit of gossip, and worse, invited opinion. Opinion offered in formal appraisal was just about bearable, but opinion given by the inexpert with a fraction of the salient information at their fingertips was unforgivable. Sitting in his train seat, leaving the countryside behind him and hurtling towards a minefield of unwarranted and unsought viewpoints, Danny massaged his temples while counting his inhalations and exhalations, desperate to rid himself of the idea of other people's inexactness.

Danny switched his attention back to the view and wondered, very briefly, whether he had attention deficit disorder. He hadn't finished a book for years, let alone a train of thought. Sam blamed his tendency to flit from one thought to another on a very demanding job that prevented him from switching off but Danny feared a deeper-rooted problem. Danny's life was a carefully choreographed mesh of entrenched worries and self-taught coping mechanisms and he zigzagged precariously between the two whilst maintaining an outward appearance of introverted competence and sincerity. Now, as he applied a small amount of antibacterial gel to his palms, rubbing his hands together methodically, he sought inspiration and answers from his new routine. The view from a train window might be soothing, mightn't it? If he secured this seat on this train, five days a week, he'd see the seasons change, notice the small differences that made the fickle landscape predictable, providing you were prepared to commit to the long view.

He really *did* like this seat. He didn't like to face the direction of travel, he found the information too quick to process – just as he would find something to focus upon, it would already be behind him, particularly those objects in the foreground which raced past him alarmingly, barely taking shape. Seated backwards, he could spot something of interest: a small terraced house with an unlikely boat in its garden; the curious storage area of a big brand DIY centre, and then, as the train roared towards the city, a twisted oak dead and dead-centre in the middle of a square field. He liked this geometry amid the swirls and curves of nature. He hoped these features would become reassuring waymarkers on his journey and he vowed to focus his attention on these new pointers and then watch them for as long as his eye-line remained uninterrupted.

Danny had always felt more comfortable with a plotted course in front of him. But it was complex, wasn't it, he thought, as he eyed his fellow commuters, all of whom appeared to be at different ages and stages, but had all similarly committed to adding several hours to their day's work in order to achieve more and live a better version of their lives. They probably all wanted many of the same things as each other (houses, wives, husbands or partners, holidays, children or pets, a car, a bigger car, two cars… each milestone coming with its own special power to validate one's existence) but surely they couldn't all succeed? Some would have to succeed at the expense of others because both economics and evolution had determined that the pot of success must be finite, and as such they couldn't possibly all have their desired share. Danny wasn't going to fail, it wasn't an option, but it might mean that somewhere in this carriage, somebody with similar conviction would have to lose. Danny shook his head almost imperceptibly, banishing the thought. There was nobody on this train with similar conviction. And this was why it was acceptable to add this journey to his working day and this was why he would succeed.

He looked out of the window again, beyond his fellow commuters who were still just about visible as silhouetted reflections in the glass. The view now was less vast and less alarming.

Danny had always understood that England's green and pleasant land would be just that: green and pleasant. And in order to qualify as pleasant, he had imagined a single wash of colour, coating the countryside and masking its caprice. Instead, each tree added its own hue and the hedgerows, whilst providing occasional promise of order, tended to immediately break their own rules with their sudden requirement to follow the contours of the rolling fields. The countryside was an eyeful of greens, a mindful of greens, a bewilderment of greens. Endless versions of green when just one would have sufficed.

Fortunately, however, as Danny hurtled through the landscape the greens were gradually replaced by the soothing tones of man's welcome intervention and he grasped these and watched them fold into each other until all memories of green had been vanquished.

The train thundered on.

Danny hadn't liked green as a child. It was his house colour at school, which happened to be that of the lowest achieving house. The 'greens' were neither sporty (red) nor academic (blue) nor theatrical and artistic (yellow). His house was the one that seemed to soak up the unallocated remnants, once the other houses had made their selection. In Danny's eight years, the house cup had never been held aloft with a proud green ribbon tied to it.

Since he'd first pinned the green badge to his lapel, Danny had never felt he belonged there, and he found himself quite incapable of finding solace or camaraderie in the shared disappointment that was meted out at the end of each academic year. It was almost as if his fellow house-members felt they *deserved* their low ranking.

This was all very unsatisfactory to Danny. From his earliest years, he'd been considered an all-rounder, comfortably competent at anything he tried, so would have felt equally at home amongst the sporty reds, the arty yellows or the clever blues. Green had felt like a clerical error and his long years cast out from the winners had made him feel powerless and friendless. He realised, after much tortured analysis, the misallocation could only be because of his lack of early specialism, and his interminable exile in the green wilderness taught him to mitigate outcomes by being in control from the outset and from that moment on he committed to communicating his intent with as much clarity as possible.

Perhaps that's why he didn't like green, he wondered, as the train began to rattle and jar as it slowed to a crawl for his station approach. He must find a way to love it, though, for

Sam's sake and because living in the countryside was now part of *the plan* and it signified a milestone in the journey he'd mapped out in the steadfast direction of success.

Danny wasn't always honest with Sam, but he knew he couldn't be honest and hold on to her and there was almost nothing he wouldn't do to earn her approval. Sometimes that meant disguising his worst traits or hiding his worst truths from her. But sometimes small incremental approvals could be won at comparatively little cost to himself. This felt like one of those occasions: if he needed to embrace green in order for her to love him just that little bit more, then he would do it in a heartbeat.

The carriage darkened, shadowed by the station roof as they entered the platform. Danny folded his laptop neatly back into his bag and, once again checking his ticket was still in his inside pocket, he prepared to leave the train to begin the next section of his journey.

Chapter 5

Leaving the church-like quiet of the study behind her, Sam was now preparing for a walk. She had already familiarised herself with the route from her front door to the village shop (she'd made the journey several times). Today, though, she was determined to explore the land beyond the cottage in the other direction by following the footpath that led from her garden gate. She had taken delivery of a pair of wellington boots and was just snipping them free of the polythene they'd been wrapped in when the doorbell rang. She was not expecting any more deliveries and her heart sank, she didn't feel quite strong enough to interact with her neighbours yet, although she knew from a steady increase in the number of recognisable faces locally that these encounters were both inevitable and imminent.

She opened the door to find a tall woman on her doorstep. This visitor was not one she had seen anywhere before, she would have recognised the memorable combination of above average height and unusually sharp features. Her cheekbones were angular, her nose and chin both long and pointed and she clutched a pile of yellow envelopes in alarmingly claw-like fingers.

'Anne,' the visitor said with absolute certainty. 'I'm collecting for St Catherine's,' she continued, by way of an introduction. 'You're new to these parts,' she added, after a brief pause, as if the clarification were for Sam's own benefit.

'I am new here, yes, this is my third week.' Sam smiled warmly, conscious that her withdrawal to the countryside was symptomatic of a wider re-set required and she could put her good intentions into practice right now, with this neighbour.

Anne assessed the new arrival critically, observing and assimilating Sam's T-shirt, jeans and Converse shoes. She nodded, having seen enough to draw her own immutable conclusions. 'About time you immersed yourself in the community. We're reasonably close knit.'

Within a moment, Sam felt herself beginning to bristle, conscious that she had been judged and found to be falling short at the very same moment she had determined to be open and likeable. Fighting an internal battle to flee, her resolution to start afresh won and she stood her ground, smiling with as much submission as she could muster. 'Of course, I fully intend to. I've been busy settling in. It's taken a while to get myself straight, but I'm getting there.' Sam knew she must sound defensive and with her confidence waning under the gaze of her visitor, she wasn't quite sure what should happen next. Sam's mother had instilled in her the manners required to coexist with different groups of people, including the older generation, and she'd told her on many occasions to allow her elders to dictate the rules, as they were probably more wedded to their ways than she was to hers. This was good advice, Sam was certain, but Anne wasn't giving any signals as to the correct protocol. Sam assessed the woman's neat skirt and round-necked jumper, her pristine white collar, her tan tights and sensible shoes. Rather than inviting her in, she stuck her arm out and shook Anne's hand.

'I'm Sam.'

'Samantha,' said Anne, correcting Sam with absolute certainty.

Sam nodded, squirming inside at her own pitiful acquiescence. Nonetheless, she clutched Anne's hand tightly, hoping to transmit both dependability and authenticity through her firm grip whilst demonstrating that she was neither prejudiced nor fearful of talon-like fingers.

Perhaps Anne perceived those very qualities because she nodded briskly. 'Very well. You can get involved in one of our projects, that will get your face out and about. St Catherine's Hospice is one. Super one. Dignified. Lucky to have it on our doorstep.'

'Sure,' said Sam, with a trace of a question mark, alarmed that she might already have formally engaged into some sort of contract, as she appeared still to be shaking Anne's hand. And Anne must have concurred because she'd already moved on to other subjects.

'Things to watch out for: Cathy in the corner shop will short change you every time. She's not a bad person, *per se*, but she'll rob you blind habitually. She can't appear to help herself. Just count your change in front of her and if you spot an error, she'll correct it immediately with no hard feelings. And steer clear of the woods,' said Anne, nodding her head in the general direction of the copse that Sam had felt sure she would soon appropriate as her own.

Sam was much more alarmed by the delivery of the second

warning than the first. She'd already popped into Cathy's shop a number of times and had always used a contactless debit card, so counting out change really wasn't an issue. 'Really? The woods?'

'Oh yes. I'm surprised you haven't already been warned. There's a mad woman there who took up residence a number of years ago. Either batty as a fruitcake or downright evil. Never quite sure which. We've tried to raise the issue with the council on a number of occasions, but we seem to be dealt short shrift. I'm not sure if the woman in the woods has somehow enchanted the *entire* local authority, though it seems unlikely, they're Tories and I doubt very much that Tories are susceptible to enchantment. They certainly weren't in my day.'

Anne dropped her voice, leaning in close enough for the bergamot of a recent cup of tea to be distinct on her breath. 'But some do say she's involved in the *dark arts*, so it's entirely possible. Strange, inexplicable things have happened – a couple of scrapes and falls immediately after visiting the vicinity. And Bea Burdess, God rest her soul…' Anne quickly crossed herself at the mention of the name, '… Bea dropped dead of a heart attack having filed a complaint against the woman in the woods. They say Bea was cursed by some type of spell and although I find that very hard to believe, it's rather *suspicious* as Bea was a vigorous and somewhat dynamic member of the community and I can't think of any other reason for her to expire quite so emphatically.' Anne's eyes darted all around her, eventually straying behind Sam into the house beyond her, as if not quite sure whether Sam were aligned with the good or the bad. 'And things do go *missing*.'

Sam looked around her anxiously, fearful stolen goods might be littering her driveway, awaiting discovery.

'Yes, sorry to be the bearer of bad news but lock up at night, and don't leave things out and about. Garden equipment, that sort of thing. Particularly given your extreme proximity, to the you-know-what.' Again, Anne gestured towards the wood, this time with an exaggerated thrust of her pointed chin.

Sam, who had never seen anyone indicate with their chin before, nodded, wide-eyed.

Anne, meanwhile, was pressing an envelope into Sam's hand. 'I'm collecting for St Catherine's,' she declared as if she had only just arrived and Sam might well have imagined their entire preceding conversation.

'The hospice,' said Sam, nodding encouragingly.

'You've heard of it. Excellent. That's a start.' Anne looked pleased for a moment but was clearly impatient to move on.

Sam patted her pockets vaguely, but Anne did not look sympathetic.

'One moment.'

Sam disappeared inside, and keen to show she'd heeded the advice about being vigilant carefully closed the front door behind her, leaving her visitor on the step. In the kitchen she rooted around in her shopping bag before retrieving a ten-pound note from her purse. She put this in the envelope, sealed it and took it back out to Anne, who felt the envelope approvingly and tucked it away at the bottom of her pile. 'Cheerio then,' she said, already turning to leave.

Unsettled by talk of *the dark arts*, Sam hovered on her doorstep, waiting for her visitor to disappear completely before she closed the door. Anne had only walked a few paces away, however, before she stopped and turned back. She appraised Sam carefully in her doorway and her gaze took a sharp inventory of the windows, as though calculating the house's capacity. 'You're married?' she barked, with barely a question mark.

'I am?' said Sam, offering one in return, in an act of unintentional uncertainty.

'Excellent.' Anne looked her up and down, affronted anew by Sam's casual clothes. 'Family house.' She observed before asking with a disconcerting brusqueness, 'Children?'

Sam faltered and swallowed. 'No,' she said, willing herself to leave it there. She dug her fingernails into the palms of her hand. 'Not yet,' she added, unable to resist a qualification to fill the screaming silence that flooded the space between them. She felt a gushing deluge of self-loathing release in a rush with the words.

'You're young. Plenty of time,' Anne said with a small nod of permission. She turned and walked off, this time without stopping or looking back.

Sam retreated to the cool welcome of her house and locked herself in. She leant against the door and closed her eyes, breathing slowly, allowing the adrenalin to subside.

Chapter 6

It was possible that the throng of a busy station might feel shocking to Danny as he became used to the still of the countryside. But right now, he felt confident as he left the comfort of the train carriage, bracing himself as he took his place amongst the cascade of commuters all destined to spill down the same narrow holloway that descended to the underground platforms beneath them. Danny liked to feel in control, so this vast confusion of feet, hurtling at pace as though a starter gun had been fired, could have been prohibitively difficult for him to face. But years of practice had led Danny to understand that he could feel in control of most things providing he'd devised a rigid system to follow. When he achieved this, he felt accomplished, and when he felt accomplished, he felt in control.

Most things, it transpired, Danny could learn, and Danny had not just *learnt* to cross London at its busiest, he had *mastered* it. Sometimes he could even believe he had pulled the trigger on the starting gun, and that the mass of humanity was moving forward at his own command. And now, far from being horrified by the swarming herd, he relished the sense of belonging that came from travelling in the same direction at the same time as so many other people. Now and then, the occasional unpracticed ditherer, out of step with the rest of them, might upset his stride by coming to an abrupt halt in front of him but that was rare on the morning commute and he had found a path that he could tread quite reliably to help him execute his journey seamlessly.

Danny loved London. This morning, as he took his place on the tube platform, he quietly contemplated the pure genius of the underground map. He didn't need to refer to the one somewhere behind him on the tiled wall, he was able to reproduce a near-perfect rendition in his head. Danny had endless admiration for the brilliance it must have taken to reduce the messy meanderings of the tube trains' literal journeys into this elegant portrayal that in no way attempted to describe the truth below the surface but somehow allowed its millions of users to navigate its many paths by only focusing on Harry Beck's linear and infamous graphic retelling. The masterpiece had spared Danny from ever contemplating the messy truth that surrounded him and instead he calmly awaited his turn before jostling his way on to a crowded carriage that pretended to take him northwards in an entirely straight line.

As he hurtled towards his office he wished that somebody could apply the same logic to the twists and turns of the countryside and present to him instead a navigable grid. Perhaps that would help reduce the dizziness that he seemed to experience when he reversed the journey and abandoned London's structures that helped to anchor him safely into place. Sam seemed to have adapted to the countryside so effortlessly but for Danny its mysteries and unexpectedness continued to frighten him.

Danny wondered how long it would take him to learn and then master his new habitat. He was impatient to develop a system, but there were no obvious moorings from which he could begin his education. If only he could be honest with Sam, he could ask for her help, but the idea of betraying his weakness to her filled him with a greater fear still. He briefly imagined opening up to her, talking to her about the night terrors that kept him awake, and his heart immediately began to race and his palms immediately began to itch with the prickle of perspiration.

The tube lurched, once falsely and then truly as it drew in to his station. Danny's previous thoughts were aborted as the carriage tipped him out on to another busy platform and, joining the current flowing there, he found himself carried along the windy tunnels, rising to the ground level and spilling out finally into the comparatively still London streets. Danny breathed in deeply, appreciating the reassuring familiarity of the myriad smells. It was clear to him that he hadn't begun to get used to the countryside. This paved ground beneath him, the certainty of the slabs, was where he felt most at home.

Chapter 7

With no firm plan in her mind, other than to escape the pull of her laptop and the possibility of any further visitors, Sam departed the house in a hurry. She turned left out of the gate at the back of her garden and followed a narrow path, darkened by thick holly trees on one side and an oppressively tall wooden fence on the other. She followed the footway for a couple of hundred metres before it abruptly ended, revealing to her blinking eyes a vast field that dipped down to another distant hedge at the very lowest point of this bowl. Here she had a choice, to continue on the path down the hill beneath the cover of the trees or to climb over a stile and track the tree line of the wood to her left. She chose to take this higher path, finding relief in her new horizons and particularly the view the drop of the field afforded her. Restored again, she was immediately intrigued to see how quickly she could immerse herself in real countryside. There was little sign of animal life, but the ground was broken up around the fence she'd crossed and there were a number of fresh-looking cow pats on the grass, so she kept a wary eye out for the field's occupants. She hugged the top of the field, looking up to admire her surroundings as often as she could but conscious of the uneven surface beneath her, which if it was a path, was a poor one, as it was broken by rabbit holes, fallen timber and ankle height brambles that tumbled from the base of the tall trees like spillage. The woods she walked beside were dark and impenetrable, knotted with a bulwark of dense foliage. Twice Sam disturbed a pheasant which, at her approach, clattered clumsily and shockingly out of the undergrowth, ill-equipped – apparently – to make a dignified escape.

The woodland formed a square and at the far corner she could now choose to follow the footpath across the field to another stile she could see at the far side or take a narrow footpath that led diagonally back through the wood. She looked at her watch. She'd only walked for twenty minutes and she calculated that this path should get her home very directly (by walking the third side of a triangle) but, she reasoned, learning a quick route to use in the morning might be useful, particularly if Danny were ever able to overcome his allergies so she could have a dog, so despite the unwelcoming darkness, she ducked into the trees and followed the path beneath them.

Where the field had been still, the woods were fizzing with activity. Birds rattled above her and squirrels darted around her feet. As she got closer to what must have been the centre of the wood, she looked up at the pine needles high above her and she felt both dizzy and small. The gaps in the trees allowed glimpses of the sky above but never before had the sky looked so beyond her grasp. In London, the sky was something that clung oppressively to the tops of buildings, threatening to drop down to street level and engulf her, but here in the woods she could see the great expanse of nothingness between the highest branches and the clouds and, as she craned her neck back, she could sense the void beyond them.

She stepped over a tree that, unable to find a direct path upwards or thwarted perhaps in an earlier effort, had grown horizontally low to the ground before seizing a better opportunity and reaching up once again towards the light. She stopped to examine it, having never had cause to notice nature's resourcefulness before. Now it was before her, this audacious determination to be a tree despite the obstacles seemed to Sam the greatest of achievements. She felt overwhelmed by them, by the sheer vitality of these plants that, left unchecked, had grown to become giants all around her and she admired their success, envied it perhaps, knowing instinctively that their will to flourish was far greater than her own.

All around her small saplings had taken root and, despite the fierce competition for both nutrients and light, some were well on their way to future greatness. She looked at one closely, an oak, still wearing its winter colours. She admired its miniaturist excellence, each of its ten leaves shaped exactly as its acorn had intended with the centremost leaf a smaller version of its future self. She wondered if this tiny tree held within it all of its future boughs and each of its future leaves, in the same way she had been born with all of her egg cells in place. The tree wasn't wasteful though, was it, each intended leaf had the capability to fulfil its whole purpose where she had been born with so many *more* egg cells than required. A couple of million jostling to be one of the few hundred to mature and all of them, as it turned out, surplus to requirements.

Whilst Sam felt insignificant in this fecund habitat, she liked the truth of her paltry inconsequence. The woods didn't care about her. They were egoless and allowed her to be still, without the need for prominence. If she remained motionless for long enough these trees would, quite without malice, entwine their branches around her and carry on growing regardless. She wondered if they would hoist her with them as they grew upwards or if they would absorb her into their heartwood instead.

In the city, she always seemed to be in the wrong place at the wrong time, battling her way upstairs from the underground with a stampeding scrum descending upon her; crossing a road against the flow and finding no plausible pathway through the onslaught of pedestrians; looking left to guard against cars only to be mown down by an unseen cyclist swinging around a corner shouting abuse at her whilst she had one foot still on the pavement and the other mid-stride. Though contradictory, she had felt simultaneously hippopotamian and invisible and she had never dared to pause for fear of being trampled. Consequently, she'd kept moving, despite never being quite sure of where she was going until the sheer tumult of pace had overtaken her, mowing her down impatiently.

The countryside, Sam decided, particularly the woodland, afforded her a better sense of scale. She felt *proportionally* represented. Here, the wood was teeming with energetic wildlife but her irrelevance felt appropriate, more like an escape than an exile. The trees had taken a hundred years or more of steady, focussed growth and she was of no importance to them. Sam felt emboldened by the thought. She peered into the darkness between the boughs, wondering if she might spy something bigger than the frantic squirrels, something that might account for the feeling of being watched that she'd felt since joining the path. It wasn't an uncomfortable feeling, but she couldn't quite ignore Anne's warning and she felt herself snubbing the fear self-consciously, whistling tunelessly under her breath and swinging her arms with a little more gusto than she might have employed had she not felt this invisible scrutiny.

The woods were much cooler than the field and with more obstacles to impact, the wind appeared to make more of an impression here. Heavy limbs waved above her and smaller branches swayed at eye level, occasionally looming towards her as if they were shaking their fists. Still, she refused to be cowed by the woods and continued at a confident pace, until a movement to her left caught her eye and she stopped to investigate. Ten metres or so away from the path the frayed edge of a blue tarp snapped in the wind. She followed its line, tracing it to the corner of a large, low caravan. The vehicle didn't look habitable, a mossy excrescence appeared to be reclaiming it, pulling it into the undergrowth and providing a slow, creeping camouflage. Stout trees surrounded the dwelling, providing no obvious entrance or exit.

It was unlikely that anybody could live here still, and yet, troubled by Anne's warning, the sense she was being observed felt stronger than ever. Sam shuddered, and hurried on, imagining the terrors you'd need to escape to find life in a rotting caravan preferable to a life elsewhere. She thought of the London equivalent, the street dwellers, whose carefully guarded prime sites near the tube station could guarantee a bewildering delivery of food, compassion and contempt. Would this be better?

The path narrowed even more as she followed its lead out of the woods. On either side thick undergrowth reached out to her and she wondered if she might have to turn back. But after only a couple more minutes she found she was able to join the main path back to her home. The unnecessarily tall wooden fence was now to her left as she walked back to Broome Cottage. The woods had felt impenetrable, and their grandeur excused them. But this fence gave the impression of something far more sinister as if only the most shameful of secrets required so much shielding. A small knothole, no bigger than an acorn, presented itself and Sam took the opportunity to put her eye to it.

Behind the fence was a long sweep of immaculate lawn. It was notably green and well presented for the time of year, perfect stripes running the full length of the grass. Generous herbaceous borders, almost the width of Sam's entire garden, flanked either side of the lawn. Half way up the border a gardener worked. He looked like he belonged to another era, Sam thought, the kind of gardener you'd find in a children's picture book. He had a wheelbarrow full of dung beside him and he was methodically working it into the soil around the base of the plants. Many of the shrubs were cut back to just a few inches from the earth so Sam was unable to identify the individual components of the overall scheme, but she could imagine the splendours to come in the weeks ahead. The gardener wore thick corduroy trousers, a tweed jacket, and a tweed flat cap. He was curiously old-fashioned and in no hurry, apparently, but it was evident that he knew what he was doing, and he carried himself in a way that suggested he had been doing it for a very long time.

Beyond the garden was a large white house. There were a couple of lights on downstairs but no real sign of activity. The garden had none of the usual trappings of life – no children's toys or play things, no outdoor seating areas. Just grass and flowerbeds. It was stark but orderly. Sam liked it but much more for its potential than its current state.

The house itself was pleasantly solid. Grand but with no frills of pretension. Sam felt guilty, peering through a hole in a fence at a house, imagining the busy goings on that must justify a building of that size. She wondered who lived there and wondered what sort of people they might be. As the crow flew, they were near neighbours, but Sam couldn't imagine ever being invited in to such a grandiose house. Perhaps it would be different when the house was in use and she could hear life being lived in full, perhaps then she could imagine being shown around the garden by a delighted and proud homeowner. She imagined herself navigating her way to the corresponding front door and ringing on a doorbell, introducing herself.

The gardener straightened himself up slowly, his face suggesting a silent groan. He was now looking directly towards Sam and even though he couldn't possibly see her, she backed away from the fence, apologising under her breath for snooping.

She headed home, thinking a little fancifully about the two homes she'd witnessed: the caravan and the mansion. Each one had been silent, barely suggesting any habitation at all, but so different in every other way. That caravan, dripping with mould and moss, scarcely a shelter and that great big house, equally empty but a conspicuous symbol of wealth and success and achievement, nonetheless. Who lived in these two homes, so unlike one another yet equally isolated? Sam wondered.

She entered the gate that led from the footpath into her own modest garden. She looked up at the small house, a flood of warm pride filling her senses. She brushed her hand across the top of a tatty box plant, happy with her house that, whilst perhaps a little bit too big for just the two of them, felt perfectly right.

Chapter 8

With Sam back in the comfortable confines of her own home and Danny luxuriating in the lack of intimacy that London afforded him, life continued in isolation for the woman in the woods.

Diana did indeed live in the woods, and her home at first glance was a hovel, but she was not a witch. She had little patience for the occult, and had even less interest in the comings and goings of her village neighbours, but she did have a *past*. And it was this life-already-lived that the villagers saw in her eyes and chose to fear. Nobody liked a woman with a past, particularly one that lived in a mildewed caravan in the woods, woods that had hitherto only really had a reputation for bluebells, which was reputation enough, the villagers thought.

Diana lived just a few hundred metres from Broome Cottage as the crows flew, though when the crows rose from her woods they never actually chose to fly in a direct line, rather scatter themselves noisily in every direction before settling close to their starting point, in a clamouring rabble, as if their short and separate journeys immediately demanded urgent discussion.

Diana was an expert in woodland noises and had heard the screech that had so alarmed Danny, recognising it immediately as the shriek of a barn owl. She'd been able to accurately envisage its circuit, knowing how it routinely called out as it quartered the field, but rather than feeling fear she'd lain awake, alert, knowing that within weeks she would hear the accompanying sound of the owlets as they rasped their grating chorus, beseeching the swift return of their mother with more food. Anticipating the young birds' croaking calls served as a reminder that she had survived yet another winter in her sparse dwelling, and she smiled.

Diana loved those night noises. The winter was a challenge but the spring, now just about upon her, was a treasure trove of recompense. There was a nest high above her, and she expected to soon hear the insistent complaint of those barn owl chicks, indignant at their mother's absence. The sound was unlike anything else in the woods and it was always such a surprise to hear the guttural scratching noise that would in adulthood evolve into the low hoot more associated with owls. Diana knew the ways of the owls. The mother would take off to hunt quite routinely, before returning to mollify her young with small sounds of comfort while bringing them their food.

For some years Diana had lived in close proximity to her family of barn owls. Their territory was the many big fields that fell away from the woods and seeing the female take her circuit before deciding on her hunting ground was one of the great thrills of Diana's life. She was not superstitious, nor religious, and yet she attached some sort of idolatry to the barn owl. It felt like a guardian angel and a sight of it lifted her spirits, and its absence – sometimes for periods that stretched over many days – gave her a tremulous anxiety that increased her feeling of vulnerability.

Living amongst the birds was to be witness to a fast paced and violent cycle more gripping than any soap opera. She knew all the nests of course, from the barn owls' to the goshawks' and the woodpeckers', wrens' and thrushes' in between but she knew better than to have favourites. Wildlife living was not for the emotionally fragile. She had learnt to be pragmatic as she watched the mother's fierce nurturing come to nothing with the first few outings for a newly fledged chick. It was hard to love all of the birds equally; her loyalties were so torn. She loved to watch the songbirds fledge and rooted for them all, the mistle thrush particularly who, undaunted by wet and wild weather, would continue its fearless song and in gloomy moments could lift Diana's spirits with a surge of optimism. Watching a juvenile mistle thrush picked off by a sparrowhawk would give her a sharp stab at the injustice but before she had even finished mourning the unsung songs she would be applauding the sparrowhawk's success which was, by her own reckoning barely one in ten strikes. These hunters favoured speed, agility and surprise over accuracy and would barrel themselves low and fast at their prey, and Diana never tired of watching their stealthy attacks. Meanwhile the misses, which were much more common than the hits, similarly pained Diana because she had come to love those sparrowhawks fiercely. But then, Diana reasoned as she ran through her ornithological hier-archy in her head, when the goshawk took a sparrowhawk she'd quickly be celebrating that triumph, too. The goshawks were dynamos who whipped amongst the trees like gung-ho jet pilots, never choosing a straight route when an obstacle course was available. Perhaps the goshawks were her favourite of all. Diana had seen a goshawk take a sparrowhawk who herself had been in pursuit of a fieldfare. And she'd barely known who to cheer. Thank goodness, she thought, that the thrushes and the tits and the robins and the warblers all had enough sense to produce more young than necessary to keep their numbers stable.

Though Diana exerted plenty of energy during each day – walking, foraging, cutting down the hazel whips that she liked to weave into ever more complex shapes – she slept very little at night. The hours of darkness were the most thrilling in the woods. The nocturnal birds and mammals gave it a vividness, depicting a three-dimensional nightscape that she could picture as clearly as if it were bathed in sunshine. She liked to lie in her bed and allow her mind to paint the detail that the noises described, and she was usually wide awake for the opening bars of the dawn chorus, certain she could sense the puffing of the first chest a moment before the inaugural note was sounded. Often, she'd compensate for her lack of sleep at night by dozing in the daytime and her favourite time for this was when it was raining heavily enough for the drops to penetrate the dense beech and conifer canopy, hitting the roof of the caravan hard and tapping out its rhythm that she'd then fall asleep to. She loved those hours, when it rained, when nobody used the footpaths and the animals had taken shelter all around her and she could burrow down just a few feet from other sleeping forms looking for the same comforts: a dry, secret bed and a sleep free from fear or conscience.

In the winter months, Diana spent a lot of time lying in the warmth of her bed, her blankets pulled up to her chin. Sometimes she would write her diary entries from there, leaving only her head and one hand exposed to the cold.

Echoing Sam's own instinct for escape, Diana had moved to the woods in a resolute search for a simpler life and she'd made great strides in pursuit of this, although much to her surprise it transpired that a truly simple life was really quite demanding. Her daylight hours were almost all accounted for by the practical requirements of survival. Diana had imagined a life of quiet meditation, interrupted by occasional forays further afield with some sort of trug or other basket over her arm, so it had come as a bit of a surprise to find that even the most basic of needs took considerably more effort when you chose to live lightly. But, though she'd managed to find all sorts of clever ways to rid herself of the constraints of capitalism and dismiss any urge for the pursuit of the material, she still retained a few of her old habits. One of these in particular she found very hard to resist even though she knew that until she could stop this practice entirely, she could never be the free spirit she aspired to be.

This most destructive habit was her unhealthy obsession with her *bête noire*, Rebecca, who lived in the big house on the hill. (Diana was very fond of the description *bête noire*, it seemed to be so much more *exotic* than some of the other words she might reach for. Rebecca was also a thorn in her side, the bane of her life, a bugaboo, a rival, a foe. But *bête noire* was the most pleasing.)

Whilst Diana had moved to the caravan to escape Rebecca and all the people like Rebecca, she couldn't quite stop herself from spending quite a lot of each day thinking about her. Diana could look at the clock on the wall and immediately have an instinct for what Rebecca might be doing at that very moment. Rebecca was Diana's most visceral manifestation of the civilised world she'd left behind, and, drawing on the details of her own past-life, she could conjure up her image with ease. If Diana glanced at the clock at 7.30 a.m., she would imagine Rebecca with her head down, umbrella up, rushing for a train. Later, after a forage in the fields Diana would come back into the caravan to her notebooks and a sharply contrasting image of Rebecca would emerge. She'd have her head down, computer screen ablaze, pale green flashing against a dark green screen, those intoxicating numbers tripping over themselves in their bid to multiply like some resilient, toxic lifeform. Later as Diana ate her lunch, she liked to imagine Rebecca despondently stabbing at a piece of chicken with a plastic fork, fishing it out of its polystyrene container, the food barely observed by the torpid eyes of an automaton and barely tasted by the numbed taste buds of a perpetual dieter.

But what, for Diana, had begun as a guilty pleasure, occasionally indulged in to add contrast to her own feral existence, had become a compulsion. Diana could now lose a whole morning, perhaps even a day, just thinking about Rebecca. Lying on her bed and looking up at the blank white ceiling above her she could imagine Rebecca going about her day in highly defined, Technicolor detail. Focusing intently, Diana would not just see Rebecca getting on the train but could almost hear her clip-clopping along the station platform in her high heels, feel the wheezing puff of the train door opening and sense the brush of Rebecca's knee-length skirt as she found her seat, before pulling it tightly across her knees as she crossed her legs and opened her laptop in one seamless movement. Sometimes Diana would feel like a fellow passenger, watching Rebecca as she tapped at her keyboard furiously, the commuter quite unaware of the arrivals and departures of her fellow passengers or their own stories unfolding around her. Rebecca would always insist on being the first to the office and the last to leave and Diana, satisfied by her own choices she'd made, revelled in the contrast of her quiet pace.

Then the sudden bark of a fox or the startling alarm call of the goshawk would tug her back to her small oblong world, unsure of quite why she'd strayed so far or how she'd managed to return.

Diana was *not* a witch, but she was a realist, and there were actually many areas that she failed to fully live the wholesome life she had promised herself. She knew she hadn't been able to rid herself of everything, she hadn't managed to achieve quite that, for here she was dozing in a caravan which in itself was inarguably 'stuff' but she'd gone to extraordinary lengths to overcome her obsession with personal wealth and here in the woods she lived very lightly. But she'd been less successful in ridding herself of the thought of Rebecca and the choices that woman had made, and Diana knew that obsessing about her was not too far removed from living that life herself and making those choices.

She scolded herself, out loud perhaps, though it was often difficult to discern between the words she spoke in her head and those she used to address the notebooks, pictures and other small comforts of her caravan. 'We all choose our individual paths,' she reminded herself. 'I am not superior to Rebecca, she does what she has to do. I do what I have to do.' But Diana *did* feel superior, she knew in her heart that eschewing that other way of living was a step further towards the enlightenment that she felt might reveal itself if she avoided the distraction of modern life.

Diana took a notebook from the shelf, turned the page and admired the opportunity its blankness presented her. She knew that her quest for nothingness would be a painstaking one, but here in the woods, at least she was no longer in a hurry. When she compared her new life to her past one, she could congratulate herself on the many giant strides she had taken. She'd coped with the reality of solitude here, and she reasoned that holding on to a few home comforts wasn't such a great failing. If, after shedding her obsession with Rebecca, it still felt important to get rid of her last few material props, she would complete her purge then. For now, though, she had her owls, her goshawks, her foxes and her herbs to focus on, and perhaps, if she spent enough time in their company, Rebecca would begin to conveniently fade away into the past where she belonged.

Chapter 9

Sam knew nothing, yet, of Diana or their similarities, but she was already drawn to the path and the woods it led to. She was about to leave to explore it further when the phone rang. Sam sensed it would be her mother. Only her mother and the personal accident claim companies ever rang the landline, but her mother rang, uniquely, when Sam was least likely to want to talk to her whilst the personal accident claim companies weren't as discerning.

'Darling, how *are* you?' her mother asked down the phone, purring her peerless blend of faux cheeriness and exaggerated concern.

'I'm good, Mum. How are you?' Sam replied, neutrally, whilst sinking down to the floor, her back against the wall.

'Exhausted,' she said with a heavy sigh. 'Your father and I are off to the Dordogne.'

'Lovely, have fun.' Sam knew that her own contribution to this conversation was merely punctuation for her mother's monologue and it could be a while before the underlying message would be revealed.

'We'll stop and see your cousins in Felixstowe. I expect we'll have a bite to eat with them before the ferry. It will help break the journey and, these days, my tummy doesn't agree with ferry food.'

'Did your tummy ever agree with ferry food, Mum?'

'Very true. But I'm even more sensitive these days. It will be lovely to see your cousin, Lucy is a super cook.'

'Great. Send my love.'

'They always ask after you. Gerry and Lucy. It would be rather nice if you went to see them one of these days rather than holing yourself up all the way over there. The children are growing up so fast. I worry you won't ever *know* them and that feels like such a great sadness. They're *family*, darling. And, you know what I feel about *family*. These early years are just so precious, but they do go so quickly. I just worry that you're going to miss this opportunity to take part in their childhood and, whilst you might not see this now, you'll almost certainly come to regret it.'

'I can't see myself popping to Felixstowe in a hurry.' Sam felt herself tensing. She had very little interest in Gerry and Lucy or their children, and she doubted they had that much interest in her. She'd barely heard a mention of Gerry, or Lucy, or her cooking or their children until a couple of years ago and now her mother seemed to talk to her about nothing else.

'Darling, you sound very brittle. Are you all right? It's been such a long time since we've seen you. Your father and I do worry about you so.'

Sam propped the telephone receiver between her ear and her shoulder and examined her fingers while she spoke, running their tips across her nails, searching out rough edges for future examination. Her nails, she realised, were in a terrible state. She wondered, in the moments it took to form her response, whether this was because she had more important things with which to occupy herself or whether she had stopped caring about her appearance. 'Well,' she said, slowly, cautiously. 'We've moved in to the new house. That's kept me busy. It's an upheaval, moving. And we're new to the area so it has taken a while to settle in; there was so much to do, so we haven't had much time at the weekends to stray very far. But you could always come and see us here, I've asked you over countless times. And we're probably closer than the cousins. I doubt we're much more than an hour from you on the motorway.'

'But, darling, you're in completely the wrong direction.'

Sam stopped looking at her nails and gripped the phone more tightly. 'I'm in the wrong direction for what? It's not completely in the wrong direction if you're coming to see me. In my new house. With my husband.'

'Oh, well, yes, I thought you meant on the way to the Dordogne.' Sam could hear her mother's deep inhalation before she spoke the next sentence. 'Why don't you come on holiday with your father and I? I think if you saw the cousins on the way that might break the ice.'

'I don't really need to go to the Dordogne to see the cousins, that's ridiculous. And, regardless, I can't just up sticks and go to France!'

'Whyever not? You have no *ties*.' Never had so much pitying judgement been squeezed into one tiny word.

'But I *do* have ties. I have plenty of commitments. The garden for one.'

'You have a garden now? Lovely, darling. I'm so pleased for

you. That will take your mind off things. We have the lovely Mr Jones who does for us. Perhaps you can find somebody in the village to keep an eye on it. If you're going to have a garden, you'll need a Mr Jones, otherwise something that should be a pleasure can quickly become a burden.'

'A *tie*, do you mean?' asked Sam, quickly, smiling at her own riposte. 'A Mr Jones? I don't think so, it's all new to me. I'm not ready to delegate yet. And besides I'm busy at work, too.'

'You're working? Oh,' Sam's mother paused dramatically before finishing the sentence with a hesitant, 'good.' Sam marvelled at her mother, the mistress of intonation. Never had the word 'good' been laden with so many syllables and so much disapproval.

'Well, actually, I'm volunteering. At a hospice.' As a younger woman, Sam hadn't been a natural liar, but it was something she turned to more and more when confronted by other people's disappointment in her. Even as she spoke the words, she could feel the heat rising into a fully formed blush. She mentally crossed her fingers behind her back by squeezing her eyes tightly shut. She had never stopped feeling like a small child when she spoke to her mother and she didn't know why she had this compulsion to pretend she was better, more *valuable*, than her own truth. She was like a small child, she realised. A small child trying on different outfits in a hot changing room and coming out each time to a wrinkled nose or fierce shake of a head from a mother who had a very fixed idea of who and what she was expecting to emerge from the changing room each time.

Her mother, though, was indifferent to Sam's fictional hospice work. 'Good on you. And how is poor Danny?'

'*Poor* Danny?' asked Sam, her eyes that a moment before had been squeezed tightly shut now widened to their fullest possible stretch of incredulity even though her mother couldn't see them.

'Well, yes, life has been so beastly to him. Rotten.'

'I'm not sure he sees it that way, Mum.'

'No. Quite. I'm sure you're *more* than enough, darling. I've got to go. Your father is calling for me.'

Sam said, 'Bye, Mum,' softly down the phone but wasn't convinced her mother hadn't already hung up. 'Wow,' she said, more forcibly to herself before standing up, replacing the phone in its cradle and stretching herself out.

Chapter 10

Giving the rage time to peter out, Sam paced up and down in the kitchen, thinking furiously. She had left London for the countryside looking for somewhere to hide. The recent intrusions, both from her neighbour and her mother, had infiltrated her defences.

The trouble with homes, she realised, is that they had too many entry points. There were doors to knock on, windows to peer through, telephone wires to creep down and a full electromagnetic spectrum of pulses and waves through which communication could reach her, regardless of whether or not she invited it in. She looked out of the window at her small neat lawn and its simplicity beckoned.

Leaving the house to fizzle and crack with unspoken sentiment, she headed into the garden. She inhaled and exhaled deeply through her nose, turning slow circles at first but then spinning around in the middle of the lawn and revelling in the fresh air that was now, inexhaustibly, hers. She still couldn't quite believe she owned this plot. Not just the house, with its roof and its tiles and its walls and its bricks (so many bricks!) but the garage and the neatly laid path that led to the garden and the made-to-measure space for the wheelie bins and the sturdy fence and the lawn.

The lawn! That was perhaps the strangest of all realisations. The grass that grew each day, that would be cut and would grow again, was all hers. She owned this grass and all the future grass yet to be, and it seemed unfathomable to be in possession of something so mercurial. She owned the shadows too, she reasoned, particularly those cast by the trees to the east of her south-facing garden, as the sun fought its morning battle to hoist itself high above her. These shadows were hers alone to sit in, which, she decided, gave her some small right to the trees that cast them and with this astonishing revelation she left her garden, propelled by the urge to stretch her legs and further explore the intricate nervous system of public footpaths that intersected with her own small patch and should lead her to expand her domain in almost any direction without going near a road.

Sam could reflect on her scars that had never quite healed, and worry at them until they reopened but really, she realised, alone in her garden she had few responsibilities other than to touch the bark that shielded the trunk that led to the leaves that cast her very own shadows.

She joined the path she'd recently discovered and even as she closed the gate behind her she felt a disproportionate thrill of anticipation at the knowledge that she would soon reach that house with its big lawn. She knew already that she would once again stop and spy on it and she knew, too, she wouldn't be able to talk herself out of it. She also knew she'd want to go and look at that other house, too.

As she reached the high fence she slowed down, stopping

at the knot hole she'd discovered before. Once again the gardener was hard at work but this time he was working much closer to her, just a few large paces from the boundary fence. She studied him carefully as he dug. With each spade-full he'd bend and sort through the earth, pulling out small roots and discarding these into a big low sack beside his barrow. He worked slowly and methodically but looked neither beatific nor anxious. His face was entirely neutral.

Between each thrust of the spade's blade he'd stretch himself tall and then lean forward with both hands on the spade's handle to maximise the downward force. His method was honed and it was clear he'd found a rhythm to his work years ago. Occasionally he'd stop and pick something up, examine it carefully only to throw it dispassionately into the centre of the lawn where a number of small birds, hopping hopefully nearby, would swoop competitively to retrieve it, as if part of a practiced routine. Snails, Sam decided, judging by the flash of contempt on the gardener's face.

As she watched him, Sam became aware of a disturbance from beyond, a young woman was emerging from the back door of the house. The rear entrance was just below garden level and she came up the two deep steps confidently, carrying a mug in each hand.

Sam studied her carefully. She was her age, certainly no older. The man's daughter, she wondered at first, but she dismissed this theory as unlikely as quickly as she'd fallen upon it. The young woman walked the full length of the lawn with an easy pace and handed a mug to the gardener. She wore neat black trousers and a white shirt. Her hair was scraped back into a ponytail and she wore no make-up. She looked a little apologetic as she approached. The gardener frowned and looked like he might even refuse to stop working but after some hesitation he thrust his spade into the ground, leaving it anchored in the soil.

'Cuppa,' the woman said, with a pleasant smile, extending the mug towards him.

Now with his back to her, Sam couldn't quite hear the gardener's response but he shrugged heavily and motioned towards the barrow where a thermos flask leant against the wheel. He took the tea regardless.

'When are you going to grow some flowers I can use in the house?' she asked, brightly. She looked around the broad borders. 'It seems silly that you work as hard as you do, and we still pay to get the florist in once a week.'

Sam held her breath, trying to hear the gardener's mumbled response but it was impossible to make out. The young woman spoke quite clearly, however.

'I know she doesn't. But I'd love to come out here in the summer for an armful of something I could use. Could she be persuaded, do you think?'

There was another exchange before Sam could hear the woman's words again. 'But I've only worked here for a short time. She might listen to you, you've been here for ever.'

The woman listened to his response and took a sip of her drink.

'Great, thank you. It's worth a go, anyway.'

Sam was intrigued. This great big house had staff and an enigmatic owner, a woman. A woman who liked gardens enough to hire a gardener but not to grow flowers for the house apparently. Sam once again imagined herself tracing a route to the front door, and hearing this conversation had allowed the idea of ringing on the doorbell to become a little more concrete as a possibility, not just a fantasy.

Glad she'd witnessed this exchange, however simple, Sam wandered on to explore more footpaths, knowing that whichever one she took, it would inevitably lead her to the woodland dwelling. She was as curious about its inhabitants as she was about those who lived in the fine, big house with its perfect lawn, and she felt nervous as she entered the thick of the trees, but it was a nervousness borne of excitement not fear.

She quickened her pace as she recognised some landmarks, knowing she was closing in on the caravan but when she arrived, she slowed right down, walking past gingerly and looking all the time for a glimmer of life from within.

Once again, it seemed forlornly abandoned. Despite this, she thought she could smell a trace of wood-smoke in the air which hinted at habitation, but the sheer degradation of the structure suggested otherwise. She imagined knocking on this door but knew that would take much more courage than arriving uninvited at the big white house. Those bigger houses insisted on visitors, despite their many deterrents in the shape of fences, gates, intruder alarms and staff but this caravan wasn't suggesting it wanted to be disturbed. Quite the opposite, this caravan was making it very clear that the whole purpose of being there was to avoid disturbance.

Resigned, but strangely disappointed that Anne's witch in the wood was probably a myth with no more reality than an abandoned caravan, she turned and repeated her previous walk but in the opposite direction and, once back at Broome Cottage, she applied herself to Danny's paperwork.

Using the methodology she had employed before, she tipped the boxes out and sorted the contents into piles. It became immediately clear that Danny's paperwork trail told a far more accomplished story than her own: paperwork relating to pension plans, ISAs and mortgage tracker funds; membership of various professional organisations; an invitation to a foreign conference; letters of congratulation; confirmations of pay-rises; contracts stating new job specifications. And each one of these steps up the corporate ladder required its own heightened bureaucracy to capture the greater responsibility that came with increased income and benefits, so that each increment, in turn, generated further paperwork and an accumulation of the necessary administration that was associated with safeguarding and protecting his wealth, his health and his life.

Sam found small pockets of sadness too, amongst the paperwork. An order of service, a faded wedding photograph, correspondence with the executors of his father's will (the prescriptive provisions for an only son spelt out with the painstaking precision by a tidy mind and the certain knowledge of its own imminent demise). But somehow Danny had wrestled order and his own carefully considered future from these ashes.

Sam was so proud of Danny. Orphaned in his early twenties, some young men would have used it as a reason not to work, or to go off the rails entirely, but not Danny, he had barely wavered from his self-determined path. His approach to adulthood had always been systematic. Even his choice of career had been thoroughly researched and investigated. When they'd first met, Danny had told her, with pride in his voice, that long before settling on a university degree, he had filled out a spreadsheet that detailed the number of years of education (and associated costs) and matched these with the lifetime earning opportunity for any career that he might be equipped for. He knew he was a competent all-rounder so would not have been daunted by any number of different directions, but his A Level choices had ruled out medicine and science and his cost-versus-benefit study had ruled out architecture and law so he'd settled on a career in actuary and had never deviated from that path. He was doing extremely well, earning promotions and the remuneration that went with it, and he was fulfilled by his role.

Though she found it baffling, Sam was full of admiration for such a structured approach to responsibility. Where she had stumbled and lurched from each emotional milestone to the next, shocked when people talked to her as though she might have adult sensibilities, Danny had purposefully set out to greet maturity at a pre-determined destination and time, allocating himself along the way a whole raft of astonishingly specific benchmarks by which he could measure his progress. These criteria were quite alien to Sam, who always felt like she was adopting the mannerisms of an adult, rather than actually becoming one.

Sam reflected on their different paths while she carefully filed Danny's paperwork. Once done, she opened her own drawer again and was pleased to see that her medical folders already looked less dominant now they were filed away. She wondered if Danny hoped her years of ill-health could be filed neatly away to be forgotten and that perhaps a miracle might yet happen, but this was just speculation. Danny had continued to insist that a family was not important to him, that he had all the family he wanted with her. And whilst Sam had initially been suspicious of his insistence on buying a three-bedroomed property, his argument rang true to his character when he maintained that a larger house was the more prudent investment.

Sam continued to work attentively, finding a quiet pleasure in preparing folders and file names and making sure there was plenty of room left for the many chapters life would yet deliver. It was a quality of pleasure that she believed, sincerely, might be able to prevent her reaching for her laptop, plugging it in and transferring the poison from within it to the crevices of her fragile mind.

Chapter 11

Birds ferried nest material back and forth, flitting past the windows of Broome Cottage. Had she been aware of it, the busyness of their purpose and the urgency of their quest would have panicked Sam who was in search of a restfulness that she believed belonged uniquely to the countryside.

Quite unconscious of the ferocity of activity all around her, Sam had been kneeling on the spare room floor for long enough for her skin to take on the cross-hatched imprint of the carpet. She had been having an argument with herself, fighting the urge to power up her laptop and check the messages that she knew would be amassing like ants around a crumb, but she was talking to herself in a stern voice, reminding herself that she was quite strong enough to resist the pull. When the doorbell rang, bouncing her out of her reverie, she hurried downstairs but seeing the blurred outline of a woman through the distorted glass of the front door, and suspecting a repeat visit from Anne, she took a few deep breaths to calm herself and, regretting her choice of a short skirt that morning, took a further moment to rub futilely at her red, patterned knees.

She composed her face into an untroubled look of welcome and opened the door.

Anne was not on the doorstep. Instead, another shorter altogether more dishevelled woman with the ruddy complexion of a farmer, was standing there. The visitor had both arms outstretched, thrusting a plated cake towards her. Sam noticed her broken fingernails and torn, sore cuticles as she took the plate and she immediately warmed to her, recognising the blatant evidence of a worrier. Meanwhile the visitor garbled her introduction, in a voice giddy with its mix of anxiety and excitement.

'I'm your neighbour, Hattie. Two doors down. It's a bit old-fashioned, but I thought I'd welcome you with a cake.'

Sam smiled generously and welcomed her visitor in. 'Cake's not old-fashioned, it's right on trend. Come on in,' she said kindly, whilst inwardly amused at the idea that people still took cake to their neighbours. She led the way into the kitchen, allowing Hattie to follow behind her. Aware that the kitchen was too warm to sit in comfortably, she went immediately to open the window above the sink, allowing a rush of cooler air to enter and bathe her face. She addressed Hattie over her shoulder as she fixed the window latch in place. 'Assuming it's gluten free?'

Hattie, who was already taking her place at the kitchen table faltered, stammering her reply. 'Oh gosh no, how insensitive of me. I'm so sorry.'

'I'm teasing,' said Sam, with a laugh. 'I love cake, all cake, particularly the glutinous type.'

Hattie smiled, relieved, but was now on edge, finding Sam's flippancy unnerving.

Sam busied herself opening the cupboard to take out the teabags and plugging in the electric kettle. The kettle had been in their London home and Sam felt a surge of affection for it as she flicked the switch down. Reinventing herself as a country dweller capable of welcoming cake-bearing neighbours with no cynicism was going to be a challenge but little reminders of her past life gave her the small boost of power she needed.

She looked at Hattie who appeared to be appraising the cake in front of her intently as if it were a complete mystery to her. 'Do you want a slice now?' asked Sam, not exactly sure of the etiquette involved in neighbourly cake deliveries – there hadn't been too many of those in SW11.

Hattie glanced at her watch and pulled an exaggerated expression of horror. 'Bit early for me. The sugar will send me wild and I'll spend the rest of the day rooting through the back of cupboards searching for sugar fixes and popping the children's vitamin chews like a demented addict. A cup of tea would be perfect if you've got the time.' She nodded towards Sam as she fussed around the kitchen and was now adding several unnecessary procedures to a routine she usually found quite straightforward.

As Sam moved from sink to cupboard, Hattie stood and replaced Sam in front of the window, looking out at the neat lawn, the bare beds and the high wooden fence that enshrouded it all.

'What a lovely kitchen, and a gorgeous garden,' Hattie gushed. 'They did a super job here, didn't they? I came and had a nose around when it went on the market the first time around but, goodness me, it needed a lot of work. This is gorgeous – it's like a new-build but with all the old-world charm. I'm really jealous, it makes mine look like a complete slum. You must be thrilled!'

Sam smiled affably. 'Yes, it's been a dream of ours for an absolute age. We're just glad to be in the countryside finally. I'm not sure my husband and I could have survived living in London for very much longer,' said Sam, quite deliberately filling in some gaps for her visitor.

Hattie looked relieved, allowing her shoulders to sag in the knowledge that she was talking to a kindred spirit. 'How long have you been married?'

'Four years,' said Sam, as she squeezed the teabags against the sides of the cups.

'Gosh!' said Hattie with a shy, hopeful smile. 'So, you must be thinking of starting a family soon. Unless...' She hesitated, first noting Sam's trim figure and swiftly moving on to scan the kitchen for signs of children's artwork on the fridge door, or the tell-tale signs of bright plastic toys in the garden. Seeing none, she carried on enthusiastically as Sam stopped her preparations and turned to face her guest. 'This house is going to be perfect for raising a family, in the heart of the countryside but with a nice safe garden.' Hattie's voice trailed off as she saw the change in Sam's face. Two pink spots had formed on her pale cheeks and though she was leaning back against the kitchen units, Hattie saw her clutch the edge of the work surface as if to steady herself.

Sam's palms had started to sweat. She knew it wasn't Hattie's fault, she knew the questioning was entirely innocent. She knew she was already harbouring resentment that should have been neutralised some other way, at some other time. Yet she also knew that she might be incapable of preventing an inappropriate response.

'We're not planning to have a family,' Sam said, amazed by her own calm delivery despite the instantaneous racing of her heart. She tried to inject some warmth into the statement, but its delivery was cooler than she'd intended.

Hattie stammered her reply, 'Oh, sorry, I just assumed...' but Sam quickly cut her off with the conversational equivalent of a blow to the back of the head.

'I can't have children.' Here Sam was looking for disarming nonchalance, but she knew from Hattie's downward glance that again her words had landed with more weight than she'd meant.

Hattie had looked momentarily crestfallen but quickly brightened, pulling herself taller and looking quizzically at Sam. 'But have you explored IVF? You're very young still, so there's plenty of time. I've heard so many stories of miracles recently. A friend of mine...'

Sam could hear her heartbeat in her ears as she ploughed on with a resolve she felt unable to control. Her anger should not find release with this visitor, it was unfair, unkind. But still she pressed on, responding not just to Hattie but to the multitude of similar sentiments that had paved the path to this moment. 'I don't have a womb so plugging that particular gap is probably an obstacle beyond the reach of a miracle.'

'Oh gosh.' Hattie lurched in Sam's direction and Sam thought she might be about to throw her arms around her. Instead she stopped, stock-still in the middle of the room looking devastated. 'I'm so, so sorry,' she said, her eyes filling up with tears. She returned to the kitchen table, sitting down heavily. 'I simply can't imagine,' she said, shaking her head.

Sam chose not to relinquish the safety of the kitchen counter quite yet, which she continued to lean on heavily. 'You have children yourself,' she acknowledged, in a misguided effort to turn the focus away from her own womb and towards Hattie's.

'Yes, three,' said Hattie apologetically, quickly adding, 'they're a handful. Honestly. Be careful what you wish for,' with a wincing smile that, fortunately, she barely allowed to materialise.

Sam sighed impatiently, recognising that other trait that so often followed when mothers stumbled uninvited into the labyrinth of Sam's absent reproductive organs. City or country-side, she was beginning to understand that she couldn't avoid this all too familiar pattern, though she calculated quickly that she could perhaps nip it in the bud before she spread it, like a virulent weed beneath her, wherever she trod. 'You don't need to apologise for your children. But I would really appreciate it if you didn't make assumptions about what I should do with my body. One of the main reasons I left office life in London behind was my colleagues' relentless obsession with my family planning. Or lack of it.' Sam put a cup of tea in front of Hattie. She had presumptively added milk but didn't offer sugar. She returned to the safety of the kitchen counter, liking its support and favouring its dependability which seemed far more appealing than sitting with Hattie at the table.

Hattie nodded but appeared not to be listening to Sam. Instead, she addressed the cake in front of her, turning a tea-spoon in her fingers as she spoke. 'I suppose you could adopt?'

Sam sighed again but this time with greater emphasis, a sigh that just about swallowed an oath. 'Well, yes, I suppose I could, if that would make you happier.' Sam spoke her words calmly, but now several notches louder, as though somebody out of sight had switched the volume up with a remote control. The increase in volume surprised Sam as much as it surprised Hattie. 'But tell me, Hattie, I'm intrigued to understand *why*, after knowing me for such a very short time, *why* you are so determined for me to have a family?' The rise in pitch betrayed the thundering chasm of emotion bubbling just below the surface as if Sam's veins carried molten lava that might find their way to her mouth before erupting without mercy.

Sam turned to stir her own tea and talked one notch still louder to make sure her words found their mark, realising with a rush that she didn't need this woman's interpretation of friendship and that her words would banish any such notion. 'You know absolutely nothing about me. Has it occurred to you that I might actually be an awful mother? I might not even *want* children. What on earth gives you the right to assume anything about me? I might have already had a baby, but had it taken away from me because social services had to intervene. My husband might be sterile. We might be celibate Shakers.' As she said this, Sam felt a trill of passion imbue her words with a quaver that might be mistaken for ecstatic fervour and she wondered, for a second, if she might have just received a calling to a remote religious community that practised non-procreation. She cleared the distracting thought with a shake of her head and returned to her rabid soliloquy with dogged zeal.

'I might, God forbid, not even *like* children.' This was the heresy that couldn't be spoken to a mother and Sam saw Hattie stiffen in horror, colour rising at her throat and travelling swiftly up to her cheeks. Sam turned the volume button one click to the left, softening her tone.

'You've made a number of pretty basic suppositions about me already and I just don't think it's remotely appropriate to come into my house and just presume to know what I want or to assume that I want what *you* want.' Sam thought this finale was quite generous and she was proud of her coherence. In her experience, words that had been stored for later use often spilt out in a far more unruly fashion.

Hattie, barely able to see the table in front of her through a blur of tears, put her tea down clumsily, catching the edge of the teaspoon and, spilling a bit of liquid on the table. She burst into noisy sobs as though the spilt tea was a final personal assault that had taken her over the edge, and, pushing her chair back and standing up in one clumsy action, she fled the kitchen.

Sam heard the sound of Hattie's wail as the front door slammed. She sighed and mopped up the tea. She didn't chase after her neighbour. Instead she wondered out loud, if these conversations would ever end.

She climbed the stairs wearily and sat at her desk, her head in her hands. She was cross with herself for letting that interaction escalate so quickly but not surprised. It was all there, bubbling under the surface all the time, waiting to be lanced. Disgusted by what she was about to do, but knowing her actions were inevitable now, she lifted her laptop from the floor and set it in the middle of the desk. She plugged it in and let its rousing lights tell the slow blinking story of its resurrection. She logged on, typing her password with one finger, a feeling of revulsion sweeping over her as she pressed return to confirm it and the computer whirred noisily to life. She hadn't meant to do this again, she'd hoped to leave it behind her for good, but she'd been wrong to think that escaping to the country would be escape enough.

Saliva ran high in her mouth, a sensation she associated with all of her bad habits. She typed the URL to a Wordpress blog. She was invited to type in her user name. Rather than her own name, she carefully typed in the name 'Libby Masters'. She entered Libby's password and, feeling a rush of adrenalin that gave her a purpose she'd missed, she waited for the page to load.

Chapter 12

Sam should have felt wracked with guilt, but she didn't. Instead she'd written twelve hundred words of impassioned complaint, proofread it carefully, posted it live and then before waiting for the inevitable flood of comments she had logged out. She had taken a few moments to delete her history, checking her desktop for tell-tale signs of her activity before powering off. She'd showered and washed her hair and let any brief thoughts of self-loathing drain away with the soap suds.

It was a fair exchange, she decided, as she towelled herself dry. She'd been subjected to a crescendo of assaults in her own home and, considering the gravity of this most recent invasion, she believed she had been fairly lenient with her assailant. But she knew from previous experience that she couldn't trap that feeling of intrusion inside her, allowing it to fester and propagate. Who knew what damage it would cause if it were allowed to advance unchecked? Instead, she had, in a well-practised methodology, cauterised it effortlessly by unleashing some provocative words into the ether. Writing honestly, painfully and self-indulgently had proven to be an excellent outlet for Sam's inner demons but she knew that there were consequences, too. She'd grown up amongst a whole generation of frail, anxious, broken women who had turned to the internet for solace and instead found a new torture. Sam knew that there would be people who would find her words and use them to fuel their own discontent, perhaps to ill-effect, and still more would find those words and rally an angry rebuttal. She hoped, in desperate delusion, that there might be a few who would find comfort from the words that Libby had written, by sharing some feelings that they might be unable to convey themselves.

While she dried her hair Sam justified her actions to herself quite fully and by the time she was ready to begin the day anew she had let some of the poisonous feelings dissipate completely so it was with a lightness of step that she hurried downstairs, renewing a promise to herself that now she was in the countryside she would commit to finding a healthier habit to replace this destructive one.

Sam washed up and tidied away the cups, erasing all traces of her visitor. She glanced out of the window at the bare garden and immediately saw what Hattie had seen: a garden pregnant with potential, awaiting the arrival of noisy children and discarded toys. She looked at it intently, until she could see it again as she wished to see it, a place of growth and renewal, a place for her to channel some of the energy she'd been using on her writing into something altogether more positive. Building something out of nothing seemed a fitting metaphor.

She let herself out of the back door and paced the lawn. The grass was definitely growing so she'd soon have to consider the possibility of mowing it. The flowerbeds, on the other hand, were stubbornly bare. She'd rather hoped that the property developers might have planted some bulbs and that she'd have a season of growth to revel in but there was nothing but a fine dusting of weeds, barely big enough to name but rampant enough for Sam to know no good would come of them.

She tugged her short skirt down around her thighs and sat in the middle of the grass, the cool of the morning just about reaching her core in a way that made her feel alive. She undid her laces and wriggled her trainers off, and then removed her socks, throwing both shoes in the direction of the house and then, less effectively, both socks. She thought about taking more clothes off. She looked around, assessing any potential risk of onlookers. Nobody would see her. But then she remembered her own moment of snooping on a neighbour's garden and felt exposed. Country dwellers seemed to thrive on noticing the activities of their community where in London it was quite possible to ignore your neighbours and pretend they didn't exist. Though she'd never tested the theory, she was quite sure that when in London she could have stripped naked and lain on the pavement at the front of the flat and passersby would have simply stepped over her. For a fleeting moment, Sam glimpsed the solace Danny seemed to find in anonymity amongst a crowd.

She lay down and looked up at the sky and then flipped over from her back to her front and examined the grass beneath her, paying particular attention to the flattened area that had been crushed under the back of her head. She ruffled the blades with her fingers, encouraging them to spring back and take their place in the lawn again. Tracing the leaves down to the soil, she could see that each grass tuft was its own little multi-leafed plant where she had always assumed that grasses were solitary blades, each fighting their own splendid battle for survival within their regiment. Sam looked more closely still, and saw immediately that at the base of the plants, insects toiled. Ants tumbled over each other in an attempt to investigate the interruption and small flies landed and took off in quick succession. In just a small circumference, she size of the back of her head, a whole universe scrabbled to right itself. Sam drew herself up to her knees, now aware that her body was probably suppressing a multitude of life that needed her to move away in order to continue its business.

On her knees, she surveyed the scene. Now she'd been in the woods she could imagine what the grass hoped it might become one day. She supposed that even a lofty beech tree must start as a tiny shoot but look what happened when it was left unchecked. Grass was vigorous, it seemed unlikely that it would bother to grow with such steadfast determination if it didn't have a greater ambition. Each individual plant had aspirations far loftier than her own and the thought astonished her. Left to its own device, this lawn might be a wild place where not just ants could get lost in its midst but bigger animals too. Sam liked the idea.

Sam also liked the idea that the growth was happening out of sight, deep beneath the surface. That was where the propulsion was really materialising, in the dark depths below her. There, amongst the damp, warm wormcasts, the core of the plant was thrusting ever upwards in a constant quest for light. What was visible to the eye was never the whole picture.

79

She continued to idly brush the grass back and forth, loving its pliability. 'This I can do,' she thought. 'It's not much, but I can do it.' The words repeated in her head, a mantra to keep her rooted to the lawn and its busy knot of life rather than racing back to the study to read the comments that she knew would be flooding in.

As Sam was dwelling on this new beginning, and convincing herself of the rightness of her actions from start to finish, she heard a car door slam. Jumping to her feet she walked down the path at the side of her house, to find Anne walking towards her, her face already set in a familiar look of consolation.

'Gosh, you're keen. Can't wait to recruit me?' Sam joked, as lightly as she could.

'My dear, I've come to apologise.' Sam drew back a bit, surprised.

'You have?'

'Yes, you must think I am terribly insensitive, trying to press-gang you into working in the hospice. Had I known of your condition, I would not have had the discourtesy to mention it.'

'My condition?'

'Hattie Jacobs told me. You're… ' here, she dropped her voice to spare the neighbours, 'you're barren.'

Sam nearly laughed out loud. Hattie had described her as barren? Sam rubbed her forehead absent-mindedly, as if trying to coax the right words out.

'Anne, for medical reasons I've had a complete hysterectomy. But I don't like to be described as barren, it makes me sound empty. And I'm not empty.' Sam swallowed heavily, submerging the emotions that were fighting to erupt as words.

Anne leant in further, conspiratorially. 'Of course you're not, dear. You're a *survivor*. Which is why you must have thought me terribly insensitive offering you volunteer work at the hospice.'

Sam was starting to shift her weight from foot to foot as her fight or flight reflexes coursed through her veins, vying for supremacy. She said quietly, patiently and with as much polite curiosity as she could muster, 'I'm actually really struggling to follow your train of thought.'

Anne had pulled a cotton handkerchief from her handbag and was now using it to excavate her not inconsiderable nostrils. Sam waited while her visitor completed her ablutions, eventually tucking her handkerchief into the cuff of her shirt. 'Well,' she said, oozing sympathy, 'that's the very last place you'd want to work, I imagine. You'd be better off volunteering for something that puts you in touch with the young, I'd think. There are plenty of worthwhile programmes I can introduce you to, we're a very *inclusive* community.'

Sam's shoulders hunched involuntarily, the weight of this new assault settling on her and pressing down relentlessly. She sighed heavily. 'I have absolutely no idea what you're talking about and why any of it is remotely relevant to me. I feel like I've just been sacked from a job I haven't yet applied for. I don't need this. I really don't need it. If I want to volunteer, I'll find something that suits me. If I don't want to volunteer and God knows why I would, quite frankly, then I won't. Is that fine with you and Hattie, do you think?'

Anne took Sam's hand in her own and squeezed it gently before dropping it. She shook her head slowly, the seep of compassion threatening to drown them both. 'My dear, I can understand what a difficult time you must be having, with your whole life destroyed at such a tender age. And your poor, poor husband. It must be even worse for him.'

Despite knowing she would sound deranged, Sam allowed a small laugh to escape. Tears were battling to form just out of sight and Sam desperately didn't want them to find an escape route. She wished she had allowed Anne to ring the doorbell. That way she could have opened the door to her and then, when she'd heard enough, she could have slammed the door in her face. But instead, they were standing in front of the garage, and Sam found herself completely incapable of ejecting her visitor, who was now peering at her closely, as if she might find traces of cancer, infertility or loss etched amongst her freckles.

Desperately, Sam seized upon the word 'husband' grabbing at it like a drowning woman grasping a lifebuoy. 'I'm very sorry, Anne,' she said carefully, 'but I'm right in the middle of preparing supper for my *husband*. You know what these men are like.'

'Oh my, don't let me get between a man and his supper. Cheerio and, you know… ' here, she squeezed Sam's unresponsive hand once more, 'well done.' Anne turned to leave, already snapping open her handbag to retrieve her car keys.

Sam ground her teeth into a smile. Once Anne had driven off, hesitantly, whilst checking her rear-view mirror repeatedly before slowly pulling out into the quiet country lane, Sam went back into the house and wearily trudged up to the office. Instead of allowing the tears to fall, she turned to her laptop with the quiet despair and inevitable submission of a seasoned addict.

Chapter 13

While Sam was learning that it would take more than a new home to reinvent herself, Danny was learning that a tight rein on his environment did not necessarily extend to his feelings.

He had secured his favoured seat, he had nodded at some familiar faces and the damp, grey day stretched ahead of him with reassuring predictability. And yet here he was, fiddling with his cuffs, adjusting his shirt collar and bristling with dissatisfaction. Danny had left for work feeling guilty and he wasn't enjoying the sensation. He was looking at his laptop but found himself quite unable to focus on the spreadsheet in front of him, nor could he lose himself in the view from the window. It was a small thing that had triggered this discontent; an observation that now wriggled between him and his focus like a bit of dust caught in his mind's eye.

As he left the house he'd noticed Sam's wellington boots, paired neatly by the door and as he'd reached down to pick up a lump of clay that had dried and dislodged from the boot's sole it had struck him that he had a wife who walked in the muddy fields each day and that this daily activity was a life quite separate from his own.

He would not walk with her, he could not immerse himself

in the vagaries of nature in the way she seemed to enjoy and they knew this about each other. But there was something about the angle of the wellington boots that seemed to hint at an absence. Perhaps there should be another larger pair, his, next to hers. Or perhaps there should be a couple of pairs in miniature, scattered haphazardly for him to right impatiently.

The memory of the dried clay between his fingers nagged at him. He wiped his hands carefully with sanitiser, hoping to erase the feeling the introspection evoked.

He should, he admitted to himself as he looked at the fields from the train, allow her to have a dog. This was where the guilt came from. A dog would be the answer. A lead hanging on the hook above the wellington boots would complete the tableau, negate the absence.

No. He scolded himself. He should confess to Sam that there were no allergies that would prevent them from having a dog. This was where the guilt came from.

But that admission would be too great. It would not be the admission of a small betrayal, it would be the disclosure of his cavernous frailty, and with that acknowledgement, everything he had built might crumble. The truth he dare not share was that he could not have a dog because he could not bear to lose a dog. A dog's life was pitifully short as it was. And how would he avoid losing his heart to a dog? He would love it, of that he was certain, he would not be able to avoid that love. But the dog's potential death would feel imminent every day he loved it. And then it would die. He would not cope.

His capacity to love was already stretched taut with his love for Sam. And she had already tested it, pulling at it beyond all elasticity. And when she had been so ill he thought it would snap, or she would snap, or he would snap, but then they had been given their reprieve, a chance for her to live, for the two of them to continue loving as they were. And he couldn't risk any more of his heart. All he had was already used up fully.

So, no, he couldn't have a dog. And he'd reasoned himself into a sensible solution. Allergies were non-negotiable and Sam respected his ways. And in his own way, he was allergic to dogs. He was allergic to the thought of a losing a dog. The idea made him feel ill. He ran a finger around the front of his collar to loosen his shirt where he felt strangled. See? He felt ill now, just contemplating that loss.

He was allergic to dogs. He needn't over-complicate things.

Chapter 14

Sam had spent the rest of the morning responding to a couple of hundred comments on her blog, the lawn forgotten. Whether the readers agreed with her or were vehemently opposed to her, the comments were visceral in their anger and the vitriol had nourished her. Her rage was further inflamed by the abhorrence she felt for finding herself back in this cycle again but more than this she was seething with blame for Hattie and Anne, for sending her back there. Actually, she reasoned, she was furious with all the Hatties of the world, the judgemental women and men who firmly believed that their choices were the only choices and that anyone that didn't endorse and subscribe to their pattern for living was in some way impoverished.

She didn't *feel* impoverished, she actually felt rather lucky, but she was riddled with resentments all of which were becoming increasingly debilitating. She was confident that she and Danny could feel complete if they weren't constantly reminded that they were a disappointment to everyone *else*. Sam had lost count of the people she could no longer tolerate but the number of people who could not tolerate her was far greater still. The biggest hurts were within her own family, her parents particularly, who wore their own scars of deprivation far more heavily than she wore hers. Her mother tried to pretend that her sorrow was strictly vicarious, but it was patently clear that her desolation was all her own, a sadness that she had invested all her energy in this one child who had stubbornly refused to thrive and deliver the grandchildren she felt she deserved.

Sam tried to blame her mother. She should have mitigated risk and had more children of her own if her future happiness lay in seeing her successors recreate themselves. Look at ducks – they played a numbers game, didn't they? Nature was good at those prescient checks and balances to ensure it allowed for wastage, so why hadn't her own mother (who after all should have been blessed with more common sense than a duck) used foresight to compensate for potential failure?

Sam left the house through her garden and joined the footpath. Despite her time online she still felt poisonous. Not angry or out of control, but bitter and twisted and with a foul taste in her mouth that she assumed when she applied basic rationalisation to the sensation was psychosomatic but it felt very real.

She marched down the path, but rather than following the route down to the fields, on impulse she immediately ducked left into the narrow opening that took her directly into the woods. Sam had not walked the path in this direction before, as usually she headed for the open expanse of the fields at the end of the tree line, but today she'd not come for the view or the smells or the birdsong. She'd come to chide herself for a trilogy of missteps. She'd embarrassed Hattie, she'd allowed Anne to provoke her and she had briefly hated her mother.

And now she was cross with herself because she knew they weren't to blame. They were doing what everyone did, they were making the same assumptions that had plagued Sam since her diagnosis.

She stopped in the thick of the woods. The footpath was marked clearly ahead but a smaller, unmarked cross path intersected this one and she stopped, tempted by the density of trees. She turned right without hesitating and continued her brisk walk before stopping, for no other reason than she felt, finally, small again.

The beech trees that formed most of this wooded area had given way to taller, darker conifers. Ivy-clad scrub, bramble and recently coppiced hazel filled the gaps. Holly trees, wearing their full length skirts like a misjudged ballgown, straddled the path. Sam liked the impenetrability here. There was no glimpse through to the fields beyond. Instead, just endless trees. She kicked at the ground beneath her foot and picked up a handful of small pine cones. She threw them, one by one, into the briar. They were light in her hand, so travelled very little distance and didn't deliver the satisfaction of a heavier object but nonetheless she enjoyed a sense of recklessness and then, spurred on by the sheer futility of throwing small pine cones into a wood, she accompanied each throw with insults.

'Interfering busybody,' Sam said, immediately liking the sound of her voice out loud. 'Nosy, meddlesome do-gooder,' she said, a little louder, throwing a pine cone with an equivalent increase in force. 'If that's what having kids does to you, who wants them?' she said, bending down to scrape some more pine cones into her hand. 'Stupid, gormless country bumpkin,' she said, a bit of spittle flying from her mouth as she threw the next.

From the woods came a low growl followed by a barked command. 'Stop that.'

Sam, startled, dropped the cones to the ground and looked around wildly. She was rooted to the woodland floor, her stomach dropping as quickly as she'd dropped her ammunition.

Some twigs snapped within the thicket barely two metres from her and as she looked into the boscage, the top of a brown floppy hat appeared shortly followed by a mop of straggly grey hair partially covering a weather-beaten face.

The hat, the face and the woman took a step towards her, using a hooked stick to clear the undergrowth out of the way, revealing her from head to toe in dark cotton dungarees, a patterned shirt that might once have been beautiful – though paired with the denim was disturbing – and stout leather hiking boots. In one hand she held the stick, which in turn pinned back the brambles and gnarly plant life that thrived in the woodland. Over her other arm she had hooked a basket, and in this lay a small selection of sculptured leaves, green and glossy, and a couple of more spindly plants with their thin roots still attached.

The woman stared intently at Sam and then glanced down at her basket. 'I can help you, you know.'

Sam looked at the contents of the basket and back to the wizened face. The face was challenging her, holding a stare with pale, translucent eyes.

Realising that this strange woman must have heard her terrible outburst, then realising with a jerk that this must be the woman in the woods Anne warned her about, Sam turned and fled, retracing her path back through the wood, veering left and then sharply right on to the main footpath and only slowing to a walk once she was in sight of the gate that led to her garden. She was painfully out of breath and as she shut the gate behind her she bent over, a hand on each knee, breathing deeply and replaying the scene over and over in her head. Even though she was moments from the calm sanctuary of her own home and a door she could triple lock behind her, she sank down and sat with her back leaning against the gate, her head on her knees.

Once she had enough breath to do so, she burst into tears and though the shaded ground was damp beneath her and she could feel it seeping into her skirt, she indulged herself and settled into a liberating expression of self-pity.

The genuine impulse to sob became replaced with a dissolute choke that approximated a sob, and this in turn quietened to an occasional artless hiccup. Her face was wet and her nose was running and when she eventually stood and walked back into the house she became overwhelmed with grief and engulfed by righteous indignation. She picked up her mobile to call Danny, framing the words in her head that would spill out. She'd been insulted by a neighbour and accosted by a witch all within the space of an hour and she wanted him to come home and tell her she was perfect with or without a womb and she wanted him to come home and rid the wood of all witches and their dark arts once and for all.

'What's up?' Danny asked in his meeting voice.

Sam hesitated.

'Sam?'

She cancelled the call and texted him immediately. 'Sorry! Pocket dial!' Followed by a blushing emoji and a kissing emoji. He responded immediately, replying with a single kiss.

The letter x morphed into unplumbed responses that piled in on her. She felt ashamed, foolish, childish, embarrassed and alone.

Floundering, she went immediately to the study and switched on her laptop where she feverishly Googled woodland plants, looking for those that might have medicinal purposes, unsure if the witch in the woods was offering her something to cure or to kill.

She flicked through the images of poisonous plants, some of which were very familiar to her though she had never realised they could be so toxic. She was alarmed by the violence of them. The foxglove, which she knew and loved and certainly featured prominently in the gardens of her childhood, would cause vomiting and diarrhoea. It could slow the heart down or cause a heart attack. How could anything so pretty be so destructive? Wolfesbane and hemlock were quite common too, but at least they *sounded* deadly. But the lily of the valley? It gave the impression of such an innocuous plant. She zoomed in on its leaves and though she couldn't be certain, she feared they might well be the leaves the witch in the wood had been gathering. She looked back once more at the description of side effects that accompanied the image: blurry vision, diarrhoea, vomiting, nausea, disorientation, drowsiness, headaches, rashes, excessive salivation, sudden alterations in your cardiac rhythm and possible death were all listed.

Sam was using Libby's profile to do her research, but even

so she wiped her Google history between every new search, terrified at the thought she might leave a trail of murderous intent behind her. She didn't know what she was looking for but gradually found some sort of pain relief delivered by the warren she'd entered. She had spent a lot of time thinking about the plants she might want to grow in her garden but her impulsive delving into the more damaging impact just served to heighten her respect for nature.

She looked out of the window at the top of the trees beyond her fence. Their branches were still winter bare and she tried to imagine them clothed and sun-drenched. It was a vision that was hard to believe, as dark and dead as the boughs appeared, but each twig seemed like a promise of better days to come and Sam was beginning to believe she could trust the trees.

Chapter 15

'There's a witch living in the woods apparently,' said Sam, lightly, pushing her plate away from her, having scraped it clean.

'Not funny,' said Danny, pulling the plate towards him and stacking it upon his own. He adjusted the knives and forks so they lined up neatly.

'Really. I had a visitor, a couple actually. But the first one, Anne, who quite frankly looked a bit witchy herself, told me there was someone practising *dark arts* in the woods.'

Danny performed an exaggerated shudder.

'Which woods?'

'Our woods. *My* woods. The woods right by the house.'

'I hate witches,' said Danny, without humour.

Sam looked at him and laughed. 'No you don't, you've never considered witches. Why on earth would you hate them?'

Danny looked at Sam carefully. She was carrying on blithely and had missed the suggestion of confession in his eyes completely. 'If you can't put them in a column, they don't exist. Right?' she said, laughing.

Danny chewed his lip thoughtfully as he considered this.

He was scared of witches, he had suffered from nightmares about them throughout his childhood. He'd love to talk to Sam about this, it was just the sort of thing he should talk to his wife about. He nodded decisively.

'You're right, sweet pea. I have never considered witches.'

'And dark arts?'

'Definitely not.'

Sam sighed, a little disappointed. 'Oh. Don't judge me but I was actually quite excited by the thought.'

'Don't go courting trouble, Sam. If you're excited by the dark arts then that probably means you're bored. You've got too much time on your hands, you should get a job.'

Sam looked sharply at him. 'But I'm busy here, I've got so much to do with the cottage and everything. And besides, we agreed I didn't have to.'

'We agreed you didn't have to until you're ready. But you might not recognise when that is, and you might not know until you try. I think you should think about it. You'll go crazy here on your own, and perhaps being excited by dark arts is probably a sign that you're well on your way to being crazy already.'

'I don't know, champ,' said Sam sadly.

'Do you remember how well you were doing at work before you quit? You were a star. You were going places.'

'Until I didn't conform,' said Sam, the bitterness still evident.

'They didn't want you to leave, Sam, I seem to remember them trying quite hard to keep you.'

'Of course they wanted to keep me. I was ideal, wasn't I? A hard-working woman with no prospect of maternity leave?

But it wasn't my bosses anyway, it was my colleagues. They were the ones that made me feel uncomfortable.'

'Being different *is* uncomfortable,' said Danny, from experience.

'Too uncomfortable for me,' Sam said with a heavy sigh. 'I'll get another job, but only when I find something where I never have to talk to another human being about my reproductive organs. Maybe I can find something where I never have to talk to another human being about anything at all. Perhaps I'll join a convent. That's ideal.'

Danny shuddered again. 'Nuns,' he said, darkly.

'Oh, now you hate nuns too?' Sam laughed at her husband who smiled weakly. He picked up the plates and took them to the sink.

From the kitchen window he could see a sliver of yellow moon through the trees. It was rising and would soon be illuminating the garden brightly. He imagined the moonlight making its strange bright dance on the woodland beyond the house. He frowned as he washed up. It was vital to him that Sam continued to believe that he was a rational, sensible man as that is who she believed she had married. But the truth was, he hated witches and yes, he hated nuns too.

Chapter 16

At home in her caravan, Diana felt sorry she'd scared away the young woman from the cottage in the lane. She didn't need friendship, in her gradual separation from Rebecca she'd proved she didn't need anyone anymore, but she had recognised something in that primordial shout into the woods. She couldn't remember the words the young woman had used but thought they had been directed at womankind and she felt (or hoped) that everything she'd learnt in her five decades might distil to be of use to this woman. After all, the knowledge she'd amassed in her life was of no use or consequence to her life in the woods.

After the woman had scarpered, Diana had withdrawn her stick, allowing the undergrowth to fold back in front of her, screening her from the path once again and returning her to her woody neighbourhood. The ground that had been bare was now full of the first shows of garlic and the scent was heavy in the air. In ten days' time, the whole ground would be carpeted but for now she just picked the tips of the tender new growth, leaving behind enough of each plant to replace itself.

Diana looked at her laden basket with pride. She had

taught herself so much in her four years in the wood. This was her favourite time of year because not only had she got a whole month of wild garlic to enjoy with every meal, it heralded the start of the most bountiful seasons that would see her well-nourished right the way through until she'd plucked the last blackberry from the hedgerow in October.

The preceding winter had been a particularly harsh one. It hadn't been terribly cold, but it had been interminably long and relentlessly wet and the wind had rattled through the trees without mercy night after night. There were many times when Diana had been tempted by Rebecca's life, by the draw of a roaring fire in a well-ventilated room; by food cooked by somebody else – ideally a professional – and by a decent bottle of red wine served at the right temperature. All of those things taunted Diana but the vision of them were all accompanied by an image of Rebecca. Rebecca sitting in front of the fire, eating the food, drinking the wine. Diana couldn't imagine any of those things without the other woman and that was simultaneously why she was tempted and why she resisted.

But winter was well behind her, and she had a good six months of bounty ahead of her, and she could now look forward to her busiest and most rewarding months of study. If, she argued, she could pass this summer without reaching for Rebecca's company at all, then perhaps she would have truly moved on without her and perhaps she could resist her pull permanently. And if she could move out of Rebecca's orbit permanently, then perhaps she would find the enlightenment she believed was there for her. It was hard, though, as thoughts of Rebecca constantly teased her and nagged at her, pulling at her like a child's fingers on a mother's skirt.

Diana thought again about the young woman she'd frightened off. Had she recognised something of Rebecca in that anguished call? Diana shuddered. She didn't need to invite that sort of trouble into her life, and was glad now that the woman had not accepted her offer of help. Somewhere near was the grating screech of a jay, sounding an alarm call. Diana put her basket down on the ground and waited for just a few moments before she was rewarded with the distinctive flash of white on the rump of the bird as it whistled by.

Yes, Diana thought, bending down to pick up her basket. There was quite enough drama in the woods without the vitriol of an angry young woman adding to it. She looked at her gatherings and, satisfied she'd done enough, headed back to her caravan for lunch.

Chapter 17

While Sam had been writing, it had begun to rain, the sort of rain that hemmed you in. The reality of the rest of the day indoors, all alone, was less appealing than Sam had once imagined. Every now and then she glanced at the curtainless window and watched the rain drops collide haphazardly with the glass. Sam sat at her desk with her chin in both hands, staring blankly at the screen, transfixed by it, despite its toxicity. She sighed heavily, disgusted with herself.

Like many harmful addictions, Sam's writing had been quietly innocuous to begin with. It had been cathartic, essential even, and it had been very easy to justify any hateful debate she'd provoked as the unfortunate by-product of her own healing. She never targeted individuals, but she knew that the people who read her blog would and she was also aware that they took her arguments and used them as weapons against other women who were quite innocently finding their own way to cope. And God knows, being a modern woman seemed much harder than her own mother had made it look. Writing, launching and finding an audience for her blog really had marked Sam's first signs of emotional recovery but, with her mounting influence, her blog had then morphed into something more addictive than she had intended and it was now potentially out of control.

Engaging with real people, as opposed to shouting into a void, had thrilled her, filling her with a sense of self-worth. She had drawn strength from discovering so many people who agreed with her but she had also found relief in the open combat she waded into with people who *didn't* agree with her. But to continue to attain an equal level of participation, she found herself stretching her views further to shock and having enjoyed that initial feeling of impact, striving for continued effect had proved irresistible.

Now looking back at the various steps that had led her to her blog, the whole process seemed unavoidable and the conclusion inevitable. Sam had started to write soon after returning to work, confident that she would quickly re-engage with her career after her long-term absence for surgery. Initially, she had floated on a cloud of infallibility that came, unbidden, with her return to health. She could still recall the sense of shocked euphoria after her physical recuperation.

Sam's initial diagnosis was a stage three ovarian cancer that was rare enough in a woman of her age to cause a barely disguised ripple of envy amongst the doctors who hadn't had the opportunity to get their hands on it. It was in fact so rare that the doctor responsible for identifying it, and the care team that had been poised to treat it, had ultimately been required to stand aside while, knight-like, the senior consultant oncologist had sailed in through the pale green corridors to take Sam under his own watchful eye. The requirement for surgery had been urgent and the whirlwind of doctors' appointments, each one resulting in an escalated version of the earlier prognosis, had left the newlyweds feeling that they were hurtling headlong, out of control, towards an inevitable, dismal conclusion.

At the time, it seemed that the entire episode had been swiftly dealt with but of course it had taken a number of months. Immediately after her diagnosis she'd had six weeks off work for treatment. Being ill took time, it filled your day with appointments regardless of how you felt. And she'd felt surprisingly well throughout that period. She had then required a further six weeks off work after surgery and during this time of recuperation she had been astonished each day by her body's willingness to repair itself. Sometimes she could feel herself becoming stronger even when her mind lacked the motivation she thought recovery would require. Her tidy scars were an unobtrusive reminder of her body's resilience and there was no other evidence of the brutality of the surgery she'd undergone. She'd of course anticipated deep emotional trauma (everyone had told her to steel herself for it) but she and Danny had been so delighted by her survival that any other demands she might make of her body, or any sense of longing for the parts she'd lost, felt really quite churlish.

Sam had surprised herself by coping with the physical surgery extremely well. Each day had provided a new obstacle to overcome but each of these hurdles she'd stepped over, unthinkingly. She had been quietly thrilled by the praise her consultant heaped on her and eagerly did everything asked of her, including making a full recovery. And when she felt too apathetic to heal herself, she knew she could rely on Danny's devout belief in her to carry her forward without any real impulse of her own.

Sam knew that Danny had been terrified by the process and knew he'd had to find his own way to cope but she'd been so focussed on the role she'd been required to play, she'd not had the additional mental capacity needed to ask what that coping mechanism might be. Whenever she'd reached for his hand, he'd been there, and that was all that she had required. His calmness had been a source of great strength to Sam, who sometimes believed it was *his* faith in her that was helping her recovery because she wasn't certain she'd ever quite mustered her own self-belief that people seemed to think would help.

When they'd found themselves, three months after her diagnosis, in a position for Sam to return to work, they were both elated. Sam had tried to raise the issue of her unambiguous infertility to Danny, but he had quashed the conversation rigorously.

'Sam,' he said, holding her by both shoulders and looking so deeply into her eyes that she couldn't tell whether the blurred vision was from his tears or her own. 'I nearly lost you. I would much rather spend the rest of my days celebrating your life than mourning the non-existence of beings I have never met.'

That was enough for Sam. She felt emboldened by her survival, inviolable even. She'd never felt more alive, or more capable than the day she returned to work. She'd swaggered into the office, imaginary club in one hand and dragging the corpse of her disease behind her with the other. 'Look,' she said to herself as she wandered through the office, hugging her colleagues and accepting their congratulations, 'the fierce warrior returns, and she is officially immortal!' Sam took the warm welcomes in her stride, loving the feeling of power her survival had imbued her with. But, to Sam's surprise, the congratulations had barely lasted as long as the flowers on her desk. Instead, they were quickly replaced by pitying glances, by conversations that halted abruptly when she walked into a room and by the drying up of invitations to office get-togethers. Sam's leave of absence had been quite short, considering the gravity of her illness and yet within the time she'd been away her colleagues had apparently all become pregnant or parents and now she was back amongst them, she found there was no place for her in this huddle of excited expectation. Bewildered by her change in status amongst her peers, a repositioning that left her feeling awkward and without purpose, she'd floundered then faltered and had eventually been invited for a meeting with her line manager, accompanied by their head of HR. Delivered with textbook compassion, the HR director offered Sam additional time off for the therapy she undoubtedly required to come to terms with her loss, which whilst offered with the very best intentions, simply served to make Sam realise, unequivocally, that nobody believed she was cured. Instead they thought she was fatally flawed.

She *had* seen a therapist. She was curious to understand why she didn't feel the impairment as keenly as her colleagues appeared to feel it. Sam began to wonder if she had some shortcomings she'd not yet identified. This therapist also suggested that she had not yet come to terms with her true suffering and that she should start to prepare for it, perhaps go as far as to invite this new wave of pain to show itself and to welcome it head-on as part of her healing. Sam left the session even more confused and sought a new therapist. The second therapist suggested Sam keep a diary of her feelings to be shared at the next meeting. This therapist was also certain that Sam was withholding her true sadness, perhaps out of shame. Sam didn't honour this therapist with a second visit either, but she did begin to keep a journal.

After a month of diary writing, she read her words back to herself and was shocked by the vehemence of her own feelings. She hadn't realised how incredibly angry she had become but she was rather pleased with her ability to express these deep feelings, and there was little held back to ulcerate. Contrary to everyone's prediction, the anger was not directed at herself, at her loss of her uterus, at her disappointing ovaries or her inconvenient fallopian tubes but solely at the people who had felt those losses and disappointments more acutely than she had. A conversation with herself that began, 'I'll show them,' ended with, 'No, really, I will actually show them,' and she wrote her very first blog piece. Entitled 'Why other women mourn my womb more than I do', it was both angry and eloquent. She had paused before she posted it publicly, though, realising that this sort of truth, whilst therapeutic for the writer, could be cataclysmic for Danny. She feared his colleagues might read it and judge him, and that this might impact his career and, even more truthfully, she feared Danny might read it himself and conclude she was unhinged, or certainly in the process of becoming unhinged. She was about to delete the blog but ashamed at her weakness, berated herself, telling herself – as she'd often done in times where she lacked conviction – her old university friend Libby would just publish it, regardless of the consequences.

Libby Masters!

Libby Masters had been on Sam's English course for the first year and Sam, an immature eighteen-year-old compared to some of her more worldly peers, had immediately admired her, although always from a safe distance. Libby had been everything Sam hadn't at university – a passionate advocate of every cause, campaigning loudly, picketing when necessary, sleeping out in a tent to protest some new atrocity performed by the government or bureaucracy or by the university establishment or capitalism or whoever or whatever had offended Libby the previous week.

Libby had been prepared to challenge everyone and everything and was frequently absent from class because of some injustice being served elsewhere on campus. When she returned from these political jaunts she would have already caught up with her work and this made her beyond reproach from her tutors and out of reach of mere students, such as Sam. Libby was not only politically active, she was diligent. Sam was in awe of this feisty young woman who had the confidence to stand up for every wrong served upon the oppressed and she recognised that Libby was both her intellectual and moral superior. Sam was often tempted to befriend Libby but was terrified of being rejected, ever since she'd heard Libby publicly brand a mutual friend as a 'bourgeois phony'. Sam felt quite certain that she had the predisposition to be bourgeois and she had absolutely no doubt that she was a phony, so the fear of denunciation made an approach in the direction of friendship out of the question. Libby's brand of activism had always made Sam feel quite inadequate. But that same activism had been powerful enough to leave a lasting impression.

For years Sam had used Libby as a silent moral compass, often asking herself 'what would Libby do?', and now, with her first blog written and with her finger poised over the delete button, she knew exactly what she'd do. Taking her thought process through to a wholly unnatural conclusion, Sam found an old picture of Libby and using some crude Photoshopping tools had added a hat (one she'd taken off a picture on the front of a novel) to disguise any recognisable features. Sam then used this as her profile picture and, empowered by this assumed identity, felt more enabled to access some of Libby's political fervour, using it to channel her own frustration through the filter of Libby's synteresis.

Admitting she had neither her own audacity or conviction, she now wrote her articles from the liberating perspective of this fearless young woman who Sam knew would willingly have jeopardised her partner's career in pursuit of justice. When writing in Libby's name, Sam became gracefully irate, focusing her attack on both the smug stay at home mothers and the working parents who believed they could have it all (who Libby argued were merely slaves to the opiate of a creativity-stifling parenthood). Out of respect for Danny she had covered her tracks carefully, making sure that nobody could link the choleric ramblings of Libby Masters with the pleasant young wife of the successful actuary. Sam had become quite artful in her disguise and now, through the complex backstory she had imagined for Libby, Libby was no longer recognisable either, so both women were safe from discovery.

In this guise, Sam had written increasingly provocative opinion pieces. Falling on it quite by chance, she had cultivated a strategy whereby she deliberately engaged with those she thought would disagree with her views. Her notoriety spread rapidly until, almost accidentally, she had amassed a dedicated following of nearly 100,000 readers around the world, all of whom either passionately agreed with her or who vehemently despised her and her views.

Her writing had become her therapy and the confidence it afforded her bolstered her enough to enable her to leave the office job she loathed (and the co-workers she loathed more) to find work in a florist. And the job in the florist made her realise her life was a sham, represented as it was by twenty-five square metres of countryside within a cement-filled metropolis and she'd decided to reignite her campaign to leave for the countryside. She vowed to leave her blog behind her once her mission had been accomplished. She had invested a lot of hope in the rural idyll, believing it would mark a new, more tolerant chapter in her life, so it had been unsettling to be immediately asked to confront, once again, the stigma attached to childlessness.

Sam looked outside and despaired. The raindrops seemed to be hitting the window with renewed force, occasionally landing in a clattering rush as if thrown from below not above. Using its full force, the rain refused to allow Sam to find any solace in the outdoors, forcing her to look instead at her screen. To Sam, the rain felt personal, so she submitted and addressed her readers once more, in a deliberate provocation of a pain she believed she deserved to feel.

Chapter 18

The rain in London had stopped, and Danny was eating his packed lunch on a favourite park bench, one among a number that lined a diagonal path that bisected a small square near his office. He watched a woman walk a dog on a lead, talking to the animal in an encouraging voice as she passed by. He couldn't make out the words, but he believed the tone to be conversational. He cursed himself for his cowardice. Of course they should get a dog. Sam would love a dog. It would die. She would be sad. They would get another dog. That is what people like Sam and Danny did all the time.

He knew his allergies were spurious. But his phobias were real and even they could be overcome if he put his mind to it. Look at him, he didn't like green, but each day he would voluntarily board a train that hurtled towards it. He didn't like woods and trees either and here he was, the owner of a house at the very end of a lane *right by a wood*.

He thought about the many things he didn't like or couldn't tolerate. Perhaps his aversions just weren't as great as some people suffered. Perhaps his were just measures he took to cope. It was coping he struggled with. He thought about Sam. She had coped. Look at her. She had been through so much and continued to be so effortlessly resilient. He didn't really know how she managed. Next to her he was just a jangle of no hope.

He chewed his lip as more people walked past him. He feared witches, but that fear was born of a childhood nightmare. And he associated nuns with the death of his mother. The nuns had always been there at the hospital and he knew they were allowed to visit her when he was no longer able to. It was so unfair. So in many respects those were two quite rational fears. Frogs. Danny remembered that was another phobia. He shivered just thinking about them. And because he didn't like frogs, he didn't like pots in the garden, or any mess at all that might give safe harbour to frogs. Their garden was perfect as it was. No obstacles, no hiding places.

Did phobias have to be irrational to qualify? His fear of frogs was rational. It had a root and he could trace it. He'd once killed a frog accidentally as a child. He'd shut the front door and it wouldn't quite close and he'd tugged and tugged at it, not understanding what was causing the resistance. And then he saw it, a frog right at the base of the door, stuck now in the hinge, and he'd been pulling and pulling at the door, nearly sawing the poor thing in half. And it was clearly dead and yet its eyes looked at him with such surprised *hurt*.

Was that a real phobia? Or did frogs just remind him of his innate ability to cause harm when all he was doing was minding his own business?

There wasn't a person he'd loved that hadn't either died or been close to death. He was too rational to believe he caused it but sometimes he wondered if he and disaster were inextricably linked. As a precaution, he wanted to protect

Sam from himself and thought he ought to warn her, but he didn't know where to start. She didn't like to talk about her cancer, she said it mustn't define her, and that made it very easy to justify his silence. Besides, talking about things sometimes made them materialise and he couldn't risk that. And what if talking opened the floodgates, and once he started, he couldn't stop? He'd held things from her, things that had the potential to make her hate him. No, he couldn't risk that, either. His job was to mitigate risk, that was what he specialised in.

Another dog and its owner ambled by, companionably. The owner had a baby strapped to her chest. He felt the pang of loss. No. He couldn't have a dog. What if he hurt it in the way he'd hurt that frog? Accidentally, mindlessly, repeatedly? He watched the woman walk confidently away from him. Fraying straps crossed her back and were tied in a careless knot at the side. The fabric that suspended her baby above the ground seemed insubstantial but the mother, apparently unconcerned, moved with a surefootedness that reminded him of Sam. He scolded himself for his timidity. He could never admit it to his wife, but he knew he was not cut out to be a father. Before shame could engulf him he checked his phone and reminded himself of his reassuringly busy schedule that afternoon.

Chapter 19

Grief was new to Sam. Having tried a number of different mechanisms she'd settled on a means of earthing her pain by sharing it angrily with strangers. Danny, however, had been coping with the immense sadness of loss all his life. His self-taught method ensured he felt as little as possible and this lack of outpouring simulated success in his mind. Any aspect of his life that veered from a managed path could be boxed up, locked up and put into long term storage while he focussed his attention instead on those things he felt able to control.

And his move to the countryside was one of those things.

With many successful journeys under his belt Danny was well on his way to establishing a satisfactory routine and was beginning to feel confident that there was ample predictability to allow him to master and then excel at this lifestyle. On Friday morning he had exchanged a brief conversation with a fellow commuter and on Friday evening he had followed the same two cars out of the station car park as he'd noted on both Wednesday and Thursday. In fact, his transition to commuter had been so smooth that it was actually the weekends he feared and as he had hurtled towards the next one he'd come to dread the arrival of those mornings at home with no framework to which he could anchor himself.

But, much to his surprise, he had enjoyed the early hours of his first Saturday mornings. This morning he had accepted a cup of coffee in bed gratefully and had been buoyed by Sam's enthusiasm for the weekend ahead of them. He had luxuriated in the slow start to the day in a way that he'd never entirely achieved in London. He lay in bed, flicking his phone to catch up with the headlines, idly wondering what there had been to fear.

When he did surface, Sam was in the kitchen, cooking herself some breakfast. 'Eggs?' she asked, innocently.

'No thanks,' Danny replied patiently.

'Fried eggs are so good,' she said.

'Er no,' Danny said, smiling to himself and shaking his head, while taking a bowl out of the cupboard for his cereal, resigned to the inevitable routine.

'Not poached, or boiled?'

'Nope.'

'Or what about scrambled? Are you sure I can't tempt you with some delicious scrambled eggs?'

'Never gets old, does it?' he said, pouring milk into the bowl.

Sam laughed. 'Not until you admit you don't have an allergy,' she said. She carried a pan of water to the sink and, having tipped it carefully out, was now looking out of the window, her hands on her hips in a pose Danny immediately recognised as dissatisfied.

'What's up?' he asked, joining her at the kitchen sink to rinse out his coffee cup.

'Those bloody developers. They laid out the garden but all that green coming up in the beds? They're weeds not plants. They could have at least planted some bulbs or something.'

'They look very much like plants to me,' said Danny, peering out of the window to examine the low carpet of green growth filling the beds on either side of the small lawn.

'Well, I'm afraid they're definitely weeds. I didn't want to start on the garden as I wanted to see what we already had, but I don't think there's anything there at all. It's fine, I'm not really worried, I'm just going to hoe and then plant. We'll put in annuals to give us some colour immediately and then some spring flowering bulbs and hardy perennials in the autumn, so we've got something to look forward to next year.'

Danny looked at his wife happily. 'When did you learn to speak gardening?'

She tossed her head impatiently. 'I've always liked gardening. You know that, Danny. I would have gardened much sooner if I'd had more than a couple of window boxes to play with.'

'I know you lasted a whole six weeks in a flower shop, but I didn't know you knew the *Latin*. That's a whole new level of gardening.'

'I don't know if the word perennial is Latin, it just means it comes back each year. But, still. I'm glad you're impressed. I plan to get *very* good at this.' Sam *was* glad Danny was impressed. There were very few areas where her knowledge was deeper than his and she was hoping to make gardening one of those areas where she shone, both in theory and in practice.

'So,' Danny said, still examining their garden with idle

curiosity. 'What exactly is the difference between a weed and a plant?'

Sam was busying herself around the kitchen while she spoke. She felt competent and fluent and at home. 'Technically nothing. A weed is just a plant in the wrong place. That said, there are some really invasive weeds you have to look out for. Knotweed, bindweed, that kind of thing. It's really nasty stuff. Bindweed would cover most of this plot in a single season. If that takes hold, you might as well wave goodbye to any chance of ever having a garden.'

Sam shrugged and turned to put the milk back in the fridge while Danny remained at the window. Sam was oblivious to the tensing of Danny's shoulders, and with her back to him she also missed him clench and release both fists several times before burying his hands in his trouser pockets to control the compulsion.

Danny tried to block the cacophony of thought as he studied the small plants through the window. They weren't conscious thoughts, the musings or wonderings of an inquisitive mind. Rather they were hostile bombardments by individual words, swiftly followed by brutal images that were as real to him as the short grass outside. The lawn still showed traces of the outlines of turf squares, laid barely a month ago and still awaiting the warmth of early summer to really bed them in. These outlines were pleasing in their regularity and could be counted, which helped to calm him, but they were not as compelling as the noise in his head.

Invasive, she'd said. He imagined the weeds growing at pace, stretching out in every direction and strangling first the fence before turning their attention to the house itself.

He imagined the plants thrusting their tendrils into the small crevices in the brickwork and crushing the mortar to dust, letting the powdery residue crumble to the ground. He imagined the newest shoots reaching out claw-like, grasping the ironwork on the back of the house, the drainpipes popping from the wall like buttons from a tight shirt. He imagined the roof giving in to the weight of the boughs of the weeds.

'Knotweed,' she'd said. 'Bindweed,' she'd said. He didn't know what either of these plants looked like, but he could imagine the damage they'd do. He suspected their thick sinuous stems were covered in tiny hairs, like the nettles he used to hate as a child. Plunging headfirst into those vivid memories of his childhood (tiny scars, barely remembered, prised open to become deep gashes of pain under scrutiny), he imagined those childhood nettles with stems as thick as his wrist and he imagined them now pushing their growing tips through the tiny gaps between the bricks and the windows, plunging the frames inwards and rushing towards him, a frothing surge of poisonous green.

'Danny?'

'Uh-huh,' he said, quietly, his eyes still fixed on the flowerbeds.

'I said, do you want toast?'

'Sure,' he said, unenthusiastically, unable to tear his eyes away from the droning threat lurking in the garden.

Wave goodbye, she'd said. He imagined the slow sad shake of the estate agent's head as he declined to offer the house for sale. He imagined the bank's letters piling up, fighting with the invasive plants for space on the doormat. He'd be stuck with this house, that's for sure. And if he couldn't sell this house, he'd lose the opportunity for the next house and the one after that. And all of those things were part of the *plan*. If he were to falter at the first hurdle, then he really might as well give up now.

'No,' he said, imagining Sam must have spoken again. 'No to toast. I'm going out.'

Sam watched Danny leave, puzzled by his sudden exit but she was fully committed to micro-managing his happiness, so was pleased to see him heading off with purpose. She had been worried he might feel a bit out of control without the bustle of a city backdrop but she watched him reverse the car out of the drive with confidence and he looked very much like a man with a mission which made her feel grateful.

Sam waited for the car to disappear before heading out to the garden. She smiled as she knelt down to pull the weeds from the soil. They barely had roots, just little white threads like the ends of carrots and they left the earth with no resistance. She thought about Danny, her hard-working, capable husband, as he drove off to explore the neighbourhood for the first time. This is what she'd always wanted for him, somewhere he could properly switch off and live a life that didn't have to shrink to the few centimetres of screen to become three dimensional to him. That world (the office, the deals, the politics of it all) fuelled him, she knew that, it was as important to him as the food she ate. But she wasn't always convinced it was a healthy diet.

Having cleared a small space of weeds, she stood and admired her work, looking around the perimeter of the lawn trying to imagine this garden in the summer, when the surrounding trees were all in full leaf and the flowerbeds were bursting with colour. She wondered what sort of gardener Danny might become in this space. It would be nice to see him with a bit of earth under his fingernails. He was so competent, so *accomplished*, but she suspected he suffered from his own worries from time to time and she felt that here in the countryside, he could diffuse those worries and fill his head with more practical concerns, the sort of concerns that might be fixed with a hammer and a nail. Everyone needed that, she reasoned. Everyone needed some utilitarian distractions to help them feel in control.

Sam had sketched out a broad plan for the garden in her mind. Her initial disappointment was already being replaced by a wilful optimism. She had a completely blank canvas and could look at the whole as a single artwork that she could complete, and it would all be her own. It was horribly dull now but with a couple of weeks of warmer weather the garden centres would be full of instant colour and she was committed to cheating this year with some bedding plants while she thought about what she might be capable of achieving for the long term.

She was so happy in her work, weeding and humming to herself as she did so, that she was startled when she heard the sound of the car arriving back. She hurried out by the side path to greet Danny. By the time she had reached him he was already lugging a large box out of the car and he beamed happily at her as he set it on the ground.

'What on earth have you been up to?' she asked, delighted by his pleasure.

He shook his head in mock despair. 'You've lost me, I'm afraid. That's it. I'm a goner.'

'You are?'

'Yup. You thought you were going to lose me to corporate life, didn't you? That's what you feared. Or as I got a bit older and fatter, to golf. But no, you've lost me anyway.'

'What on earth are you talking about?'

'To DIY! That store! What riches you've been keeping from me! I've never been anywhere like it. It's a goldmine! The *tools*! There's something for every imaginable project – there are scythes and shears and sledgehammers, mallets and maces. I can have my own jackhammer if I want. I barely knew where to start.' He grinned at her as he set the box the right way up.

'And you're starting with?' She eyed the box suspiciously.

'A mower.'

Sam put her head on one side, looking at the box.

'Oh, no, not in here. This isn't the mower. I've ordered it, they'll deliver it next week. But I managed to pick up some basics.' Danny reached into the car and dragged out two full carrier bags which he lifted to the ground and put next to the box.

'What on earth have you got there, it looks like you're waging war?'

'Just the essentials.' He tore at the top of the box and heaved out a large plastic contraption with a big water canister attached.

'What on earth is that?' asked Sam, genuinely puzzled.

'It's a pressure hose.'

'And we need one of those, because?'

'Look at this cobble,' he said, stabbing at it with his toe. 'They've done a nice job, granted, but each one of these are individual stones. Grass will grow up between them, moss will encroach, and before you know it, saplings will have seeded themselves and will be twisting their roots around our foundations.'

Sam looked at the cobbled drive beneath her feet. The builders *had* done a good job – they could have chucked down a bit of tarmac but instead the stones were really nicely laid out and they stretched all the way from the lane to the garage, giving a generous apron on which you could park two cars side by side, with ease.

'But there are no weeds here, Danny,' said Sam with the slightest trace of concern in her voice.

'And that's the way I intend to keep it. Can't be complacent, now.'

Sam, realising this was not a battle she needed to concern herself with, laughed and headed inside. Before closing the front door, she paused to watch him as he attached the pressure hose to the tap by the garage and carefully unravelled an extension lead, walking it backwards and concentrating furiously as if laying dynamite. She was glad he had found a task to involve himself in, but equally, she couldn't help wondering how she had managed to marry somebody so completely different to her. Her instinct was to plant and to grow and encourage some sort of natural chaos to spring from the garden, creating a wilderness that would reveal new splendours daily. His was to hold it all back.

Chapter 20

The weekend had passed in steady activity. Danny had waged battle with an as yet undeclared foe and had felt calmed by his pre-emptive strike. But stepping on to the train to mark the start of another week as a commuter reassured him. Standing on the platform, nodding to his fellow passengers, finding his seat and opening his laptop all contributed to the quiet knowledge that, amongst all of this change, he could find ways to corral the unfamiliar and break it, taming it to behave in a way he could manage.

Arriving at the office, Danny walked up the three flights of stairs to his floor, taking two steps at a time and counting as he went. He put his head down to make the climb, and didn't break his stride, matching each step with the rhythm of his steady tally. He was confident he wouldn't meet anybody coming down the other direction, these were service stairs, concrete and uninviting, but he had recently discovered they were a viable alternative to the lift which had become intolerable to him recently due to the endless variables he had identified. If other people were as meticulous as he was, he might be able to work out which lift was best to use in the morning, but his peers' arrivals were haphazard, anarchic even, and the lifts tore up and down spilling people out on their floors and paying no heed at all to the order in which they'd arrived. The stairs, on the other hand, were solid and reliable.

Once he reached the third floor he paused to straighten his tie and smooth down his hair before pushing the heavy fire door open and emerging into a small lobby next to two unnecessary chairs and a large notice board. He ignored the posters and announcements, having never even considered there might be anything of interest to him and headed straight towards the small kitchen to make his tea as quickly as possible, hoping to escape to his desk before the arrival of the throng. There was one person in the kitchen already, which frustrated him, as he really liked to be first, but she had her back to him and seemed preoccupied with own preparations, so he took his cup from his bag and set to work as briskly and quietly as he could.

The woman immediately turned around and her face lit up with a bright smile.

'Morning there, Danny. I didn't hear you come in.'

'Morning, Zoe,' he said, warmly. He liked Zoe, she was straightforward and easy to work with. Other colleagues confused her directness with abruptness or aloofness but Danny considered her something of a kindred spirit.

'You've changed your hair,' he said, 'I didn't recognise you from behind.'

She reached a hand up to her hair and smoothed it down, nervously.

'Well observed, Danny. It's a new colour. Do you like it?'

He took a step back as if to observe her more closely and tilted his head to the side while he examined this question seriously. 'Yes, yes I do. It's lighter, isn't it?'

'Yes. But don't get attached to it. It'll change again soon.'

'It will? Don't you like it?'

'I like it, but I've recently begun to work with a therapist to see if I can become a bit more adaptable. She's identified a few issues that she believes makes it hard for me to navigate a workplace like this.' Zoe shrugged emphatically. 'She thinks I am "uncompromising" apparently and believes I can help accept change in others if I get used to change in myself. So, consider my new hair colour my homework.'

Zoe's conversation was light and bright but Danny was fascinated by Zoe's revelations. He found the idea of therapy strangely alluring but the idea of undergoing any for himself appalled him. To accept that he needed help would mean either admitting his fallibility to his wife or lying to her yet again. Neither of which he was prepared to do. Being married to a strong, adept woman was both a blessing and a burden. And, besides, allowing somebody to poke around inside his head, possibly messing up the neatly ordered files, just felt like opening a can of worms.

'How many changes will you make, and how often?' he asked, assessing Zoe's hair.

Zoe laughed, recognising herself in Danny's questioning. 'Now that is exactly the sort of detail that I tried to pin down myself. Frankly, she has been a little vague on the matter and rejected my proposal to lock down a schedule out of hand. But it seems that she has recommended a crash course of big noticeable changes each week to get used to people's comments and then a series of minor ones to keep myself flexible thereafter. It all seems a bit nebulous to me. But still, here I go, following another course of action blindly. But thanks for noticing, Danny, you're one of the first to comment, so consider yourself a pioneer in my therapeutic journey.'

'Interesting,' said Danny, genuinely. He fished the teabag out of his cup, and squeezed it against the side before throwing it in the bin. He replaced the lid on the cup and turned to leave.

'I'll see you at Peter's barbecue at the weekend,' said Zoe as he left. 'Look out for the redhead!'

Danny began to laugh but turned back to Zoe sharply. 'When's Peter's barbecue?'

'This Saturday, isn't it? You are invited, aren't you? I haven't put my foot in it? You've definitely been before. I've seen you there. We've chatted.' Zoe looked stricken by the thought that she might have been insensitive to somebody she considered a fellow outlander.

'This Saturday? No. No, I haven't been invited actually. No harm done,' he added when he saw the confusion on Zoe's face. 'I've moved away from London so I probably wouldn't have been able to make the trip back into town at the weekend anyway.'

'Oh, that's probably why you weren't invited,' said Zoe, relieved.

'Probably,' said Danny, who had already set off towards his desk.

He walked the long way around, deliberately passing Peter's desk. Having just arrived, his colleague put his coffee down to shrug off his jacket.

'Morning, Peter,' said Danny quite confidently, as he passed.

Peter nodded briefly, leaning down busily to log on before he'd even sat down. As Danny walked on, he reflected on that small exchange, categorising it in his mind as *uneasy*.

He wasn't rude or dismissive, but he looked distracted and, Danny wondered, perhaps even embarrassed.

He sat down, logged on, and put his headphones on. In the last building he'd had his own office but when they moved, they had adopted an open plan arrangement regardless of position within the firm. This was designed to be progressive, removing hierarchical barriers and encouraging collaborative working but he knew it to be significantly less efficient for the company and considerably more stressful for the individual. He had found some crowdsourced research online that supported his theory and had even contributed to it in the hope that eventually senior management would understand that the most efficient strategy was to allow employees to work independently and to come together occasionally to pool ideas and reject or promote the best ones. For the time being though, he had to toe the line. Earphones weren't encouraged as they were believed to contribute to a feeling of isolation, but his work was largely mathematical at the moment and he had demanded the right for white noise to help him focus on the job.

He picked up from where he'd left off the previous day and as he scanned the rows and columns of numbers, he felt himself starting to relax. He loved the certainty of mathematics. As he scrutinised his work for patterns he could use to predict outcomes for a client, he allowed just these to flood the front of his brain and all those other bewildering issues, the issue of therapy, the issue of Peter's barbecue and the issue of Sam and the knotweed, to gradually reduce in size until they were no longer of any significance.

Chapter 21

Sam had been looking at her empty flowerbeds and wondering, in despair, where to begin. Her confidence with Danny had been feigned to reassure him that the garden was in safe hands but today she felt overwhelmed by its barrenness. Looking at the sky and pulling on a jacket, she headed off down the path for a walk, hoping to clear her head and find inspiration amongst the lofty trees.

Without hesitating, she stopped to spy on the big house and once again the gardener was at work. It was like a long drawn-out version of the childhood game, grandmother's footsteps. Each time she looked he was working on a different part of the garden, as if suspended in time. Today, he was towards the house, his barrow beside him once more. The work looked relentless and there seemed little joy in it.

She looked at the beds, admiring the richly worked earth and the tightly pruned shrubs. There was some warmth in the sun today and everything seemed poised to surge. She remembered the exchange she'd overheard. It seemed to her that both the gardener and the young woman were disappointed by the owner's lack of ambition for the garden.

She wondered if the gardener was dispirited by the futility of working for somebody who perhaps didn't care.

Sam felt a flicker of an idea and, emboldened, she turned and continued on the path, ignoring the turning that would take her through the woods and the stile that crossed to the first big field. Instead she continued downhill. Eventually she reached a small gate that took her out on to the road and now she turned right, using the pavement and stopping occasionally as cars came and went from the driveways that intersected the road that led to the village. She looked carefully at each house name. As she walked, the houses thinned out and the gates became larger and the driveways more oppressive.

She discounted the houses she could see from the roadside and soon came to one that she believed must be the one she was looking for. The house name 'Willow's Fortune' wasn't displayed proudly in white paint on oak boards as with so many of the other homes. Instead it was engraved deeply into a large pink stone, which itself was inset into one of two sandstone pillars that cradled tall, wrought iron gates. The gates were firmly closed to cars but the matching pedestrian entrance was only latched and Sam went through, closing the gate carefully behind her.

She walked up the gravel driveway. Neatly clipped box hedging bordered both sides and as she turned the corner she was welcomed by the front aspect of the large, white Georgian house. She was certain it was the house she had spied from the path and she looked around for the gardener, expecting him to be watching her and aware of her entrance.

The front door was painted a glossy black, and the brass

door-knocker shone proudly. She rang the bell and the door was answered very quickly by the young woman she had seen before. She wore the same black trousers and white shirt, and slippers on her feet. Once again her hair was scraped back from her face into a neat ponytail.

The woman didn't greet her but waited silently at the open door for Sam to explain herself.

'I'm looking for the owner of the house. Is that you?' Sam asked. A rumble of anxiety arrived deep in her belly, triggered by the lack of warm welcome. Now she was here, she wondered what on earth had prompted such boldness in the first place.

'No, it's not. She's not here.'

'Are you expecting her back? I'd love to chat with her.'

The young woman shook her head quickly. 'No, I don't expect to see her today. She is at work.' The woman moved as if she was about to close the door but Sam, determined to remain courageous, spoke again.

'I'm your neighbour, Sam.'

The young woman opened the door wider and for a moment Sam thought she might be invited in. Instead the woman waited for further explanation, her eyebrows raised in question.

Sam smiled. 'I've just moved in and I know this probably sounds a bit strange but I have a garden for the first time in my life and I've spotted your gardener and wondered if I might chat to him about where to start. There's nothing quite like seeking the advice of experts.' Sam smiled again, but beginning to lose confidence, faltered. 'I'd like to grow flowers. Flowers for my house,' she said, hopefully.

The young woman hesitated and for a moment her face looked like it might soften, but it quickly reset itself in hard, professional disdain.

'That's not possible. The owner of the house is a very private woman and she doesn't care for visitors. The gardener is paid to tend to the garden here, not to offer advice to passersby. I suggest if you want help in your garden, you advertise locally. I am sure there are plenty of people who would be happy to help.'

Sam was taken aback. The woman was younger than she was but spoke with absolute confidence. It was clear she spoke for her boss and it was clear too, that in doing so, she believed her visitor to be beneath her.

'Sure,' said Sam, half-heartedly. 'Sorry for disturbing you.' Inexplicably, she felt her eyes sting with tears as she turned to leave. The door shut behind her and Sam retraced her steps, acutely aware of the imposition of her visit, amplified by the sound of the gravel crunching under her feet.

She chewed her lip as she walked. She had assumed, from the conversation she'd overheard, that they all wanted more from the garden and she had also thought, naively she now realised, that she could somehow fulfil that for them whilst learning about the garden herself. She felt embarrassed by her presumption now.

She passed through the gate back on to the footpath and headed home. She felt foolish and sorry for herself but there was another more nagging concern. As she reached Broome Cottage she realised what it was. Her neighbour, Hattie, had visited with honest intentions too. She'd even baked a cake. Sam hadn't just rejected her coolly, as the woman at Willow's

Fortune had done, she'd humiliated her and sent her away in floods of tears.

Opening her front door, Sam remembered Hattie's chewed fingernails and sore cuticles and wondered guiltily how much courage it had taken to come and ring on her doorbell that morning.

Chapter 22

That night, Danny lay in bed listening to his wife's soft breath. She slept on her back with her head tilted slightly towards him. She'd been quiet during the evening and she was now frowning in her sleep.

Danny knew Sam as well as he knew himself. He knew her worries, and he wished he could make them go away. He knew the pain she'd been through and he wished he could have borne it for her. He knew the hopes that had been dashed and he wished he could have kept them alive.

He studied her face carefully. He knew her so well, it was true, but meanwhile he'd kept secrets from her, the sort of truths that might make her hate him if she ever found out. He wondered whether she'd kept anything from him. He hoped so. It would make his own duplicity easier to bear.

He moved on to his side and watched her face, wanting to smooth her frown away with the tip of his finger but knowing he'd wake her and then there would be two of them lying there, hurling their anxieties into the night.

Knowing he couldn't solve Sam's, Danny flipped his attention back to his own worries, flicking through them one by one, as idly as if he were choosing a film to download.

He couldn't decide which one to focus on, they were all so compelling and deserving of the 3 a.m. limelight – truly the most cherished time for any anxiety to take a foothold.

He thought about his career, something he often brushed past without scrutinising it carefully. It was easy to dismiss it as under control when in reality there were all sorts of obstacles lurking in the wings, capable of derailing his steady progress. There was Peter, for a start. Danny was certain now that Peter didn't like him.

Danny had been invited to Peter's family barbecue for the last three years. Within their office, Peter's barbecue had become a bit of an institution. Peter had successfully managed that delicate blending of work and home life that some people navigated seamlessly whilst others, Danny included, would like to separate with yellow and black 'do not cross' tape. In fact, if Danny had his way, he would pay particular attention to ensuring his home life had an impenetrable exclusion zone clearly marked all around it.

Not being invited to Peter's barbecue was fine, Danny didn't particularly mind. He didn't need to like his colleagues, he just needed to respect them. But the exclusion did bother him because he wasn't sure why this had happened. Peter and Danny were peers, and in all likelihood, they'd continue to be at a similar grade for many years before one of them was elevated above the other. So why had Peter now rejected Danny's company?

Danny flipped over to face away from Sam. The curtains were closed but he could make out a sliver of night sky between them. It was dark, but not pitch black; a curious colour that was neither one thing nor another.

Having discarded a number of possible causes for Peter's sudden aloofness, Danny alighted on the obvious one. Peter had three small children. He had passport pictures of them in a little fold-out frame on his desk. They were present in Peter's workspace environment but not embarrassingly so. Other colleagues had taken their commitment to paternal excellence further, posting their own portraits in crayon on their pinboards, with the nauseatingly inoffensive, carefully spelt out letters of early expressions of love. 'I heart daddy', this sort of thing. Ironic, wasn't it, that by the time the children were old enough to express a more sophisticated understanding of their familial pull, they no longer felt it strongly enough to write it down, and even if they did, the words would never find the public prominence of a shared office wall. Which was a shame, Danny thought; it would be certainly be more interesting: 'Dear dad. Despite the fact you let me down from time to time and I'm increasingly suffering from overwhelming shame whenever you are in the same room as my friends, I realise that you are a good role model, making the right choices to ensure my own career is as easy on me as yours has been on you. If I recoil from you now, rest assured, it is only in recognition of my future self, not the physical revulsion you must sometimes suspect. P.S. Thanks for the tenner.' Now, Danny thought, that sort of transparency *would* be interesting.

Peter's children were still small and malleable, and probably made very few demands on their father. Peter was the sort of dad that did his bit. He took a bit of time off for the carol service, left early for parents' evening (parents' evening? What on earth did they discuss at a parents' evening? Danny wondered. The children were barely out of nappies). He was a good example of the new breed of dad, still privately certain that his children were best cared for by their full-time mother whilst being careful not to refer to babysitting when he meant fathering.

Danny let these thoughts drift around his head, finding their own nooks and crannies to fester within his brain. He was a long way from falling back to sleep, but his heartbeat was quite calm and the thoughts weren't spiralling out of control. Glancing at the clock, he calculated that he could maintain this status for an hour or more without it impacting on his well-being.

Danny allowed his attention to stay focussed on Peter. Peter should feel superior to Danny, shouldn't he? He'd fathered three children whilst enabling his wife the luxury of a decade or more at home to launch them confidently into the world with the best possible start in life to cushion them from future blows. Peter couldn't feel threatened by Danny's lack of family, could he? In fact, hadn't Danny always been the one to enthusiastically uphold Peter's right to dip out of a meeting to watch a nativity play? Hadn't he suggested they avoid half term week for a conference, so that the dads wouldn't have their family time compromised? Thinking about it, Danny felt quite indignant that not only should Peter like him, he should be *grateful* to him.

Danny looked at the clock again. Eight minutes had passed. Eight minutes was enough to spend on Peter and his progeny, surely.

But nothing else felt pressing. Danny wondered if Peter ever lay in bed worrying about him. Whether the pressure of work was enough to rattle him as it rattled Danny or if Peter sailed through life, oblivious to the little concerns that could derail Danny if he gave them any room to smoulder. Danny's coping strategy had always been to closely examine only the things he could analyse scientifically and resolve them through the structure of *process*. Everything else he locked away firmly, determined to leave it there, with no further scrutiny. Now, as Danny lay watching the minutes tick by, he wondered what to do with Peter and the barbecue. Peter, his barbecue, his wife and three children were not obliging by immediately becoming a resolvable problem. Danny thought some more. Empathising with those unlike him had never been a skill Danny had honed but he was aware that perhaps he needed to look at the issue from Peter's perspective. Perhaps, whilst he had decided that Peter was not a threat, Peter in the meantime had come to the opposite conclusion.

A further two more minutes had passed but Danny felt he had made progress. Now it seemed clear. He was a threat to Peter. And as such Danny needed to rise to the challenge, not evade it. He needed to compete with Peter at work, respond to the duel that Peter had declared by not inviting him to his barbecue. He and Peter were colleagues, not friends. That was the distinction. He didn't need Peter as a friend, he didn't need friends at all. They only let you down.

Danny tried to fall asleep.

Chapter 23

Sam's ability to mask her worries was the product of her upbringing.

Her mother came from a long line of mothers who did not think it was tasteful to share one's anxieties or, as she would prefer to describe them, weaknesses. When facing the randomly spaced hurdles of adolescence, Sam had learned to deal with her own problems quietly, stoically and privately while other girls flexed their teenage angst noisily all around her. But the events of the last few years had tested even Sam's resilience. At the point that her head was full to bursting with a lifetime of things unsaid, she'd needed to write her blog to deal with the overflow. But of course, this wasn't something she could ever risk her mother encountering – let alone Danny, who shared her mother's suspicion of emotional outbursts. So when she had started writing her blog it had been an easy decision to adopt another character to front her public display of outrage.

And it was an obvious decision to adopt a façade in the shape of an old university friend, the sort of person who would have discarded her own mother alongside her decorum.

She clicked on Libby's profile picture and a new window

popped up, magnifying the image. Sam looked at the third of Libby's face visible under the brim of the big felt hat. Libby had never been conventionally pretty, but she had a handsome, strong face and the eighteen-year-old Sam had certainly found Libby's conviction attractive.

To add to her mystique, Libby had vanished, inexplicably, at the end of her first year of university but nobody but Sam had seemed particularly perturbed by, or interested in, her absence. Sam had asked a number of people where Libby had gone, but nobody either knew or cared which had surprised Sam as Libby had made such an indelible impression on her. Libby had been a supernova in Sam's life, her orb of light could only have been extinguished fully or it would still be visible, of that Sam was certain. She had always assumed that Libby must have died that first summer and, though she had no proof of her hunch, she assumed she could only have died a tragic, poetic death.

Had Libby lived, she might well have written an angry blog but Sam doubted very much she would have allowed it to become her sole source of comfort, as Sam had.

Now, sat in her study, Sam felt sickened by herself. She'd lost two hours to browsing on the internet. The comments that had come in during the night included one from a woman who suggested she examine her commitment to her faith while looking for a cure for her childlessness. The woman had quoted Genesis 11:30, reminding her that God had repaid Abraham's faithfulness by granting him a son and suggesting that she and her husband try to truly put the Lord first in their lives. '*That old chestnut,*' Sam had thought, at first, and was about to respond glibly but she'd clicked on the next comment and the next, finding a barrage of accusation and judgement and a bitter argument between the childless, the childfree and the mothers and the fathers who thought both categories of women were failing in their duty to men, to God or to each other. There were so many angry people out there and she was sickened that she'd actively gone out of her way to invite them in. Now she spent too much time in their company, in a vicious cycle for which she was solely responsible. A cycle that saw her first fuelling their fire and then stoking it, whilst all the time watching the resulting drama in voyeuristic horror.

Sam knew she had coerced Danny into leaving London for a better life but now she wondered whether there could ever be such a thing. What if there was just this one? Wherever she went she had to take her problems with her, she couldn't just leave them behind and even if she wanted to reinvent herself there would always be the Hatties of the world to remind her who she was and who she wasn't. Sam felt more than sick. She felt unnecessary.

She paced up and down like a caged animal. The garden, which had once felt glorious and burgeoning with possibility, now felt petty and pointless. Furious and confused she could not stop thinking about the rejection she had received from her neighbour. She switched from this thought to the woman in the woods whose pale eyes had appeared to see right through her. Sam revisited the encounter over and over again. She had thought the woman was dangerous, she'd responded by running away, but now, when she thought of her eyes and tried to accurately recall the words that had been spoken, rather than the subtext she'd imagined, she wondered if the woman in the woods was just offering her help.

'God knows, I need help,' said Sam to herself as she applied mascara to her lashes and blinked back at her reflection in the mirror thoughtfully. Her thoughts up until this moment had been quick firing, meandering from one unlikely scenario to the next but now she found herself in the bathroom with her hair brushed and make-up applied, she knew she had resigned herself to paying the woman a visit. She needed to talk to somebody. She'd chosen to withdraw and she'd chosen this quiet retreat over a busy life full of colleagues with their own busy lives to share but she hadn't quite taken into consideration how very little her husband offered in terms of conversation. It was fine, she thought, to be a good listener, but it was not fine if your good listener wasn't helping you to process your thoughts and make your worries go away. She needed a friend. She was a little startled by the realisation that her instinct was to choose the witch in the woods over the well-meaning neighbour with her cardigan and cake but she knew her mind was made up. Putting her glasses back on, she checked her reflection in the mirror before heading downstairs and out of the house.

She walked beyond the point on the path where she'd thrown the fir cones into dense thicket, until she found a spot she could see more clearly through the trees to the blue tarp and the caravan. There was no obvious route to the door, and she wondered how the woman ever left it to join the path. Perhaps she didn't. Perhaps she didn't even live there, and it was just a coincidence she'd been nearby. Nerves gripped Sam's stomach but she remained determined to see this through.

She called out, looking around self-consciously. 'Hello?' She noticed the quaver in her voice and tried again, injecting a bit more certainty into the call. 'Hello?'

After a few moments, the door to the caravan slowly opened. The woman, once again wearing dungarees and a brightly coloured shirt, poked her head out and didn't seem fazed to be disturbed. In fact, she greeted Sam quite neutrally. 'Come in, I've been expecting you,' she called.

The words should have been welcoming but given the context Sam was alarmed. She knew she could still retreat but the same feeling of recklessness that had got her this far propelled her further forward. She tried to use this sense of abandonment to approach the caravan door confidently, but the coppiced hazel appeared to be impenetrable and having tried one possible entrance and then another she faltered. From the other side of the dense young trees, the woman took a step towards Sam and, using her stick in a sweeping motion, she pushed a cluster of young boughs to one side. Sam could see the path now and stepped through, embarrassed that she'd found the simple act of negotiating a path through undergrowth so difficult. Having made it into the sanctum of the clearing, she felt she needed to greet her host with a handshake or a hug but whilst deciding which, she realised that her companion had already moved ahead into the caravan.

Sam took a deep breath and followed her up the rotting steps, and gasped.

There were many versions of the interior of the caravan she'd run through in her head. She'd imagined abject poverty, squalor and dirt or worse – but nothing had prepared her for this.

At one end of the caravan was a small double bed, made up with a duvet in crisp white linen, four big comfortable pillows and a camel-coloured cashmere blanket folded neatly at the bottom. At the other end of the caravan was a small kitchen, with a hob, a small fridge and a couple of good quality units on the counter. A Nespresso machine sat next to a Dualit toaster.

In the space between the bed and the kitchen there was a very small table with a comfortable chair on either side. The table was covered with a very good quality linen tablecloth and on the middle of the table sat a delicate porcelain jug holding a spray of wildflowers. On either side of the caravan were bookshelves which held leather notebooks of some sort, with delicately inked roman numerals on the spines.

The woman pulled out a chair from the small table.

Sam was spellbound and speechless. She looked around, trying to take it all in and was aware that whilst she would like to set her face in a look of polite interest, she was probably gaping. She was conscious, too, of her racing heart and dry mouth, and wondered if either were obvious to her host. She knew neither would permit her to speak for a while. She wondered if she could still flee but she felt light-headed.

She wanted to introduce herself politely but stammered, instead, 'Who are you?' which she knew sounded wrong, but she felt incapable of correcting herself.

'I am Diana,' the woman replied, solemnly. 'Goddess of the hunt, the moon and nature. I am sister of Apollo, daughter of Jupiter and Latino, wife to no man, maiden for all women.'

Sam swallowed noisily but before she could process any of

this information, Diana broke the uncomfortable silence by roaring with laughter. 'I'm sorry. That was mean. You look like you've seen a ghost. Let's start again. I'm Diana. Shall we leave it at that?'

Sam said quietly, 'Sam.' She attempted a smile and looked at Diana apologetically as she sat down at the table opposite her. 'This is not what I expected,' she said.

Diana looked crestfallen, the previous light in her face vanishing as she leant heavily on the table between them. 'I know,' she said sadly. 'I let myself down. I try so hard to rid myself of all material comfort, but it really is much harder than you think. I'm in constant conflict with my flaws.'

Sam was listening to Diana but she continued to look all around her, absorbing as much detail as she could. However hard she tried, she couldn't reconcile it with the deteriorating exterior shell of the caravan. The space was dry and warm. But more strikingly it was immaculate and smelt so deliciously clean, but not the acrid clean of cleaning products, more, Sam imagined, like the dressing room of a wealthy and successful actress. Sam could detect Chanel No. 5 and talcum powder but there were other opulent scents she couldn't place.

'It's just so lovely. I think I could live here.'

Diana looked around as if trying to see her home through her visitor's eyes. 'Oh, I think anyone could live here. It's all about deciding what you absolutely can't live without. For me, it's my bed linen. I blame my circulation which is shocking, not my willpower which is really quite strong. I get terribly cold in the winter. But that duvet keeps me gloriously warm regardless. It's my den. I feel like a bear hibernating when I climb under it.'

Sam eyed the kitchen fittings. It was all very beautifully designed. Thinking of Anne's warning, she wondered if the expensive toaster and coffee machine were stolen and then felt immediately ashamed.

Diana saw her looking at the coffee machine. 'I'll make you a coffee, shall I? Decaf or fully leaded?'

Sam, who had braced herself for something made of mushrooms or acorns, replied with a more confident 'whatever you're having', and the small space in the caravan quickly smelt of rich, dark espresso.

Sam was still looking around, narrating the experience in her own head, desperate not to miss a single detail. Eventually she asked the one question that she felt had to be asked. 'What are you doing here exactly?'

'Just living,' said Diana, taking a sip of coffee and smiling back at Sam quite contentedly.

'But in a caravan? On your own? In the middle of the woods? That's not usual. That's much more than just living.'

'Oh, I rather hoped it was less not more. I spent a few years – decades even – racing through life in heavy shoes. I'm trying to tiptoe for a while.'

Sam looked around her, at the pristine bedding, at the small but deliberate comforts and the leather-bound volumes on the shelf.

'And how do you spend your time?' she wondered, out loud.

Diana smiled warmly. 'With research. Let me show you.'

She pulled down the first of the leather-bound notebooks and flicked proudly through it before handing it over to Sam. The book was over an inch thick and must have had a couple of hundred pages of creamy smooth paper inside. Occasionally there were small drawings in ink, but the majority of the pages were filled entirely with even-handed writing. Sam absorbed the book as a single entity and then began to look at occasional pages, pulling out words and phrases. Each entry was dated, and each page noted sightings of animals and birds, plants and flowers, with carefully scribed names given both in their popular and Latin forms. Periodically, numbers accompanied the words.

'These are just beautiful.' Sam stood up and pulled another volume off the shelf.

'Careful,' said Diana, reaching towards Sam as if to stop her. 'Some have flowers pressed inside.'

Sam handled the book assiduously and Diana relaxed again. Gingerly, Sam opened the diary and read a couple of entries to herself. 'These are so lovely, what an astonishing record.'

Diana smiled gratefully. 'I call it my research, but it's not really research, as such. Just observations. Nothing more than nature notes. But I like to think that somebody with a more scientific brain might be able to analyse these and establish the patterns from year to year. Prove my assumptions if you like. I plan to continue,' said Diana, scanning the volumes proudly with her eyes. 'When these shelves are full I will move them to storage and then will simply carry on. I plan to document every day of my life here.'

Sam put the notebook back and carefully took down another, opening it on the table in front of her and turning the pages over, admiring the commitment as much as the content. 'Are you hoping to prove something specific? What *are* the assumptions you've made?'

'Gosh,' said Diana, as if she had thought about this a lot but hadn't had cause to speak it out loud for a while. 'I think I lived before in a world where I trusted other people to use their brains to understand and solve these great big environmental problems. I never really felt the problem was on my desk, either literally or figuratively. But when you live with your nose to the ground, as I do now, and you feel the impact of decline everywhere you look, you realise the problem is very much your own to solve. If I don't notice and record these things, who else will?' Diana paused and said, with a dismissive wave of her hand, 'Of course, the problem is always money.'

Sam had been absorbed by the small detail of the caravan, the comfort of it all, but of course, she reminded herself, Diana must be living in poverty. She asked kindly, 'Yours? Your lack of money for your research?'

'No, not mine,' said Diana a little impatiently. 'I have all I need for my own research – it costs nothing to notice and to note. I'm talking *globally*. And it's not a lack, it's a misdirection. There's plenty of money for research, but the money tends to be spent on those things that improve efficiencies or are capable of making money in their own right. The things I study are more whimsical, but I fear there's very little money in whimsy.'

Diana thought for a while, and her gaze seemed to reach beyond Sam, beyond the confines of the caravan, beyond the woodland even. 'Take orchids, for instance. If the lady orchid or the lizard orchid disappears for ever, does it actually matter? If the cost of improved yields, more mouths fed, cheaper food on the table is the disappearance of a couple of species that, at best produce a few flowers per hectare within a rarefied landscape each year, that – let's face it – only a handful of people really get the benefit of looking at, then that is probably a price most people are prepared to pay. And we all want our farmers to stay in business, don't we? We need our farmers to be efficient, to make enough money from their land to keep farming, don't we? And if a farmer, whose meadowland has been grazed for livestock for centuries finds himself with cattle at risk of TB or the supermarkets are offering him less for milk than the cost of production, can we blame him for prioritising those immediate concerns ahead of maintaining the biodiversity of his meadow for the good of me and you? So we must support the research that gives every possible chance of that farmer thriving. And yet, and yet…'

Her voice trailed off and she reached for yet another volume and flicked it open. 'I care about these guys more and more.' She showed Sam a picture of a flower, a graceful, characterful plant with flowers clustered at the top of its elegant stem.

'Well, it's certainly very pretty.'

'But I can't do justice to it. In real life each of the flowers looks like a tiny lady in a pink crinoline ballgown. Here, you see, are her slim arms, and here's her head, composed of sepals and petals. But even if my pen could capture her luxurious hair and graceful posture, I couldn't capture her scent.'

Diana traced her finger over the pen lines and smiled indulgently, the smile of the proud mother of a wayward but brilliant teenager. 'She's elegant but she's mighty obstreperous too. You can't force her to make an appearance, you can simply suggest she might want to drop in. And even then, the invitation has to be absolutely right: subtle, never overt. She'll visit fresh ground that has recently been cleared of scrub. But she won't appear if you watch and wait, she likes you to turn your back and then she might just deign to visit. She's both belle and bellicose. I'm learning her ways, though I'd never take a visitation for granted. If you're very lucky, I might be able to introduce you. But,' said Diana, changing her tone abruptly from dulcet to forceful, 'you'll have to behave yourself.'

'Behave myself?' asked Sam, alarmed. She had been so transfixed by the drawing and by Diana's description of this prima ballerina she hadn't quite remembered the reason she'd come to visit in the first place.

'Well, you need to be a little less *angry* perhaps? I'm not sure she'd take kindly to being introduced to someone who habitually vents her fury on nature.'

'Angry? Me?' said Sam, quite indignant.

'Yes, you! The first time I met you, you were throwing pine cones at me and calling me all sorts of names.'

'But that wasn't directed at you, I didn't even know you were there!'

'Of course it wasn't directed at me. How on earth could it be directed at me when you had never met me? Though you'd be surprised by the leaps people make. But you were angry nevertheless and angry people don't tend to be people who care about wild orchids. Besides, if you're going to hurl insults into the woods, I recommend you wait for a really windy night. That feels marvellous, the trees suck up your words, spin them into a blustering vortex and fling them to the heavens. That's the right way to dispel anger.'

'Actually, that sounds great. Perhaps I'll try it,' said Sam, liking the image.

'You should. It's much more effective. If you shout at a tree on a calm day, the insults will just bounce right back at you.' Diana sounded pensive and very much as if she were talking from experience but she quickly shook her head and continued.

'Our relationship with nature is precarious. It's a very delicate thing. People far more brilliant than me have been looking at these issues since time immemorial. The task has been to expand the earth's production to feed seven billion people and it's pretty astonishing that this has been achieved. OK, granted, there are people going hungry all over the world, but that's not a food production issue, we throw away a third of everything we produce. I imagine the same clever people who have managed so capably to increase our planet's capacity will now turn their attention to infrastructure and spend a few generations getting food grown where it's actually needed. That way, we don't have to plunder the earth's core in pursuit of oil, just so we can move the food around, which just exacerbates the problem. You and I can both do the maths, if the population is yet to expand to nine billion, we are already producing enough food to feed those extra mouths. But, my fear is that we are barking up the wrong tree. So much money is being ploughed into futuristic solutions, but I don't believe technology is the answer, I think attitude is the answer. I believe we need to think smaller, not bigger. We need to protect our pollinators, look after our immediate environment, whatever small bit we've been allocated, and we all need to learn to tiptoe through life.'

Diana stood up again and reached for another notebook, flicking through the pages until she found another entry. She pressed the book open and put it on the table between them. The ink drawing showed a bird on top of a post. She carried on talking, 'The gradual decline and eventual extinction of animals tells a very relatable story. We can look at their eyes and see their souls and we can mourn for them as we mourn for ourselves. A picture of a female goshawk tearing some flesh into smaller pieces to feed her chicks, or the male coming back from hunting to drop off a kill for the female and chicks to share, well, those are scenes that can move us. You'd have to be a philistine not to understand with alarm that we must protect these things as we must protect ourselves. We see families fighting for survival and we feel their struggle, regardless of the species.'

She sighed heavily. 'But wildflowers disappearing? They don't really pull on our heartstrings in quite the same way. Once this whole landscape would have been full of hay meadows, but they are few and far between now. They are no longer part of the fabric of our countryside and within my lifetime, flowers that were once considered weeds are now extinct to all intents and purposes. Our industrial grassland is not much better than concrete. But who mourns the cornflowers? Not the farmers, it's not their job. For a farmer these weeds reduce the palatability of his grassland for cattle or reduce his cereal yield. But for the pollinators and the birds, those wildflowers are a life source.'

Sam looked at the picture of the bird. Somehow with a few lines, Diana had caught the bright eye of the goshawk and with that she could see its ferocity. She spoke apologetically, in awe of Diana's fervour. 'You'll have to be patient with me, I've only just moved to the countryside. To me it is all so green and glorious, it's hard to imagine any peril.'

'You're right. We are very lucky here. You only have to fly

over the land in an aeroplane to marvel at its greenness. Seventy per cent of our land area is occupied by agriculture. And we have over 1,500 flowers that make up British flora. But to understand the peril you must understand that of those 1,500 species, around 580 of these are considered threatened or rare.'

Diana sighed a deep lament of loss. 'The wild strawberry, ragged robin, harebell... they've all pretty much gone. They were here in the first place because our traditional methods of farming, the grazing, the mowing, were all beneficial to the land.'

'And what can be done?'

'By civilisation as a whole? Absolutely nothing. But by you and me? Everything. Look at me? I've reintroduced three species since I've been here and I'm not stopping there. If we all did that...'

'How long have you been here?'

'Four years. So that's three quarters of a species for each year I've been here. But I'm only fifty-four. I might well be here for another thirty years or so if I'm lucky. I might be able to have a go at establishing more than twenty species, do you think? That would be something, wouldn't it?!'

Diana noticed Sam flinch at the mention of her age and now watched her scanning her face and hair.

'You thought I was older?' said Diana, a trace of disappointment in her voice.

'I suppose so, yes. I'm sorry,' said Sam, embarrassed. She was certain her face had already betrayed her but she knew that any backtracking would seem disingenuous.

'Well, there's no reason to apologise. Infirmity and weakness come to us all. We must make the most of every strong day.' Diana looked around, and Sam realised that the caravan did not contain a single mirror. 'I think my skin is really quite good for my age but it's the colour of my hair that you're not seeing past. I had to let myself go grey when I got here. Trying to keep myself any other colour artificially wouldn't have been practical and would have gone quite against the spirit of my journey of discovery. And vanity isn't necessary here. The trees don't care. And, besides, my grey hair makes me invisible which I like. Sometimes I tie my hair into a knot on the top of my head and put a decent dress on and walk into town and nobody gives me so much as a glance. There's nothing quite like being a grey-haired woman to put you at the bottom of a pile of interesting people. And I do so love being anonymous.'

'Doesn't that make you sad? Being invisible? It happened to me and I hated it.'

'No! That's the whole point. I'm here because I wanted to find *value* in my life. I have a friend, Rebecca, who insists on keeping me up to date with what's going on out there and I don't envy her one jot. Quite frankly, I'd rather not know.' Diana looked thoughtful. 'But for her it's probably vital. She's still got her nose to the grind, she's constantly working and worrying herself to death. She's likely to keep on going until she drops, but I don't quite know what the point of that is. If she were doing something useful, mapping the wheat genome or something practical, I'd get it. I'd applaud her. But she's not. She's just amassing personal wealth. It's all so ludicrously futile. She doesn't even have family...'

Sam wrinkled her nose, detecting a judgement she felt obliged to fend off. 'Is it excusable, working as hard, if you have family? I'm not sure we'll see eye to eye on that...'

'I have no personal knowledge, I have no context. But I think that is often the driving force for empire building. That urge to stake your claim to a plot for the future with the family as motivation.'

'And if you have no family?' asked Sam, leaning forward and running a hand through her hair.

Diana looked flustered and then angry, her eyes flashing from pale blue to indigo as she appraised Sam. 'This isn't about me, Sam.'

Sam drew herself upright, shocked. 'No! I was talking about *me*.'

'Well,' said Diana, relieved but still a bit irritated. 'It certainly isn't about you. It's about Rebecca. Just Rebecca. I'm talking about Rebecca here.'

'Oh,' said Sam, completely caught off guard by Diana's stern rebuke. Sam, silent for a few moments, thought hard before asking, 'But how on earth do you manage financially? If you're so young, you're not even claiming a pension yet! How on earth do you live? Benefits?'

Diana looked crossly at Sam. 'Goodness me, what do you take me for? Heavens, no. I have my means.'

What an enigma, thought Sam.

The conversation had become slippery. There had been a principled objective at the start of the conversation, Diana had seemed open, energetic, but now, since talk of Rebecca, it had become almost unbearably tense.

'I'd better leave you in peace. But I'd love to come back?'

Diana stood up abruptly to signal that she too thought they had reached the end of the conversation but then, to Sam's surprise, she smiled quite warmly. 'You've been a lot less troublesome than my visitors in the past, so I don't see why not.'

Sam said goodbye and walked slowly back to her house, conscious that something new had happened. She'd spoken at length with another woman who had not tried to categorise her. Diana had assumed that Sam was one of the good people! She'd shared her notebooks, her thoughts, her dreams and had promised her glimpses of rare flowers and birds as if she might be worthy of such access. Diana had neither asked her if she was married, or a mother, or in some other way attached to people in a manner that made her less not more. And the moment she'd tried to wade in with her own defence of childlessness, she'd been told, categorically, 'This isn't about you.' How *refreshing*! Sam thought. Diana hadn't tried to understand her or fix her. Instead, Diana had talked about the things within her control that only she could fix.

Sam realised with a jolt how much she'd enjoyed both talking *and* listening. There were so many subjects that had become off limits with Danny and the cordons around those restricted areas seemed to have widened with time, preventing them from approaching the topics themselves or any others that might lead inadvertently towards those exclusion zones.

After being submerged for so long, the sheer breadth of their conversation felt like oxygen and the intellectual challenge felt like light. And Sam felt taller.

Chapter 24

Danny was getting ready for work, packing his laptop away and winding a cable neatly around a battery pack before sliding it into place in an internal pocket in his rucksack. He had a lunch appointment so wouldn't need to take his own food into the office, but he checked his watch and then hesitated at the fruit bowl, wondering if he should pack a piece for later regardless. He eyed up the selection and frowned. Sam didn't compromise. She knew he didn't like satsumas but she bought them anyway. She knew he didn't like eggs, but despite this, she regularly cooked them for her own breakfast.

He picked up a satsuma and lifted it to his nose, inhaling deeply. A flood of memory accompanied the unmistakable scent and he closed his eyes briefly, remembering.

The associations were all good. A wooden tray lined with purple, crinkly tissue paper, each fruit individually nestled into its own compartment, like a precious jewel. The wooden tray, rough with splinters, was kept out of his reach, high up on a dresser, Danny recalled, but he could just about get to it by stretching up on his tiptoes. He would fumble around, biting his tongue in concentration, his small fat fingers meeting nothing but the tissue paper until perhaps the third or fourth attempt when they would find their target, the cool, dimpled touch of the satsuma under his fingertips.

Danny would crouch down beyond the dresser, just out of sight, and work his thumb nails through the skin until rewarded with a sharp spray of juice in his face, the scent so strong he could taste it in the air before he'd eaten a single piece. And then he would unwrap it, sometimes trying to remove the peel in one unbroken piece, though he was usually too impatient to be successful. He was never too impatient to remove the pith though and would pull at it conscientiously, discarding each white thread as he separated the segments, liking to prepare the whole fruit before consuming it.

The fruit meant so much more than a rationed sweet treat. It was Christmas; a tree with lights and paper chains; a bunch of mistletoe strung in the kitchen doorframe for his mother and father to squeal beneath; it was the penultimate gift in the toe of his Christmas stocking, just before the cool touch of the coin that was his alone to spend. It was the very best of his childhood.

Danny opened his eyes and looked critically at the satsuma, weighing it up in his hand, before returning it carefully to the fruit bowl and choosing an apple instead. Apples were easy to select, the colour and the texture combined to give you an accurate assessment of the taste to come. Even without a visual clue, that slight give under your finger tips described exactly the brown, pappy flesh you could expect in a bruised area. But a satsuma? Satsumas were liars.

This was a lesson that Danny had only learned as an adult. He remembered no disappointing fruit as a child. He was quite certain that they had been consistent, the perfect blend of sharp and sweet, with each segment swollen balloon-tight with juice. But as with so many other truths of adulthood, satsumas had the ability to underwhelm. There was nothing about the scent or the feel of a satsuma that could accurately describe the level of acidity you could expect to find within. It could feel perfect to touch, the skin just loose enough for you to predict it would peel easily; the scent could be strong and citric, the feel of the fruit itself, once peeled, could offer a promising degree of plumpness. And then, even as you salivated, knowing exactly what was coming, the taste would dismay. An alkaline, dry disappointment, the juice barely running, and with no tangy bite to shock the tastebuds.

Danny packed the apple carefully into his bag, zipped it up and hoisted it onto his shoulder. He checked his watch. With four or five minutes to spare before he needed to leave for the station, he climbed the stairs to say goodbye to Sam.

Chapter 25

Sam couldn't wait to see Diana again. Danny was now routinely leaving the house at just after six to catch his early train which gave Sam an extra pocket of time she had never anticipated. She felt too guilty to go back to bed so instead she hurried around the house, cleaning it and dealing with her outstanding paperwork, impatient for it to be a respectable enough time to visit. She imagined Diana would be up early, busy also, and she feared she might have lost her already to her woodland wanderings but nor did she want to appear overly keen. Eventually she allowed herself to head out, pretending to herself that she might just be going for a walk but knowing she was craving more conversation.

Diana was beside the caravan, tending to a fire. 'I was just about to put this out, I'll stoke it up a bit and put the kettle on, shall I?' she said, brightly. Sam relaxed, aware suddenly that she'd been holding her breath.

Diana was wearing her ubiquitous dungarees and another vividly patterned shirt. Bright red concentric circles interplayed with black numbers and gold swirls, scrolls and, somewhat incongruously, pairs of fish.

'I like your shirt. Pretty bold for a hermit,' said Sam, sitting down cross-legged by the fire.

'This old thing? I've had it for ever. It's silk.'

'Fancy!'

'Rather practical actually. It dries quickly. I'm not blessed with a laundry service here.'

Sam looked up at Diana from her seat on the ground and imagined coping with day to day living in such a small space. 'I can help, I mean, if you ever want me to take some things home to wash them, I wouldn't mind at all. I don't have much to do at the moment.'

Diana shook her head vigorously. 'Good heavens, no. That would defeat the purpose, don't you think? My objective is to live self-sufficiently here, I can hardly take on a cleaner and then go to sleep with a clear conscience.'

'If you change your mind, let me know.' Sam was still puzzling at the swirls and features on the shirt. She thought she might have seen the pattern somewhere before. Diana stepped into the caravan to collect the cups and tea she needed. Sam followed her and stood on the threshold watching Diana busy herself.

'What's it like, being a recluse?'

'It has its moments.'

'What do you miss?'

'Surprisingly little. I have given in to a few small luxuries that I didn't seem able to cope without, so I look after myself reasonably well.' Diana looked around the caravan, a little proudly.

'Television?'

'Good lord no. I never watched it anyway. Poison.'

Sam, whose sanity often seemed to depend on the relief offered by other people's problems was horrified by this. 'Poison? I think of it as a merciful escape.'

'But I have escaped, I hardly need to escape from this, do I?' said Diana, as they stepped out of the caravan. Diana added another log beneath the kettle, prodding it into position with a short iron poker.

'True,' said Sam, settling into the warm spot by the fire and thinking how far removed she felt from her own life which was really so near.

'Are you ever lonely?' Sam asked, determined to get as many of her questions answered as possible, before Diana tired of her.

'Lonely? No. Never. I was much lonelier before, when I was surrounded by people.'

'I know that feeling.' Sam remembered the sensation of being cast out by her office when she returned from her recuperation. That crushing feeling of isolation when nobody would even look her in the eye.

'Oh, it is entirely possible. Believe me. Take my friend, Rebecca. She has a very active life and look at her, not a single friend in sight. She is one of those women who likes to think she has it all – but as far as I'm concerned, she's severely lacking in several departments.'

Sam smiled at the slight. 'You talk about Rebecca a lot. She is your friend, so you must be hers. She has you, at least?'

Diana paused while she stirred the tea and handed Sam a cup. 'Well, not really. She had me but then I chose this life. In order to fulfil this obligation to myself, I had to reject her entirely.'

Sam narrowed her eyes as she looked at Diana, searching for traces of a past betrayal or deeper wound. She could see none. 'That must have hurt her hugely. Real friends seem hard to come by these days.'

'I needed to reject her in order to save myself. That is something that became very apparent and I don't think I have had a need to regret my decisions.'

'And you really are happier here on your own in the woods?'

'I feel *better*. In the past, every weekday my diary was full for months and months in advance, but the panic I felt when I woke to a featureless Saturday could simply overwhelm me. Now, I have absolutely no idea what will happen tomorrow, but I feel in complete control of today. And that is a vast improvement.'

'You make it sound so easy. It can't be. There must be moments when it feels difficult to be out here on your own all the time?'

'Sometimes I doubt myself. Sometimes I fear that my life as a happy recluse is just one more charade in a lifetime of charades, but most of the time when I wake up and I do a quick top-to-toe assessment of worries I find myself to be more or less carefree. Or at least, if I have cares, I have limited them to ones I believe I have the power to fix. There's not enough kindling to light a fire, I need vital supplies I can't find in the woods so will have to make a trip to town, that sort of thing. But I never find myself worrying about the things that used to keep me awake at night. My greatest achievement, I think, is that I no longer care what people think.'

Sam studied Diana. She still couldn't quite equate the sheer volume of opinion and the wealth of ideas with this humble life. Diana seemed to hold more thought than anyone she'd ever met. She seemed, somehow, beyond human. 'Do you remember when we first met?' Sam ventured. 'You said you could help me. What exactly did you mean?'

Diana looked at Sam blankly. 'Just that. You were standing right in the middle of the woods shouting insults and crying. I simply thought I might be able to assist you.'

'How?' asked Sam, peering over her glasses a bit at Diana, remembering the basket of herbs and wondering if Diana would have the same recollection.

'By talking!' said Diana, a little impatiently. 'By being a friend!'

'Oh,' said Sam, unable to hide her disappointment. She'd expected something a little less pedestrian than friendship which, in her recent experience, was lamentably contingent on a number of things she could not offer.

'Do you mind if I ask you a personal question?' Sam watched Diana brace herself for something tough. 'Nothing like that. Just, what do you *believe* in?'

Diana looked thoughtful and her eyes darted around the room as if examining her past in small chapters.

'Belief. Belief kept me going for a number of years.' Diana closed her eyes, to better describe her old self. 'I suppose I was once a neo-classicist. But my big break with society made me reconsider. I toyed with Keynesian theory, but it never went quite far enough for me.'

Sam frowned, puzzled.

Diana, frustrated, exhaled in reply. 'Well, I'm not a Marxist, if that's what you're thinking?'

'A Marxist?' Sam suppressed a laugh. 'No, I was thinking nothing of the sort. I was thinking a bit more, well, *spiritually* I suppose. You're not a *witch*, are you?' said Sam. It was as much a statement as a question and there was a trace of disappointment in her voice as she acknowledged this truth for the first time.

Diana laughed loudly and drained her cup. 'I am most certainly not a witch. Forgive me, I rather thought you were asking me about my economic leanings, I am neither a Marxist nor a witch. Though frankly I'd rather be either of those things than the neo-classicist I once was.'

Diana looked down at Sam. 'Whatever, or whoever, gave you the idea I was a witch?'

'That's what they say in my road. My neighbours. Apparently, they don't let their children into the woods because a witch lives in a hovel.'

'Goodness me. Well, would you mind doing me a favour and not mentioning I invited you here. I'd be quite happy to let them carry on thinking that for a bit longer. I'm more than happy if their children don't play in the woods, they'll only disturb my birds and, besides, I don't much care for the villagers. Anyway, they will all have much more to worry about than mere witchcraft by the time I've finished with them,' she said, a little mysteriously and, Sam thought, betraying a trace of threat too.

Sam remembered her recent introductions to her village through Anne and Hattie. 'So, it's all very well you wanting to discard society, but your job is made much harder if society refuses to ignore you, isn't it? I just don't think they're going to let you be.'

'Ha! Yes, I'm aware. I think they are quite obsessed with me, locally at any rate. I've been waiting for them to tire of me, but it's only a matter of time before somebody else is more interesting than a woman in the woods.' Diana eyed her guest with renewed interest. 'Perhaps you? You're a bit of an oddity, aren't you? Perhaps you could distract them. You might well live in a house, but something tells me you'll be fascinating to the village.'

'Fascinating? That actually sounds quite appealing, I don't think I've ever been fascinating to anybody.'

'Be careful what you wish for. I didn't mean fascinating in a *good* way. I meant in a curious, not-quite-our-type way,' said Diana, with no trace of a smile. 'Now, leave me be. I've got an extremely busy day ahead and you've already taken up a quite enough of it.'

Sam rose to her feet and brushed the woodland debris from her jeans. She tipped the dregs of her tea out on to the ground and handed the empty tin cup back to Diana with a grateful smile of thanks. For a very long time, Sam had wanted to disappear, but suddenly the thought of being fascinating held a surprising attraction. She didn't feel admonished, she felt *accepted* and a glow of happiness accompanied her all the way home.

Sam was oblivious to the groundswell of change all around her. Even as she walked the bluebells were pushing up their green leaves, the advance guard of foliage that laid a welcome mat out for the flowers to follow. A few green shoots had already appeared, cautiously raising their tips to check that winter had left for good and now, confidently, the others were following, quickly replacing all remnants of brown woodland floor with a fresh new look for spring.

Chapter 26

The delivery had arrived mid-morning, timed to coincide with the weekend when Danny would be there to receive it. He had been pacing up and down, looking out of the window, anxious not to miss a moment of its entry into his life. Sam was entertained by his excitement but was also aware of a sombre anxiety humming in the milieu of her mind, wondering if his proprietorial stance signalled some unnamed danger she needed to guard against. As if to illustrate her fear, Sam could hear the reverse warning alarm beeping as the flatbed truck inched backwards into her drive.

The lawnmower was strapped on to the rear of an improbably large vehicle. Had Danny picked it up from the garden centre, Sam now realised, there was no way he would have been able to fit it into the car. From her view at the front door, the lawnmower seemed very large.

'It's very big, Danny.'

'She's a monster!' he agreed proudly. He felt Sam stiffen beside him and quickly attempted to justify his decision which now, looking at it in the context of his driveway, seemed disproportionate. 'You'd actually be surprised by the range, Sam, and by the complexity of the various attributes.

There were many appropriate models I could have chosen, so I had to do some extensive research but I'm confident I got the right one for the job.

'She's a beauty, isn't she!' He looked at it with admiration as it was pulled slowly backwards down a metal ramp. 'It doesn't just cut, it mulches and collects and see those high rear wheels? They will help with manoeuvrability. It's not a difficult machine to handle, thanks to the ball bearing wheels, which will make for pretty smooth rolling, and they're much more durable too. It's got a powerful engine, so it really won't need much muscle and you can cut the grass at four different heights.' He looked on proudly as the driver of the truck lifted the ramps and loaded them back on to the flatbed. Sam smiled indulgently but felt something rip at her insides as she looked at the ferocity of the machine.

Danny signed the delivery note with a flourish and folded his copy of the paperwork carefully into his pocket before proudly pushing the mower up the garden path. Sam watched in despair as Danny crouched over it. She knew the grass needed cutting. The lines marking out the turf squares like tiles in a bathroom had all but disappeared. While Danny read the instruction manual, working fastidiously through the book and familiarising himself with each feature by referring to the numbered diagram on a pull-out flap, Sam studied the lawn. New grass was weaving its way over and through the cracks, knitting it together and finding its own compulsion to grow.

Sam dropped to her knees. It was still cool, but it was early May now and she was happy enough in jeans and a T-shirt. She sat and looked at the grass, studying it carefully. It wasn't just grass, there were tiny white flower heads trying to make their way to fruition. Clover perhaps, Sam mused. She stroked the green, loving its resilience as it bounced back to full height as soon as her hand left it. It didn't mind being trampled on, it didn't mind being rolled on. It took whatever you gave it. But it wouldn't like being cut.

Sam studied the grass further. There were all sorts of different plants racing away ahead of the grass. It was punctuated with the occasional single blade that had risen a good ten centimetres above the grass height, and each of these single strands supported a tight knitted crown, the suppressed bud of something yet to flourish. Sam shuffled forwards on her knees from bud to bud, finding one that was beginning to reveal the bright yellow promise of the flower to come. She looked at the leaves beneath each strand and now recognised dandelions and realised that within a day or two her lawn would be a little solar system of bright colour. She called out to Danny.

'We could let it grow a bit longer, Danny. We don't have to cut it just yet.'

He frowned, but perhaps at the lawnmower rather than at her suggestion. 'That's not practical.'

'Why not?'

'Because it will quickly get out of hand. And the longer you leave it, the harder it is to keep under control. Look at it already!'

'I quite like it this length,' Sam said with a wan smile, trying not to let desperation creep into her voice which she knew would only alarm Danny.

'That's definitely not the point of a lawn. A perfectly mown lawn is symbolic. Our lawns represent us – both our desires and our ability to keep our desires under control.' Danny smiled broadly at Sam, but she wasn't sure if he was joking. She wondered why anyone would want to keep their desires under control.

'Oh,' she said, neutrally.

'People's lawns aren't just an extension of their homes, they're an extension of themselves, particularly in England. We love our lawns, we must treat them with respect. Besides, if we let our lawn become unruly our neighbours will judge us, they'll run us out of the county.'

'But *why* do we love our lawns?' She felt petulant. She directed the question at Danny but continued to stroke the grass around her, knowing her own answer to that question but keen to hear his.

'Because we work hard to earn them. And once we've earned them we like to sit on them, to play on them, to kick a ball around them. But mostly, we just like to admire them. We're proud of them. They're a mark of our success.'

Sam nodded, trying to understand. 'But if we let it grow just a bit longer we could let the clover grow for the bees… '

Danny laughed as he filled the mower with petrol. 'I don't think our tiny patch is going to save the bees, but I love you even more for trying.'

'But if everyone… '

'Not everyone is. You can't singlehandedly save the planet and, quite frankly, you have even less chance of overturning hundreds of years of British culture. For years, men have been rushing home to cut the grass. It's a rite of passage. You've earned your lawn, you get to keep it under control.'

The word hung in the air between them. That was it, wasn't it? Sam thought. It's just a control thing.

Danny put the cap back on the petrol tank and yanked the starter rope. The lawnmower roared to life and quickly spluttered back to inertia again. Twice more he tugged at the rope until the motor caught convincingly and the engine began to idle happily. Danny released the throttle and the machine jumped forward, powered by its engine, not his muscles. He set off in a slow deliberate line.

Sam watched him. This would make him happy, she mused, and she knew it was important to give him a role to play in the garden. She should give him this. The lawn could be his project, it would suit his temperament, and she, in the meantime, would get going with the planting and the long-term vision, which would suit hers. But as she watched him make a careful turn and come back towards her, she felt a sense of regret. That had been her grass. He didn't need the grass, she did. She felt sullen and spoilt and his frown of concentration irritated her. What right does he have, she thought, to saunter off to London all week and then come home to cut *my* grass?

She paced, absent-mindedly pulling up small weeds from the flowerbeds between her thumb and finger but she still felt aggrieved. He waved happily to her at the next turn, encouraging her to admire his work (so far, three unwavering lines, the prized stripes of contrast showing his steady hand to full effect) but she found it hard to swallow her disappointment in him. This wasn't gardening, this felt like the opposite.

After another couple of minutes, Danny waved again,

with five stripes now under his belt. She waved back and smiled. She pulled at the weeds, accelerating her progress by alternating between her left and right hand, her technique improving as she moved along the bed.

The lawnmower continued to roar.

The noise of it drowned out any hope of tranquillity. When Danny next made a turn away from her, she left the garden and walked with purpose towards the woods and then immediately towards the caravan.

Chapter 27

After the roar of the lawnmower, the shady woods seemed hallowed and Diana, who was removing her own weeds steadily with a hoe, seemed to be in the midst of worship.

She stopped and looked at Sam without a greeting.

'Can I help?' asked Sam quietly.

'If you like. I'm weeding.'

Sam dropped down to her knees beside the plants, trying to identify the patterns that distinguished the growth that Diana was cultivating and the plants she was busy removing.

'It's so hard to tell everything apart at this stage. How do you know which ones are good and which are bad?'

'I've planted these brassicas in a couple of long rows,' Diana answered, indicating the seedlings with the edge of her hoe. 'They're both paler and more glossy than the weeds around them. Take everything else out, roots and all if you can.' Diana bent down and plucked a weed out of the loose soil to demonstrate.

'So this really is gardening?' It was no different to the gardening she'd been doing at home and she now felt foolish.

'Yes. This is pretty much all there is to it.'

'I feel let down. Gardening is simply the constant

eradication of small plants, all that burgeoning growth, just trying to find its own way in life. It's the opposite of what I expected, it's all so much more destructive.'

Diana carried on hoeing, without agreeing or disagreeing.

'And it must be subjective, too. What's good and what's bad. Why should we get to decide which ones should live or die?'

Diana leant on her hoe, looking down at the younger woman.

'When you're gardener, you're lord and master. You plant what you want and in order to give everything a chance of thriving, you get rid of everything else. It's all a battle for light, for food, for space to put out your roots. There's not much more mystery to it than that.'

'Does it make you feel powerful?' asked Sam. The tiny plants showing growth seemed very frail in the context of the giant trees all around her.

'Well, I had never considered it in those terms, but I find the act of growing things very helpful.'

'But what about these guys?' said Sam, gesturing to the growing pyre of wilting weeds beside her. Their limpness made Sam sad.

'Those are simply not your concern.'

Sam sighed. 'I want to garden but I don't think I'm quite ready for it. For all the ruthless killing required. It all feels a bit discriminatory to me.'

'What are you hoping to grow?'

'It doesn't really matter. I just want to grow something, give it a chance to get going. That would feel like a bit of an accomplishment at the moment. I spend too much time engaged in negative activity and I need a bit of displacement. I know it probably sounds silly, but I was really getting a bit attached to the grass, and now my husband is cutting it, it makes me feel so sad. I liked it.'

To Sam's surprise, Diana didn't blanch at the mention of a husband. Nor did she ask any of the questions Sam had come to expect when people discovered she was married – there was no 'what does he do?', no 'how long have you been married?', and certainly no 'Oh – and do you have children?'

Instead, Diana just continued to look calmly into her face, and asked, 'How big is your patch?'

Sam looked around her, squinting, trying to imagine how big her garden was. 'I think maybe from that that beech to the other big beech in length? And maybe half as much in width?'

'Oh, small,' said Diana, sounding rather underwhelmed.

'Big enough for me. I had a couple of windowboxes below the level of the pavement in my old flat, so it's like Richmond Park as far as I'm concerned.'

'And is it a nice sunny spot?' Diana asked, watching the dappled light play with the ground at her feet.

'Pretty much, it gets sun for much of the afternoon certainly.'

'Well, you can probably grow anything you want.' Diana eyed Sam critically. 'You don't sound very ambitious though.' Diana carried on with her task as if Sam's lack of ambition might be incurable.

Sam stopped weeding to protest. 'I am, I am. It's just, it's mostly lawn and that will now need cutting all the time. That's all I seem capable of. I watch the weeds grow and then pull them out. I watch the grass grow then we cut it. It all feels futile.'

'Then why not just let the grass grow?' said Diana, with a disinterest that Sam felt quite unable to ignore. She had begun to pull at the weeds half-heartedly again but on hearing Diana's question, she suddenly became excited. 'Could I do that?'

'Of course. Long grass is glorious and it's much better than short grass for your insect life. You'll attract all sorts of visitors. Butterflies and bees, even crickets in these parts. And they in turn will bring in the birds.'

'I thought the bees would like the clover but, yes of course, longer grass could be a haven for all sorts of things.' Sam smiled, imagining the possibilities.

'People tend to cut their grass far too short these days anyway. If everyone allowed their grass to grow by just a couple of inches we could make a big difference to some of the damage we've done on this planet of ours. And when there's a drought, short grass will scorch and die, so it's prudent to let it get a bit longer if you can. But we're obsessed with control. We love our lawns.'

'That's what my husband said,' agreed Sam, thinking of Danny. 'What would it look like, if I let it grow?'

'I'm afraid you'll learn that growing grass isn't entirely passive. You won't be able to leave it be, it's not quite as simple as that. Nature fights fiercely and plants will use every trick they can to establish themselves at the expense of others and it can be pretty resourceful. Some things are better at naturalising themselves, so you can't just ignore it, or you'd quickly end up with a mess of nettles, thistles and dandelions.

They all have their place but that's probably not what you're after. But if you manage it carefully and put in a bit of thought and effort, you could grow a meadow in miniature. It would be pretty and would provide not just colour but plenty of movement. A bit of long grass is gorgeous to look at when the wind picks up. It would take a while to get a good mix of wildflowers dispersed though they'd come eventually. You could hurry it along by adding some wildflower seed. That would be nice. You'll attract a few more varieties of insect life that way. Perhaps that's the answer while you get to know your garden.'

Sam tried to imagine it. She looked back at the careful rows Diana had planted. 'What are you growing here?'

'All sorts. Cabbage and broccoli for the winter. You'd be surprised what you can get away with with a bit of care and attention. I've had success with kale and kohlrabi, spinach and celery.'

She looked around her at the shielded clearing in the copse, admiring the small healthy beds Diana had coaxed from the earth.

'There's nothing too fanciful or indulgent. I tend to start a few things off under my watchful eye. I grow a bit of veg and a number of herbs that I think should do quite well without much sunlight, but once they're established I shall move them out into different areas in the hope they'll naturalise. They'd probably have come from this sort of landscape in the first place. I've got angelica, horseradish, rosemary and lovage and in those pots there I'm growing some chervil, chives and sweet woodruff. But my priorities are different these days. Trying to establish plants and let them thrive where they are happiest is a great motivation to me. Yes, I grow a few veggies I want to eat, carrots, leeks and mustard do well, but I've cultivated a couple of sunnier patches elsewhere and trying to learn from season to season is my real motivation. I'm up against it with the rabbits and the deer but I have a few tricks up my sleeve. I've had a tremendous amount of success introducing some berries into the margins here too. Not just the blackberries you'd expect to find but lovely wild bilberries and some currants too. I do what I can to harvest them all but quite frankly I'm growing them for the animals half the time.' She shrugged. 'But perhaps that's a fair exchange. I've put in a few fruit trees too, some damsons and greengages and a couple of hazelnuts. But I won't see much from them for a few years. It's nice to know I have them in store for me, though.'

Diana had allowed a bit of pride to creep into her voice. Sam wondered whether what Diana was doing was legal, but it seemed so completely harmless it was impossible to imagine anyone objecting. She looked at the caravan and wondered how Diana could possibly use such a small space to store and preserve food to keep her going all winter.

In turn, Diana was watching Sam's assessment. 'Are you wondering if I'm allowed to do what I do?' she asked.

Sam was startled and stammered her denial. Diana quickly interrupted her, before Sam could form a lie. She closed her eyes as she recited a passage.

'"The first man who, having fenced in a piece of land, said, This is mine, and found people naïve enough to believe him, that man was the true founder of civil society. From how many crimes, wars, and murders, from how many horrors and misfortunes might not any one have saved mankind, by pulling up the stakes, or filling up the ditch, and crying to his fellows: Beware of listening to this impostor; you are undone if you once forget that the fruits of the earth belong to us all, and the earth itself to nobody.'"

Sam remained silent, in awe of Diana and her knowledge.

'Rousseau,' said Diana, by way of explanation.

'Oh,' said Sam, who felt more ignorant than enlightened.

'He was a philosopher in the eighteenth century,' Diana said kindly, 'and I'm an admirer. You should read him. Not everything, of course, but perhaps think about his version of self-love. That might help you.'

Sam knew she needed help. Of course she did. And while it was a bit alarming to know it was that obvious to Diana, who'd met her just twice before, the idea that she might be able to help herself rather than rely on therapists, medicines or even Danny, was appealing.

'Well, that's my homework for the weekend. Grow some grass and read Rousseau,' said Sam, lightly. 'I'd better head back. I'm going to go home and have a rethink.' Diana continued to weed her vegetables and acknowledged Sam's departure with just the slightest incline of her head.

Chapter 28

Sam devoted the next three days to reading, alternating between researching everything she could about Rousseau and, in equal measure, meadowland. Both often seemed beyond her grasp, but she persevered, motivated by a desire to please Diana. She also spent a good part of each day pacing up and down her lawn, thinking about who she'd become and where she might end up if she didn't make an effort to alter her course. Though she wasn't entirely comfortable with some of the conclusions she was coming to, she hadn't felt the need to interact with her blog and this felt like a small step forward in the direction of progress.

There was more light in the evenings now and Sam, quite unaware of how late it was, had looked at her watch and rushed in to prepare an evening meal. Danny had come home, kissed Sam briefly, changed out of his suit, put on some comfortable clothes and gone straight out to mow the grass, all within ten minutes of arriving. Sam had been chopping onions in the kitchen and had barely noticed his movements, it was only the sound of Danny rattling the mower up the garden path that brought her out of her reverie and back into a world where the struggle of man versus nature was waged with relentless tenacity. She swore under her breath, wiped her hands hurriedly on a towel and ran outside.

Danny had lined up the mower in the far corner, facing the machine to the house and was just bending down to yank the starter.

Sam walked up the lawn towards him and stood in front of the mower with her hands on her hips.

'Thought I'd get on top of it before the weekend, give it a little trim.'

'Don't, Danny. It doesn't need cutting.'

'No? I think it's best, it will start to get a little straggly if I only get to it once a week. This way I can really focus on the sharp edges and the lines on Saturday. We'll be able to play tennis on it by Wimbledon week at this rate.'

'I don't want you to cut it. Not now and not at the weekend.'

Danny seemed puzzled and looked at Sam, the grass, and back at Sam again. 'Really? Why? What's up, sweet pea?'

Sam still had her hands on her hips. She looked and felt combative which she knew was unfair because she'd not yet warned him that this was no longer a lawn, but a battlefield. 'I'm going to take charge of the lawn, if that's OK?'

Danny looked disappointed. 'But I thought we'd decided the lawn was my thing.'

'No,' said Sam, shaking her head certainly. '*You* decided the lawn was your thing. I think it is *my* thing. Or at the very least, it is *our* thing. But I don't want you to unilaterally decide to cut it. This is not a dictatorship.'

Danny laughed loudly but stopped suddenly when he saw the look of forbidding conviction on her face. He had never seen such blatant resolve in her eyes, not even in times of dire need. 'Are you kidding?'

'I've never been more serious.'

Danny gestured at the grass which had already grown a couple of centimetres since the weekend and to Danny it now looked on the brink of anarchy. 'It needs cutting, Sam. It's fine if you want to cut it, you're more than capable. But I don't want it to get unruly.'

'I like unruly,' said Sam, unreasonably.

'Well, I don't,' said Danny, equally unreasonably.

'I just want to let the grass grow a bit.'

'Is this a feminist issue?' he asked, seriously.

'No,' she paused. 'This is a *me* issue. A Sam issue. I want to grow this grass and I want to grow some more grass.'

'Where?'

'In the beds. I don't want to grow plants and flowers there; I want to grow grass. I want to make it all lawn.'

'Oh!' said Danny, relaxing. 'That's a different matter. That's not a bad idea at all. It's not like we're not surrounded by the whole of nature if you want to go and find it. Turning the whole thing to lawn will make it much more manageable and we won't have to worry about the weeds in the beds anymore. That's actually a great idea, Sam. But if you are going to commit to this project, it's important to keep an eye on the quality of the grass. I picked up some lawn fertiliser, it's in the garage, I'll go and fetch it. It will suppress the weeds that will do their very best to infiltrate, the dandelions and whatnot.'

'I don't want you to worry about weeds, Danny. The weeds aren't on your desk, they're on mine.'

'But I've noticed some are already getting away. That's one of the reasons you need to cut the grass regularly. If they get big enough to grow a flower and that goes to seed then *'puff'* he said, mimicking an explosion with his hands. 'Seeds dispersed everywhere with the first gust of wind.'

'You just don't have to worry about it. You're banned from gardening. You can come home and sit in the garden and have a glass of wine, but I don't want you cutting, digging, pruning, spraying or anything else. I am not going to let the weeds get away. I'm on it.'

Danny hesitated. He thought about his beautiful new lawnmower and the pride he was ready to feel for the maintenance of his immaculate lawn. He would have liked to put up a fight but Sam looked so wild. He wondered whether there was something else going on that he had missed. Sam stared back at him intently. She could see the imminent capitulation in the set of his jaw before he stiffened again, realising there was another skirmish yet to be waged.

'What about the front, the drive area? What about the weeds there?'

Sam considered this, trying to weigh up any possible consequence of a hastily agreed settlement. She pictured the front of the house and decided this was an area she could afford to concede. She nodded decisively. 'You can have those. I won't touch that area. You can pressure hose them to your heart's content.'

Danny was mollified. He surveyed the garden again. The back of the house was immaculate, the gutters were clear, the paintwork still shone. The brickwork was solid. Putting the whole garden to lawn was an excellent idea. One less thing to worry about.

'OK, you've got a deal. I'll take care of the front of the house and you take care of the back. But don't take your eye off the ball.'

Sam stepped around the lawnmower and kissed Danny noisily on his cheek. 'I won't. I promise. Thank you, Danny. This lawn and this garden are going to help me heal. They're going to make me better. I'm going to *grow* something.'

Danny pulled Sam into his arms saying into her neck, 'You promise you won't let it become a nightmare out here?'

'I promise.'

'What about the mower? Shall I put it away?' Danny didn't seem ready to relinquish control altogether.

'It's fine. I'll pop it back. You can go and check the front, maybe use the pressure hose or something. I've got this.'

Danny shrugged and wandered off towards the front of the house. She could tell from his back view that he was disappointed that she'd taken this job away from him and she felt a bit sad, she hated to hurt him. But she couldn't really afford to let him loose with the mower. She looked at the grass, admiring the even spread of clover that had reclaimed its hold since the weekend. Above it, insects hovered busily, liking the longer evenings too. This was her garden. Her grass.

Chapter 29

Sam had wandered into the woods to find Diana and had suddenly been struck by how different everything looked. 'Just look at this!' said Sam, excitedly, sweeping her arms around her to take in the lush green growth underfoot. The residual autumn debris of fallen leaves, fir cones and dry or wet mud that had carpeted the woodlands since Sam had first encountered them had now been completely resurfaced with the glossy green leaves of the bluebells. To Sam, it seemed as if the transformation had happened overnight.

'Isn't it magnificent?' replied Diana, proudly. 'This is one of my favourite times of year, the rebirth and renewal of late spring. Each day is one of immense change and progress, you can't take your eyes off it for a second for fear of missing something.'

Sam inhaled deeply. The scent in the air had changed too, there was a promise captured in its sweetness.

Diana lowered herself into a folding chair beside the fire. She looked thoughtful as she considered the bluebells-to-be. 'It's funny, for the many years I commuted, the bluebells were a bit of a thing for me. I'd jump on a train in the dark and I'd return in the dark too. I had very little time for anything other than the relentless business of adulthood. But I'd always try to keep my eyes open for the bluebells. I'd congratulate myself if I remembered to look and, better still, if I caught a glimpse of that uniquely ephemeral blue. I think the first time I noticed them as an adult, it must have been a very late spring as for the longest time I associated them with May and so usually I'd barely start looking until they were already nearly over. Years would pass with just one glance of the blue carpet gleaned from a train window as we rushed by.'

Sam looked closely at the green all around her. There was no evidence of blue in sight but she waited patiently, knowing Diana hadn't yet finished.

'And they're still a big part of my calendar today though not always with such positive associations. The bluebells in flower are a bit of a thorn in my side. They bring out the fair-weather walkers of April and May. They flock here in their droves to take pictures of the bluebells, they marvel at nature, they "ooh" and they "aah" and they impress themselves with their ability to immerse themselves in the moment. But they're not really immersing themselves in it, are they? All they're doing is taking pictures with their phones as proof they were here. And, I can tell you this for nothing, I know for a fact that nobody has ever taken a decent picture of bluebells on a phone. Nothing captures the true depth of field that the bluebells create. Bluebells are a fleeting manifestation of their own elusive myth. They are like a rainbow, you can't ever quite reach its source, as you walk towards it, it skips away from you.'

Diana looked out at the green lawn beneath the trees.

'Now that I live in the woods, I have a very different

relationship with bluebells. They appear early, those first green shoots. They push themselves up in February, giving promise that whatever the winter still has to deliver, spring *will* arrive and they will be here to herald it. I love that moment, their assertion. Once I used to congratulate myself if I managed one glimpse of blue in a whole year. Now I give myself a much harder challenge. It's my job to look for the very *first* bluebell. Not the first handful, not the first haze of blue, not the moment before it becomes an explosion. But the very first. There's always one, a scout sent ahead on behalf of the army that follows. And being witness to this first is being witness to the arrival of a season in one precise moment because it is solitary for only a second. Almost as you find it, you'll then find a scattering wherever you look, as if they'd been hiding shyly, turning their heads but now you've found them, they will hold your gaze. And then the next moment they're everywhere. There is a moment when they appear, the beech trees come finally into leaf – and there's nothing greener than a beech leaf is there? – and there it is, sunlight filters through and the wood isn't brown anymore. That's the moment to savour because shortly afterwards they'll be followed by the throngs of onlookers with their cameras. They lose their shine so quickly. They droop their heads, their green skirts are folded away, their colour fades, they lose their gloss and they wilt. And then they're dead.'

Sam felt sad, grieving for the loss of her bluebells before they'd even shown their faces.

'Don't look so hard done by, Sam. Do you realise how lucky I am? I have prolonged my life by slowing it down to a pace at which I can actually live it. Once, that flash of blue seen from a train marked a whole year's noticing. And you have, at best, seventy of those moments in a good lifetime if you discount your early years where all growth is rightly taken for granted. Seventy ticks on the clock's countdown. But now, I have taken that one moment and turned it into so many moments from the first brave shoots, to the last pale, wilted death throes.'

Sam didn't stay long, she walked home to Broome Cottage with her eyes on the green shoots all around her. She had walked in the woods daily without noticing these incremental changes and she realised she was no different to a busy commuter, charging around, attacking everything she did at pace and barely slowing down enough to watch a whole season arrive. She wondered how many more bluebell years she had and understanding she probably had fewer than others, she vowed to notice each one in the detail that Diana had described.

Chapter 30

Each morning offered a little more daylight and each morning, as soon as Danny left for work, Sam headed straight to the woods to find Diana. She didn't pretend to be passing or hover in the area hoping to get the timing right. Instead, she pushed the hazel boughs to one side in a decisive sweep, stepped through and took her place by the fire, in a space that she now considered her classroom.

She had been admiring some drawings in one of the leather notebooks, flicking through to find the next sketch and asking Diana for the stories behind them. Eventually she closed the notebook and said, with an envious groan, 'You are so *talented*, Diana.'

Diana considered this. 'I can draw, yes, but I'd very much like to paint. I'd like to put something beautiful into the world that came purely from within me, that nobody else had seen or dreamt.'

'You definitely have the skills. These drawings are captivating. You make it look so easy but to distil the essence of these creatures with just a few pen strokes is such a gift.' Sam shook her head admiringly and handed the notebook back to Diana. Diana left her seat by the fire and went in to fetch another book. She flicked through it and holding it open with her thumb, passed it carefully to Sam. The picture showed the base of some trees, the gnarled convolutions of bark depicted with swirls and whorls of brown ink and a fox peering through, staring with intensity at the artist.

'That was here.' Diana pointed to the base of two big beech trees close to them. Sam could recognise the trees immediately and sense the space left by the fox.

'I was sitting here, writing my diary and it appeared – what is that – three or four metres away? No more. And I only had a few moments to capture it. I drew that in less time than it would have taken me to fetch my camera.'

Sam looked at the ink strokes on the page. 'You've captured him beautifully. Watchful and sly.'

'It's a she. That's the vixen. I had just finished my lunch and she came to see if there was anything interesting in the pan for her. She watched me, I drew her, and then she was gone. All within a couple of minutes.'

Sam studied the picture again. She thought she could see the imminent retreat in the hunch of the fox's neck.

'So why don't you paint, if that's an ambition of yours?'

'I wouldn't get that instantaneous response, would I? By the time I'd set myself up, it would have gone. There's no such thing as still life in nature. All I can possibly do is try to capture the essence of something I've noticed. Noticing is my job.'

'If that's your job, you're excelling at it. Not that I'm an expert or anything but you've got a real talent. Is that what you did before living here? Were you an artist or a writer or something?'

Diana laughed. 'There's no such thing as a before or an after if you're truly creative. You can't stop and start. There's just a beginning and an end, and in between, a life.'

'Did you teach?' Sam felt like Diana's student, so the question didn't seem daft, but Diana roared with laughter.

'Can you honestly imagine me teaching?'

Sam looked at Diana, and imagined her teaching. She felt like a pupil at the feet of a great guru in this woodland academy. Everything Diana said was imbued with the sadness of experience. The best teacher, Sam concluded, was a sad teacher, haunted by her subject, defeated by time.

'You could *definitely* be a teacher.'

Diana remained silent.

'So, what *were* you?' asked Sam, boldly.

'Why your obsession with what I *was*? I am much more interested in who I am now.'

'But if I understand what you *were*, I can better understand who you *are*. I want to know where you've been, I want to trace the paths that have led here. I think your whole story is interesting, not just your ending.'

Diana looked cross. 'This is not my ending and you're entirely wrong about me. My story is not at all interesting. I was a fierce young woman, then a cross middle-aged woman. Now I'm an old woman looking for peace. That is my story.'

'You're not old, you're fifty-four. You're in your prime!' Sam thought of her own mother, who was a few years older. Her mother looked much younger than Diana, she dyed her hair and dressed with meticulous care, but her attitude was much more wizened. Sam's mother wasn't interested in learning.

'I've lived much more than many, and that makes me feel a bit older than my years. But, regardless of birthdate or longevity, this is definitely my final phase. Some people don't make that shift, the shift towards reconciliation and then dissipation until it is forced upon then, when their bodies give them no choice. I made that choice sooner, while I still could.'

Diana got up, taking the book she had been holding with her back inside the caravan and she quickly emerged with another. She flicked through it looking for a specific entry. 'This is early on,' she said, already eager to share her notes before she'd yet found the page. 'This is when I began to think about these things earnestly. It was just me and the foxes and I found myself here, alone for my first long winter, wondering what I had done and what I might miss by being here.

'Here we are: I split my life into its phases, as perhaps we all can. She counted down a list. Nine in all. Nine phases. Firstly, Birth then Growth. Neither of those I could control, they happened to me without my input. Then Expansion. That was my first conscious phase, taking what I had – either naturally or from my early education or from my family – and specialising by expanding my knowledge into certain areas. That was me, all on my own, though I needed others to lead the way, to show the way if you like. Professors, mentors, books. Then there was a period of Accumulation. The amassing of wealth, material things, knowledge, power, family, friends – all of those things you add as proof you're a successful adult. They're your trophies, your medals, your validation.'

Diana looked towards the trees, as though seeking their corroboration. Sam waited patiently until Diana, with no obvious trigger, shook herself out of her reverie.

'Where did we get to? Accumulation. Yes, I was good at that phase. I accumulated well. Then Creation, Reflection, Reconciliation, Dissipation and Death.'

Death hung in the air between them.

'Death doesn't count as a phase of course. Death, like birth, is just a moment. Too brief to be a phase. But death is so much easier to face if you've done the reflecting, the reconciling and the dissipation beforehand.' Diana looked at Sam who appeared puzzled.

Diana tried to explain. 'Imagine that those first phases – Birth, Growth, Expansion, Accumulation are all on the way *up* and Reflection, Reconciliation, Dissipation and Death are all on the way *down*. Then Creation, yes, well that's the blanket that covers the peak and can drape right down on either side. You might be creative throughout all the other phases, they might overlap or run concurrently but it is very unlikely to be seated in isolation. It will develop because of, or despite, those other phases.

'Birth is just a moment. It's not the opposite of death, it's the same as death. A step forward from one thing to another, nothing more nothing less. My phases demonstrate that you could live a very short life completely providing you consciously move through those stages. Reflection is much the hardest in modern days. We find it very hard to look at ourselves objectively without wanting to kill ourselves in despair.'

'Not all of us,' said Sam defensively, despite recognising that despair in her own response to self-examination.

'Yes, all of us. If you examine your life carefully and don't want to kill yourself in despair, then you're simply not doing it right.'

Sam frowned, shocked by Diana's vehemence. Even if there was a grain of truth in her verdict, supposing Diana did speak for her, then she certainly didn't speak for Danny. Danny was steady and true and respectful of life. She didn't want everyone to be cursed by the same familiar blight. She didn't quite know how to answer Diana though so settled with a very tepid, 'You're cheerful today.'

Diana scoffed. 'It's not my job to be cheerful. If you want to be cheerful go and play tennis or watch television or do one of those other mindless activities people do when they don't want to think about the short time they have left to reconcile their purpose with their actions.'

Sam didn't respond. Instead she sat quietly, watching Diana's face darken and become light again as her thoughts swept across her mind. The woods were still, it was hard not to settle back into a peaceful truce.

'So, I wonder where I am, in terms of your phases?' Sam lay back on the ground and looked up at the leaves above her. 'I was born, of that I am certain. And I grew.' Sam laughed self-consciously. Her long legs were stretched out beside the fire and she propped herself up to look at them, in wonder, as if she'd missed that phase altogether and had only just realised it had happened. She flopped back down again. 'And then what?'

Diana consulted her list. 'Expansion.'

'Hmmm.' Sam thought about her early adult life, her stint at university, then her career with its flare of early success, her illness, her secret writing. She'd expanded, certainly.

'Yes, yes, I suppose I've done that phase, though if I had realised it was a necessary stage in life and that one day I might be asked to account for it, as I am now, I might have tackled it very differently.'

This piqued Diana's interest. She had recently been thinking about the different choices you could make to impact your outcome. 'How?'

'I've always worked better to a deadline so I'd probably have tackled it with a bit more determined gusto. If I'd treated it like coursework I'd probably have got an A star. As it is, I'm thinking more like a C plus. Certainly I'd have been more positive. More useful.' Sam frowned in concentration. 'I'm competitive so I'd probably have tried much harder. I haven't really expanded, I've just followed a slow spiral, circling away from the core of me, gradually moving outwards, but never far enough that I couldn't just leap back to here. Contracted again.'

Diana seemed to understand this because she didn't ask for any further clarification. 'And Accumulation? You're still young, I suppose, but what have you accumulated?'

'Not much. Surprisingly little.' She thought of her followers, her 100,000 subscribers who regularly interacted with her blog. She had been busy accumulating these but she could close her account tomorrow and they'd all disappear immediately. They were fleeting. She could only count them, not know them. She probably wouldn't be able to find them again. 'Almost nothing,' she concluded finally.

Diana considered this before answering. 'Well, that's not a bad thing. I think the period of Accumulation might be the least impactful in the overall scheme of things. It's the one to which we often attach the most importance, but it doesn't actually contribute to our well-being particularly. The more successful you are within the Accumulation phase, the more time you'll have to devote to the Dissipation.'

'And it all has to go, does it?'

'Yes. Yes, it does I'm afraid. Because you can't take it with you.'

'But what about your family, your friends?'

'Well, you obviously don't have to get rid of them, but you should devote some time to undoing any harm, getting rid of regret. That's why Reconciliation is important. That's the time you decide who and what is important, what you can live without, what you can't. What you can die for, what you can't. My Reconciliation is ongoing.'

Sam was pensive. She thought about the friends she'd made and lost: the childhood ones, the family ones, those she'd made at university and then at work, before she'd become ill. She'd let them go quite deliberately, neglecting them before they'd had a chance to neglect her, aware of the sullying impact her illness would have on their glowing, burgeoning health. Some, she reasoned, might not even have realised she'd cut herself off from them.

Sam tried to imagine what Diana might have been through, prior to her current Reconciliation. The conversation had become hard and spiky again, so she softened the edges by returning to an easier subject. 'I think I'd like to try being more creative, too. I look at that picture of a fox and know I could never do that.'

'Drawing just takes practice. I write and I draw every day. Could you write do you think?'

Sam laughed. 'I do write. But I need a distraction from writing. It's eroding me.'

Diana didn't see any paradox in this. 'Then do something else.'

'I think I must. If I don't have the confidence to draw and I want to reduce the amount I write, then perhaps I could just tend to my garden. What do you think? Would that count?'

'Would it count? *Would it count?* Are you joking? There is nothing much more creative than gardening.' Diana picked up a small pine cone and tore it apart carefully before holding up a seed that had been buried amongst the tough layers of shell. 'The seed is one component. Choosing between the seeds, adding light, water, nutrients and then nurturing it through to adulthood. Yes, I think if you devoted yourself to that then you could tick the creative box, most certainly.'

Diana passed the small woody seed to Sam who rolled it between her thumb and forefinger thoughtfully.

Chapter 31

As soon as the alarm went off Sam reached for her phone and looked at the weather forecast, scrolling forward to look at the prognosis for the next fifteen days. Each day showed a mix of sun and showers. 'Yes,' she said, under her breath and she jumped out of bed enthusiastically. She called to Danny through the bathroom door. 'I'll drop you at the station this morning if you don't mind. I need to borrow the car.'

'No problem,' he shouted back, through a mouthful of toothpaste.

At the station, Sam pulled the car into the drop-off zone and waited while Danny gathered his backpack and came around to the driver's side. She wound the window right down.

'I like this,' he said, reaching his head right inside the window and kissing her on the lips.

'Have a good day at work, dear!' she said, ironically but pleased with him and her day ahead.

She was about to close the window, but Danny leant his forearms on the car window sill. 'I feel,' he looked around, 'I feel *enviable*.' He grinned happily. 'Everyone now knows I have a beautiful wife who drops me at the station. I've become *somebody* in their eyes this morning!'

Sam pulled a puzzled expression. 'Do you really think they've noticed?' she asked, motioning through the railings towards the static commuters, each with their eyes down on their phones as they waited for the train.

'Oh, of course they have noticed. They're just pretending not to stare because they know their wives aren't as pretty.' He leant in and kissed her again. 'The routine has changed this morning and it's only Monday. It doesn't get more exciting than this around here. People will be talking about me *for ever.*'

Sam laughed. 'I'm off, I'll leave you to your fantasy life. I've got stuff to do.' She hit the button to close the window, driving off with a wave into her rear-view mirror. Danny watched her go and lifted his arm a little self-consciously before turning towards the ticket office.

Sam drove home, immediately putting her wellington boots on before setting off through the garden gate. She walked down the longer path and circled the perimeter of the big field, taking her time to allow Diana the chance to have her breakfast before stopping at the caravan on her return.

'Knock knock!' she shouted through the closed door. 'I've come for the good stuff you promised me,' she called. A moment later the door opened, and Diana handed her an orange plastic bag.

'Be extremely careful,' Diana said sternly. 'They'll spill. They're packaged separately. If there are only a few in a package, be extremely frugal. Don't waste a single one. They will have taken me a huge amount of effort to get them so use them wisely. If there are plenty, then they are easier to come by but, still, be careful. Each one matters to me.'

Sam looked grave as she took the precious parcel, and thanking Diana she hurried off home, clutching the plastic bag to her.

Once Sam was back at Broome Cottage she still had some time to kill before the shops opened so she used it to hoe any last weeds she'd missed from the flowerbed. Eventually she'd passed enough time and was able to drive to the garden centre where she was the first through the doors.

She walked past the greenhouses and the rows and rows of pots for sale, ignoring the beautifully planted hanging baskets and burgeoning displays, and heading instead to a big enclosed shed. Here she spent a bit of time reading the backs of several different packages, before settling on a 25 kg sack of grass seed and lugging it clumsily into her trolley. From the same building she bought a rake, a watering can and a sprinkler attachment for the garden hose before heading home to get to work.

Using a saucepan from the kitchen she took a scoop of grass seed at a time, scattering it methodically on the bare beds. She ignored the occasional weed she'd missed, figuring that if it had got this far, she'd give it a chance to meet its potential.

Once she'd covered all three sides of the beds she then mowed the lawn on the highest setting, taking just the top centimetre off. Rather than carrying the grass cuttings to the compost as she'd seen Danny do, she detached the collector from the back of the machine and removed a handful of grass at a time, spreading it on top of the newly seeded beds, hoping the seeds from the clover, dandelions and other naturalised flowers would intermingle with the rather uniform grass seed she'd just bought.

When she was happy with her progress, she went back inside and collected the plastic shopping bag from the kitchen. Within the bag were a dozen different parcels, each carefully taped up. She tackled them one by one, carefully peeling back the tape, unfolding each reverently and smoothing them out being careful not to spill any of the contents.

The paper the seeds were wrapped in were pages from a glossy magazine: expensive houses with immaculate lawns; society pages with glamorous couples staring vacantly into the camera; huge pale kitchens with suspiciously empty worktops, stripped pine tables adorned only by an elaborate vase of flowers and implausibly big dressers showing off china that had probably never been used. Briefly Sam wondered why Diana would have such a magazine in her caravan, her lifestyle was so diametrically opposed from these, surely these wealthy people with their improbable happiness must seem alien to her, but then, she remembered, didn't we all love to gawp at people that were different to us? Isn't that difference the very thing that had drawn Sam to Diana in the first place?

She dismissed the thought and focused instead on the treasure inside the wrapping. The first package contained a vast amount of seed. Fashioning a funnel from two edges of the paper, Sam poured it carefully into a cup which she carried out to the garden and there she spread it extravagantly, taking generous pinches and flinging them with abandon onto the bare earth, letting it mix with the grass seed but also throwing it joyfully around her, allowing it to land on the lawn.

She returned to the kitchen for the next parcel. As she worked methodically through the packages, some revealed just a pinch of minuscule seed, each one so insignificant that it was impossible to imagine they might contain life of any sort and Sam handled these with particular care. She used a biro to drill small holes in the lawn, dropping just a seed or two in by rubbing them between her thumb and finger and when she was certain they'd found their mark, she covered them each up with a bit of earth, working fastidiously. This was slow, laborious work and by the time she had finished she realised she'd lost all of the morning to the process.

Not risking stopping for lunch she then paced up and down the garden with her watering can, treading heavily and watering as she went, helping the seeds to settle and find their home.

She took tiny incremental steps, making sure each one overlapped, leaving nothing to chance and being absolutely certain that each seed had the benefit of her weight on it, so they couldn't be carried off by the wind.

When she was satisfied she'd done a thorough job, she assembled a number of bird feeders around the fence line.

'That will keep you off my lawn, you little beauties,' she said, hanging the last one.

Once she had finished, she admired her work. There was nothing to see but she felt the most enormous sense of achievement, as if she had just materially altered nature itself. She squeezed her eyes tightly shut, in part to allow herself to imagine the fruits of her labour but also to cast some sort of spell that she felt entirely unable to articulate. 'Come on!' she said, eventually, to the lawn in general, before going into the house to pay it a fraction of the attention she'd just paid her garden.

Chapter 32

Danny and Sam had gone to bed and were lying in the dark, chatting quietly. 'You're not lonely here, or bored?' Danny asked Sam.

'No, I'm happy, really. I've got loads to do in the garden and I've started to make some friends…'

Danny sounded pleased and a little relieved. 'Great! I'm not surprised, you're such a social thing. Who have you befriended, our neighbours?' he carried on, without waiting for an answer, but sounding a little less delighted as the logical conclusion of this new reality occurred to him. 'Oh. I don't have to make friends too, do I?'

'Heavens, no. It will be a while before we find ourselves on the dinner party circuit.'

'Phew,' said Danny into the darkness above him.

'Don't worry. I know that's not your scene, but I'm not actually convinced it is my scene either, so we can remain in our rather splendid and completely untested isolation for a while longer if you'd like.'

'It *is* your scene, sweet pea, but you know it's not mine and you're an absolute angel not to make me do it. That's love, that is, not dragging your anti-social husband out to meet your friends.'

Sam tutted dismissively. 'You're totally social, Danny, you just have a huge and busy network as part of your job and that completely fulfils you. I know that socialising is the last thing you want to think about when you get home and I respect that.'

Danny flushed guiltily in the dark. 'I appreciate it, I really do. But I don't want you to suffer from loneliness here, so I am glad you're meeting people, I really am. So, who are these new friends of yours?'

Sam remained silent for a long time before answering. 'Well, there's Hattie, she lives just down the lane in the small house with the lean-to garage.'

Danny squinted trying to imagine it.

'The one with the "unkempt" front garden?' Sam prompted.

'Oh, that one. Yes, I shudder every time I pass it.'

'Hattie's fine, just a bit overwhelmed, I think. She's got three small children and I don't think she gets any help from her husband.'

'Well, nice she's got a friend in the lane who can empathise.'

'Hardly!' said Sam, squeezing his hand. 'You do so much for me. The obsessive-compulsive partner is the best catch,' she said, glibly.

Danny squeezed her hand back and asked, quietly, fearing a truthful answer, 'Do you think I have a disorder?'

'No, I was using the term lightly and probably a bit disrespectfully. But still, you like a tidy kitchen and you're pretty handy with a hoover.'

'And I'm going to keep the garden in check,' he added, hopefully.

'Hmmm,' Sam said, worried that any other words or noise might sound like consent.

'Who else? Hattie with her messy garden. Are there others?'

'There's Anne. She's a bit of a straight-laced thing. All angles and edges. She's trying to rope me into all sorts of volunteering.'

'Might you volunteer?'

'Sure. Maybe,' Sam said, non-committally and to avoid further scrutiny from her husband or, worse, from within her own conscience, she raced on. 'And then there's Diana.'

As she spoke the name, Sam flushed. Saying 'Diana' out loud with such casual indifference felt like a betrayal. She wanted to share Diana with Danny one day but she wasn't quite ready yet. Besides, it had occurred to her lately she had no concrete proof that Diana was even real. If she only existed in Sam's mind, like some *alter-mother*, there to fill the gaps in a conversation she needed, then talking about her out loud might make her disappear. She wasn't ready for that, either.

'Does she live in the lane too?' asked Danny, trying to place their neighbours to help give them form.

'No. The other side, beyond the wood,' said Sam vaguely.

'Is she your type?'

'Gosh, what's my type? If I have a type, then perhaps yes, she's the most like me of all of them I think. She's sort of *earthy*.'

'I don't think of you as earthy, I think of you as the high-achieving career girl type.'

Sam was shocked. 'Do you, still? Even now? I mean, I'm here, moping around in the countryside, not having a job, let alone a career. I don't even know if I've got it in me anymore.'

This time Danny squeezed Sam's hand. 'Of course you've got it in you. You're the cleverest person I know, you're hard working, you're lovely and you're resilient.'

Sam flinched a little, unable to recognise herself in his description, and terrified at the idea of going back to work.

'Well, I'm… I am working on something…'

'What sort of something?'

'I'm writing.'

Danny sat up and put the light on and looked at his wife with a broad smile on his face. 'Oh Sam, I'm so pleased! That's just the best news, really. You're so, so talented. What are you writing? Poetry, I hope, you always had such a gift.'

Sam shrunk with guilt at her husband's support. She thought with shame of the awful tripe she'd written at university, back in the days when she still believed she had something original to say. She cringed internally now at the audacity she must have had to share her pathetic little scribblings with anyone – let alone her boyfriend who she'd so wanted to impress. She felt the colour rising in her face as she remembered some of the most pretentious and excruciatingly flamboyant phrases as she tried to wrestle something meaningful from her oh-so-inexperienced world view.

'Something a bit more long-form actually,' she stammered, wishing she'd said nothing.

'A novel? You're writing a novel, aren't you! Fantastic! You have my full support.' Danny's eyes shone with pride. 'And what are you writing on?'

'It's early days.'

'No, I mean what are you using to write? Your laptop?' Danny shook his head, answering his own question. 'That won't be good enough. It's too slow, it will crash. You need something better and you'll need something with a much more up-to-date operating system so that you can live edit, and keep a version on The Cloud. I'm going to sort that out immediately. There's not much I can do to help you, but that's something I am entirely capable of.'

'Oh champ, no, it's too soon, let's see how I get on.'

'No, my wife, the author, will have the very best. No compromises for you.'

'Thanks, Danny.' Sam lay quietly while Danny turned off the light and settled down again. She flinched with embarrassment at her lie and wondered what he would feel if she knew how her writing betrayed him, the man who had been so indefatigable in his loyalty towards her. Sometimes she hated herself.

'Night, sweet pea,' he said softly beside her.

'Night, champ,' she replied, quietly.

Chapter 33

Sam and Diana were sitting in the caravan, either side of the small table. They had a number of Diana's notebooks open in between them and had been leafing through the pages, chatting occasionally about the wildflowers depicted there while they waited for a shower to stop. The two women were growing comfortable with each other, as happy to sit in companionable silence as they were to talk.

Sam turned the pages slowly before asking, carefully, 'What about children? You mentioned having children in the accumulative phase of living? Isn't that a bit odd? Wouldn't most people argue that having children falls into the creative phase?' Sam studied Diana as she answered.

'Well, *I* don't think so. Anyone can have a child. Most manage it rather easily – it certainly doesn't require much creativity. And people don't seem to get better at it necessarily, you're not better at producing children by child three or four or by number seventeen, are you? And it doesn't make you *special*. It's just the job of the body, assuming your body is geared up for it. It's just *birth*, isn't it? And we've already agreed that Birth isn't a phase, it's just a step.' Diana closed her eyes to think more deeply and then opened them again, fixing them on Sam. 'The nurturing phase? Yes, that can be creative, but all you're really tasked with is to ensure your children are conscious about living their own lives fully and independently of you. You want them to *feel* like they matter until they are old enough to know *why* they matter, with or without you. And then you'll want them to navigate their own phases of life. You would want your child to expand, to accumulate the right things, to be creative but also to be sensible to their own Reflection, Reconciliation, Dissipation and Death. It would be a crying shame not to inspire them to do these things consciously. Those who live without conscience really are the scourge of the planet.'

Sam nodded, chewing the inside of her cheek. She was curious about Diana, but she knew it would be hypocritical to ask Diana if she had her own children and if so where they were in her life, so whilst the question nagged at her, desperate to be asked, she pulled herself back from its brink. This was the first time since she'd had her womb removed that she'd been able to have a conversation with another adult, other than Danny, without being drawn into the childlessness question herself, and whilst she was aware how liberating this could be, she was also beginning to see how compelling the question was and with that, she was beginning to develop a small amount of empathy for the many women who hadn't been able to stop themselves asking.

'I wonder,' said Sam, cautiously.

'Go on.'

'Who influences you?'

Diana looked puzzled. She threw her arms around her

as if the broad encompassment of the caravan and the trees could answer her. 'Have you listened to nothing I've told you?'

'I believe I've listened to every word.'

Diana sighed heavily. 'Bringing you into my world might have been the most terrible decision I've ever made.'

'No, no it wasn't. Bringing me into your world was the *best* decision you've ever made,' beseeched Sam earnestly, willing that to be true.

Diana smiled at Sam warmly. 'I have come to the woods to practise positive self-love. To disassociate myself from any idea that self-value must be defined by being viewed through the eyes of others.'

'Rousseau again,' said Sam, glad to be able to recognise the philosophy.

'But here I am, vexing myself over my ability to mould and shape you, worrying that you view me in the way I want to be viewed. This goes against everything I'm trying to achieve.'

'Not at all. You care nothing of what I think of you. You have never once given me an insight into who you are, why you matter, what you have achieved in your life before the woods. If you wanted to impress me, I bet you could, but you have never bothered.'

'I wish I had that much power over my reason, Sam. The truth is, I fear, that there was nothing very impressive about my life before being here in the woods, that's the real reason I won't talk about it. And the truth, too, is that I am desperate to make an impression on you. I don't think I would have invested the time in you otherwise. It's very hard to move away from the pride that drives us. Perhaps as a species we've evolved beyond a point of no return. There is nothing I can do or achieve that doesn't secretly beg for some sort of recognition or praise. Take my diaries, for example. I couldn't wait to share them with you, to finally get some sort of external validation.' Diana shook her head sadly.

'Your diaries might have a bigger purpose, Diana. If they were to disappear with no trace, you'd be doing a great disservice to nature.'

'Don't flatter me, it's unbecoming,' said Diana sternly.

'I understand what you're trying to achieve here, Diana, and I understand that you don't want to see yourself through the eyes of others. But, equally, I think, it is important to matter. That is why you talk to me. Because you want to save me. I want to *matter* too.'

Diana recoiled a little, looking displeased. 'I might be old enough to be your mother, but I don't want to be a mother to you.'

'That's the last thing I want,' said Sam, indignantly. 'I don't know what I want from you, except perhaps I've come to believe you can help me change direction. I want to follow a different path and I'm happy to have come to that realisation now, at my age, rather than in twenty or thirty years' time. That's a real gift you've given me. But sometimes...' Sam hesitated.

'Sometimes what?' prompted Diana.

'Sometimes I think you might exist only in my imagination. I have no real proof that you exist in any other realm and it all seems a bit convenient that you're here in the woods, offering me guidance and help and not judging me but letting me work it all out for myself. I don't know if you are real, or dreamt or some sort of shamanic spiritual guide, but whoever or whatever you are, you have made me feel like I matter.

Me. Not the deranged woman trying to find an outlet for her internal rage, or not nice Sam, the wife of Danny, but *me*.'

Diana pursed her lips and rocked her head from side to side, as though considering this theory seriously. 'Mattering to somebody *does* matter. It's true. And if you've found some comfort here in the woods, with me, I'm glad. But that somebody can be yourself, you know. *Feeling* like you matter is good enough.' Sam waited patiently while Diana paused to frame her next thought.

'Besides,' Diana continued. 'Rousseau was far too literal. He was right on many counts. Being able to value yourself only in terms of how you compare to others is destructive. Far more so today than in the 1700s. Wealth is amassed so quickly and so disproportionately these days, and so arbitrarily, that it can only leave the rest of humanity feeling inadequate. I made the right move, coming here, and valuing myself simply through my own ability to survive. But of course,' she said, quickly, 'Rousseau was wrong on many levels too.'

Sam feared she was out of her depth but didn't want to be discovered. She'd studied some philosophy at university and since Diana had first mentioned Rousseau she'd tried her hardest to explore the topic properly, but one of the books still remained unread on her bedside table and the other she'd read too quickly to assimilate. While she mentally filed through the words she'd read to find an appropriate response, she raised an eyebrow in a non-committal invitation for Diana to continue.

'His insistence on the preservation of the patriarchy and the subordination of women,' said Diana, patiently.

'Of course,' said Sam, quietly renewing her vow to continue

with her studies and to stop leafing through illustrated books featuring wild meadows.

'Rousseau considered that women must be constrained by modesty and shame. The idea that men are somehow unable to control their urges, and that women must be held accountable for distracting them seems barbaric. It was a laughable idea then but it's a dangerous idea now, as men continue to rely on it to defend their own behaviour. But, if anything, his views on self-worth are almost *more* relevant today than in his own time.'

Sam nodded in agreement before cautiously adding her own conclusion. 'Sometimes I wonder if we're regressing. My generation has taken external validation to a whole new level. I hate to imagine what Rousseau would have made of social media.' Sam thought of her own dependence on the engagement she had with her readers.

Diana looked at Sam sagely and dismissed her train of thought with a sympathetic shrug. 'That's just not my battle, Sam, and I'm so glad it's not because I just don't think I'd have the energy for it. You're testing Rousseau's theories to beyond their very furthest imagined boundaries. The idea that even the simplest of everyday actions have no value if they are not shared broadly and endorsed widely exceeds the scope of his philosophy.' Diana blinked slowly at the realisation and Sam now felt guilty of narcissism not at an individual level, but at a societal level. She was an integral part of the ruination of a generation. Diana, however, was not blaming her, but instead distancing herself from the inevitable conclusion. 'I've picked my fights, I've fought a principled fight, I've sacrificed myself to a cause. But this solitary battle, the one

I'm waging here, is the only fight I have left in me. You might believe I am a coward and you might interpret my withdrawal as retreat. But it's not. I've just picked a battle I believe I might win.'

Sam thought about this. She'd faced a battle or two herself and she'd definitely retreated. Rather than assemble an army, she'd simply turned and run for the hills. And like Diana, she'd decided to maintain her distance from her detractors. But Diana had found a crusade and Sam hadn't.

'The rain's stopping,' said Diana, cocking her head to tilt an ear towards the roof of the caravan. 'Haven't you got a garden to grow?'

Sam looked at Diana intently as if the older woman had all the answers for her, even to questions she hadn't yet asked.

'I have,' she said, slowly. 'I've got a battle to fight too.' She closed the book in front of her, wriggled her way into her anorak and headed back to Broome Cottage.

Chapter 34

Danny and Sam were in the kitchen. Sam was sitting at the table with her book and Danny was standing at the sink, washing up. Sam was aware of Danny glancing out of the window towards the garden, so she grasped the opportunity to raise the issue of the lawn before he did.

'I'm thinking of growing it,' she said boldly, congratulating herself for taking a bucket of unspoken words and tipping them out on to the table between them.

Danny turned and looked at her carefully. 'You know I love you whatever you do with it, don't you?'

She grinned, relieved. 'Really? I thought you might put up an argument!'

'Me? Pick a fight over how you wear your hair? Does that sound like me?'

'Oh. You misunderstood.' She turned her book upside down on the table, immediately deflated not to have won her battle after the false promise of an easy victory. 'Not my hair. Though, actually, I might,' she said, patting it and wondering if she should. 'No, I meant the lawn. I'm thinking of letting it grow a bit longer.'

'Hmmm,' said Danny in an attempt to sound non-committal. He paused before adding, 'That sounds a little risky to me.' He was immediately concerned but was trying valiantly to retain a degree of calm so as not to alarm his wife. He came and stood behind her, stroking her hair, remembering it when it was longer, when they'd first met.

'Risky how?' Sam asked, tipping her head back to look up at him.

'The weeds might get a foothold.' He leant down and kissed Sam's forehead before looking towards the window and imagining the horrors awaiting him. 'We need to keep on top of things. We can't take our eye off the ball for one moment. What about the bindweed for instance? Have you even *considered* the bindweed?'

'We haven't got any.'

Danny squeezed Sam's shoulders and went back to the window, running his hand through his own hair anxiously. 'You don't know that for sure. Bindweed can penetrate to a depth of five metres. It could be burrowing underground at this very moment and you wouldn't know it. And once a shoot appears it can spread a couple of metres in just one growing season. We might not have any now, but if we drop our guard for a day we could soon be smothered.'

Sam sighed patiently. 'Well. We haven't got any. I'm certain of it. But I'll keep my eyes peeled.'

'And ground elder… ' suggested Danny.

'What about ground elder? What on earth do you even know about ground elder?'

'I know enough about ground elder to know we don't want it anywhere near us. It's irrelevant if we have it here at Broome Cottage. You really need to do a thorough check of all the gardens locally to see if we are at risk. Have you inspected the gardens in the rest of the lane? Take your friend's house further down towards the road with the very unkept front lawn. If that's the bit they let their neighbours see, I hate to think what horrors they might be hiding in the back. Ground elder can easily spread from neighbouring land. I can show you an image online so you can recognise it when you see it, but I'm just concerned you'll miss its arrival altogether if the grass gets long. It's pretty pernicious.'

Sam smiled, a little puzzled by his knowledge of ground elder but not entirely surprised that he'd researched it; it was the sort of thing he would like to understand. 'I'll look it up. Put it on my pinboard of most wanted.'

'It's not a joke. You promised you wouldn't allow our garden to become unruly. What about giant hogweed? Have you considered *that*? I bet you haven't given it a moment's thought. If you are going to keep your side of the bargain you will need to familiarise yourself with *all* potential enemies and mitigate *all* possible risk.'

'Are you kidding me? Do you honestly think I'd fail to notice giant hogweed in our garden? I'm pretty familiar with every single *blade of grass*. I think I'd notice an outbreak of a two-metre high cow parsley, don't you?'

Danny laughed briefly. 'I'm sorry. I'm being silly. But promise me you'll be vigilant, won't you? I'm not comfortable with the idea of letting the grass grow longer. It actually...' he paused, and took a deep breath. 'Just the thought of it makes me extremely anxious.'

'I shall be vigilant. I promise.' Sam turned back to her book, wondering when Danny had taken such an interest in weeds. She had always known her husband to be cautious and he certainly liked to prepare for any eventuality, but she had never considered him *anxious* and certainly not *extremely anxious*.

'Long grass, huh?' she said, casually, picking up her book. 'Well, I suppose you need to worry about something.'

While Sam went back to her reading, apparently oblivious of the perils all around her, Danny thought about their obvious differences. Danny could present her with a range of menacing dangers and she could listen, absorb, process and dismiss these threats with barely a frown. Danny was cut from very different cloth. He studied his wife carefully as she leafed through her book, her unfurrowed brow confirming her ease. He was worried about the prospect of untamed long grass, yes, but then he worried about so many things.

He worried about the big things and the little things with equal dedication. He worried about the things he could control and he worried even more about the things he couldn't. He looked at Sam as she read and wondered if there was any possible way that he could have successfully hidden his relentless anxieties from her for all these years. And he wondered too, whether now was the time to broach the subject and talk to her about the many, many fears that plagued him every day and most nights. But she had considered him with such kindness and right now there was an air of serene calm about her as she turned the pages of a dense-looking book with a battered old cloth cover and he didn't want to get between her and her carefree reading. He wondered what she would think of him if she ever knew. She glanced up, smiled, and turned another page. Now was not the time to talk to her, he had dismissed the idea as soon as it had formed. Instead he headed outside to apply the pressure hose to the drive.

Chapter 35

'Can I come in?' Sam had knocked but the caravan door had remained firmly shut so she leant close in towards the door, rapping with her knuckles while calling out, instead.

'Must you?' shouted Diana from inside. Her voice sounded hoarse and was tempered by impatience. Sam felt a flush of embarrassment; she was clearly intruding but Diana had always welcomed her in so willingly up until now.

'Shall I come back another time?' she shouted, unsure if she should just turn and leave.

The door opened.

'Come on in, though just because I invited you in once doesn't mean I want you dropping in all of the time.' Diana turned to take a seat at the table in the middle of the caravan.

Sam hesitated at the threshold. 'I can come back another day if that would be better but how will I know when it's convenient?'

'That's just a risk you will have to take,' answered Diana, sternly. She beckoned her impatiently. 'Come on, you're here now, come in, sit down.'

Sam sat down and matched Diana's tone in seriousness.

'I planted the seeds, thank you.'

Diana acknowledged this with a quick nod of her head.

'It's a waiting game now, I suppose?'

Once again, Diana nodded.

'And I've been thinking about what you said to me.'

Diana interrupted Sam with a dismissive flick of her hand. 'Oh, ignore me. I talk a lot of nonsense.'

'Specifically, I've been thinking about what you said about truth,' Sam continued, undeterred.

Diana scoffed noisily. 'Particularly about truth. Ignore anything I ever say about truth, I'm not qualified to talk about it. I'm the biggest liar you'll ever meet. We're all liars, either to ourselves or to strangers or to the people we love. It doesn't matter which, we're still liars.'

Sam knew that Diana was preparing to dig her heels in, and she knew her well enough now to understand which topics might be safe, so she changed tactic. 'Are you satisfied with your life?'

'Now? How I live now?'

'Generally. You talked to me about living consciously, to make sure you ticked off those phases you'd defined. But if you died tomorrow, would you be satisfied with the way you've lived your life?'

'If I died tomorrow, I'd be fine with that, I'm prepared. And besides… We have to assume that we will know or care nothing of our preparedness beyond the moment of death. Those we leave behind, though, for them our departure is a very different matter. Our own death is not something experienced by us, it's something experienced by all those who knew us. You have the power to leave those you love satiated or incomplete, rejected or accepted, settled or floundering. Leave no regrets.' Diana waited as though she was processing the impact of her own words before answering herself. 'And I have none of those. But still, I'd like just a bit more time. I think I have more work to do. I want to rid myself of some of my very worst habits. I think, *I hope*, by replacing those bad habits with some better ones I might leave a reasonable account of myself. And I hope that I might one day be able to say I'm satisfied with the way I've lived my life, yes.' Diana looked far away.

'I'm living a very shallow life. Meaningless, utterly meaningless,' said Sam, more certain of this than ever before.

Diana snapped back to attention, interested in her visitor for the first time since Sam had sat down. 'Are you really? You're a bit too young to have come to that conclusion, aren't you? Most people are busy growing, expanding, accumulating, creating, at your age; they haven't yet considered any sort of Reconciliation. You could live a bit before completely writing yourself off, perhaps?'

'Not at all. I'm quite certain that I'm ninety per cent superficial. The thing is, when I was little, I was very confident that I was the centre of the universe. My parents completely adored me, I was popular at school, I was considered to have good *prospects*. And even when they were fully occupied worshipping me, I used to look at my mum and dad and think how boring they were. How I'd never grow up to be like them, that I'd do something rather wonderful with my life, where their lives had seemed so dull.'

'And have you?'

'I planted some seeds yesterday... ' Sam paused and shook

her head assuredly. 'Absolutely nothing. I went to college, got some A levels, went to university, got a husband. The thing is, I had a moment at university when I might have really made something of myself. I could have. I met a lot of amazing people there, but the truth is, I knew as soon as I met them, they were simply better than me. They were smarter, I mean a *lot* smarter, brilliant and with a zeal for learning and a sort of mental reach that I not only didn't have but had no desire to have. I wouldn't have known what to do with it. Meeting them didn't inspire me to be better, I just thought I wouldn't bother competing in a competition I couldn't win.'

'Were you jealous of these people? These smart people?'

'No! I admired them far too much to envy them. And they were not just smarter, they were prettier, funnier, more ambitious, more passionate, *far* more daring. All of them were daring. There was one girl in particular. Her name was Libby. I had a bit of a crush on her if I'm honest. She was so *dazzling*. I would have liked to be like her, abstractly, but I was never prepared to make the effort to *actually* be like her. I'd have had to work so much harder, I'd have needed to be in so many different places. I didn't have the bandwidth.'

Sam thought some more. She had never really articulated any of these thoughts out loud, so the words excited her as they landed.

'Up until I met Libby, I thought I was the main character and that everyone else was an extra. I honestly believed I was the centre point from which everything else radiated. I'd think of people like that, particularly when I was at college. I'd look at these ordinary people and think, "You're going nowhere, you're a nobody, you're nothing." And then I went to university and quickly realised I would be lucky just to be a bit part in *their* lives.'

'Well, you're young. You can still have a stab at life, surely?' asked Diana, although there was a hint of hesitancy in her voice, as though she, too, doubted it.

'I don't know. My life has so far been a series of endings. I thought I might be able to make something of myself at work, but the truth is I always felt like a sham, that I was just acting the role of a successful career girl. And then, as if in answer to my doubts, my colleagues told me in no uncertain terms that I wasn't good enough. I wasn't a whole enough person to join their club. I think I was a bit of an embarrassment to them, I could make people feel awkward just by being in the same room, breathing their air. In order to cope with me, collectively, they cut off my oxygen. And I hoped to find more oxygen here in the countryside but I've only just begun to notice that Danny and I don't really talk, not about the important stuff. It's entirely my fault, I've held back from telling him what an utter mess I feel inside as I don't want to burden him but in the meantime, I don't really know what's going on inside him either.'

Diana looked pensive before asking, quite sharply, 'Do your parents still adore you?'

'Not really. I'm a terrible disappointment to them. I haven't got a womb. My mother despises this about me and my father just finds the whole thing rather tasteless.'

Diana shrugged, unimpressed. 'I can't imagine it makes much of a difference to them, does it? Wombs are terribly overrated in my opinion. Mine has caused me nothing but trouble.'

'Mine too.'

'And men seem to have got on terribly well without them, don't they?'

Sam smiled. 'Yes, I suppose so.' But she quickly became serious again. 'But I don't want to live an ordinary life.'

'Well, don't.'

'But how can I live an *extraordinary* life? I don't seem to be skilled at anything. And I don't see the point of any of it. I already know what's going to happen. It's like I've read the last page.'

'What? What's going to happen?'

'I'm going to carry on doing just what I'm doing. Getting out of bed, seeing my husband off to work, twiddling my thumbs, pretending I have a purpose, cooking some supper for him, going to sleep and starting all over again the next day.'

'That's enough for lots of people.'

'Of course, I know that. I don't want to be greedy. And I have a lovely life, so I mustn't complain. But I just sometimes feel like I didn't get the memo.'

'The memo?'

'Yes, maybe everyone else got a memo telling them what to do with their lives and off they went, in pursuit of their purpose, and perhaps I just didn't get one.'

'Or you got the memo, but you chose to ignore it?'

'But I'd remember what it said, surely?'

'Would you? Not if it told you something you didn't want to hear.'

'Like what?'

Diana shrugged. 'What if your memo simply told you

that all you needed to do to fulfil your obligation was to live an *ordinary* life.'

Sam felt a physical stab of pain, truly understanding for the first time what it meant to be hurt by words. She'd been incensed and enraged and disappointed and dismayed in her time, but it was a visceral smarting she now felt from this wound delivered by somebody she really wanted to please. 'Wow. That's tough.'

Diana had set her face determinedly into the look of somebody unprepared to compromise her stance just because her companion had a wobbling bottom lip. 'Sam,' she said, 'you want to talk about truth, but have you really tried being honest with yourself?'

Sam put her hand to her heart, as if to demonstrate that she would swear an oath to the very notion of truthfulness. 'That again! How can you talk to me about truth when you yourself have told me you're a liar?'

'It's because I'm a liar that you should listen to me about the truth. Do you want to end up like me? I'm living in a caravan in the woods. I have no friends.'

'But I also know that you have no regrets.' Sam looked around the caravan, breathing in the warm, clean air, making a mental sweep of the bookcases. 'Your lifestyle actually seems quite appealing.'

'Exactly. Which is why you should listen to me. It really isn't necessary to live an extraordinary life. You're better off living an ordinary life truthfully, than living an extraordinary life dishonestly. If you're untruthful, not even you will be able to like yourself. Perhaps set your sights lower, make your goals a little more realistic and then see if you like it. Try to make just a little bit of difference. Take control of something you can control.'

Sam thought about this quietly for a while before asking of Diana, 'What makes you so certain I'm a liar?'

'It takes one to know one. You and I are exactly the same, Sam. We're both so well disguised, we've hidden the real self from ourselves. I bet you don't know which version is the authentic one anymore.'

Sam blinked steadily as she looked at Diana. She thought of Libby Masters and wondered if there was any possibility that this woman in the woods could possibly know of her parallel existence. Diana was seeing all the way through her. Perhaps she was a figment of her imagination after all.

Chapter 36

Sam wandered around the perimeter of the lawn, holding her mug in both hands for warmth. It was early and there was still a chill in the air and she was only wearing a light shirt over pyjama bottoms. She felt listless and despondent. She hadn't been to the woods for a few days, she'd felt exposed and wracked with self-doubt. It mattered to her that Diana liked her but instead she'd seen right through her and called out her duplicity.

Sam knew she was a fraud. She wrote but didn't have the courage to use her real name. And she couldn't use her real name because Sam didn't have the courage to write. These were Libby's opinions, scribed by Libby's fluent hand. These issues mattered to Libby, not Sam. Libby was prepared to die for them, Sam wasn't.

She chewed her lip and then stopped, suddenly alert. Quietly she crouched down and put her cup on the lawn beside her. She peered in closely. A single shoot of grass, perhaps a centimetre tall already, had caught her eye. And another, just beside it. And then more, wherever she looked. Tiny protestations, thrusting up towards the light, each one almost impossibly vulnerable but together, the makings of a forest. Sam grinned. She tried to reach out to stroke one, but it was not yet substantial enough to resist her touch, it was still just a sliver off life to be.

She stood up and re-walked the rest of the lawn's verge. The grass was growing everywhere she looked. It hadn't been there yesterday, of that she was certain. But here it was. Not a lawn yet, but the promise of one.

Sam desperately needed to share the good news with somebody. Danny might care but he wouldn't be home until later and he wouldn't think it would warrant a phone call at work. Diana might not care quite enough but she would almost certainly listen. Sam looked down at her pyjamas, chided herself for her own inertia and headed with purpose back inside and then, focused again, back to the woods.

When Sam arrived at the caravan, Diana didn't ask where she had been but welcomed her as though she had barely left. Sam, emboldened by Diana's warmth, quickly told her with pride of the new life in the garden.

'I know it's a simple thing, Diana, but I'm not as confident as I once was. Seeing those little shoots of life made me think I might actually be able to do something again.'

'You've lost confidence already? At your tender age? Well, I suggest you get that under control now because it certainly won't get any easier as you get older.'

Diana sat down heavily and continued. 'Aging is a terrible thing. There's no easy way for a woman. Grow old gracefully they say. Grow old *disgracefully* they retort. But there's no such thing. You're racing along, feeling infallible and one day, quite out of the blue you pick up a packet in the supermarket and you find you can't read the list of ingredients. No warning at all. You move it away six inches, and there it is, legible again and you carry on like that for a while because you don't really want to admit that your eyesight has gone. It is an admission that you've begun the slow, inevitable, decline towards death.'

'Gloomy this morning, aren't you? I came to be cheered up.' Sam had come clutching her borrowed copy of Rousseau's *The Social Contract*. Since she'd last visited she'd read it cover to cover and the book was now swollen with Post-it Notes and scraps of paper; the scribbled questions, thoughts and arguments that the philosopher's discourse had provoked but Sam now needed Diana's help to resolve.

'Oh, but that's not my role!' said Diana emphatically. 'Please don't ever come to me to be cheered up. You can come to me for many things but don't expect me to spend my energy making you feel better about yourself.'

Sam laughed. 'That's fair enough. Truthful as ever.' Sam said this pointedly, knowing that Diana claimed to lie habitually. So perhaps what she was saying now was also a lie. She squinted carefully at Diana and took a slow sip from the cup of coffee Diana had handed to her on arrival.

'Carry on. I believe you were talking about a slow decline to death.'

'Well, that's it really. A woman's life is terribly hard, it's so much harder for us than it is for men. Take periods for instance.'

'I don't get them,' said Sam straightforwardly.

'I don't often get them either.'

'No, I mean I don't have them at all.' Wanting Diana to acknowledge the special position she had earned post-surgery.

'Well, of course you don't, you don't have a uterus. But I do! And they cause me nothing but trouble and here I am now battling the next ten years feeling like absolute death. I don't know when they're coming and I don't know when they'll end and I have absolutely no idea what havoc they'll wreak on my mind or my body from one month to the next. But what I do know is that it is much better here, alone in the woods. Here with no one to bother me I can reach out to the feelings – the night sweats, the impending doom, the cramps and the sheer, physical onslaught and I can say, "Bring it on, do your worst," which is some sort of comfort. Particularly if I yell it at the top of my voice, which I'm prone to do. Poor old Rebecca on the other hand… She must be having a terrible time of it. It's hard to go through a career pretending you are not at the mercy of a woman's great burden. You cope once a month, battling through, trying to manage the sheer practicalities of it and then this – the final insult. At work you have to pretend you are not enraged by your colleagues' knowing glances, the looks that say, "Oh here she goes again, must be the time of the month," as if they are the ones suffering.'

Sam nodded and took another sip of her coffee. 'I know what you mean – I've been through the same. It's not easy but of course mine has been associated with part of my treatment, if you like, all part of the same thing. Where yours has come as a bit of last hurrah.'

'Ha. That's a better name for it. The last hurrah. Our bodies start letting us down much earlier than you'd think.'

'Oh great,' said Sam, with a roll of her eyes.

'It's true. Your eyesight goes first… '

'Mine's gone already,' said Sam taking her spectacles off and waving them at Diana.'

'Your ovaries go haywire...'

'I haven't got any,' said Sam, adopting a bored, repetitive tone.

'Obviously not. But still, the vast majority of us have to cope with that, and it's no wonder we feel a bit vulnerable.' Diana shook her head before continuing. 'And our digestion changes. The very foods we used to enjoy suddenly turn on us and attack us,' she sighed and despaired.

Sam watched her quietly, knowing better than to interrupt.

'But the worst thing of all is that finally we lose our bravery. You have it, you've earned it and then – whoosh – you're this timid thing that doesn't really know where to put a train ticket or how to navigate simple machinery. Suddenly, everything is terrifying.'

Sam thought of her own mother and that maddening dithering she did when it was time to leave anywhere. The sheer panic on her face as she tipped her handbag out looking for keys or her card. And they were always there, every single time. And she found herself talking to her mum like a child, 'They'll be there, just take a deep breath, take your time, let's go through your bag slowly. There they are! Clever you!' when inside she was thinking, 'God, you decrepit old fool.' Sam felt bad.

'And the more we dither, the more we're treated like fools,' said Sam, helpfully.

'Exactly, and the more we're treated like fools the more we behave like idiots.'

'And so the decline begins,' finished Sam, looking at Diana's wrinkled, drawn face.

'Yes. That's what you've got to look forward to.'

'Thanks,' said Sam, nonchalantly. 'Well, like you said. Your job isn't to cheer me up.'

Diana actually looked very cheerful and her eyes twinkled as she said, 'I've dodged the bullet of old age by being here.'

Sam looked at Diana, at her greying hair, her glasses perched on the end of her nose.

'No really, I have. It's only now, with you looking at me like an old mad thing that I feel remotely old. Day to day, I'm a warrior. I'm learning new things every day. I don't really lose anything, I write it all down, *everything*, and every time I write something down I lock into my memory. And if my memory does fail me one day, then it doesn't matter, does it? It's all there in black and white. Diana nodded at the books, at her memories.

'But you're not actually old, Diana,' said Sam, remembering that Diana was only fifty-four.

'But I will be soon and I fully intend to do it well. I won't be surprised by it. I'll be prepared because there's no shame here in the woods. I'm young compared to these trees. I'm a baby compared to the land. Feeling old and useless is something imposed upon us by younger, more useful things. Us older folk should feel brave not timid. We've got a lifetime of experience and all that coping behind us, so nothing should give us any fear. And what have we got to lose by being courageous? So what if we mess up? Does it really matter if we occasionally lose our keys, or get on the wrong train, or drive off a cliff?'

'Well,' hesitated Sam, wondering if driving off a cliff perhaps was a very real problem.

'Here on my own I am strong. I am powerful. I feel very alive. And if I screw up, if I go foraging for mushrooms and end up eating a panther's cap instead of a blusher then that's fine too. That certainly wouldn't be the preserve of the elderly, you could make that mistake when you're young, too, it's a very easy one to get wrong.'

Sam looked alarmed. She'd often arrived at the fireside for her morning coffee with the smell of freshly cooked mushrooms still hanging in the air. 'But you won't mess up, will you? You forage daily, you're unlikely to make a mistake.'

'I know what I'm doing and I'm certainly more knowledge-able now but, the truth is that my eyes were good once. My hair was chestnut once. Things change. My mind could go. But you'll never know, will you, you wouldn't know if you find me dead tomorrow, the stem of an *Amanita phalloides* clutched in my lifeless hand, whether I ate it deliberately or not.'

'You're scaring me.'

'Well, don't be scared. That's the whole point. And in reality, if I should choose to top myself, I'd be very unlikely to deliberately poison myself with mushrooms. Terrible way to go. Your vital organs go into failure long before your heart stops pumping. No, that would be no good at all.'

'And what is *Amanita* . . .'

'The Death Cap. The clue's in the name. That's not one you want to confuse with something else, but it's easily the most deadly mushroom in this country so plenty of people *do* get it wrong. The symptoms start a few hours after eating. It begins with severe vomiting, diarrhoea and stomach pains. Then you get completely better, you think you're fine and then within a few days later you'll die of kidney or liver failure.

Very cruel but in reality, getting to the hospital in between time wouldn't do you any good. There's no known antidote.'

'Perhaps you could take me foraging one day, show me the basics,' said Sam, whilst silently vowing never to eat a wild mushroom again in her life.

'Happily. There won't be anything much until the autumn now and then I'll take you to all the best hunting grounds and show you which ones to avoid.'

'Thanks,' said Sam. After all of this talk of old age and death, she rather liked the idea of an appointment in Diana's diary for the autumn.

Chapter 37

'Do you fear old age, champ?' Sam asked Danny, her words landing heavily amongst the silence. They were sitting on either end of the sofa, facing each other, their toes touching.

Danny looked startled. This wasn't a conventional topic of conversation. He scanned Sam's features for signs of illness, as though new traces of disease might be found right there on her face.

Sam saw his discomfort but pressed on. 'I know you don't like to talk about it, but we should, shouldn't we? I mean, just sometimes, we should broach the big stuff? We're in this together, after all.'

Danny blinked a couple of times to help him order his thoughts. 'Are you OK, sweet pea, you're not feeling poorly, are you?'

'No, no. I feel good. Great. I just realised that we've got out of the habit of talking or we never really got into it. You're such a closed book, Danny, and I respect that, but I'd like to take a peek inside from time to time. You know, just scan the chapter headings if nothing else.'

'And so, you're starting with death?'

'It feels like a good place to start. We'll work backwards from there.' Sam shrugged glibly.

'Rationally, I do not fear death,' he said, carefully.

'But? There's a but in your voice... ' Sam said, applying pressure on his toes with her own, urging him on.

'I have no cause to fear death. I can only assume I will return to the same state I occupied before I was born, whatever that might have been, and I have no reason to believe I was either afraid or in pain then.'

'But?'

'My father faced his death stoically, he prepared everything so practically in order to give me as little inconvenience as possible. He knew he was dying and he used his time to sort out his affairs and to leave nothing to chance. I'm grateful to him for that. But I think he would have approached it very differently if my mother had still been alive. He wouldn't have wanted to leave her.'

'Were they very much in love?'

'It's hard to say, they were just my parents, I didn't really have any point of reference. But I think her death must have broken him. She took all capacity for him to love or be loved with her, I think.'

Sam blinked back the tears that formed, not wanting to startle him.

'I don't think I really understood any of this until I met you, sweet pea. My father was a practical man, he gave me everything I needed. But he never put up a fight when he was diagnosed. I think he must have been looking forward to joining my mum. And I might have resented that if I hadn't met you but I'm beginning to understand, now, what he must have felt without her. His own death might have been a relief.'

'But he had you.'

Danny didn't respond. Instead, he carried on speaking without looking Sam in the eye. 'Love can complicate things, sweet pea. It can make life harder to live and harder to leave. But in answer to your question, I fear living without you far more than I fear death.'

Sam thought hard about his words, surprised by the passion in his voice that had been impossible for him to disguise. 'You should take great comfort from those feelings, Danny. You'd never really know, from the way you act, quite how much you love me. I mean, I do, you give me no real cause for doubt. But nobody else would know. You're not exactly one for grand gestures, are you?' Sam smiled, remembering how quietly strong he'd been when she'd been ill, he'd been her champion when she'd been at her lowest, with more than enough strength for the two of them. 'Your dad probably loved you very much too, and he showed you by making sure you were safe without him.'

Danny nodded quietly and thought about his dad. He felt a pang of recognition and hoped his dad had never feared the pain of loss as keenly as he did. He would rather tell himself his own version of that story, that his dad went peacefully towards his mum, than imagining him facing the double wrench of separation from his wife and then his child.

Danny glanced at his laptop. It looked tangible, reliable, solid. He looked at his wife. She looked ethereal, vulnerable, elemental. Like the sweet peas he'd named her for. 'I've got a bit of work to do this evening, you don't mind, do you?' He drew the computer to his lap and opened it up. The bright light on his face blanched out his features.

Sam recognised the look. He had shut down. And when Danny shut down, she had to reach for that other outlet. She stood up and stretched. 'No problem, champ. I've got some writing to do myself.'

Chapter 38

Sam and Diana were sitting on a plank that had been balanced on two upturned logs. In front of them a small fire warmed a kettle and the smallest trace of steam was beginning to rise.

Sam, who now felt more at home in the woods than she did in the fields or lanes of her area wondered of Diana, 'Do you ever feel oppressed by these trees?'

Diana leant forward and stoked the fire with a heavy stick before looking up to the canopy above her. 'Oppressed, heavens no. Listen to them. They're my orchestra, my ballet, my soap opera. They're my derring-do adventures *and* my lullabies.'

Sam looked up also and watched the tips of the trees sway harmoniously, as if choreographed by Diana's words.

Diana continued. 'And I love their vigour. The way they just grow regardless. A crack in the concrete, a patch of dappled sunlight, an acorn dropped by an absent-minded squirrel. And whoosh, they don't wait for a second invitation. They're off.'

Sam recalled her very first visit to the woods. Long before she'd met Diana. 'That's funny. That's the feeling I first had when I got to the woods. But they made me feel so apathetic in comparison. I wonder though, if when they're swaying above you at night you're fearful. You know, when the wind picks up.'

Diana inhaled deeply, loving the scent of the conifers and the sound of the kettle. 'Oh I'm not daft, and some of those trees are what, thirty metres tall? And golly, if you saw the size of the root systems it's a wonder they stay upright at all. But no, I'm not a fool. When it's really stormy in the autumn and the winter, I occasionally run for the hills, then I'm not too proud to find a more solid roof to sleep under.'

'You do? I'm really glad to hear that. I rather imagined you holing up in here through thick and thin. Where do you run to, when it's stormy?'

'Rebecca's,' said Diana, a little curtly, as if it were obvious.

'Oh goodness. I somehow thought Rebecca and you had fallen out, that you no longer spoke.'

'Whatever made you think that?' Diana used her stick to lift the kettle off the fire by its handle. She didn't look like she wanted to make Sam a cup of tea anymore and Sam wondered if she'd overstepped the mark by making assumptions.

'You told me you'd needed to reject her entirely. But perhaps I misunderstood.' Sam said lightly, 'I'll fetch the teabags, shall I?'

Sam stepped over the makeshift bench and headed into the caravan to find the tin with the teabags in it. She reached up to the shelf, pulling down the caddy and in doing so knocked over a small pile of unopened post that had been wedged between the tin container and an earthenware pot of sugar. Sam stood the envelopes up again before realising that this was the only clutter she'd ever noticed in the caravan. Guiltily, she grabbed an envelope and studied the address. 'Ms Rebecca Downing. Willow's Fortune, Hambledon Hill.' The address was handwritten in ink. She reached up and looked at the other envelopes. The same name and address, but the typed addresses of bills or statements. Helping herself to two teabags, she put the tea caddy back and the envelopes in place, hoping it didn't look like she'd disturbed them. A flood of realisation swept over her. Willow's Fortune. Rebecca. The woman with the gardener and the housekeeper was Diana's friend, Rebecca. She wondered why Diana would have Rebecca's post. She'd never yet seen any trace of personal life or interaction with the outside world inside the caravan. And now she knew that Diana made a dash for the big white house on a stormy night. Perhaps, she mused, this was a letter from Diana to Rebecca, though it didn't look like Diana's careful script. Sam frowned as the small pieces of information she thought she knew jostled to take shape in her head.

She went back out with the teabags. 'Ta da!' she announced brightly, brandishing them.

Diana was still looking at the kettle as if she hadn't even noticed Sam's absence. Ignoring Sam entirely, she fished a couple of teabags out of her dungarees pocket, dropping one into each of the tin cups sitting on the ground beside her. 'I rather like the idea,' she said, towards the fireplace but perhaps to Sam, 'that when we've really screwed up and we've finally done the decent thing and killed ourselves off, then everything else will have another shot at life. Perhaps the waters will have risen, drowned us all and subsided again leaving nothing of note but our urban debris. Then the trees will soon be back. At first it would be the turn of the weeds and the fast-growing oxygenators. They'd soon fill the planet up. They'd break up the concrete, pull down the skyscrapers, the bridges would succumb. But the trees would be fine again.'

Sam was only half listening. She was still puzzled as to why Diana would have Rebecca's post in her caravan. It was unsettling her, but she wasn't quite sure why. She lay down on the dry ground. She used her jacket as a pillow and folded her arms underneath her head, looking up at the canopy directly above her. In the gaps between the leaves, small clouds scuttled across the blue sky and she could feel the coolness of their shadows pass across her face. She pushed the niggling concern to one side and tuned into Diana's words, responding at last. 'I love the shape that the spaces between the tops of the trees make. I've never been aware of them before, but it looks like they're afraid to touch.'

'They are,' said Diana, looking up. 'It's called "crown shyness". The uppermost branches of the trees can sense that they are approaching another tree and the growing process halts.'

'The trees are shy!' exclaimed Sam, delighted. She thought about the implication and asked, in awe, 'The leaves can actually *feel* the presence of another tree?' She looked with greater scrutiny at the patterns made by the branches and sky above her.

'Apparently so. It feels so respectful, doesn't it? Each tree allows the next the space they need to be a tree. The science behind it is that each tree needs to ensure light can penetrate the canopy and photosynthesis can continue for the good of all. Effectively they all sacrifice their own personal growth for the long term benefit of the whole community.'

'Wow,' said Sam. 'That sounds like the sort of communal living humans often aspire to but always fail at.' Sam looked in awe at the branches above her head. 'What's your favourite tree, Diana?'

Diana, who was still sitting on the bench, holding her tea in two hands, looked around her, examining each tree in turn critically.

'I mean tree *type*,' said Sam, feeling an oblique answer brewing. 'What's your favourite *sort* of tree?'

'Species?'

'Yes. Species,' said Sam, happily. She could detect Diana's impatience and knowing this about her, knowing how predictably quick she could be to contest Sam's vagueness, lent a familiarity that Sam was beginning to recognise as friendship.

'What an utterly ludicrous question,' said Diana, dispassionately.

'Why is that ludicrous? It's a perfectly reasonable question to ask in a wood. OK, let me frame it differently. If you could only have one tree survive, which one would you want to save?'

Diana tutted. 'Trees don't work like that. Woodland certainly doesn't work like that. You can ask me a more specific question. Which is my favourite tree to look at, which is my favourite tree to sit under, which is my favourite tree for firewood, which is my favourite tree to draw, which is my favourite tree to hide behind, which is my favourite tree to eat from, which is my favourite tree for birds, which is my favourite tree *en masse*, which is my favourite tree to climb, which is my favourite... '

'I get it, I get it,' laughed Sam. 'Let's start with which is your favourite to look at?'

'Day or night? Sun or cloud? Heavy rain or drizzle. Spring, summer, autumn or winter?' asked Diana.

'Seriously?'

'Yes, seriously.'

Sam turned on to her side and propped herself up on one elbow, looking at Diana carefully. 'You have a favourite tree for each season? A favourite tree for each weather condition?'

'Of course. Trees change all the time and daily too, depending upon the amount of light on them. Trees at gloaming and trees at night are completely different beasts. Come and visit after dusk and I will show you. The leaves are no longer green, they are the *absence* of green, and yet they retain the memory of the colour from the day. At night they *approximate* green in the best way they can. In the dark, each shade is completely different and yet I know of no names to label the colours.'

Sam chewed her lip, wondering if she had ever looked at trees in darkness. She could only imagine them as shapes with no colour so realised she probably hadn't. 'Your favourite tree to look at, Diana. You're being deliberately obtuse.'

'I can't narrow it down entirely. I like the hardwoods, for obvious reasons, but it wouldn't be fair to lump those in with all other trees in the same category. So, shall I give you three hardwoods that I wouldn't want to live without?'

Sam nodded and though Diana probably hadn't seen the assent, she continued regardless. She thought about her answer carefully, with a deep frown on her forehead, as if she feared offending a tree with a flippant answer. 'The

240

oak of course. Who doesn't love the oak? I love the oak for its grandeur and its resonance. I love it for its symbolic importance. There are oaks all around the world, but I truly believe the English oak is its most spectacular form and a single oak tree in the middle of a field is one of the most emblematic sights in the British countryside. But I hesitate to make the oak my outright favourite. There are just too many caveats.'

'There are?' asked Sam, imagining squirrels running in and out of an oak tree's caveats.

'Do you know how old a plant must be to be considered native?' Diana paused and answered her own question. 'Old. So very old. They need to have colonised these islands during the retreat of ice at the end of the ice age or they need to have been present when the English Channel was created.'

'They're ancient,' said Sam from her leafy bed. 'It's hard to fathom.'

'It is, isn't it? It's hardly surprising, given its history but I can't help but fear the oak is rather *entitled*. I suppose it *is* nobility, it is very much the landed gentry. It's been here for ever, long before the upstarts that came in and settled around it and it carries on so successfully. It rarely concedes any territory. However, I can't help fear that the English oak might be the most terrible snob. It's aristocratic, of course, but I think it might believe that aristocracy still matters when the rest of the world has moved on.'

Diana chuckled as if laughing at a private joke but she quickly shared her thought with Sam. 'It's a bit naughty, but sometimes I can't help but admire an ivy that has successfully rooted itself and is using an oak as its support, wrapping itself around those broad trunks like some sort of social climber. The ivy is pernicious, I know, but it really is the equivalent of an audacious tech start-up that has somehow turned a stately home into its head office. We shouldn't actually celebrate the ivy, but I can't help but admire the pluck.'

Diana paused quietly before continuing. 'But then, the oak is such a marvellous thing to sit below.' She sounded wistful as she considered the question.

'But goodness me, the silver birch is a gem.' Shaking her head in admiration she continued, oblivious to everything else around her. 'It's consistently beautiful in every weather, in every season, in bright sunshine but in the darkness too. Oh, a silver birch in moonlight is a wondrous thing. It's known as the Watchful Tree, literally, I think because of the "eyes" formed by dropped branches that seem to gaze from the trunks at you but, regardless of their bark markings they seem watchful to me anyway. Watchful and *knowing*. There's a wood near here that you should visit one day. It's only few miles away, so you really should go. You could go at night-time perhaps. There, there are 1,729 silver birches, planted in rows. Or so I am told. I'll take their word for it, I've never felt the need to double-check. But my goodness, it really is a breathtaking thing. Depending on how you look at the trees their magnificent trunks make different forms. They can line up in exact rows so they all but disappear or you can look at them on the diagonal and the seemingly never-ending sequence will play mind-boggling tricks on your eyes. Usually I'm all for nature in its most natural form: tumbling and turning, tripping over itself in its requirement to grow and yet, sometimes, to see so many trees planted out in regimental formation can be absolutely glorious. Just stunning. Yes, the silver birch is indeed the lady of the woods, a very dainty thing. And as old as the hills of course, but without any of that elitist entitlement that the oak seems to wear on its boughs.'

'I'd love to see that wood. Could you show me perhaps?'

'I could, of course. But I think that's something you might want to do with your husband.'

Sam winced a little. 'I'd love that, but he's not overly fond of nature, I think he finds the prospect of all this…' She cast around for the word and gestured with both arms to capture the sentiment she was looking for '… *wildness*, quite alarming.'

'Ah, but in that case, he'd almost certainly appreciate the precision of this particular patch. And he might not like the prospect of nature, but it's important to put the two of you into the landscape from time to time. That's where you can catch a glimpse of your past selves and your future selves.'

'Meaning what?'

'Well, your home is your home now, isn't it? But there might be other homes yet to come. And fortunes change so homes can come and go. But the landscape isn't going to go anywhere, it's been there for ever and it will be here long after you and me. If you immerse yourselves in it, you'll catch glimpses of yourselves from time to time when you revisit. I can find myself crossing a road and, all of a sudden, I'll see the faintest trace of my past self walking down the pavement, striding confidently away with purpose and I like to catch that glimpse. Finding shadows of your former selves in the landscape is a very good thing for the two of you, it means you'll always be there, regardless of what happens.'

'And you think I'll catch a glimmer of our future selves also?'

'Oh yes, by the same reckoning. Do plenty of different things together and you'll quickly see which small joys are those you'll return to again and again. Being able to imagine your future selves doing something together, despite the dulling of time, provides a roadmap of how to get to that point later in life.'

Sam closed her eyes. There were so many things, already, that she could imagine doing again and again with Danny. She'd known, right from the beginning, that they had the potential to grow old together, health willing. She wondered about Diana's own past self but couldn't quite grasp an image of who she might have been. Instead she turned the conversation back to the safer ground beneath them. 'So, the three you couldn't live without are the oak, the ivy and the birch?' – summarising Diana's previous meander through the woodlands.

'Heavens, no! The ivy was a mere postscript, not an actual contender. There are many ahead of the ivy, I'm afraid. It's a lovely thing but it doesn't have the stature of the other great trees. My third would have to be the beech. I mean, just look at them,' she said, tipping her head back and gesturing towards the tallest trees around them.

They both stared up at the shocking green of the leaves, which in their luminosity appeared to reach out into the sky, capture the sunlight, and focus a warm green light back down to the shadowy forest floor, allowing them to bathe in its warmth some thirty metres beneath those bright tips. They both marvelled quietly at the furthest leaves and the intricate pattern the bashful leaves made against the deep blue sky.

'The birch is all about new beginnings, it's one of the first in leaf so it has always been there to herald spring, and traditionally it was thought that sweeping out a building with birch will rid it of any past negativity. It was the first thing I did when I moved here. I tied some old dry birch twigs into a brush and swept out the caravan. Then I burnt those twigs on my very first fire and used their heat to cook my first meal. I wasn't following any particular tradition but if felt ritualistic and as ancient as the hills. I think I might even have walked clockwise around the fire and recited a few blessings. If anyone from the village had seen me they'd have run a mile!' Diana laughed happily at the memory before continuing more gravely. 'But whilst the birch is about renewal, the beech is associated with learning, with study and creativity. I'm very glad to have found my home amongst them for this next chapter of my life. I couldn't wish for a better classroom. The beech is supposed to be the sum of the wisdom of all the other trees.'

They both looked around them.

'You can just see it, can't you? The ash is positively *stupid* in comparison.'

Sam laughed at the idea. 'I'd like to learn more. I could listen to you for ever.'

For once, Diana didn't extinguish Sam's enthusiasm with a cold splash of reclusive retreat. Instead she matched Sam's acclamation with relish. 'We can take a number of walks and I'll introduce you to a few of the others, so you can befriend them. I'd like you to meet the ash and the elm, the sycamore and the walnut. There are of course plenty of oak and beech to keep you company without straying too far, so you can soon decide which you like the best, but I'd also strongly recommend a visit to the silver birch wood to see it in all its splendour.'

'I'd like that.' Sam closed her eyes and allowed the memory of the bright sky to paint light jigsaw pieces on her eyelids. She loved her beech classroom and she loved Diana's melodious teachings. *This is belonging!* she thought, with joyful recognition. She felt an odd little flurry of jealousy that Diana was friends with the woman in the big white house. Somehow, she had allowed herself to believe that she was Diana's only friend. She had allowed herself to feel chosen. Perhaps that was why she felt unsettled.

Chapter 39

The phone rang and Sam wanted to ignore it, but both guilt and duty (one indistinguishable from the other) swept through her and propelled her towards the phone which she picked up with a tremor of prescient anger.

Her mother, shrill with delight, appeared to be already mid-flow as Sam answered. Her parents had returned from their holiday to the Dordogne and the highlight appeared to be the extraordinary coincidence of running into a couple they'd met many years ago on a holiday to Cyprus.

Sam listened, trying to detect a purity in her mother's pleasure but, rather, her tone was laced with a sort of spiteful joy that Sam recognised as her mother's favourite flavour.

'Now Simon, I recognised immediately. He hadn't changed a bit. Charming. *Charming.*' She oozed generously before sliding in for the attack. 'Pamela, *Pam*, however, was a completely different story. For a moment, I thought Simon might be dining with his elderly *mother.* I barely recognised her. She looked absolutely dreadful. It wasn't just that she'd put on weight, which I don't mind telling you, she had, but she'd squeezed herself into a sundress that was at least two sizes too small and she'd completely let herself go. She looked ghastly. Old and *sallow*. I felt rather sorry for him. And I have to say, I'm rather glad I had that new hair-do done just before we left.'

Sam allowed her mother to continue flattering herself and she realised with a jolt that it was a very long time since she'd actually liked her mother. She must have liked her as a child, and she couldn't remember not liking her as a teen. She supposed she had liked her until suddenly, one day, she didn't anymore. She wondered if this was normal.

'Your father was positively preening with me on his arm. The truth is I knew I didn't look a day older than when we met Simon and Pamela in Cyprus. Your father said she was looking me up and down like something the cat had brought in. We roared with laughter afterwards.'

Sam felt outrage on Pam's behalf. How dare her mother shame her! Poor old Pam, thought Sam, in a rush of solidarity.

'And we had such a delightful time with your cousin that we stopped on the way back too. The children are completely adorable. And Gerry is doing terribly well. He's been promoted again. I think he must be earning an absolute fortune. Lucy's very proud of him, it's rather sweet.'

'Good old Gerry,' said Sam, half-heartedly.

'He's a dear,' said Sam's mother quickly.

Sam experienced a surge of competitive, protective, proud love for her own dear husband, who had probably been promoted a number of times without her mother's recognition.

'I just hope it's enough for Lucy,' said Sam, allowing a detectable trace of pity to creep into her voice.

'In what sense, darling? I would say Lucy has more than enough to cope with.'

'I do hope so. She had plenty of potential.' Sam's voice, she hoped, suggested that it was all probably far too late for Lucy.

'Oh darling. She had *some* potential. But her brain was never quite on a par with yours. You're the career girl, aren't you? But not everyone has it in them. Luckily, she has Gerry to provide for the family.'

No, thought Sam. Not everyone has a career to throw away at the first whiff of struggle. Not everyone has ovaries to throw away either.

'She sent her love,' said Sam's mother.

'Good, good. Got to go, Mum. I'll be late.' Sam hung up and breathed through her nose, knowing solace could only be found amongst the trees.

It was dry outside so Sam slipped her trainers on and let herself out of the house, heading off to the woods, grateful for a haven to retreat to. When she got to the caravan, there was no sign of Diana but the embers in the fireplace, though cool-looking, were still slightly smoking and it only took a few well aimed breaths to puff it back into life. Sam emptied her mind completely, and instead focussed fully on feeding the fire tiny twigs and leaves until the flames caught convincingly. She became bolder, adding larger bits of wood before she was confident the fire was ready to accept a dry log from the woodpile. She knelt down beside the fire and let her mind remain empty and still while the flames licked the new fuel tentatively, finding its way into the grooves of bark before grabbing it wholeheartedly. Sam smiled at this primordial pleasure.

'Oh hello,' said Diana, appearing through the trees, carrying her basket laden with leaves. 'Honestly, I thought I'd made my home here to escape society but these days it's like living in some sort of commune.'

Sam didn't mind being told off by Diana. Her scolding was earnest and straightforward and because she sidestepped confrontation, Sam now felt confident that Diana would just say if she didn't want her to visit.

'I kept the home fires burning,' she said, proudly, grinning up at her.

With barely a pause Sam's smile disappeared. She broke a stick she'd been poking the fire with into smaller pieces and dropped them systematically around the burning log.

'Is your mother still alive, Diana?'

'Goodness, no. She died a good ten years ago.' At some point during Sam's visits, two fold-out chairs had appeared in the shelter, to the side of the wood pile, where before Sam was certain there had only been one. Diana now fetched these and unfolded them one by one while talking. 'I don't know if I'd be here in the woods if she had lived longer. I doubt it. It's hard to know, isn't it, how the twists and turns of life impact us. Where you find yourself at any given point is sometimes the only place you could possibly be, given those thousand different decisions you've made along the way. I'd be fascinated to see my life now, plotted out, having given the opposite answers to all the significant questions I'd ever been asked. Imagine if you'd said yes, each time you'd said no and vice versa. Where would you be, Sam?'

'Gosh. Weirdly, I know I might be mistaken for an adult but I don't think I've made many significant decisions yet.

I said yes when Danny proposed, so my life would have been very different if I hadn't married. I certainly wouldn't be here, in the woods with you. And perhaps I wouldn't be anywhere.' Sam thought about the consequence of that decision as if for the first time and acknowledged the enormity of it. 'I suppose, if I hadn't married, and hadn't wondered why I hadn't conceived I wouldn't have gone to the doctor and I wouldn't have had my cancer diagnosed as early, so I'd probably be dead.'

'That sounds like a significant decision to me.'

'Yes. But when Danny proposed I never truly thought about the consequences. I just said "yes". I was waiting for him to ask me and it never occurred to me to say no. I've always assumed my life was dictated by ultimatums. Mostly I've had decisions made for me and the rest of the major upheavals in my life have been a result of things that have just happened to me, so all of those have been quite out of my control. The truth is, Diana, I've drifted through my life until quite recently but perhaps if I'd been more assertive, more certain of who I wanted to be, I'd be a better person.'

'Who is this better person you lust after? What does she look like, what does she do?'

'She'd look like me. – I can't really change that. I'm just this collection of cells, organised in this particular configuration. But she'd speak up. She'd have a voice. She'd be doing something with her life.'

'But you do have a voice, don't you? With your writing.'

'But that's not me, that's Libby. She's just my alter-ego. Typical of me that my alter-ego is a better version of me. More proactive, more vocal, she has opinions and she's not afraid to express them. I'm passive and weak and I let people trample all over me. Take my mother for example.'

'I assumed this was leading there.'

'I just can't quite be the person she wants me to be. I am such a constant disappointment to her.'

'Are you sure? Is it possible that's just a role you've chosen to adopt?'

'No, really, I am. She quite likes Danny, which is a bonus. But she thinks he deserves better than me which is not what you want from your own mother. I suppose me not having children has been a real blow to her. That was what she wanted for this next stage of her life and I've let her down. She's sort of adopted my cousin – her brother's daughter Lucy, and her children. She's channelling all of her love into them... '

'And how does that make you feel? Jealous?'

'Um.' Sam really didn't know. 'Jealous? No. I don't think I'm jealous. Jealousy is a spiky thing, isn't it? That's not it. I feel a bit baffled, I suppose, that she's been so quick to swing her attention from me to my cousin. I mean, I don't think I'd heard a word about Lucy and Gerry until they had children and now I never hear the end of them.'

'You are jealous.'

'I wish I were. That would imply some sort of natural response. I don't actually care which is probably quite unhealthy.'

'I think you care about plenty of things but you are trying very hard not to care about this. That's OK. But I think maybe, just *give* your mother this.'

'How do you mean?'

'You haven't quite lived up to her expectations, she's found an alternative family. Another daughter and some grandchildren. It's fantastical, of course but it doesn't really impact you. Let her have them.'

'Oh. Is it as easy as that?'

'Definitely. You're going to have some battles to fight in your life but this isn't one of them. You don't want to be loved by your mother at the moment, but don't stop her loving someone else instead. That's just selfish.'

'Is it bad that I don't want to be loved by my mother at the moment, do you think?'

'It's a necessary phase. You'll get over it. You'll discover a reason to love her again.'

'Oh, OK.' Sam continued to poke at the fire. Bringing the flames back to life was incredibly therapeutic and Diana's words now seemed irrefutably sensible.

'Are you sad or are you angry?' Diana asked.

'Sad. Angry. No. Sad. Actually angry. I don't know.'

'You can be both or neither.'

'Then sometimes I'm both but right now I'm neither. Here, in the woods, with you I am not being judged. I feel fine. I feel nice.'

Diana smiled in recognition. 'Nice is a great state to achieve. It took me over fifty years and a major breakdown to move myself into a space that allowed me to feel nice.'

'Well, the school of Diana works then, doesn't it? You've helped me get there sooner, minus the breakdown.'

'Good. Something positive has come out of my own collapse. But, Sam, it's really OK, though, to feel angry. Anger is natural and important. Being angry can help.'

'But what can I be angry about? How can anger help me? I can't regret things that I have absolutely no control over. It's like being angry about being too short or too tall. Where does anger fit in?'

'So you never rise, never get flooded by a version of anger that takes root in a helpful, indulgent version of self-pity?'

'Of course. I'm not immune to that. But what I do with it isn't very healthy. I take it and I write these provocative pieces, designed to inflame people. That's healthy for me because I am washing myself of those feelings. But it's not good. It might be fine if I were doing no harm but I think I probably am. When I feel a wave of what you describe as anger it is very rarely true anger. It is more, as you say, self-pity and that is the thing that makes me angry. But the self-pity doesn't come from the obvious routes, it's not that I pity myself because I was ill or couldn't have children or – God forbid – came through all of that treatment only to plunge headlong into the menopause while other people are still starting out in life. It's none of that. It's that I'm never understood. Nobody ever really asks me how I am. They just look at me, see I'm a bit broken and then run a mile in case whatever I have is infectious.'

'That sounds hard.' Diana stood up and started walking, motioning Sam to follow. Sam walked beside her, falling into step quite comfortably.

'It is but it's confusing, too. Because, what I'd really like, is the right to choose not to have children. And be respected for that choice. People know I can't have children and they immediately pity me, or they run away from me, or they try to suggest ways to fix me. Their assumption that not having children is a complete disaster is unhelpful and offensive. I would like, just for once, to say that I am absolutely fine not having children, thanks. But I never get that chance. That's why I write what I write, that's where I vent. And I'm never truthful. I lie to myself, I lie to Danny. And when I write a version of the truth that I feel comfortable with, I pass it through Libby's filter, and hand over the authorship to her. I let her write it for me. It's her truth, it never feels like mine.'

'You are angry. I'm not judging you, I've been angry myself in the past. I'm curious that you have chosen to subsume your anger with passivity.'

'I really don't think of myself as angry. I think of myself as provoked. I am capable of being at peace with the cards I've been dealt but other people don't seem to accept it. Their response to me makes me angry.'

'So, can't you just ignore them?'

'No, I can't! They just won't let me. I can be minding my business when a neighbour comes to introduce herself and before I even know her last name she's telling me how to fix myself. She's telling me I must find a way to have children or I can never be the neighbour she needs me to be.'

Diana and Sam walked out of the woodland and began to wander slowly around the edge of the large field to the north of the copse. Sam fell silent as they walked, letting Diana point out the names of wild plants as they went. She used her stick as both a pointer and a hook to pull a plant closer to them for inspection but now she hung it on a branch and they were perched on a fallen ash, looking back up at the woodland that cushioned Diana's home from the rest of the world.

'If you don't want to be judged by a neighbour, don't answer the doorbell.'

Sam smiled. Diana had appeared to be immersed in the wildlife surrounding them but had clearly not forgotten Sam's plea. 'You know how hard that is. You removed yourself entirely and yet people still found a way to harass you, they tried to chase you away and you don't even have a doorbell.'

'Perhaps I'm talking metaphorically.'

'Oh.'

Sam thought a bit more. 'Oh. I see.' Although she wasn't sure she did.

'Tell me, Sam. Which aspect makes you angry, the interference from other women or your lack of womb?'

'Definitely not the lack of womb. That doesn't make me angry, how could it? I'm alive because of my lack of womb. I made that sacrifice willingly. But ever since my cancer I've been pitied and I have been denied the right to not *want* children. There's a big difference between childless and childfree and nobody seems to let me be both.'

'So, you wouldn't have wanted children? They weren't in your plans?'

'They were abstractly, but I just sort of assumed I would go on to have them. There wasn't a burning desire. I wasn't focussed on having children as part of my big plan but then I wasn't really focussed on anything. I was just stumbling blindly forward letting life happen to me. When I found I couldn't have children, I just didn't feel a great loss, I readjusted very easily, readily even. And then I started to feel bad because everywhere I looked, people told me that wasn't a healthy response.'

The view across the field was beautiful and the sun was high. Neither of them felt any great urge to start walking again. 'What about you? I assume you don't have children?' asked Sam, casually, trying to make the question sound as if it hadn't been fighting to be asked for weeks.

'No. Never. And I don't feel a loss. I might have been a good mother once I suppose but I'd be awful now. I'd have had to turn my back on them eventually. I fear that even with children, I'd still be here, talking to you, not there, picking up the pieces of their lives. They'd have hated me eventually, regardless of how hard I'd tried.'

'You can't possibly know that, you might have become somebody entirely different, surely. Perhaps right now you'd be baking a cake ahead of a weekend visit.'

'I don't think so. I think I was always on this path.'

'And how do you define this path?'

'To go at life hard, fast, headstrong and wildly in the wrong direction. To crash into a crisis like a train hitting a wall. To pick myself up, alone, without help from anyone and to contemplate and meditate, to face these last phases like this. But not without effect, not without impact. I will leave a report.'

'Your notebooks.'

'Exactly.'

'I envy your determination. I've never led life fast or been headstrong. I've been so passive. I haven't felt like I'm wading through treacle, just drifting along.'

'But you're not doing that now, are you?'

'I am; I very much am doing that. I'm almost compulsively ordinary. And I'm completely pliable. I can't imagine ever crashing into a crisis. I'll just walk slowly up to it, apologise and change direction.'

'I don't think you're ordinary. I think you're extraordinary.'

'Me?'

'Yes, you.'

'But I'm not!' insisted Sam, though desperate to believe she could be.

'You are the first person I've known in all my adult years who I've liked more, not less, the more time I've spent with them. That makes you extraordinary in my eyes.'

Sam glowed with pleasure.

Chapter 40

Now Sam was carving out so much of her day to sit in the woods with Diana, the weekdays flew by and the grass grew resolutely, marking out the passage of time in millimetres not seconds. The newly planted border, whilst not yet as lavish or lustrous, was bright and vigorous and had now caught up with the height of the older grass of the turfed lawn which had been trimmed twice more. There was nothing much Sam could do for the new grass now other than to watch it flourish.

Standing on the paving stones at the rear of the house and squinting at her garden through half-closed eyes, she could already imagine it in all its majesty. She still had no proof that any flowers would appear from amongst the green, but she accepted that she would simply have to bide her time. Waiting was a challenge that Sam felt she could overcome by being respectful of nature and its ways. Her other challenge, that of keeping Danny at bay, was much harder to surmount.

Fortunately, each evening for the past couple of weeks, a light warm drizzle had fallen vertically from the breezeless sky, leaving no trace other than the earthy scent of burgeoning growth. The weather had delighted Sam. She knew the combination of gentle rain and gleaming sunshine would create the ideal conditions for her wildflowers and it also made it much easier to keep Danny indoors when he got home in the evenings. She had deflected him with carefully prepared dinners and diverting conversation and had concocted a series of increasingly convoluted distractions to keep his mind off the garden.

Meanwhile, Danny was not oblivious to Sam's scheming. He had allowed her to manipulate him willingly, fully aware that his every moment was being managed until darkness fell and she could finally allow him to wander the house unescorted. He had of course been keeping a watchful eye on the height of grass, it was impossible to ignore, but her progressively complex recreations had amused him and had gone a long way towards nullifying the alarming prospect of the wilderness that Sam was cultivating behind his back.

A couple of midweek twilight hours were easy to fill but the weekends were impossible. Now Danny joined Sam, handed her a cup of coffee and they stood on the paving in silence, observing the long grass together.

'Gosh,' said Danny, as if it had sprung upon him unnoticed.

'It's amazing how it's grown, isn't it?' said Sam, cheerfully, but looking firmly ahead, unable to face him.

'It's a savannah,' Danny said, trying not to pass judgement but needing to name it.

'A small one.'

'And you're not going to mow it.'

'Not yet. No.'

'Do you have a timeline?'

'No.'

'Right. I see. But I assume we can't really walk on it at the moment.'

'Not really, it's in a bit of a delicate state. But you can enjoy it by *looking* at it.'

'It's just long grass. I am not sure it will hold my attention all summer.'

'Yes. Yes, it is just long grass. But let's see what happens over the next few weeks. I already find it quite captivating.'

They both fell silent.

Sensing Danny's tension, Sam realised she needed to urgently remove Danny from her lawn, away from the lawnmower, away from the potential wildflowers.

'Shall we go for a walk? Or find a pub?' she suggested.

'Sure,' said Danny, not sounding sure at all.

'Apparently, there's a beautiful wood locally. It's near enough to go on foot if you fancy it? I think it's about a four-mile walk, we could head there, see if there's a pub nearby and walk back?'

Danny frowned.

'What do you reckon? A long walk would do us both the power of good.'

He turned away from the lawn and headed inside. Sam followed him, hopeful that the hardest piece of the negotiation was now behind her.

'Well?' she said once they were inside again. 'A walk to the woods?'

Danny scrunched up his face in barely disguised disgust. 'Walk to a wood? Why on earth would we do that? We've got a wood right here on our doorstep, haven't we? How about we Google the top pubs in the area, jump in the car, and head for one of them? We could work our way through the list over the next couple of weeks. That might be a fun thing to do. Over a period of time we could survey all the pubs in the area. We could come up with our own scoring system and see if we agree with the published reviews.'

Sam nodded encouragingly whilst silently dismissing the idea. 'That's a possibility too, but I was thinking you could do with the exercise. Now you're living here you're not going to the gym. It would be ironic if you were to drop dead of a coronary because you moved to the countryside.'

'But a wood? I'm not sure woods are my thing.' He looked quite frightened by the idea.

'Perhaps not.' Sam was disappointed. 'It's just something my friend Diana mentioned, she said it was particularly beautiful. It has 1,729 birch trees laid out and… '

Danny, who had been fussing around the kitchen in an unfocussed frenzy of activity, stood stock-still. '*One thousand, seven hundred and twenty-nine trees?* You have got to be kidding me!' he said, looking and sounding astounded.

'I know it sounds crazy, it would be nearly impossible to count trees in a normal wood because they're always so higgledy-piggledy, but in this one, all the trees are the same species and it is laid out formally apparently.'

'Well, of course it must be a *formal* wood, one thousand seven hundred and twenty-nine is a really *great* number.'

'I know; that's one of the reasons I want to check it out. It must be huge, can you imagine? What kind of a nutter plants so many trees at once?'

'No, no, no,' said Danny shaking his head impatiently.

'I don't mean great as in *huge*, I mean great as in *powerful*, because one thousand seven hundred and twenty-nine is an extremely *interesting* number. This is not a coincidence. This is not an accident. This wood cannot have been planted by a nutter, it can only have been planted by a mathematician. I'd *love* to see this wood.'

Danny was quite animated. He walked around the kitchen several times, looking for his wallet and the car keys but, in his excitement, failing to find either.

'Well, great. Let's do it,' said Sam, jumping up to get her anorak before he changed his mind.

'What I'm intrigued by is how it might be laid out. I imagine it must be a long narrow wood. That would be my first guess.'

'We don't really need to speculate, we're going to look, aren't we?' said Sam, zipping up her anorak impatiently.

'Nineteen trees planted in one direction, ninety-one in the other. That's the obvious solution. Given that it is the largest number which is divisible by its prime sum of digits and reversal.'

'Cool,' said Sam loudly over her shoulder, looking for a pair of boot socks that she thought she'd left in her wellingtons.

'But that would be a very narrow wood, wouldn't it? Not really a wood, more of a corridor. But you know that's not the *only* interesting thing about the number 1,729.'

'You're kidding.' The sarcasm was high in Sam's voice but Danny, in his enthusiasm, failed to notice it.

'It's also the *smallest* number expressible as the sum of two positive cubes in two different ways.'

Sam dropped the car keys into his palm and then handed

him his wallet. 'Compromise,' she said firmly, 'we'll drive there and then go for a walk. We'll look out for a pub along the way. I refuse to Google the pub first though. I don't care if it's in the top three or the bottom three, it will serve warm beer and adequate food if we're lucky. Regardless, it will be *our* pub.'

'OK,' said Danny, puzzled.

'And no more speculation about how the trees might be arranged.'

'Really? That's not interesting?'

'Really. And no spreadsheets for the pub. Let's just leave it all to chance.'

'Weirdo,' said Danny, with a broad smile. They left happily. Behind them the grass continued to grow. Beneath the earth, the yellow rattle fixed its own roots on to those of the grass, extracting the minerals and water for its own growth and holding the grass back to give itself a greater chance of survival. Above the earth the cornflowers, poppies and malopes pushed their growing tips through the damp soil, racing each other towards the light.

Chapter 41

The weather, talisman-like, played its part in Danny's first real venture into the countryside, beyond the boundaries of his own small slice of it. Up until then, Danny had barely ever asked a favour of the elements, although he had recently begun to look at the weather forecast each time he thought about his new lawnmower lying idle in his garage. So perhaps it was Sam's plea that was heard.

Regardless, luck was on their side as they pulled up into a layby just at the outskirts of the birch wood. They had parked and pulled their boots on, leaving their shoes in plastic bags in the boot to appease Danny's uneasiness at the whole excursion, but even out of the car, shoes stowed, wellington boots and coats on, they were hesitant, as if unsure how best to tackle this uncharted territory together. While they stood by the roadside, paused, the sun pushed its way through the clouds unexpectedly and bright shafts of sunshine immediately illuminated the woods as if from within. Strong shadows provided stark contrast between the bright white of the trees' trunks and the dramatic darkness of the nooks and crannies that the sunlight failed to reach and the whole panorama, a collision of dark and light, amplified by a lampshade of luminous green from the new birch leaves above, brought the sheer majesty of the formal planting into vivid reality before their eyes. Sam gasped and Danny reached out and took her hand as they moved towards the first of the birch trees and then took a few paces into the woodland itself. Danny stood still and allowed his eyes to trace the tree trunks diagonally, helping him to get his bearings before sweeping his eyes in both directions, watching the patterns form in every direction.

'This really is quite something,' Danny said, marching confidently more deeply into the woodland. The trees were at their best, the impact long ago imagined by their architect now fully realised in a splendid display of regimented order, each trunk entirely hidden by the next or revealed in a trick of the eye that played havoc with the senses.

The impact of these gorgeous pillars was compounded by the even carpet of green beneath them and the ceiling of green above them, each as vivid and constant as any artist could aspire to, but painted there not by any hand but by the bluebell foliage beneath and the still-crumpled new leaves above.

'This was definitely planted by my kind of guy. And not as I'd imagined it at all. It's broadly square, wouldn't you say, sweet pea?' Danny continued forward, checking and counting, trying to find the centre point. 'And yet I can't really see any out of line. So, either he's been very clever in disguising a few extra, or perhaps it's more like one thousand seven hundred and twenty-two. What do you think, Sam?'

Sam had wandered off. The trunks of the trees were extraordinary. On each one the white bark was peeling back in layers like pencil shavings, revealing in places diamond-shaped fissures and the dark grey stretch marks of expansion. She felt herself absorbing the detail greedily, trying to commit to memory each tree's own fingerprint. She was aware of Danny's singular fascination but walked deliberately out of earshot, able but unwilling to verify her husband's calculations.

This wood was the opposite of the wood she had learned to love, its unruly sprawl dictated by each species' own mad desire for growth, spurred on by its relentless search for sunlight. This wood had a power, too, but its potency seemed to be fuelled by consensus.

'Ha!' called Danny. 'I found them!' Danny was walking towards her, a broad grin stretching across his face. He looked strong, amongst the trees, Sam thought. 'Seven sneaky blighters planted in their own row, but on almost the same line so you'd barely know they were there. Clever. Forty-one trees on one axis and forty-two on the other, plus seven on their own. One thousand, seven hundred and twenty-nine. You were right.'

'Phew, I was worried,' said Sam.

They held hands and walked out of the woods together, the bluebells springing up behind them unnoticed, so that, despite the impression the landscape had made on them, they made no lasting impression on the landscape at all.

Chapter 42

A shaft of sunlight found its way through the leafy canopy to the base of the beech trees, illuminating the tin kettle that swung above the fire around which Sam and Diana were seated. Sam had been pensive, breaking a twig into smaller and smaller pieces and feeding each piece in turn to the small flames that occasionally reached up to lick the kettle.

'The thing is, Diana,' she said, eventually, 'my marriage is a complicated thing and your birch tree wood confirmed that.'

'You went? I'm delighted!' Diana beamed with pleasure.

'We went, and yes, it's a beautiful wood. Regimented and peculiar, but sombre like tombstones.'

'Yes, I can see that, like one of those vast burial grounds you get a glimpse of from the window of a fast-moving train.'

'Exactly!'

Sam smiled and then shook her head sadly. 'Danny loved it.'

'He liked the precision?'

'Oh yes, he loved the precision, but more than that he loved the maths. He walked up and down excitedly, talking in tongues. One thousand seven hundred and twenty-nine is a magical number, apparently. I have never seen him so animated. He actually said he thought that the countryside might finally make sense to him.'

'And that surprised you?'

'Well, it's such a narrow representation of the countryside, isn't it? One wood that a mathematician had a bit of fun with thirty years ago? It hardly feels like Danny is embracing the true breadth and bounty of nature.'

Diana was quiet for a moment before asking, 'Are you in danger of wanting him to experience the countryside through your eyes, not his? Beauty is subjective, you must allow him to find its allure for himself.'

Sam nodded. 'You're probably right, but I realised how different we were, in that wood, we're polar opposites. He couldn't have been more excited to find that order, it was a homecoming for him. In the meantime, I am most at home *here*, in the chaos of it all. I realised, to my shame, that he had probably found it harder moving here than I'd ever made allowances for. I've been so wrapped up in my own world, I've barely given his response a second thought. And yet he's always thinking of me. Gosh, I can be incredibly self-centred sometimes. I won't even let him cut the grass at home, which is all he really wanted to do.'

'Perhaps next time your husband is feeling frightened by the wildness of the countryside, mention Fibonacci,' Diana said, mysteriously.

'Fibonacci?'

'Your husband will know him, I expect,' Diana continued kindly. 'Go easy on yourself, Sam. You're preoccupied, not self-centred.'

'You're right. I am.' Sam threw a cone into the fire and watched it flare, its resin fuelling the flame. 'My mind is so full, all the time. I have so much to process but Danny and I don't really talk. Not about the things that matter. But it's a hard habit to break. If you've grown up being taught to subsume your feelings in order to reflect well on your parents, you soon learn to hide it all. If only my mother had taught me to yell out loud on a stormy night, I might not have retained so much resentment. It's all there, somewhere, still inside me. I fear it's sitting where my womb was. I haven't ever found a way to expel it. And I am beginning to worry that Danny's just the same. He's had to deal with so much sadness already and I always thought it was such a credit to him that he was able to carry on with this indefatigable strength. He has this inner force, propelling him ever onwards and upwards but now, I wonder... '

'If he's dealt with it?'

'Exactly. Perhaps his sadness is sitting somewhere deep inside him too.'

'So perhaps you're not polar opposites?'

'No, I think we might be as different as we are the same.'

'Do you think it's time for both of you to yell out loud on a stormy night?' suggested Diana, kindly.

Diana prodded the fire and dropped a number of pine cones into the flames. The flames leapt high, engulfing the pine cones and the surrounding timber. A spiral of steam escaped from the spout of the kettle. It seized the wood smoke and the dust and there they all danced unabashedly in the spotlight of sunshine for their audience of two.

Chapter 43

Sam wanted to talk to Danny about their differences but she couldn't find the words. Without meaning to, she found herself once again turning to her blog for solace and conversation and there, the words arrived unbidden. She had been writing, uninterrupted, for about an hour. Her fingers were flying across the keyboard and she'd been mouthing the words to herself as she typed, as if she were dictating out loud although her fingers moved almost quicker than her brain. She was trying to temper her anger, to retreat from the fury, but it was hard. Her readers were still commenting on her last post, pestering her, poking her, nagging her for more. She tried to block them out and focus instead on some of the things she'd learnt from the woods. The words toyed with her, as if appearing in her peripheral vision, and she wrote furiously before they escaped her sight altogether.

She was angry with her mother. It needed to pass. And in order to allow it to pass, she needed to give it voice. She needed to find a way to express this anger, in order to quell it. She blocked all extraneous noise out and focussed in, realising as she wrote that of course she mustn't temper it, she must tease it out. As she wrote, she wondered if she'd find the courage to write this next piece under her own name.

Since moving to Broome Cottage, Danny had taken to removing his shoes when he came into the house, so she simply hadn't heard him climb the stairs swiftly, two treads at a time, and he was standing over her before she'd had time to log out or shut down the laptop.

'Hello, my love. Glad to see you're writing. Let me have a peek?' He put a hand on each of her shoulders and dropped his head down parallel with her own to look at the screen.

Sam could feel the colour rise in her cheeks and she leant forward, tipping the screen down a few inches and mumbling apologetically, 'It's really nothing yet, I'd much rather you didn't.'

'Oh come on, Sam. Let me be that person for you, the person that reads your first drafts and gives you the encouragement you need. I'm your biggest fan.' He nuzzled into her further and playfully motioned to open the laptop screen up again.

'No, Danny.' Sam snapped, closing her laptop completely. She swung around, surprising him. 'You can't.' The laptop was closed but it was still logged on. Behind her, it buzzed a couple of times. There was a pause before it buzzed again, three more times in quick succession.

'What are you up to?' he asked, his suspicion only aroused by her secrecy.

'Just answering email,' she said, opening her eyes as wide as she could, hoping her challenge would cow him. Her laptop buzzed again a couple more times and the constant nagging of the machine was now impossible to ignore.

'Who gets that many emails?' said Danny, genuinely curious and with such great faith in his wife that, expecting nothing remotely nefarious, he pushed open the lid and watched in awe as the notifications in the top right corner delivered message after message. His eyes swept to the Word document that occupied most of the screen and he started reading.

'Sam?' he said, confused now. She pushed her chair back and left the room.

Danny continued to read.

Much later, he came downstairs. Sam had made some soup and it was now bubbling on the stove. She had laid the table and was sitting at it, staring into space. Danny drew up another chair at the table.

'What *was* that you were writing?'

Sam said nothing. She didn't know where to begin.

'There's so much you haven't been telling me, Sam. I thought you were writing fiction and then I read on and realised you were publishing your feelings, your very most private thoughts. I cannot tell you how useless that makes me feel. If you had secrets to share, I could have been there for you. I *should* have been there for you.'

'You were there for me when it counted, Danny. You were there for me when I was ill. But you didn't have to keep being there for me. At some point I had to take responsibility for my own recovery and I'm not quite sure how it happened but writing that blog was part of that.'

'That was a blog. Open to the public. Anyone could read it?'

Sam looked apologetic. 'Yes.'

'And it looks like people *were* reading it.'

'Yes. In their thousands. Tens of thousands.'

'Anyone we know?'

'I somehow doubt it, Danny. And I didn't use my own name to write it.'

'Oh. That makes it better.' There was a question mark in his voice, as if he wasn't sure if that were true.

'I'm sorry, Danny.'

'But I don't understand why you hid it from me, Sam? I assume you were writing your true feelings… but, all that… all that *anger*.'

'Pretty much my true feelings, yes. But maybe I dramatised it a bit for effect. The angrier I was, the more attention my blog got. And don't get me wrong, I was angry. I'm *still* angry.'

'I had no idea. I always thought you dealt with it so well. You were such a brick. I wish you'd told me. I feel so stupid.'

Sam, who already felt a little liberated by the revelation, tried to explain her actions. 'But you're so together, so on it, Danny. I didn't want you to think you had a weak wife. I wanted you to think of me as happy and carefree, not demonic.'

Sam thought about the words Danny would have read in that blog. The anger and disgust she'd discharged into the world, her utter contempt for not just the mothers who had judged her, but for all mothers. The mothers she hadn't met, the mothers with the power to heal her, her own mother, and all the mothers before them. There was no woman that she hadn't expressed revulsion for.

'How much of it did you really mean?' he asked.

'Of the words I wrote?' She thought about it, trying to imagine the words, all of the words and failing dismally to recall anything much more than her most recent post. 'Some. Not all. Definitely not all.'

'Fifty per cent? Less? More?'

Sam laughed hollowly at Danny's predictable requirement to quantify the hatred. 'I can't put a number on my anger, Danny. I can't fit my emotional range into a spreadsheet for you, my love, as much as you'd like me to. I don't know. The anger was there – is there. I'm still angry. But some of it wasn't me. Some of it was Libby.'

'Libby? That's the name you write under? A pen name?' he asked, now recognising it from the blog title.

'Yes and no. A pen name but she began her life as a real person. Libby was in my English class at uni. You met her, I think. Liberty?'

'I don't remember her. I only had eyes for one English student. I didn't really fraternise with the humanities lot.'

Sam smiled, remembering the humourless and staid young maths student who followed her around devotedly until, one day, she fell into step with him and they were never really apart again. 'I'm sure you'd remember her if you thought about it. She was an activist if you can call a first-year student that. Passionate. Vehement. She was so driven and so *just* and so consistently *right*. She never let anything go by in class. She was sort of a bit of a joke actually, because she was poised to correct us all at any given moment, but I think everyone secretly admired her too because she was just never afraid to call it. A visiting lecturer said something vaguely sexist, she'd call it. A fellow student casually offended a minority, she'd call it. She was way ahead of her time – or certainly ahead of me. I felt that Libby was the last hope for womankind, that she'd fly the flag so the rest of us didn't have to. Lazy, I know, but those fights weren't for people like me. I wasn't going to interrupt a professor to campaign for non-gendered toilets at university. I wanted all those things to happen, believe me, I really did, but I kind of thought that those issues were on Libby's desk not mine. She was obsessed with Radclyffe Hall, I remember.'

'Who's he?' asked Danny, genuinely interested.

Sam glanced up at her husband to see if he was joking. She shook her head, exasperated. 'She! Who was *she*! God. Poor old Libby, that was what she was up against all the time. I never had her energy to constantly admonish, chide, correct. You'd be lucky to get an eye roll from me.' Sam rolled her eyes and looked devastated by her own apathy.

'What became of her? Did you stay in touch?'

'God, no. I honestly don't know what became of her. She didn't come back after the first year. I think something awful must have happened. She cared so deeply, had so many feelings that could have toppled her at any moment so when she didn't return I couldn't help myself imagining some grisly finale at Beachy Head because of an injustice served by one underclass or another. I never did find out though.'

'But I am still not sure where she fits into your life now? To this blog. Is that her or you?'

'I borrowed her identity and gave her a new life. I stole it really. I had a picture of her from that time Simon Armitage visited university.'

'Who's she?' quipped Danny.

Sam looked up sharply and saw he was joking. 'Funny. No really, that was actually quite funny.' She paused, recalling the visit. 'We had a group picture taken with all of us. I Photoshopped a hat on to her so she wasn't really identifiable. You can only see a bit of one eye and her hair falls around her face.'

'That's the woman in a hat on the blog,' said Danny, sounding pleased to be piecing things together but still anxious about the outcome.

'Yes, that's a little bit of Libby's face under Radclyffe Hall's hat. I know, I know, childish really. Anyway, once I'd created this identity, I started blogging. There was no way I could have said half of that under my own name. I'm far too much of a coward and the truth is, I wouldn't have wanted to do anything that might damage you or your career. I can't imagine that your bosses would approve if they found out you had a ranting, angry, feminist wife inciting an uprising amongst downtrodden women around the world.'

'And that's what you were doing. That's your writing.'

'Yes. But semi-fictionally. That is, I wondered what Libby would say and then I removed any filters, any capacity for intellectual reason and then spouted it out into cyberspace. I tagged a bunch of feminist blogsites and made sure I tagged a few outspoken right-wing nutters and some pretty vitriolic Christians too. And then I'd stand back and let them fight it out in the comments. It wasn't anything particularly clever or original that I wrote, it was the readers that gave my blog traction. All I had to do was pose a leading question, disguise it as an opinion, and then I'd let them get at me and each other. It was amazingly powerful.'

'What sort of questions?'

'Well, now you know what I've been up to, you can go back

and read them all if you must. But I suppose I wrote about anything that upset me. It started soon after I went back to work. All those women who I thought were my friends, they turned out to be so incredibly judgemental. I didn't fit into their friendship group once I'd had my op and they just *dropped* me. That's what started it off. But after that, anything could trigger it. I'd hear a really obnoxious comment on the tube or at work or somebody would patronise me and I'd just focus all my spleen on them. It was weirdly therapeutic.'

'It was?' Danny looked genuinely interested in an idea that losing control, any control, might have a benefit when he'd worked so hard all his life to do just the opposite – to use control to keep a lid on the stuff that might yet come out. He and his wife were opposites, he now realised. 'Did you hate me? Did you write any posts about me?'

'You didn't exist, Danny. Sorry. I don't think Libby would have had any credibility at all if she'd had a loving husband at work supporting her while she stoked her revolution. I am afraid I just wrote you out of the picture.'

'Cheers,' said Danny, hiding his hurt with some flippancy he didn't really feel. 'So, Libby was single.'

'God yes! She'd voluntarily removed her ovaries to free herself up from the confines of maternal responsibility.'

'Wow. That's harsh. Can you actually do that? I mean, it's not really like having your tonsils out, is it?'

'I don't know, but I really sincerely doubt it. But I don't think I ever actually said that in the blog. I just gave that to her in my own backstory. I had to create a character that I absolutely believed in and who absolutely believed in her own doctrine and then it was easy to let her say what she felt she had to say. She always had something to say – it was astonishing really.'

'You're talking about her in the past tense,' observed Danny.

Sam looked up at Danny accusingly. 'Well, I can't exactly carry on with her, can I? She existed in my mind and now she's here, sitting between us at the table, she can't exist. She's not real enough anymore, she lacks conviction. And she can hardly be fervid while she's married to you,' Sam snarled a bit, as if it were all Danny's fault. 'She can't plausibly have an *opinion* now, can she?'

Danny dropped his voice to something just above a whisper. 'I actually hate opinions, Sam.'

Sam was silenced for a moment. This was new information. There was nothing much Danny hated, other than eggs, satsumas and mess. 'All opinions?' she asked, puzzled.

'Yes.' He nodded seriously. 'I mean, apart from yours. I value your opinions. I don't always understand them, but I do try to listen to them and to try to interpret what you mean by them. But people at work with opinions, they just about kill me.'

'Oh my love,' said Sam, remembering that none of this was really Danny's fault. 'Nothing could kill you. You're such a *coper*. You just get on with everything so brilliantly. Look at how you're dealing with me now. I'm a complete mess, I'm a tangle of cheap coat hangers, so simple in their design, but so complicatedly entwined once you try to get in there and pull the individual components apart.'

'And I hate metal coat hangers too,' added Danny, for clarity.

'I know you do!' said Sam, adding this to the list of things she knew Danny hated: mess, eggs, satsumas, opinions and coat hangers. 'Why do you think we don't have any in the house? I get your dry-cleaning home and I transfer your suits on to wooden coat hangers. I am exceedingly good to you at times. I try to shield you from all the stuff that you shouldn't have to cope with.'

'You're amazing,' Danny agreed.

Sam was embarrassed now by the paltry deed. 'I don't think that's amazing. That's just a tiny act of love and respect for what you can and can't cope with.'

Danny sighed, as if he couldn't cope with very much at all. 'So, what else haven't you been telling me, other than your intense relationship with thousands of fans that read your blog that I didn't know existed.'

Sam looked at him. His shoulders were hunched with hurt. It was now though, that she had to share everything she could with him. If she could bundle everything into one tidy knapsack of misinformation, she wouldn't have to drip-feed it and he wouldn't have to confront her dishonesty again. She paused.

'I don't actually have any friends here.'

'You don't? Hattie and Anne? They don't exist?'

'They exist, but they're not friends. Hattie is the sort of woman that drives me to write my blog. She couldn't be friends with somebody like me, I'm not her type. And Anne, she's just a bitter old cow really. She's where I'm going to end up if I'm not careful.'

'And what about the other one, you had a third friend, didn't you?'

'Diana? She's real. And I hope she's a friend. We may even be very alike. If she is who she says she is.'

'But you're not always who you say you are.'

Sam looked at her husband sadly. 'That's true, I'm not. I'm sometimes me and I'm sometimes Libby and I'm always a bit of a confusion. I'm dishonest with myself but then, I think so is Diana. She says she's not a witch. But I think she might be. If she is a witch, she's not a bad witch. She lives in the woods. She's been healing me.'

Danny recoiled melodramatically. 'Now I actually think you are crazy. That other thing? That thing where you adopted the persona of an old friend and wrote caustic articles about women without telling me? That's fine. I'm good with that. But a *witch* in the *woods*?'

'Really. Diana might actually be a witch. She lives in a grubby old caravan in the middle of the wood, under a bit of mouldy old tarp and the caravan looks like it is half fungus, but inside it actually feels more like a luxury bijou apartment. I met her when I thought she was offering to kill my enemies.'

'Don't talk to mad old witches in the woods, Sam, you can't do that!'

Sam laughed at the passion in his voice. 'You don't believe in witches! That's *me*. You're the one whose job it is to tell me there's no such thing as witches and to pull myself together.'

Danny took Sam's hands into his own. 'I am frightened of witches. Genuinely.'

Sam snorted. 'You're the one being silly now. You've never given witches a moment's thought until now.'

Sam's blog, the sheer weight of those unspoken words, had given Danny some courage. She had all these feelings that she'd not dared to express. And so did he. He bounced Sam's hands on the table to emphasise just how much thought he had given witches. 'But I have! I always thought my grandmother was a witch. I had to go and stay with her every time my mother was ill, which increasingly became the dominant part of my childhood. My grandmother absolutely terrified me. She was always stirring a big pot of something at the stove, and yet it never seemed to materialise into anything good to eat. I tried to look inside the pot sometimes, but she'd send me flying across the kitchen if I went close.'

'Really?'

'Yes really, she'd push me away. But she didn't need to physically push me, it felt like the sheer force of her displeasure was more than enough to repel me. She'd put her hand up to stop me coming close and I'd feel like she'd pitched me across the kitchen with just her mind.'

'My love. You've never told me any of this. That does sound awful.'

Danny nodded. 'It was awful. My mother was so *soft*. She smelt of talc and starched linen and she wore silk with these delicate lace edges and I'd climb into bed with her if she was well enough and I'd bury my face into her neck to smell her skin. It was so smooth, even when she was really thin. Her arms were the softest thing I knew, and I can still feel the touch of her lips on my forehead. She gave the lightest, driest, kindest kisses.'

Sam felt her eyes filling up. She found it hard to be soft and kind. She was often far too brittle and harsh. 'I'm so sorry you lost her, Danny.'

Danny nodded at the memory of his mother and then

quickly shook his head. 'But her mum? Jesus. There was nothing soft about her. I swear she had hairs growing out of warts on her chin.'

Sam laughed. 'You're making that up.'

'Oh, almost certainly. I had some terrifying picture books in my bedroom in her house. *Grimms' Fairy Tales*, I think. *Hansel and Gretel, Rapunzel, Red Riding Hood*. God! *Red Riding Hood*. What was she thinking? I think the images from those books and the reality of my grandmother merged into one ghastly memory. And I expect I probably blamed my grandmother for keeping me from my mother. My grandmother was never kind. She never took me on her knee or told me it would be OK. She never told me my mum would get better.'

Sam tried to imagine Danny's childhood. 'She was probably hurting too. No mother likes to see their own child get ill.' She thought of her own mother standing out of reach by her bed when Sam had been in hospital but shook away the image, banishing it for another time.

Danny shrugged. 'That's true, I suppose. But it wasn't really my job to empathise with my grandmother. I was six or seven, for God's sake. And she always made it very clear that she hated my father.'

'That's tough too. Do you know why?'

'Because my mum turned to him when she got poorly. She only wanted to be with him. And with me of course, when she could. But Mum didn't like me to go in to see her at hospital. I only saw her each time she came home and that became less and less frequent.'

'I wish I'd known all of this, Danny. You were so great

to me when I was ill, but I never stopped to think what memories it might be bringing back. You should have told me this right at the beginning, it would have helped me understand you.'

'But then you wouldn't have married me. I wanted you to marry a strong supportive man who could look after you, not a jangling mess of nerves. You were way out of my league as it was.'

'You are a strong, supportive man but you've got your foibles too. You don't let them show too often but you should, it's attractive, I promise you.' She squeezed his hand across the table.

'But don't get ensnared by a witch, Sam. Promise me?'

'I can't promise you that, and she's really not a witch, Danny. I used that facetiously. She is just a lonely old woman in the woods.'

Chapter 44

Danny and Sam had been lying in the dark silently musing on their own separate worries when the storm began. It started without warning, a sudden, vertical deluge of rain that hit the roof of the cottage with astonishing force before the wind picked up and began to pummel the house relentlessly from every direction. Danny ran through a mental register of threat and jeopardy, picturing the guttering, the fencing and the roof and reassuring himself that all risks had been mitigated where possible.

'Five hundred pounds,' he said, into the darkness, over the sound of the wind.

'What's five hundred pounds?' Sam asked, who had been listening intently to the trees, straining to hear any sounds the screaming gale might be swallowing.

'The excess on our buildings insurance. Isn't that what you asked me?'

'I didn't say anything!' she said.

'Oh, it must have been the wind.'

'Typical you, Danny. The wind is choosing to talk to you about insurance.' She laughed, but half-heartedly. She too was hearing things in the wind and was resenting the noise of her own voice which was stopping her concentrating. She was sure she had heard a howl.

'It's getting louder.'

'Shhh. I'm listening,' Sam said, feeling an unanchored anxiety building in her stomach.

'Sorry,' said Danny but as he spoke a large crack pierced his words and the room lit up for a second. 'Jesus,' he said. 'That was close.'

Outside something snapped, a sickening wrench, the splitting of something solid.

'Oh God,' said Sam, leaping out of bed. She fumbled in the dark and threw some tracksuit bottoms and a jumper on before saying, 'I've got to go out there.'

Danny followed, putting a jumper on over his pyjama bottoms and hurrying after his wife.

'Where are we going? What are we doing?' He could now think of a number of loose items that could do with being secured. The bins for instance. And the garden furniture. He was sure it was securely stowed but he wouldn't mind checking. His mind raced, imagining heavy forms coming loose and hurtling towards the windows of Broome Cottage.

'Stay here. I'll be right back,' Sam said, grabbing an anorak.

Danny ignored her and when he called out, a little hesitantly, 'Wait for me,' she ignored him. He grabbed an umbrella but as soon as he followed Sam outside he realised how futile it was and he threw it back into the porch, where, possessed by the wind, it jumped and twisted and hurled itself into the garden, stopping and starting and disappearing into the darkness.

'Where are we going?' Danny called.

'I have to check on Diana, the woman in the woods. I heard something fall, a tree maybe.'

'You're... ' He panted as he jogged to keep up with her fast stride. 'You're doing no such thing!' His voice rose to a high pitch, but it failed to carry against the building noise of the storm. Another large crash exploded above them as Sam reached the gate and they both instinctively crouched down. Danny reached forward and pulled Sam's hood tight over her face. 'I'm coming with you.'

As they reached the path they slowed down. They were each armed with the torch from their phone only – usually so bright but now so dismally underwhelming. Each torch picked out just a small spot of wet ground in front of them.

'This way,' said Sam and she dived off left down the narrow path that led towards the caravan.

'This is such a bad idea. We're pretty much about to die,' said Danny, desperate to lead but only capable of following closely behind Sam. He held his torch up high, shining the thin beam ahead of her, picking up the glistening leaves all around them.

Sam had slowed down and was now walking less confi- dently. She turned inwards to the thickest section of the wood and swiped her phone left and right, sending the narrow beam of light erratically from side to side, which returned only glimpses of leaves and brambles as she searched for her usual passageway into the briar. Turning her torch off she instructed Danny to do the same and waited for her eyes to adjust, hoping to see the glow of the caravan, a light or a lantern, any sort of beacon to draw her towards Diana. There was nothing. It was pitch black. Around them they could feel falling debris, as leaves and twigs hit the ground. Heavier branches swayed above their heads, threatening to follow suit. Sam switched her torch back on and walked on further, sweeping the light from side to side.

Her torchlight caught the bare stems of some thin hazel trees that swayed loosely in unison. Suddenly confident, Sam dived in between these boughs, pushing herself through a slim gap into the opening beyond. Danny caught a glimpse of her anorak shining in the rain as she was swallowed by the trees and he called to her just as she shouted out to Diana. Completely obscured before, the caravan was now easy to spot, its large frame solid and still amongst the dancing limbs.

'Diana!' Sam called loudly, competing with the shrieking wind.

'Sam, this is way out of my comfort zone,' called Danny behind her anxiously. Sam laughed, finding hilarity in the moment. Despite her urgency, the irony was not lost on her that she would choose this moment, with the wind raging around them and trees promising imminent collapse, to introduce Danny to the woods, to Diana and to the reality of witches.

Sam banged on the door and pulled it open, calling as she entered and using her torch to pick out the interior. The wind caught the door behind her, banging it loudly against the side of the caravan. The bed was unmade but empty and Diana was nowhere to be seen.

'She's not here.'

'Good?' said Danny, uncertain of why they were here.

'Good, I guess, in that the caravan isn't squashed under

a fallen tree which is what I was expecting to see. But not good in that I have no idea where she is, and I hate the thought of her being out there tonight.'

'Perhaps she's moved somewhere safer than a forest in a thunderstorm?' said Danny, hopefully, quickly following his concern up with a more selfishly motivated question, 'Can we go? This place is giving me the creeps.'

'Sure. Let's go.'

Sam shut the caravan door behind her but didn't speak all the way home. The rain continued to fall and the trees continued to hurl twigs and leaves at the bedraggled walkers but they made their way back steadily, picking their way carefully as they followed the path back to the warmth and safety of Broome Cottage. The storm was no longer directly above them, the thunder and lightning were now several seconds apart, but the wind was still screaming through the trees and closing the door of the cottage on the noise and the bluster brought silence crashing between them.

'I'm worried sick about her.'

'She'll be fine. She's a… she's a… ' Danny wasn't really sure what she was. 'She's an outdoor person, isn't she?' he tried helpfully. 'She's probably better equipped to deal with a storm than you or me. Certainly me. That was the most dangerous thing I've ever done.'

'Really?' Sam had taken her anorak off and was now drying her face with a towel. She looked at her husband who was still standing in his wet coat as if in shock. Drops of water were beginning to pool on the tiled floor around him.

'Yes really. I spend my whole life mitigating risk. It's what I do. What I don't do is go into woods during gale-force winds. What I don't do is enter strange caravans in the middle of the night. What I don't do is chase witches around the countryside.'

'Get your wet stuff off. I'll chuck it in the dryer. And I'll make us a hot drink before we go back to bed. And I don't think it was a gale-force wind. And she's not a witch.' All of this was said over Sam's shoulder as she disappeared into the kitchen, her wet socks leaving damp marks across the kitchen floor.

'Still. It was risky.'

'And you survived.'

'Changes my risk profile though.'

'It doesn't change anything, does it?'

'I'm now *that* person, the person that runs into a stormy wood despite the lightning, despite the thunder and with logs crashing all around us.'

'I think it was just a twig or two.'

'You were scared too. Don't tell me you weren't scared.'

'I was scared. Am still scared. For Diana. Not for you or me.'

'Anyway, I'm now officially an irrational person. I should pay more for life insurance.'

'Well, I won't tell them if you don't.'

'Deal.' Danny smiled.

Sam poured boiling water into two cups and slid one towards Danny.

'Thanks for coming with me.'

'Pleasure. She'll be fine. I'm sure she's fine.'

'Diana is fantastically sensible. I mean, living in the middle of a wood in a caravan doesn't sound sensible, but she's clever and wise. She knows what she's doing. She must have known the storm was coming and she'll have gone elsewhere. She has a friend who lives close by, I expect she's gone there. But I just hope she got there OK.'

'Well, of course that's what she will have done.'

'It's just… Her bed was unmade. I've never seen the caravan anything other than immaculate. She definitely left in a hurry.'

'How well do you know this woman?'

'It's hard to say. She's difficult to know well, she's ephemeral. I've been spending a bit of time with her recently. She's the first person I've ever been able to talk to about anything.'

'What are you talking about?'

'Everything. Nothing. I'm probably doing more listening than talking but I'm finding the companionship a relief. The sound of another voice that's not the voices in my head. I had no idea how much I needed someone.'

'You've got me, Sam. Am I not enough for you?' Danny sounded hurt.

'No!' Sam said, her voice higher than she meant. 'We don't talk, Danny, we stopped talking after my surgery. It's like the doctors removed both our voice boxes when they removed my womb.'

Danny wanted to protest, but he couldn't even find the words for that. He picked up their cups and took them to the sink to rinse. The storm was subsiding now but the noise of the wind in the trees had been replaced by the howling of unheard words in his ears. It was true. They didn't talk. He took a deep breath before turning to face Sam.

'Go and find her in the morning. I'll take the morning off work and come and look with you if you're really worried.'

'You'd take the… No, sorry, I misheard you. I thought you said you'd take the morning off work. I must be tired and emotional.'

'Just because it hasn't happened before… '

'I'll be fine. But, you know, Danny, I count on you to be you. Now you're irrational, don't start getting weird on me. There's actuary-wizardry to be done tomorrow, it can't all come to a crashing end because of a stormy night.'

'That's true. There are risk profiles to be modelled and outcomes to be ascertained.'

'Spoken like a true actuary.' Danny stepped towards Sam and pulled her into his arms. He kissed the top of her head.

'I'm still the same, sensible guy but I know a bit more about me now.'

'You do?'

'Yes, I'd follow you to the ends of the earth, I'd be irrational for you. And risk profile be damned.'

Sam laughed. 'That's the sweetest thing you've ever said.'

Chapter 45

Sam left her garden and walked down the path. Debris from the storm littered the pathway and occasionally she stopped to move larger bits of wood to one side. The air smelt clean after the storm and the birds were singing loudly in celebration of another day. Sam walked past the turning to the caravan and carried quickly on, and she ignored the stile that would take her into the big field, too.

She rang on the doorbell of Willow's Fortune as she had done before. She hoped Rebecca would open the door, or perhaps Diana, but once again the young housekeeper was there, standing silently and staring at her.

'Is Rebecca in?'

'No, she's at work.' The housekeeper waited, paused, more cautious now this neighbour knew her boss's name.

'Did she have a visitor last night? Diana? Is she here?'

'No, she didn't have a visitor. Is there something I can help you with?'

Sam gave her a half-smile, resigned to the fact that she was about to be turned away again. 'May I come in and talk to you for a moment?'

The woman looked puzzled. 'Talk to me?'

'Do you mind?'

The woman shrugged and, much to Sam's surprise, motioned for Sam to come in. Sam stepped into a large hallway with pale walls, a shining mahogany table and a richly coloured rug, Persian perhaps. She followed the young woman through to the vast kitchen. Each surface was empty and gleaming as if it had just been cleaned. It smelt of coffee.

'I'm Sam,' Sam said. 'I live over there,' she explained, pointing vaguely through the window and out beyond the big sweep of lawn. 'I sometimes walk the path on the other side of your garden, so I thought I'd come and introduce myself.'

'I'm Hope,' said Hope, not offering Sam a seat. 'You'll have to make this quick. I should get back to work,' continued Hope, gesturing to the immaculate kitchen around her.

'I can see you've got a lot to get done,' laughed Sam. 'What time does Rebecca get home usually? I'd like to meet her, I've heard a lot about her.'

'After me, but I clock off at six. I don't live here. I never cross paths with her.'

Sam looked around for signs of life. No pictures, no personal trappings, no paperwork. None of the normal clues to personality. It didn't really look like anyone lived there.

'You missed quite a storm last night,' said Sam.

Hope smiled politely but Sam knew she couldn't stand in this kitchen making polite conversation for much longer.

'And Rebecca definitely didn't have a visitor last night?'

'No. I would know if the spare room had been used.' Hope looked crossly at Sam, worrying she was being asked to betray her employer.

'It's just… ' Sam hesitated. 'A good friend of mine comes and stays here from time to time. I think she might have come last night. I thought I might catch her here. I was worried about her after the storm.'

'Rebecca did not have a visitor last night. She is very busy, she travels a lot. She rarely stays here herself. I barely see her so I don't think she'd have time for visitors.' Hope sat down at the table heavily and looked up at Sam. Sam looked at her, puzzled, and pulled a chair out for herself. Sam recognised that look. Hope was longing to talk.

'You must get a bit lonely here.'

'It's quiet yes, but it's not too bad. It's not the loneliness that gets me. It's the futility of it all. I don't know what I'm doing here. I have a job to do, to keep this house, but it is ludicrous. There's nothing to do. When I got in this morning and saw that Rebecca had been I was actually excited to make the bed.'

Sam held her silence, letting Hope speak.

'Most of the time she barely leaves a trace. I only know she's been because she leaves a shopping list. She drinks a lot of coffee. She uses a lot of notebooks. She gets through an unbelievable amount of bedlinen considering she's barely here. But that's all I know about her. She'll realise I don't do much soon and fire me. I won't even mind. I would fire me if I were her.' Hope laughed.

Sam laughed too, but her eyes were sad and puzzled as she looked around the big cool kitchen, inhaling the scent of good Italian coffee which lingered, caught amongst the clean scent of talcum powder and the familiar scent of expensive perfume, painting a vivid picture of the person who lived there.

Chapter 46

Sam had bought a package of bacon from the butcher's and it was now sizzling noisily on a heavy cast iron frying pan over a small fire in the clearing outside the caravan. Both Sam and Diana had been sitting quietly, taking it in turns, entirely spontaneously, to stoke the fire or turn the bacon as it spat busily in its own fat. As idyllic as the scene might have appeared to a passerby, the silence was neither satisfactory nor companionable. Eventually, as the bacon began to crisp and brown and the scent called out to them, Diana broke the impasse.

'Diana's not my real name.'

'No, I figured that out myself. You're Rebecca, aren't you?'

Diana winced and looked sharply at Sam. 'I *was* Rebecca. I became Diana when I came to the woods. I left *Rebecca* behind.'

As she spoke, Diana observed Sam's face which remained passive. Her indifference gave Diana courage. 'Though that's not strictly true. Originally, when I first arrived here I had much grander ideas for my reinvention. For a while, I was to be Artemis. *Artemis!* Can you imagine?' She laughed at herself before continuing.

'I had a far-fetched notion that I may be able to begin my life over, wiping out everything that had happened before and starting with a rebirth of sorts. If I was to be reborn then I could take a new name. Not a disguise, you understand, but a whole new *being*. A new *life*.' Diana smiled at the memory, mocking herself with an empty laugh. 'I called myself Artemis for a number of days, but it didn't stick. I admired Artemis. I wanted to *be* Artemis – but her responsibilities were simply too great for me.'

Sam had sliced a white loaf and was now toasting the bread piece by piece on some hot embers she'd scraped towards her for the purpose. 'Funny. I always thought Artemis was a boy. Not that it matters of course. If you're going for a whole new life you can start again in any guise, I suppose.'

'That's true, of course, but choosing to be a man would have been an admission of defeat. It is so much harder to be a woman, don't you think? And having failed so spectacularly once, I felt I owed it to myself to try again. Regardless, Artemis was a girl. In mythology she was the Mistress of the Animals. I think I could have borne those duties reasonably well, but Artemis was a bit more of a polymath than me, an all-rounder. If you want my opinion, her remit was probably a bit too broad. But perhaps in a steep hierarchical order the top tier will always assume they are the only ones capable of vast responsibility, and there's no greater example of hierarchy than God's. "You, you and you, you can be my disciples." Which means you follow me and do as I do. Not exactly egalitarian, is it… ?' Diana drifted off and looked at the bacon and then Sam with equal intensity.

'Where was I?'

'Artemis I think...' Sam said, hesitantly, though in truth, Sam was struggling to follow Diana whose eyes had been darting all around her as if the answers were leading her to them without needing to voice the questions.

'Artemis indeed. When I first came here I was a bit like her. I thought I might be able to do it all, reign supreme in my own little kingdom, but even within this small realm I quickly realised I needed to specialise.'

'What else was she goddess of, this Artemis? I bet there's nothing much that she could do that you couldn't do, if you put your mind to it.' Sam looked around her, at the little glade they were cooking in, the bucolic haven Diana had built out of nothing more than a messy head and a need to abscond.

'Technically I probably shared a few of her skills, but I found her multifarious roles to be just a bit contradictory. She was goddess of animals, yes, but also the *hunt* – and that feels like a conflict of interest. I'm not averse to bagging myself a rabbit for the pot, but a hunt always feels so merciless, the odds seem stacked against the *hunted*. And on top of that, she was both goddess of childbirth *and* virginity which again seems incompatible. Childbirth *and* virginity? If you're looking after one, then you took your eye of the ball on the other. Bit like modern day politicians as far as I can see. An opinion on everything but a comprehension of nothing.'

Sam moved the bacon to the edge of the pan, to let it complete its cooking a bit more slowly. She leant back in her chair, allowing it to tip back fully until she was leaning against the beech tree behind her so that she could look up at the furthest leaves and their backdrop of grey sky. It was about to rain.

'Perhaps life was simpler then? Perhaps a goddess could preside over her domain and see the purpose of all of it, accepting all of those individual components without passing judgement. Virginity probably needed a goddess to a point and then, you know. Not so much. It's hardly a full-time job. And besides, you'd be an excellent goddess of childbirth. So would I. Better not to know too much probably. Goddess speaking, not practically speaking.'

Diana smiled. 'The *pansophist*. The general practitioner of deities.'

'Exactly.'

'And if I were Artemis, then do you know what that would make you?'

Sam closed her eyes tightly and rifled methodically through her entire education, beginning with the illustrated encyclopaedias of myths she devoured as a child and leafing through the pages of her brain in chronological order, desperately trying to find some nugget of intelligent response. She gave up and shook her head. 'I give up.'

'My *she-bear*.'

'I like the sound of that,' Sam said happily but felt the foreboding of Diana's silence in response, so allowed her chair to drop forwards so she could face her. 'Is that good?'

Diana shrugged. 'For the time being. It doesn't end so well.'

'Oh.'

'But that's fine. I'm not Artemis. I'm barely Diana. I should have taken the name Peg.'

'Peg?'

'A mythical old hag, "Churn Milk Peg". Lived in the

woods. Hung out in hazelnut thickets.' Diana motioned with her head to the hundreds of hazel stems surrounding the clearing. 'Peg's job was to stop children picking the unripe nuts. A nice, simple, well-defined role. I expect that, as crones in the woods go, she wasn't too bad. Unripe nuts give you stomach cramps so perhaps she was doing it to save the children some discomfort.'

'Or,' said Sam, 'she just really didn't like kids and didn't want to lose her hazelnut crop to them.'

'Sounds more likely, doesn't it?' agreed Diana. 'Churn Milk Peg doesn't sound like she got her name for being some sort of guardian angel.'

'Peg. I like it. And it suits you.' She looked at Diana's serious frown. 'I mean, so does Diana obviously.'

'The villagers see me as more of a Churn Milk Peg than a Diana, I fear.' Diana said this with a hint of pride. Sam studied her carefully while remembering the first time she'd been told about Diana. She'd been described as mad, a thief, perhaps even a witch. Somebody to fear and avoid.

Sam lifted the bacon off the pan and onto a tin plate. 'The bacon's done. Bacon butties are about thirty seconds off. I don't suppose you have tomato ketchup in the caravan, do you?'

Diana looked at Sam with a withering combination of contempt and outrage. 'Tomato ketchup? Are you *mad*?' Sam recoiled, embarrassed, and started to stammer an apology. It was hard to reconcile this erudite, capable woman with somebody who had reneged upon all modern comforts.

'I'm sorry, that was insensitive. Of course you don't.'

Diana tutted, exasperated. 'I expect I do, if you insist,

but brown sauce is far superior. Ketchup's for heathens in this scenario.' She pushed herself upright from her kneeling position and went to the caravan, returning with a couple of tin plates, some butter and a bottle of brown sauce.

Smiling to herself, Sam buttered the bread, and dropped the sizzling bacon on to it. 'Do you remember if you ever came across a villager called Bea Burdess?' Sam asked, feigning nonchalance.

Diana took a big bite of sandwich, chewing slowly and happily before answering. 'Absolutely. How could I forget her? I came across her far more than I'd have liked but I got rid of her eventually. That meddling fool in the village, she's always into everyone else's business.' Diana was about to take another bite of her sandwich but instead looked up sharply at Sam. 'Why? Did something happen to her?'

Sam eyed Diana carefully, looking for traces of knowledge. 'You didn't hear, did you?'

'Hear what?'

'She died,' said Sam, continuing with her matter of fact tone. 'A massive heart attack.'

Sam expected some sort of shocked reaction from Diana but instead Diana took a leisurely sip of tea, savouring it before responding. 'Well, that was a heart attack that was simply waiting to happen. No heart could sustain that amount of righteous indignation for very long without imploding.' Diana took another mouthful of bacon sandwich.

'They blamed you!' said Sam, apologetically, still looking at Diana carefully to gauge her reaction.

'Oh well, I was most certainly to blame then,' said Diana, rather too breezily.

'Did you *curse* her?'

'Curse her?' Diana laughed. 'Don't be ridiculous, of course I didn't *curse* her. I wouldn't know how to curse somebody if I wanted to. But I certainly got under her collar. That's for sure.'

Diana looked rather pleased at the memory, and Sam couldn't detect any outrage.

'What happened?'

'Gosh. It started a while back. She used to walk her dog on the path, which is fine. Really, I don't mind the dogs at all, but sometimes the dog *walkers* can be a bit of a nuisance. Her dog was a black Labrador, harmless enough, I think, though not particularly memorable. The owner, though, *Bea Burdess*. She was *memorable*. She had the most extraordinary habit. Her dog would do its business, and Bea would make a right old fuss of cleaning up after it, as if every other dog walker that didn't clean up their mess was a scourge on society. She'd do this loudly, commentating on her own actions as if she were the subject of an important nature documentary. She'd bundle the dog dirt into a little blue plastic bag. So far, quite normal, responsible dog owners are encouraged to do exactly that, I believe, and I don't have any problem with it. But then she'd leave the bag right here in the woods! Sometimes, she'd sort of make an effort to disguise it by hiding it under a few leaves but more often than not she'd tie it on to the fence post. Can you believe it? Why on earth would somebody do that? What goes through a mind that comes to the conclusion that parcelling up dog poop and hanging it on a fence post is rational or responsible? Apart from anything else, if she'd left the dog mess in the woods it would have disappeared in a matter of days. Instead, she took something that is biodegradable and turned it into something that was going to hang there looking just a little bit disgusting like some vile little faeces flag. People are *weird*, aren't they?'

'They are,' said Sam. She'd too noticed the little plastic bags dotting the countryside. They always made her think far more about the dogs and their owners than she wanted to.

'So, for a little while I just tidied up after her. It's not like the little blue beacons were hard to spot, you could see them a mile off. I'd pick them up with a stick and dispose of them. There's a bin for the purpose just where the footpath meets the road. Bea Burdess must have passed it every day. As caretaking jobs go, it wasn't pleasant, but it can't have been pleasant for other walkers to come across these little parcels either, so I was quite resigned to picking them up. But this carried on for a few weeks and it suddenly occurred to me that she wasn't really getting the message. Perhaps, worse, she was thinking that the poo bags were sort of magically decomposing overnight and that therefore her behaviour was exemplary. So, one day I decided to gather a whole week's worth. I strung them along the length of a stick and I walked them down to her house in the village.'

'You didn't!' said Sam, transfixed but gleefully horrified.

'I did. I rang her bell and she answered the door. Before she even saw what I was holding she looked at me like I was something the cat had brought in. Like I might bring down the value of her property just by walking up her garden path or something. And then when she saw what I was holding – honestly, her face was a picture. This was a while back, but I remember it like it were yesterday. I said to her very nicely,

303

very calmly, "I believe you might have left these behind, they are yours, aren't they?" And then I said, equally calmly, "You went to such great trouble to put them into these pretty blue bags that I imagine you must have left them accidentally, so I thought I would be a good neighbour and return them to you." I then tilted the stick and let them all sort of slide down on to her doorstep.' Diana grinned, looking absolutely delighted at the memory.

Sam burst out laughing. 'What did she do?'

'She screamed and said she was going to call the police. Which is laughable really, as there was nothing there on her doorstep that was any more disgusting than she'd left on the path. It was *her* dog poo, not *mine* so I don't really know what was quite so horrific about me returning it to her.'

Diana went quiet while she finished her sandwich before carrying on with the story. 'I didn't see much of her after that, but I knew what she was up to, and it was about then that she waged war on me.'

'What happened?'

'Just that; *war*. She began a campaign, a rather vicious campaign with the sole purpose of getting me evicted from here. She distributed a letter that said I was a menace to the village – I remember very distinctly that she called me a menace and a vagrant and she got everyone in the village to sign a petition to have me removed. I know because she put the petition through everyone's door – including Rebecca's so I saw it with my own eyes.'

'And did they sign the petition, the villagers?'

Diana looked at Sam sadly and shook her head. 'At the time there were 1,647 registered voters in the village.

And more than 1,400 names signed it! Can you believe she managed to engage with the villagers so emphatically? What a triumph that must have been, a landslide victory for Bea Burdess. She was very active in the village and she'd lived there for a long time, so I suppose it was a mark of her power and her influence, but still, it's quite hard to get people involved in activism. Even if people care about an issue, they won't necessarily put their name to it in case there are later ramifications or just because they don't quite feel strongly enough to take a position. And yet, there I was, minding my own business, living in the middle of the woods, doing absolutely no harm whatsoever and eighty-five per cent of the entire adult population cared strongly enough to sign a petition to get me moved from here.'

Sam tried to imagine herself in Bea's position. She had certainly enjoyed the feeling of influence that came with engaging with her audience, but she also knew she would never have to meet her readers, they existed in another paradigm altogether. She wasn't sure she would have the courage to take on such a local cause, where you might run in to your supporters or detractors every time you popped to the shops. Or maybe, Sam wondered, it wasn't courage but fear, sometimes the two were very hard to tell apart. 'Perhaps, Diana, she might have found the whole dog poo incident a bit threatening? I expect that gave her the motivation to get behind the campaign so effectively.'

'Oh, I have no doubt. But I bet she didn't come clean as to why I gave her that visit. I bet her petition failed to mention those little plastic-wrapped details.' Diana went quiet for a while and then nodded in agreement. 'I imagine she was mortified. If your whole purpose is to be righteously indignant, you don't want somebody pointing out your own bad habits. But even so, eighty-five per cent is pretty conclusive. At least there was no ambivalence. I do so hate ambivalence.'

Diana laughed and shook her head nostalgically, as if this unequivocal failure to get any support in the village was something to be proud of and then she continued, pragmatically. 'It wasn't a fair campaign. If we'd been head to head in a debate in the village hall and I'd had a chance to tell my story then I might have had a few more people on my side but she was on the council, so she had a huge advantage. She knew her way around the system and had it working for her. It was rather a shame she didn't use her power for something more useful, don't you think? Can you imagine how that sort of commitment could have moved things forward for the good of all – so misguided, poor old thing. I'm rather sorry to hear she dropped dead, I can only imagine what an extra few years would have done for her zeal.'

Sam looked around her admiringly. Both Diana and the caravan looked entrenched, welded to the earth by a combination of roots and gumption. 'But you're still here. That's the main thing. So, what happened to her petition? How on earth did you persuade them to let you stay?'

'Now let me get the chronology right. Let's see. The police came to see me here first of all, and I sent them away with a flea in their ear. That was a delightful moment.'

'Weren't you frightened? That must have been horrid. Didn't they have the power to move you?'

'No, not at all. Rather, it was a moment of watershed for me. Two policemen, sitting right in there, sitting at my table and listening to my side of the story for the first time. I felt *substantial*. And when I told them where I stood, legally speaking, my goodness, they really were very polite. We drank some coffee, we actually had a bit of a laugh about the whole thing. They promised to keep an eye out for me and they left. But before they went I made quite sure they knew of my rights under the privacy laws and made it absolutely clear they were not in a position to divulge the details of our conversation. I wasn't ready to share my legal position with all and sundry.'

'What was your legal position?'

'I'll come to that.'

'And was that the end of your run-in with Bea?'

'Not exactly. We met once more. She'd wound herself into a right old lather, I'm afraid. She went to the police to see *when* I was going to be removed from the woods, and they told her they had no grounds to evict me and sent her away. She had a bit of a tantrum, not quite used to not getting her own way, you can imagine how that happens with somebody as frequently *right* as Bea Burdess. I believe they then told her they'd arrest her for causing a nuisance.'

Diana looked into the distance, her blue eyes shining happily. 'Oh my, she was *incensed!*'

'Then what happened?' asked Sam, leaning forward in her chair now.

'What *was* her next move? Yes. That's right. She convened a special meeting of the council, to decide my fate. She hand-delivered a letter to tell me this was going to happen. She didn't have the courage to knock on my door, she just pinned it to a tree like I was some kind of outlaw.'

'Which you were, sort of,' said Sam, admiringly.

'I was nothing of the sort!'

'Well, knocking on your door wasn't easy. Look at it,' Sam said, gesturing to the thicket all around them.

'It was easier back then, I coppiced the hazel when I first arrived, so these trees have grown up around me in the last couple of years but back then there was nothing very much stopping her knocking on my door and talking to me like a reasonable human being. I read her notice and decided to pay her another visit.'

'Did you hurt her?'

'Of course not, but I wasn't a stranger to confrontational situations so I wore a body-cam.'

'A body-cam? Are you serious?'

'Absolutely. I didn't want her falsely accusing me of harassing her. I know how these things can escalate. I filmed the whole thing.'

'But, a body-cam? Where on earth did you get a body-cam?'

'I was somebody once, you know,' Diana said obliquely. 'I never had to use the footage, it was a straightforward enough exchange. But I have to admit that when I left her she was exceedingly upset. I remember her face, it was puce. She was so angry, she was spitting. I thought she might explode.'

'And apparently she did.'

'Yes, I'm sad to hear that, I must say, but that really was quite out of my control. I simply told her the truth.'

'Which was?'

'That she couldn't evict me, that these woods are mine. And that every time she comes to visit me and pins a notice on my trees she is trespassing.'

'The woods were yours?'

'The woods *are* mine.'

'You own them?'

'Yup. And quite a few of the surrounding fields too. Most of them. All of them by now perhaps. There's a public footpath that runs right past here, but every time you step off that path and wander through the woods, you are technically trespassing. If I were less neighbourly I'd put up signs telling people to keep their dogs on leads, but I don't really mind them having a nose around.'

Sam was still trying to digest the news. 'So you obviously couldn't be evicted from your own property. That was your legal case.'

'Exactly, it's not complex legal precedence. And I certainly wasn't breaking the law by living in a caravan. This woodland is attached to my main residence, Willow's Fortune. This caravan is technically just an outbuilding. Village life has got pretty draconian recently but there's no law against living in a caravan in your garden *yet*. Had I built a permanent home then somebody might have been able to report me for planning infringement but they couldn't even get me there. The caravan has been here for a while, it was once the home of the woodsman but of course that sort of job doesn't really exist anymore. I'm the woodsman these days. The caravan was already here when I bought the woods and had originally been installed with all the correct permissions in place and all I'd done is make some improvements internally so nobody had a leg to stand on.'

'No wonder she was angry. She must have been livid. But you could probably get planning permission now to live here permanently, couldn't you? I mean you could build something a bit more substantial surely? If you own the land?'

'Oh of course. These days, I actually have a very civil relationship with the council, they are respectful of my rights and I pay my dues, so to speak. I think, in terms of removing what is considered an eyesore from the local environment, they would almost certainly allow me to build a small dwelling but I rather like this one.'

'I mean from the inside, yes, I can see that. It's quite idyllic.'

'But from the outside too,' Diana insisted. 'I love the fact that the habitat is reclaiming it. This caravan must have been bright white once but is now almost completely green. I sometimes imagine I have built my own comfortable coffin, like the sarcophagus of some sort of extravagant Egyptian queen and providing I time my own death carefully, I shall just snuggle up under the duvet and let the woods swallow me up entirely. Instead of jewels and a sacrificial servant I'd be found clutching a bag of first press coffee beans from Arabia and a Hermes shirt.'

'Don't, Diana. That's a bit morbid.'

Diana sat upright, looking at Sam strangely, as if an irresistible thought had suddenly occurred to her.

'Goodness me. It's entirely possible this has already happened. Perhaps Rebecca is my "ka" and is continuing to live my life over there in Willow's Fortune?' She shook her head, a flash of irritation clouding her eyes for a second. 'God forbid.' Immediately she brightened again. 'Much better still, I am Rebecca's ka! The Egyptians were rather good at making sure they were just as comfortable in their afterlife as they were before death. I'm not slumming it here, you know. My bedding is simply heavenly. *Egyptian* cotton no less.' Diana roared with joyful laughter, a flurry of unseen wildlife scattering in response.

She took a sip of tea. 'I could almost believe this were my afterlife if you weren't here cooking me bacon.'

Sam remembered her own imagination allowing her to consider something similar when she'd first entered the woods. 'It's a bit morbid but actually it's not too far off a thought I had when I first came to these woods. I was probably being a bit melodramatic, overwhelmed by the trees and the relentless capaciousness of it all, and it did occur to me then that being absorbed slowly by a tree wouldn't be the worst memorial.'

'Well, there you are, we're very like-minded,' agreed Diana, satisfied.

'Do you resent the interference of the villagers now? I mean, you've got your own way, so they have to leave you alone, but do you resent the trouble they went to? The police? The council? The notices?'

'Funnily enough, they don't leave me alone. Nobody likes a smartass. That's the lesson I learnt. Even a smartass that minds her own business, pays her taxes, and lets other people's dogs chase her squirrels. They don't leave me alone. They won't leave me alone. Every now and then something sparks a new bout of interest in my activities and accuses me of some new crime. Something gets pinched, they blame me. Somebody hears a strange noise at night, they blame me. Somebody sees somebody behaving strangely in the village, they blame me. Somebody's dog has an upset tummy they blame me. The police call on me and I make them a nice cup of coffee and we have a bit of a laugh and off they go again. Case closed. They are kind, I'm lucky. And I do my bit, so they're respectful.'

'A bit irritating though?'

'Heavens, yes, but not enough to make me run away again.'

'Again?'

'Of course. I mean, what do you think I'm doing here? I'm clearly running away from something. I'm not a nutter.'

'No, of course not. I suppose you could be running away from something but equally you could be running towards something. Something better.'

'Those two responses are identical. How about you? Were you running from London or to the countryside? It's no different. I was definitely running away from somebody.'

'Rebecca?'

'Yes. Of course.'

'Do you know why? Was there a moment you couldn't live with her any longer?'

'There was a moment, certainly. I had to save myself. She came to represent everything I came to despise about myself. Here I'm learning to be me at the very most basic level, without her needs and desires, and to understand what that means.'

'And what have you learned?'

'Rebecca lost sight of why she wanted what she wanted. She would have run blindly off a cliff in pursuit of something she'd decided she needed but she no longer knew what it was. She was addicted to the pursuit. And addictions are tricky things. If you stop some suddenly, they will kill you.

Whereas others just need to be replaced. Luckily her addictions weren't fatal but I think they would have been eventually. Rebecca was sad and angry and full of hate. But most of all, Rebecca didn't *matter*. She didn't matter to anybody or anything. The first time I felt I mattered, perhaps in my life, was when those two policemen came and listened to me. They were so unnecessarily respectful. I felt like somebody.' Diana looked across at Sam, whose frown of concentration mirrored her own.

'But you know exactly what I'm talking about, don't you? Have you ever had therapy, Sam?'

'Yes, twice.'

'Did it help?'

'No! Well, actually, yes. But not in the way the therapist intended perhaps.'

Diana nodded. 'Rebecca saw an analyst. Frank, his name was. She saw him for a number of years. Five or six at least. We all did then. Rebecca became very dependent on him. Addicted to him even. She honestly believed he was her best friend, the one person she could count on. But something rather silly happened, a trite little misunderstanding. Frank's assistant called Rebecca and said something woefully innocuous like, "I'm going to pop a statement in the post from Frank." Nothing more, nothing less. But Rebecca didn't normally get calls from Frank's office, she normally *made* calls and she rather thought that he was reaching out to her in some *extra* way. And Rebecca looked forward to it, she felt chosen and special. She imagined that the statement was some sort of declaration or affirmation. But it was all a bit more pedestrian than that, I'm afraid. The regular invoice payments had become out of sync, I don't know, maybe a change of direct debit or something and everything was a bit out of whack and his assistant had simply sent through a statement of account. It was a just a list of transactions. Invoices and payments. Pages and pages of them. Invoice numbers, too, and it was the invoice numbers that struck Rebecca in a rather profound way because they weren't sequential. The invoice numbers had vast gaps which meant there were hundreds of other conversations happening in between her own conversations with Frank. There were hundreds of other relationships being forged and counted upon.

'It was a low point. The humiliating realisation that she didn't even matter to Frank. And then she became a little obsessed – it was in her nature, she was very driven, liked to get things done. So she did some investigating, realising that she knew nothing at all of his marital or family status. And then she found out that Frank wasn't even his actual name! It seems that he was a very popular man, so he had to assume a different name, in order, I suppose, to keep his private life separate from his professional one. That was a shocker for Rebecca because she hadn't realised there was any difference and suddenly, there she was, acting like one of the people he was having to protect himself against. Well, it didn't take too many leaps of the imagination to conclude that each one of her relationships were purely transactional. She didn't have a single friend that didn't send her a bill or a cheque. She lost the plot for a while. Nobody came to visit, nobody checked in on her. Nobody cared at all.'

'I'm sorry.'

'And do you know what his real name was? Frank's actual

name? It was Josh. I didn't have to work too hard to track *that* down. Terrible name for a therapist, don't you think? Perhaps it wasn't his personal security that made him change it after all, perhaps he changed his name because of a brand issue. Josh? Who wants to think about *joshing* with your psychotherapist? No, you want Frankness. That's what won it for me. For her.'

'For Rebecca?'

'Of course, Rebecca. You don't need a therapist here in the woods, I can talk as much or as little as I want here. If I want a therapist, I'll sit quietly and watch a woodpecker at work. That sorts me right out, puts my own little issues into perspective. I recommend it. If you're going to bang your head against the wall, don't do it without a purpose in sight. That's a valuable lesson to learn, and one best taught by a woodpecker. But I did bring some lessons with me to the woods and some of those things were lessons that Frank had helped Rebecca to think about and I remembered some of what I'd learnt and I think I used that when I planned my rebirth. I wanted to live the rawest version of me. The me that just needed sustenance of the very most basic level and everything else – the spiritual, the creative, the ego – could all be met by me. I didn't want to rely on anyone or anything for any stimulus.'

'And is it working?'

'I'm more fulfilled and I like myself more than I liked Rebecca, which isn't saying much, I know. I matter now. My research matters. But then again, I can't see this sort of drastic renaissance catching on. I don't suppose anyone would envy my life for a moment.'

315

'I do.'

'You can't possibly.'

'You're so truthful to yourself. I am such a sham.'

'You think I'm truthful after everything I've told you? I must say, you do have a strange way of looking at the world. And you're a sham, are you?'

'Oh yes, a certifiable phony. My husband loves me because he thinks I'm strong but I'm actually incredibly weak. The weakest person I know. I spend my whole time peddling lies to make me feel better about myself. That's my entire reason for being.'

'You and Rebecca would get on!'

'I'd rather spend time with you than Rebecca if you don't mind. I think you're better for me. And we're not so dissimilar. You say you've reinvented yourself here, but perhaps this is the real you. Perhaps Rebecca was your alter ego.'

'It's possible. Yes.'

'And I've never really thought of it this way, but I have an alter ego too. I thought it was just a pen name but when I write under her name my life is so much more interesting, so much more passionate. I am powerful, influential, I have followers who hang on my every word. Not just a few readers but tens of thousands. I'm loved and hated, and respected and vilified all at the same time. I'm popular! I matter too! But the truth is, none of it is me, it's all her. My whole life is a lie.'

Sam sighed extravagantly. 'I'd like to live more honestly. I just want to be truthful to somebody. Rebecca and Diana. Libby and Sam. Look at us.'

Diana reached out and pushed the logs together, causing a little flurry of flame. 'I told you before, we're all liars.'

'But you are honest, you're the most honest person I've ever met. You might have had to abandon your previous self but you've done it so conclusively. I'd like to be like you.'

'That's because you don't know me. You don't know, for instance, if anything I've told you today is true.'

Sam looked crestfallen. 'I want to believe it.'

'Then believe it, believe in the version you want to believe in. Like the version you want to like. Rebecca has plenty going for her. She's wealthy, successful, independent. You might like her.'

Sam thought about Hattie and about Anne. 'I don't think so. I like *Diana*. I'm not that interested in the more impressive version. This breakfast with you this morning has been one of the happiest meals of my life. Really.'

'That's because coming to terms with the broken, dishonest version of yourself and accepting that she may be better than all of the other versions is a good moment in adulthood. I was twice your age when I got there. Accept yourself for who you are and you'll like yourself more. You're the one that has to live with you, you must be truthful with yourself. That's all. And ask yourself what the other persona is really doing for you. Your alter ego. Does she make you feel good? If not, ditch her. At least you only have to press delete. It's a lot easier than dissolving several companies, liquidising millions of pounds of assets, planting a couple of thousands of trees and moving into a caravan.'

Sam sat still for a few minutes, thinking before she spoke. 'You own all of these trees?'

'Yes, I suppose I do, if you can own a tree in the material sense. But I think the trees probably own me.'

'Yes, yes, I can see that,' said Sam, thinking of her own

grass and shadows. 'You know, I think I might be able to press delete on Libby,' Sam continued, realising only then that she might be capable of such a thing, and that her life might be easier to manage when she'd got rid of all of that extraneous mess.

'And I might be able to press delete on Rebecca,' said Diana, bravely.

It might have been a sudden dip in the temperature, but Sam felt the hairs on her arms stand up. 'Four women will become just two. Will we mourn them, do you suppose?'

'Our worst selves? No, we should jump up and down on their graves, shouldn't we? I suppose we must celebrate. But it won't be easy. We won't have them to hide behind anymore, we'll feel exposed once we're out there, blinking in the blinding light.'

'We don't need them, Diana, they stopped us being brave,' said Sam, standing up to leave.

Diana stood up too and, for the first time since they'd become friends, gave Sam a brief hug as she left.

As Sam walked away, stepping through the narrow gap back on to the path, she heard Diana call out.

'Brave. That's exactly right, Sam. We must be brave.'

Chapter 47

Sam rang on the doorbell. A quick, joyous double burst at first and then a longer, lean-on, fully committed ring afterwards, the sort of ring that implied that the visitor was not in the mood to be ignored. Sam knew Hattie was in. There were windows open at the front of the house and a radio had been playing as she walked up the path but had been silenced as she reached the door. While she waited for the door to open, she looked around her at the front garden. The grass hadn't been mown and was in poor condition. It didn't look deliberate. It looked desperate. There were deadened patches of yellowing vegetation betraying the outlines of lost detritus that had been left outside for far too long, killing the grass and allowing the earthworms to colonise these dank habitats. And, Sam thought, wrinkling her nose in displeasure, it smelt a bit like all the local cats might be using it as their public convenience.

Sam leant on the bell again, noticing the slug trails that traversed the doorstep and wound their way up the side of the doorframe.

Eventually the door opened.

Hattie blocked the entrance with her body, holding the

door open just enough to use it as a barrier. She looked at Sam coldly but said nothing.

Until this moment Sam hadn't decided what form her attempt at reconciliation would take. She hadn't yet decided if she was still angry or ready for a more submissive truce, just that a confrontation of some sort must happen. Hattie's unequivocal and stubborn refusal to concede any ground tipped the scales that had been hanging, quite evenly balanced. Sam bristled.

'Are you not going to invite me in, Hattie? You were very keen to make friends when you came to see me with cake.'

Hattie's lip wobbled in an unrealised sob. 'You were very cruel to me, Sam, I've barely slept a wink. I'm utterly exhausted.' She made to close the door, but Sam blocked her with the toe of her trainer.

'I wasn't mean to you, I was truthful.'

'The truth can hurt, Sam, and you need to think about the impact your words can have.'

Sam felt something well up in her, a crescendo of outrage that began in the pit of her stomach and rose to the base of her throat, but she quashed it, forcing Diana's words to the front of her brain, allowing them to drown out Libby's predilection for combat. *'We're all liars, either to ourselves or to strangers or to the people we love. It doesn't matter which, we're still liars.'*

She swallowed, physically suppressing her instinct to rebut the slight. 'I'm sorry if I was abrupt, Hattie, but perhaps we can begin again? May I come in?'

Hattie's eyes darted around, she looked frightened, but after a further hesitation she opened the door to let Sam in.

The house was a mess. Toys littered the hall, spilling a trail of cheap, brightly coloured plastic, creating a path that led all the way to the kitchen. The toys looked abandoned as if a volcano had erupted and ossified them as they fell. Hattie pushed some aside with her foot and picked up a couple more, as if picking up a fragment of the mess might imply the problem had been dealt with.

'The littlest is taking her nap. I was just about to start picking up after them.'

'I can only imagine what it's like,' said Sam, her nose wrinkling at some unpleasant smell leaking from the cloakroom as she passed it.

The kitchen was a mess too. Traces of breakfast still hung around on the table and on work surfaces.

Hattie didn't apologise any further, she just moved the cups and toast rack off the table and put them by the sink, she brushed the crumbs on the table to the floor with a sweep of her hand. Most crumbs fell, but some clung to a small patch of something sticky.

Sam watched Hattie, whose shoulders now sagged in defeat. As she felt Sam's scrutiny, Hattie pulled the cuffs of her cardigan over her hands, which Sam interpreted as a subtle expression of shame.

She softened.

'I'm sorry. Coming to visit me and bringing me a cake was very kind. You couldn't possibly have known what you were wading into and I regret making you feel bad. I really should have kept my feelings under wraps.' *We're all liars, either to ourselves or to strangers.* Diana's words echoed in Sam's mind, as if giving her permission to speak the words Hattie needed to hear in place of the words she wanted to say.

Hattie, who had clearly felt wronged by Sam, looked like she was weighing up a peace proposal.

'I'm sorry, too. Perhaps I was insensitive. It's hard to know what to say in that sort of situation.'

Sam crushed her natural response and let Hattie continue.

'The truth is, I really didn't know what to say and I don't know what to say to you now. I was so excited to have a new neighbour, and I'd watched you walk past my house to the shops a couple of times, so I knew you didn't work. I rather thought we would be friends. But the hope that we might have something in common sort of disappeared immediately when you said all those horrible things about children.'

Sam looked at Hattie, at her sad reddened eyes that sagged in exhaustion. She looked around the draughty kitchen noticing the ingrained dirt that had settled in beneath the surface mess. She looked at the open cereal packets lying on their sides on the table and she realised what a huge effort making that cake must have been. Hattie was right, they had nothing in common.

'My lack of womb is my problem, not yours, Hattie. It is uniquely mine to deal with. More so than my husband's, even. If he wants to have kids, he can still have kids – and I wouldn't even blame him. When he married me that was very much on the agenda. But me? I will never have my own children but I believe I am much more than my womb and I don't really want to be cast out as no use to my neighbours, just because you won't be able to share a school run with me.'

Sam could feel the angry cry of injustice bubbling up

within her again, but she pitied Hattie so tempered it. 'My infertility makes people feel uncomfortable, I know that. I can see how that is. But can you only be comfortable with people who have and want exactly what you have, do you suppose?'

'I hope I'm more flexible than that, but it can get a bit lonely in this village and the thought that I might have a neighbour with children came as a huge relief.' Hattie paused. 'Life-saving, even.'

Sam assessed her again. The realisation that Hattie wasn't coping had been creeping up on her but now Hattie revealed a flash of desperation that Sam hadn't anticipated. Sam felt swamped by guilt.

'Sit down, Hattie. Let me make you a cup of tea.' Hattie slumped down at the table. Sam ran a sink full of hot water and began to wipe down the surfaces. The cloth she was using was stained brown. She opened the cupboard beneath the sink, extracted a new cloth and threw the old one in the bin, continuing where she'd left off.

'Oh God,' groaned Hattie, collapsing forward on to her folded forearms, shielding her face. 'You must think I'm disgusting. I'm just so, so tired.'

'I don't think you're disgusting. My husband is a bit compulsive in his need to keep things clean, so he spends his entire time tidying up after me. Quite frankly, it drives me a bit nuts sometimes, but I suppose I've picked up some of his habits.'

'Your husband sounds dreamy,' said Hattie, her voice muffled by the sleeves of her cardigan that she was now talking into.

Sam paused, the cloth in her hand. 'Yes. Yes, he is dreamy.'

Hattie turned to face Sam, but continued to rest her head on her arms. 'Olly's barely at home during the week, he has so much on at work that he tends to kip on a colleague's sofa. He only really comes home at the weekends and it just doesn't seem worth tidying up for the kids. It's not like they notice, and they just make a mess all over again.'

Sam felt a flash of anger towards Olly.

'Well, I hope your husband gives you a hand at the weekends. You've got a lot on your plate. It can't be easy.'

'He's knackered by the weekend. He needs to catch up on his rest and he likes to get out to the golf club on a Saturday morning. He needs to take his mind off the stress of the week. After working as hard as he does he can't really be expected to come home and cope with the kids or help around the house.'

Sam swallowed hard and opened cupboards, finding a home for the cereal. The cupboards needed cleaning. She opened the fridge and took out the milk. The fridge needed cleaning. She put on the kettle and wiped the table around Hattie, who didn't move, but just followed Sam with her eyes.

'My husband will bring the mower down this weekend. He'd love to tackle your garden for you.'

'Really?'

'Yes, really. It will probably only need to be done once. I'm sure that will prompt your husband to help a bit more. Men often tend to work that way, in my experience.'

Hattie smiled sadly. 'It's hard to talk to people that aren't the same as you,' she ventured.

'We're the same, Hattie.'

'No, we're not!' said Hattie, outraged. She sat up. 'Look at you, you're perfect. Look at me. I'm a mess.'

Sam laughed kindly. 'How long will the baby sleep, Hattie?'

Hattie groaned. 'Maybe another thirty or forty minutes?'

'Do me a favour, go and lie down in the sitting room. Close your eyes. Have a proper rest while the baby sleeps. I'll finish up in here.'

Hattie stood and looked Sam up and down. Sam wondered if she had overstepped the mark, but Hattie nodded obediently and traipsed off towards the sitting room. Sam reappraised the kitchen, looked at her watch and rolled up her sleeves.

Chapter 48

Sam took Danny by the hand when he got home from work and led him to the lawn.

'Look!' she said. The grass stood tall and proud in the evening light. It was fading now, the colour of corn and it shimmered with gold in the last rays of sunshine. There were splashes of dark green amongst the pale grass, provided by other plants as they began to make their mark.

'Gosh, it's not a savannah now. It's a forest. Well done, sweet pea.' He bent down to look at it. 'So much growth. It makes my head spin.'

'Sometimes it's easy to grow things. Sometimes it's not. Not so easy for us. We're at the end of the line, you and me.' Sam squeezed Danny's hand. Her words were untroubled and didn't tumble over themselves but appeared one by one, in an orderly fashion, unlike the hysterical clamour of Sam's thoughts when she was writing as Libby. This was not a conversation they had ever had and since Sam's operation, they'd both been quite content to leave the words unsaid. But now, with all of this new growth around them, and with only Libby's side of the story to represent her, Sam needed to redress the balance.

'That's very true – no kids for two only-children.' Danny nodded and returned the squeeze.

'I'm sorry,' said Sam, realising she'd never apologised to Danny.

'For what? To whom?' he asked, confused.

'We've let them down a bit, our ancestors, haven't we? They've been busy procreating successfully, generation after generation, since *for ever*, and we've dropped the ball.'

'I think the human population will carry on without us, don't you? And I suspect our ancestors have been more successful elsewhere. We've probably each got a million distant cousins we don't even know about.'

'I'm sorry for you, Danny. You've been so good about this. But it doesn't have to be the end of the line for you. I know you didn't sign up for this. And you can probably go right ahead and procreate without me if you'd like to. I wouldn't blame you.'

'Oh, Sam.'

They were holding hands, looking intently at the even growth of grass that stretched from boundary to boundary. Sam turned to look at Danny, pulling him closer in to her.

'I wouldn't blame you. Don't look so sad. I worry, yes of course I worry. I lie in bed and imagine you getting cold feet and rushing off to find the first functional womb. And I feel a rage of absolute jealousy, but I would get over that. But I wouldn't get over *you*. My God, I would miss you and I really don't want to live my life without you. But I'd let you go.'

'Sam.' Danny's tone had changed. His eyes were filled with tears, but the sadness was greater than the plea of his eyes. His sadness was greater than the sag of his shoulders or the downward slump of his mouth. His sadness filled the space around them.

'What?' said Sam, alarmed now.

'I've not been honest with you.'

Sam felt a rush of nausea. This is what she'd dreaded. She wasn't enough. She could never be enough.

'Tell me.'

Danny sat down heavily on the paving stones and brought his knees up towards his chest. He covered his face with his hands. She saw his shoulders heave a couple of times and she realised she'd never seen him cry before.

'Champ. Tell me. I'm strong enough. You know that.' She sat down beside him, putting an arm around his shoulders.

Danny spoke through his sobs. 'You're so strong. You're so unflappable. You're so capable, and I'm not worthy of you.'

Sam felt light-headed. 'What have you done?'

'You're stronger than I am. And I took advantage of that. I let you carry this weight on your own and I should have shared it.'

'You're scaring me a bit, Danny.'

Danny rubbed his face fiercely with both hands, as if he could fight back the tears with physical force. He turned to Sam. 'Back when we were first married, I was untrue.'

Sam's stomach lurched. Back then? All that time ago, when she was still well? When they had a whole perfect life in front of them? He'd been unfaithful back then? She stood up, took a couple of paces away from him and then returned and sat kneeling beside him. She put her hands on his knees.

'Tell me, Danny.'

'When we were first trying for a baby.'

'Yes?'

'I felt sure it was me. I thought I was the problem. I made myself sick with worry that I'd let you down, that I wasn't going to be good enough for you.'

'Well, that was a whole lot of additional anxiety you needn't have worried about!' Sam used one hand to tip Danny's face up and she prised his hands away so that she could see him. 'What a waste of worry!' she said, light-heartedly, though the fear still hovered between them.

'But that's just it. I went.' Danny stifled another sob. 'I went to a specialist, I went to see a doctor and I got myself checked out.'

'Without telling me? You brave thing.'

'I wasn't brave. I *was* the problem. My sperm was... ' He stopped dramatically, shaking his head in shame. 'It was *sluggish.*'

Sam tried to process this information but couldn't get beyond the vision of sluggish sperm. She'd never really imagined them, *en route*, but didn't think that torpidity would be a useful attribute. She stifled a small laugh. 'Sluggish? I mean, what? They lacked motivation? What on earth are sluggish sperm?'

'I was told they might not hit their target.'

'I don't understand why you're so upset, Danny. You had lacklustre sperm, but that wasn't really a problem in comparison to the complete removal of all my reproduction organs, was it?'

'But don't you see? I didn't *tell* you.'

Sam used her thumbs to wipe a tear away from beneath each of Danny's eyes. He blinked steadily.

He shook his head. 'You're so strong.'

'I have my moments.'

'And I didn't want you to see me as weak. I never found the courage to tell you. I lay awake at night thinking about telling you, but I could never say it out loud. And the longer I left it, the worse it seemed to be. And then you got your diagnosis and suddenly, I didn't have to tell you.'

'My news trumped yours, I can see that.' Sam frowned, unsure how she felt.

'I'm a coward.'

'That was, well, yes, that was a little spineless, Danny.'

'I'm so ashamed.'

'But more than that, it was *stupid*. Why did you carry that on your own, you could have shared it with me and it would have been gone in a flash. Events soon overtook your sluggish sperm. Not that it sounds like they were going to put up a fight.' Sam laughed at her own wit, but Danny was not yet ready for her flippancy.

'Because I didn't want to be less of a man for you.'

'That's one of the most idiotic things you've ever said. And besides, you were prepared to take the risk that I might consider myself less of a woman for you. That doesn't seem fair.'

He hung his head in shame, the occasional fat tear escaping and forming a rivulet in the crease between his nose and cheek.

'What do I think about your manhood, Danny? Let me be honest. I do not think less of you for having sluggish sperm, but I do think less of you for not telling me. Telling me would have been courageous.' She searched his face with her eyes, looking for other revelations she might find now they'd started to talk. 'Did you tell *anyone*?'

He shook his head vigorously, tears rinsing his face. She wiped his cheeks with the heels of her hands pushing the wetness towards the outer edges of his cheeks where it clung to the stubble growing there.

'Who on earth would I tell? You're the only person I talk to.'

'I don't know. Who do guys tell their personal problems to? Other guys, I guess. That colleague of yours, the one with the annual barbecue. Peter? I can imagine you talking to him over a beer.'

'Can you? Can you really imagine me talking to Peter about my sperm while drinking a beer? In a pub?' Finally Danny laughed. 'Oh, sweet pea. I've done a better job than I thought of presenting myself as worthy of your love.' He clasped his hands behind the back of Sam's head and pulled her gently towards him until their foreheads and noses touched.

Chapter 49

Danny and Sam were laughing again but still clinging to each other for reassurance. They'd both held back so much from each other that the watershed of revelation had allowed themselves to look at each other anew, although their mutual curiosity was still tinged with a trace of suspicion. They were both sitting on the sofa, toe to toe, talking softly and teasing each other gently.

'Peter didn't ask us to his barbecue this year,' Danny said, aware that the snub had never been properly filed away and was fizzing around in a disorderly mesh somewhere just behind his eyes.

Sam was immediately alert to a spurn. 'Any reason why not? He's quite a good friend, isn't he?'

'Friend.' Danny scowled as if struggling with the pronunciation of a difficult foreign word. I don't know how to tell. I thought so. At any rate, we've been asked to the barbecue previously and now we've not. It's puzzling me. I can't seem to formulate a clear response because I don't know exactly what I'm responding to. I thought I had dealt with it. I assumed he'd re-evaluated his career prospects and somehow decided we were in direct competition so he would need to distance himself from me to focus on his next steps.'

Sam thought for a while, concentrating on the conundrum. She flicked his toes with her own while she thought.

'I tried to file it away, in a drawer marked "work problems" but you know that thing that happens with a filing cabinet, when you can't open one drawer if another one is slightly open? It's like that. I think I've got two drawers open at the same time. It might need re-processing.'

Sam nodded seriously. 'You're right. It's not a work problem. And it's not you. It's me.'

Danny shook his head, decisively. 'Don't be ridiculous, sweet pea. He's my colleague. This is a reflection on me. I think he sees me as competition. But there might be something else, too.'

'Well, if it's not me, it's us. You make him nervous because you are married to me. I make him nervous because I make his wife nervous. We don't fit in. My lack of reproductive organs makes us unsuitable candidates for barbecue guests.'

'People don't actually think like that. Do they?'

'Oh they do. Believe me. These days I'm only surprised by people who *don't* think like that. Every time anyone learns of my absent womb, they immediately reassess me. More often than that, they reject me.' Sam shook her head and laughed lightly. 'It's times like this you want friends like Libby Masters, she'd probably campaign for the rights of my womb-shaped gap. She'd probably fight for my rights harder than I would.'

'What on earth do you think happened to Libby Masters?' Danny said suddenly. 'Has she never cottoned on to the fact you both stole her identify *and* turned her into one of the women that women most love to hate?'

'I think she might have got there all on her own, eventually. She was a young woman destined for a following. She was always going to attract a vast number of acolytes or dissenters. Who knows which she would have ended up with, she had the personality for either or both. But she never came back to class after that first year. I can only imagine she died a tragically valiant death. She just vanished.'

'What did the tutors say?'

'They said they didn't know why she'd left. And in my experience the university body wasn't exactly open about mental health problems. They didn't dwell on issues that might be interpreted as personal weakness in case it reflected badly upon the institution. Well, that's what Libby always said.'

'But didn't you adore her? If she had died you would have heard surely and wouldn't you have wanted to be at her funeral?'

'Oh, you misunderstand me. I was a little bit *in love* with her, but she barely noticed me. I was way out of her league, I promise you. Even dead she was wildly superior to me. There is no way I would have had the guts to go to her funeral. She'd have called me bourgeois from her coffin and I'd have had to leave the church in shame.'

'But you're absolutely certain she died?'

'Well, no, I can't be certain. I can't quite remember what I knew and what I fabricated to fill in the gaps. But she was incredibly involved at university and all the tutors loved her despite her militancy. Everyone knew she was preordained for great things, so only a huge disaster could have derailed her. She was very bright, very attractive and rather ahead of her time. It was rumoured that she'd turned down a place at Oxford because she was rebelling against her privilege. Honestly, ours was a good university but she must have been frustrated by the dullards around her. There was nobody on her wavelength. I just think it is entirely possible she took her own life, she felt things so very deeply and it can't have been easy, to carry everyone else's suffering on her shoulders.'

'Maybe she just went to a different university... maybe that could explain it. Perhaps you and the other dullards had her running for the steeples.'

Sam thought about this as a possibility and shook her head, solemnly. 'I just doubt it, she'd been so vociferous in her contempt for the establishment. But it's a happier thought...'

'Haven't you ever looked for her?' Danny asked. He was now tapping away at his laptop.

'Libby M.A.S—' he spelt out carefully as he typed. 'This might not be easy, there would be a few of those, I imagine.'

'She wasn't Masters, she was Sage-Forsyth.'

'Sage-Forsyth. Goodness. She sounds like she *was* the establishment. That should narrow it down a little. Where did Masters come from?'

'Her name was far too obvious, so I changed it.'

'Fair enough. Sage-Forsyth might have stuck out.

'Bingo!' said Danny only a few seconds later. 'Here's a Liberty Sage-Forsyth and she is...' He scrolled down for a few seconds, 'exactly your age.'

'You're kidding me.' Sam leapt up and came around to Danny's end of the sofa, she nudged him to move up, squeezing in beside him.

'She's still alive?'

'Liberty Mulholand, nee Liberty Sage-Forsyth. Seems she is.'

Sam frowned at the images as Danny flicked through a Facebook account dominated by pictures of happy children glowing from a combination of good health and earnest parenting.

'Yup. There's your militant, she's married with three kids.'

Sam was transfixed by the photos, both by the pictures of the children and of Libby herself who looked similar but almost unrecognisably *steady*. 'Three? Yikes. She's my age! That means… ' She concentrated while she did the maths.

'Her children are ten, nine and six,' said Danny, delighted with himself and his detective work.

'So… ' Sam tried to process the information but Danny once again filled in the gap.

'She left university because she was pregnant?'

'She left university because she was pregnant,' nodded Sam in agreement, the repetition helping the meaning to take shape. She took control of the laptop and scrolled down even further.

'Wedding pictures,' said Sam, the disappointment palpable in her voice. 'Happy wedding pictures that first summer.'

'You didn't see that coming!' said Danny, triumphantly.

'No. No. No. Actually, there are about a thousand scenarios I had imagined in a church but not one of them involved a happy smiling couple under a shower of confetti.'

'Did you never think to look?'

'I looked for news, that first term when she didn't return, but there was nothing. No sign of her. She'd just disappeared.'

'I expect she was keeping a low profile, trying not to bring a cloud of shame upon the Sage-Forsyths.'

'Maybe.' Sam sounded desolate.

Danny turned Sam's face from the screen to his own. 'Gosh, you really are saddened, aren't you?'

'Saddened. No, of course not. Look at her, she's radiant on her wedding day. Still happily married by the looks of it. Three nice-looking children, although they seem to be wearing quite scratchy jumpers,' said Sam, wrinkling her nose.

'Must have married well. Perhaps Mr Mulholand was a bit of a catch. The richer you are, the more scratchy wool you expect your children to wear.'

'I can't help feeling a bit let down, though. I mean, obviously she's not let herself down, but I feel a bit betrayed. I had rather hoped that if she hadn't died tragically then at the very least she'd be doing something incredibly worthwhile. She should have been running an NGO or responding to a humanitarian crisis. I mean, it's people like Libby that do all the good works so people like me don't have to.'

'Well, perhaps when she's not looking blissfully happy, which, let's be honest, she appears to be most of the time according to her profile, perhaps she is mourning that earlier moment of notability. It's entirely possible that nobody even listens to her views anymore. I feel a tiny bit sorry for her, she just sort of fizzled out, didn't she?' Danny continued to scroll up and down, trying to detect the qualities that had so enchanted Sam.

'But, she didn't entirely, did she? In a way she carried on,' said Sam, with a glimpse of pride. 'She might think her activism stopped the day she got married, but in a parallel universe she's been causing quite a stir. Actually, some of her ideas got more ardent not less. And what she might have lost in academic argument she made up for in hot-blooded fervour. Good old Libby,' said Sam, smiling a bit for the first time since Libby Sage-Forsyth had risen from the grave.

'Good old Libby,' echoed Danny. 'Good old Sam,' he said, more quietly, wriggling to get more comfortable beside her.

Chapter 50

Danny had washed up and Sam had been looking at a book, flicking through pictures of ancient meadow land and endangered wildflowers.

As Danny dried his hands carefully, Sam looked up at him. 'I wish I could see what goes on inside that brain of yours sometimes. You're so strong, so sure of yourself.'

Danny laughed. 'Oh, you'd be surprised.'

'I know. You are surprising. I always rather assumed that you didn't have great torrents of emotion running through you but I seem to be learning all sorts of things about you. Not just your sluggish sperm, but your fear of witches. You seem to compartmentalise everything so well. Meanwhile, look at me. I'm such a mess. If you looked inside my brain, you'd divorce me immediately. The inside of my brain is what the tumble dryer filter would look like if you didn't clean it out for me every Saturday. Layers and layers of bits of unfinished thoughts and responses. Some of it recognisable but most of it fragments of feelings, nothing substantial to grab on to, nothing as reliable as a memory.'

'That sounds very different from mine. I don't think I'd want all of my memories tangled up inside me, imagine the knots, imagine the chaos.' Danny shuddered. 'Look inside my brain and you'll just see locked drawers.'

'Your filing cabinets. Like the one we have upstairs? The big wooden one?' Sam wondered.

'Not really. Metal, and fireproof. And the drawers are slimmer. Perhaps like the cabinets in a pharmacist. Less chance of cross-contamination. And lots and lots of them. If there's anything of any interest in those drawers, you'll have great trouble getting in to look at the detail. I've made sure of that. They're locked with a combination lock. A heavy duty one made of steel. Not one of those flimsy ones that comes free with a suitcase that any old fool can crack with a lucky guess or a pair of tweezers.'

'Gosh, you sound certain of that.'

'I am.'

'Do you mind me asking, Danny, there's one thing I've always wanted to know. What about the drawer marked "Sam's illness"? What does that drawer look like? I've always wondered. I know it's a cliché, but you were such a pillar of strength for me. I didn't even need to find the fight to deal with any of it myself because of your indefatigable resilience. You were astonishing. You had such faith.'

Danny looked troubled. 'You really don't want to know what's in that drawer.'

'But I do. I've never quite understood where you drew your strength from. I don't quite understand whether it was a religious faith or some sort of inner strength. Tell me.'

'As always you overestimate me. I'll show you, if it won't make you hate me.' He sat down and flipped open his laptop, typing in a password and waiting for Excel to load. He dived confidently into files within files within files before pulling out a spreadsheet and keying in a second password.

'Here you go.' He hesitated and closed the lid partially. 'Wait. I probably have to go back in time a bit. I need to open another drawer first.' He looked pained. 'This is exactly why I don't like these conversations, it's never as straightforward as I'd like it to be. Soon you'll have me spilling out the contents of everything I've ever filed away.'

'Sorry, Danny.'

'One drawer, Sam. One drawer. If it doesn't shed some light on what I'm about to show you, I'm not going to delve any further.' He closed his eyes for a few seconds and then started speaking slowly, dragging the detail to the front of his brain word by word. 'I remember when Mum died. Not the exact day, it had all been kept from me at the time. Just telephone calls to my grandmother's house and tears and whispers. I knew, I think I knew, but Dad wanted to tell me himself, so it had to wait. I walked into his study and he shook his head and said, "Danny, your mother passed away. I'm sorry, son. The odds were just stacked against her."'

'Oh, champ.'

'Don't pity me. It wasn't actually as harsh as it sounds. *The odds were just stacked against her.* It wasn't her fault, it wasn't his fault, it wasn't my fault, it wasn't the doctors' fault. It was just a numbers thing. Those words were the ones I most needed to hear. They helped me not to feel too angry, there was no one to blame.'

He opened up the laptop and gestured to Sam to take a look.

She peered at the spreadsheet, rows and columns filled with numbers. 'What am I looking at?'

'Your odds. The odds were with you, Sam.'

Danny clicked on a couple of cells within the spreadsheet and a graph popped up. Sam peered at the graphs and the charts, not understanding them at all.

'Here's the baseline for your cancer. And then these,' here Danny used the mouse to point at a row of numbers, 'these are the variables.' He cleared his throat and wriggled in his seat, getting comfortable with the explanation. 'Your age, the doctor, your diet, your father's earnings, your mother's earnings, your maternal and paternal grandparents' age at death. Each of these factors improved your chances.' Sam followed the hovering arrow as it jumped from cell to cell. 'Here, this is you and this is your treatment plotted against your own personal timeline. Everything that happened, your early diagnosis, your swift treatment, your comprehensive surgery by a competent medical team. It all counted in your favour.'

Danny coughed nervously. 'I didn't have faith, I just liked your odds. Your odds were stacked in your favour.'

'Oh,' said Sam. Her eyes filled up with tears and she allowed one or two to fall before blinking the others away.

'I'm sorry it's not more romantic than that.'

'I'm rather glad I didn't know at the time. It's not exactly what I thought was keeping us going. I'm pretty sure it was your conviction in me that kept me strong. If I'd known that it was just work for you...' The thought trailed off.

'Sweet pea! It wasn't just any *work*. It was the most important work I'd ever undertaken. I just didn't really know how else to cope with your news. I spend my whole life talking about outcomes, that's what I *do*. I predict outcomes for corporations that take the risk on insuring people like you. If I couldn't predict your outcome fairly confidently then I wouldn't be very good at my job.'

'When I was sick, you never told me my odds were good. You could have done. The doctors didn't tell me that either.'

'Nobody wants to be the statistic,' answered Danny. He continued, 'Understanding the maths helped me cope with my loss as a child. I could have been angry with Mum for not fighting hard enough or angry with Dad for not protecting her. And then when Dad died young, well, look.' Danny used his mouse to navigate swiftly through files, pulling up another spreadsheet, typing in another password.

He pointed at a graph. 'Look, the odds weren't with him.'

Sam sighed heavily. 'That is one way of coping but Jesus, Danny, that's your *dad*.'

She looked at the spreadsheet of numbers. 'And now, don't you know too much? What about you? Both your parents died young. You've got a stressful work life. Your home life isn't a bed of roses. What's your own outcome looking like?'

Danny closed the spreadsheet and shut down the laptop. He looked at Sam earnestly. 'I haven't run the numbers. I don't need to live for ever. I just need to live as long as you.'

Chapter 51

'Have you heard of Fibonacci?' asked Sam, innocently. They were sitting on chairs they'd dragged outside on to the paving to better admire the tall grasses that swayed melodically in front of them.

Danny snorted. 'What on earth do you mean, have I heard of Fibonacci? Have *you* heard of Fibonacci?' he retorted, a little arrogantly.

'I just wondered what you know of him or his sequence...' She allowed her voice to trail off as she closed the book on her lap.

'The Fibonacci sequence is an incredibly powerful numerical ratio, named for the Italian who discovered it, though in truth it had been played with one thousand years earlier, in 200 BC. Fibonacci was the greatest European mathematician of the Middle Ages, but it was an Indian mathematician who first made the connection by looking at the numerical patterns in poetry. You love poetry, Sam, you should look into the Indian poets, you'd like them. Imagine distilling all that mathematical knowledge into verse? The numbers are significant because they bind our very being. The structure of our own DNA correlates very closely to the Fibonacci sequence.'

'Close your eyes, Danny,' Sam said softly.

He frowned, but followed her instructions obediently.

She stood up and fished something from within her pocket. She put it into his hand and closed his fingers around it.

He opened his eyes and unfurled his fingers to reveal a pine cone. He studied it, confused. Sam turned it over so that he could see the pattern made by its woody scales at its base.

'Fibonacci at work,' she said.

Danny smiled as he studied the arrangement of the pine cone's bracts. He'd never had reason to consider their perfection before.

'Clever little guys, aren't they?' Danny said, admiringly, holding the cone up and looking at the pattern in the light.

'Clever little *gal*, actually. She's a she. But yes, clever indeed. In mythology throughout the ages they've represented human enlightenment. They've certainly been around for long enough to merit the badge, in fact, three times longer than all flowering plants.'

Danny ran his thumb over the pine cone thoughtfully, turning it over in his hand. Sam remembered his joy as he counted the trees in the birch wood.

'From within the chaos of the countryside, you'll find the order you're looking for, Danny. It's everywhere. Fibonacci has seen to that.'

'In rabbits, sure,' he acknowledged. 'You can apply the sequence to the rate at which they breed. Not accounting for a hunter's trap and myxomatosis, that is,' he said, wryly.

'Trust you to think of death, Danny. But you can also apply Fibonacci to the growth of a snail shell and the pattern of a hurricane and the distribution of flower seeds on a sunflower head. And there's mathematics in snowflakes. And spider webs. Look at the symmetry and order in those two things. Every snowflake is different, which makes you think they should be endlessly, chaotically random, but each one is perfectly symmetrical. Why? How is that even possible? And as for the structure of a bee's honeycomb? Don't get me started.'

Danny laughed but Sam was serious. She drew her eyes from the cone and looked at him earnestly. 'I dismissed your joy in the woods. I was happy to see you happy but, truthfully, I thought your response was less valid than my own. I thought it was an unnatural reaction. But perhaps you were responding to something primordial.'

She continued. 'We're all a bit like those pine cones. Everything is buried deeply within us, travelling from generation to generation in a complex pattern that can *only* accurately be represented by mathematics to try to make sense of it. We try, as we grow, to unfurl in an orderly fashion. Some of us find it harder to express our inner beauty than others and for those people it's probably also a bit harder to recognise it when you see it. That's all.'

She sat down again and reached for his hand. 'That's you, Danny. So orderly on the surface. I always thought you were a simple man. But I was wrong. We're all wildly complex and you're no exception.'

'Are you going to carry on writing your blog, Sam?' Danny asked after a silence that felt useful to both of them.

'No. I don't think I need to. I'm going to try to talk a bit more, I think. I'm going to talk to you about the things that make me sad and, I'm afraid I'm going to run the risk of making you sad in the process.'

'OK,' said Danny, thinking this sounded fine.

'And I'm not going to go back to work yet.'

'OK,' said Danny, thinking this sounded fine, too.

'I want to write but I want to do something a bit more positive. I'm going to work on another project altogether. I've got an idea, a really good idea.'

'OK?' said Danny, wondering if his input would be required.

'I want to help Diana find an audience for *her* writing. I haven't talked to her about it, but I believe she'll let me help. She writes a journal every day, she calls them her nature notes. They are really lovely observations about the countryside and she draws these incredible sketches. I think they deserve to be shared. But they might be of scientific interest, too. While she's been observing the countryside around her, she's also been systematically collecting data which might be important. I thought you might be able to have a look at the records and see if you can find some patterns.'

Danny smiled. 'I love data. I love patterns, Sam. That's what I'm good at.'

'Diana's my friend. I'd like to help her.'

'I'm glad you've found a friend here, Sam.'

'We're an unlikely pair but we're learning to be honest with each other. I think that is all that our friendship requires.'

In front of them as they sat, the grasses pushed ever upwards, scattering their seed heads as they jostled for light while bees buzzed industriously from one flower to the next, spilling pollen along each twisted journey. Every tiny seed gathered with care by one hand and sown with care by another was now replicating itself with ignorant abandon.

Chapter 52

Danny awoke. The weight of the sleep had anchored him to the mattress in a way he'd never experienced. He tried to climb his way back from the depths but the ascent felt treacherous and even as he struggled to surface he was tempted to let himself fall again.

He remained groggily awake for a few moments, wondering if this is how everyone felt after a good night's sleep before realising that Sam wasn't beside him. His heart lurched.

Downstairs, Sam was at the window, admiring the garden. She turned and smiled broadly. 'You slept the sleep of the wicked… feeling better?'

'I think I slept the sleep of a man with nothing on his conscience. Or nothing that matters very much.'

He poured a cup of coffee from the pot and wandered out of the kitchen into the garden. Sam saw him looking intently at the tall grasses and she wondered what went on in that head of his. She'd just assumed he was a simple man – a bit of work, a few numbers that other people would find dull but that he enjoyed. She had always assumed that he might harbour a couple of suppressed memories from childhood at most.

But the way he stood, looking at the grass, his shoulders slumped and then, as if about to take action, tall again with both hands on his head as if he were solving a complex riddle. Sam tried to see the garden through his eyes, imagine what he was seeing and wondered whether her letting go had tied him up in knots. Something in his frame suggested anguish and she couldn't bear to look any more. She turned away to sit at the kitchen table, her head in her hands, a diminutive shadow of her husband's stance.

She waited, rooted to her chair, anxious and aware, an awareness that registered as a ragged pain in her heart, that she'd revealed so much of herself recently that he might just not like the woman he realised was his wife.

The kitchen clock had broken, perhaps it had become damaged in the move and she had just never sat still enough to notice it. The second hand made a good clean sweep of the face of the clock, only to get caught on the minute hand where it would make two or three attempts to free itself before rushing onwards again, faster for those initial seconds, making up for lost time. Sam studied the clock's behaviour for a number of revolutions, marking her husband's silence with this stifled attempt at time to battle on regardless. Gosh, Sam thought to herself, it was amazing just how much didn't quite function properly when you stopped to examine it. She wondered, sitting there in the weirdly rhythmic pattern of her broken clock, whether it was better not to notice at all.

The silence of the kitchen was broken by the roar of the lawnmower, springing to life at the first attempt with none of its usual spluttered warning. Sam jumped but remained seated. She sighed heavily. This was inevitable, she thought,

I am not an ant, I can't hide away in the messy wilderness of my own back garden expecting to continue unbidden, unchecked. The sound sawed at her soul nonetheless.

The lawnmower stalled and started again. It stalled again. Sam wondered whether Danny was struggling to make it work and regretted now not draining it of fuel, or, better still, filling it with the wrong fuel so that it would splutter to a premature but conclusive death.

The front door slammed and she wondered, both hopefully and a little fearfully, if she had pre-empted the machine's early demise with her thoughts. It was unlike Danny to give up on a task so quickly.

She could hear him go into the garage and then out again. He was busy in his activity, fixing the lawnmower perhaps, but he never stopped to check in on her. She deserved that. She'd been dishonest with him and now he was going to punish her. She wondered if there could be a reset.

Another twenty minutes passed before he came back inside. She looked up as he crossed the kitchen towards her. She cowered a little and a flash of confusion clouded his face before he reached a hand out towards her. She felt ashamed. Ashamed of her selfishness, her recklessness, but sad, too, that her garden, her beautiful wasteland, had come to such a sudden, painful end.

Danny took her by the hand and pulled her gently to her feet and led her to the kitchen door. He said nothing. He led her down the path that ran between the house and the garage but he stopped before they reached the lawn. She didn't want to see it, but knew she needed to take her punishment bravely.

He stopped her and blocked her path and kissed her eyes

closed. She kept them closed. He bent down and undid her laces, helping her to wriggle out of the first and then the second trainer. He led her forward once more, her eyes remained closed.

Sam felt the space around her, knew she was at the edge of the garden, her heels were on the stone slabs and her toes were on the grass. She could feel the shorn grass under her feet. It felt dry and scratchy with no trace of the softness of spring grass. She felt so sad for the end of her wilderness but so resigned to a barren garden that she imagined it brown and brittle permanently.

Danny tugged at her hand, gently pushing and pulling at her, inviting her with the kindest of manipulations to kneel and then lie down. Her eyes were still tightly closed. She trusted him. She'd always trusted him. The newly cut grass scratched at the back of her head. She felt a flash of irritation at his insistence. He let go of her hand.

'Take a look, sweet pea.'

She opened her eyes and was immediately confused, she had such a clear vision in her head of the vista she expected that it took a few moments for her brain to assimilate the image around her. Her meadow was still there, all around her. She sat upright, bewildered.

She had been lying in a narrow strip of mown grass, surrounded by tall grass. The cut area fit her length perfectly. A coffin of grass. She could barely see Danny, he was next to her, lying in his own mown strip of grass, with just a narrow gap connecting them, allowing him to reach his arm out towards her. By lying down once again, she could hold hands with him.

She made a series of noises that conveyed something to him, puzzlement, and creeping, hopeful joy but she still found no words. She stood up to see if she could better understand what had happened to her garden. And then it was clear, a central path, opening up to two symmetrical mown boxes for them each to lie in. The two boxes were joined by a narrow gap through which they could hold on to each other. She lay down again and stretched her arm out once again into the channel to find his hand.

'I love it.' She lay still, symmetrically, so the tear that left each eye raced down her face and reached her ears at exactly the same time.

'I love it too,' he said, from his little grass box. He squeezed her hand.

'The thing I love,' he continued, 'is the total absence of green,' said Danny from behind his curtain of grasses. Sam laughed, thinking he was joking, but she opened her eyes when he remained silent. She looked at the grasses immediately around her. He was right. There was almost no green. The sun had blanched the stems every colour of cream, gold and brown and the wildflowers added splashes of colour, red from poppies and powdery blue from cornflowers.

'Red for sporty, yellow for theatrical, blue for academic,' Danny chanted.

Sam frowned, not following his logic at all but squeezed his hand, feeling that sometimes loving him absolutely, without necessarily understanding him, might be enough.

'My ideal garden.'

'Chaos with a little bit of order?' Sam asked.

'Order, with a little bit of chaos,' Danny insisted.

Sam wondered if the freshly mown grass beneath her would become green again now it had access to the sunlight. And rain was forecast, so it would probably need cutting again in no time at all.

'Are we going to keep it like this then?'

'Of course we are. For as long as you want. You're the meadow expert. Though I might need to buy some garden shears. I cut our arm channel with the kitchen scissors this morning.'

'Danny? I think it might be the nicest garden ever.'

'Me too,' he said and she wondered if behind the privacy of his grass curtain, he might be crying also.

'Can you cope with me, Danny? Now you know a bit more about the tumbling bag of nerves that I am?'

Danny nearly laughed, a noisy smile escaped at least. 'We probably both ought to talk a little bit more. You know, nothing too over-sharing, but it's probably best that I know what's going on in that head of yours sometimes.'

'And what about your head, Danny? What should I know about what's going on in there?'

'Oh, there's nothing much there you need to worry about. You know me. Nothing much that won't fit into the rows and columns of a spreadsheet. No pivot tables, no macros. Just numbers.'

'That's not quite true though, is it? You've kept stuff from me, which means you've filed our thoughts somewhere other than a spreadsheet. Otherwise I'd have found it easily enough marked, "Things I haven't told my wife." What else haven't you been telling me?'

Danny listened to his wife's voice, a sound that he loved

more than any other sound on the planet and he looked up at the sky. It wasn't a particularly beautiful sky, it was blue in places and white in others, but there was plenty of grey too. He looked up at the sky not because the view was irresistible, but because he didn't want to open his mind to Sam.

'Danny, is there more?' she probed gently. She felt safe here, she thought she might be able to cope if there were more.

Danny closed his eyes and pictured his brain. Hundreds of drawers tightly shut. Padlocked even. He had the key now, he could open just one more for her, couldn't he? He could see what happened, surely?

He shuddered, imagining the tsunami of thoughts tumbling out, unstoppable.

'Danny? Trust me.'

Gingerly, he pictured himself turning a key, unlocking an un-shared thought. He rifled through the files, most of which he didn't dare open, he didn't particularly want to know what he'd stored away.

'I like eggs,' he said, suddenly, both gladdened and appalled by this revelation.

Sam laughed but stopped quickly when she heard the earnestness in his voice.

'You do?' she whispered, alarmed.

'I love them.'

'But I don't understand. Why don't you eat them then? Why do you say you hate them?'

'Because I love them *too* much.'

Sam pulled a face of bewildered disgust, even though she knew he couldn't see it. 'Danny. You're being weird.'

'Oh Sam. I am weird. You don't know the half of it.'

'I'm beginning to think you might be right. Come on, talk to me about eggs – what's going on there. Oh God. It's not linked… ' she asked, horrified, not even daring to speak the fear that had leapt to the front of her brain.

'No, don't be silly. Of course not. This is not a fertility issue. I've never eaten eggs as long as I've known you.'

'True. Do you remember how I used to tease you?'

'You still do.'

'And do you remember how I hid eggs in everything you ate to prove you weren't allergic to them?'

'Yes, that was a bit mean, not respecting me, not taking my word for it.'

'But you word wasn't truthful, Danny. You just didn't like them! And now you tell me you *do* like them. What is going on, Danny?' She squeezed his hand again, the small pressure reassuring him. She really didn't mind about the eggs.

'The thing is, Sam, it is hard to explain, but I find eggs very *unreliable*.'

'Go on.'

'They just can't really be counted on. I love hard-boiled eggs, they're my absolute favourite, but nine times out of ten, they're just wrong. They're too hard, they're too soft. They're so unpredictable. And don't even get me started on poached eggs.'

'This doesn't feel insurmountable, Danny. You just have to be consistent, you can get pretty close if you use the same technique every single time.'

'Not true. That's not at all true. You can use exactly the same type and size of egg, you can measure everything exactly the same but sometimes they come out with the white uncooked and stringy, which is the worst, and sometimes they're too hard. And whilst hard isn't as repulsive, it always feels like the saddest waste of opportunity, because at some point in time, the egg would have been perfect.'

'Well, that just doesn't seem a big enough problem to stop you eating eggs altogether. You're a ludicrous excuse for a human being.'

'It's my brain, Sam. If you could see inside my brain you'd know just how big a problem that is. As a young man, before I met you, I spent a good few weeks trying to get a hard-boiled egg to turn out perfectly every time. I weighed the eggs, I measured the water. I had a chart. It should have been science, but it was just voodoo. It was all too unpredictable. I had to give up.'

Sam lay quietly, watching the sky make its tiny adjustments to its colour and depth, small strokes from east to west, micro changes all for her. She thought about her husband. She wondered exactly what did go on in that brain of his.

'Have you heard about Prince Charles?' she asked him.

'In what context?'

'In the context of hard-boiled eggs.'

'No. I can't say I have.'

'Apparently, though this could be an urban myth...'

Danny interrupted her, 'I don't really think of the royals as urban...'

'A palatial myth perhaps...' Sam corrected.

'Better,' said Danny.

'Apparently his butler cooks him a range of eggs, five I think, every morning. He adds them to the boiling water at intervals and then he sets them out in front of the prince in order.'

'How does he know what order they went in?' asked Danny, picturing the process a royal butler might use to guarantee consistency.

'I don't know, he must mark them, do you think? With a pencil perhaps? One to five? Anyway, the prince then begins with the middle egg, three it must be if that's the system they're using.'

'Or C,' posed Danny, deciding with certainty that he would use letters not numbers in case the numbers were confused with minutes.

'Or C, certainly. He starts at egg 3 or egg C and then if it is a bit too runny he moves to the right, and tries egg 4 or even 5 but if it's too over-cooked he moves to the left, to egg 2 or 1.'

'That actually is genius,' said Danny, admiringly. 'A bit wasteful though,' he added, imagining himself using a similar system and immediately dismissing it for fear of profligacy.

'Well, perhaps the butler isn't so fussy and eats the rest. I'll be your butler. I mean, cooking five eggs might be a bit excessive, but three might work. And I'll eat the ones you don't eat.'

'You'd do that for me, wouldn't you?' Danny asked, knowing with certainty that she would.

'I'd do that for *me*. I love eggs. I'm happy to eat two to every one of yours.'

Sam paused. 'But there's another way.'

'There is?'

'You could just accept that one of the joys of eating

a hard-boiled egg is that sometimes they are perfect and sometimes they're not. The random nature of the hard-boiled egg is part of the experience.'

Danny considered this. 'But I always feel so let down.'

'Life isn't perfect, Danny. It will let you down from time to time. And it's going to feel out of control, mostly. And mostly it is – we can only control a tiny bit of it.'

'That's all I'm asking for. A bit of control.'

They were silent for a while.

'How long are we going to lie here?' Danny asked.

Sam looked up at the sky, it continued to change and shift, but not decisively, just little adjustments nudging it quietly across her field of vision.

'Until it rains or we get old and die.'

Danny looked up at the sky. There was no sign of rain.

'OK, sweet pea. I can live with that.'

Acknowledgements

The non-collaborative, solitary nature of writing is the point for me. It's the thing I do alone: selfishly, quietly, indulgently. It's its own retreat.

However, whilst a writer can work alone, an author really can't. There is so much more to it than the words. From the minute I've finished my bit, it's very much a team effort and having worked amongst the good folk of UK publishing for most of my adult life, I'm more thankful than ever for the wealth of experience, dedication, professionalism and *hope* that is applied to each new manuscript and at every stage of its onward journey.

I love my team at HQ – they are serious about everything they do, including partying, which is a prerequisite. Sadly, though, I've been very careless with my editors over the years. I've recently managed to lose yet another, but working with Clio Cornish was a complete joy and I am very grateful to her for the passion and skill she applied to both this book and, before this, to *Mr Doubler Begins Again*.

Having worked with Clio on my last novel, I would have been devastated to lose her before the ink had even dried on this one, had it not been for the knowledge that *Growing*

Season would fall into the temporary custody of Lisa Milton. To be a successful publisher you really do need to be good with words *and* good with people… and Lisa is great with both.

My greatest thanks must always go to my family. My husband pointed out that in my first novel the children were absent; in my second, the children were unlikeable and in the third the children were unwanted. This is as good a place as any to remind my husband and children that I couldn't and wouldn't write about them, but if there's a personal cry amongst the pages, it's a cry for the freedom of self-determination that I would wish for them all.

My four children all inspire me in different ways but I've dedicated this book to Poppy and Millie who continue to amaze me… they already seem to *know* so much. I'd love to think I was still close to the prow of our rowing boat, keeping vigil, but these girls are already sitting with their hands on the tiller, nudging us all in the right direction.

My final thanks and love goes to Jon. None of this would make any sense or be any fun without him.